AMIAYA ENTE
Presents

THAT GANGSTA SHIT
VOLUME II
Here Comes the Pain

FEATURING

ANTOINE "INCH" THOMAS

Copyright ©2005 by Amiaya Entertainment LLC

Written by Antoine "Inch" Thomas
J. Marcelle
Derrick "Blue Gambino" Phillips
Eric "E-Boogie" Ferrer
Anthony "Big Ice Nitti" Bledsoe
Brandon McCalla
Shareef
A.K.A. Big Rock for Amiaya Entertainment LLC

Published by Amiaya Entertainment LLC
Cover Design by www.mariondesigns.com
Cover Design by Antoine "Inch" Thomas for Amiaya Entertainment LLC

Printed in the United State of America

Edited by Antoine "Inch" Thomas

ISBN: 0-9777544-1-3

[1. Urban-Fiction. 2. Action-Fiction. 3. Drama-Fiction. 4. Street-Fiction.]

Dedication

To every American soldier that Bush sent to Iraq
We gon' keep it Gangsta for y'all over here!

Contents

American Me

by

Antoine "Inch" Thomas

Chapter 1

"Mutha fuckas tryna kill me, but ain't got the heart..." Some old shit by *Jay-Z* was knocking in the background while Kieser Sozay, a twenty-four-year-old, 6′ 2″, orange complexioned poster boy, who was the head blood of the set, *CK-1*, sat on his front porch, surrounded by his team, kicking some gangsta shit!

The black contacts he wore made it look as if someone had painted his pupils with a black jumbo magic marker, and if one stared at them long enough, they were guaranteed at least three weeks of sweat drenching nightmares.

"Sozay, pass me a light," Little Red Ridin' Hood, a 5′ 10″, half Dominican and half Brazilian, olive toned, ghetto princess with light grey eyes and who was a dead ringer for *Free* from BET, was making a request to her boyfriend. *Hood*, respectfully called that by her crew, was about seven inches taller and about five pounds *in the trunk area* heavier than ol' girl from *106*. Hood had a blunt in her hand that resembled a cigar. The cigar roller she and Sozay had purchased on their trip to Havanna,

Cuba, the year before was in constant use on a daily basis.

Sozay passed his *Ruby* a candy apple *Bic* lighter in which she wasted no time getting the party started. After the second pull, Hood coughed like she was trying to throw up her lungs.

Two of her underlings, *Bloody Money*, a 5 foot ink pen black, skinny ass nigga with waves that could only be seen when you stood over him, and *Sangré* (Blood in Spanish), a 6'1", Puerto Rican cat with a low ceaser, green eyes and a beard that mocked a chin strap, were laughing their asses off at how their female boss fought to take a drag of some Cali green to the head.

"Yo, son, Hood be stuntin' like she can hang when it's time to blaze." Bloody Money spoke to his cohort as Hood passed the L to him.

Bloody Money took a drag and passed the blunt to Sangré, who had his hand out and was still high from the blunt that he sucked down for dolo on his way to the block about an hour earlier.

"I know, Blood." Sangré sounded as if he were holding his breath, "Sometimes I be overlookin' her fuckin' titties and ass and shit and be viewing her as a nigga."

Neither Sozay nor Little Red Ridin' Hood ever took offense to any of the comments made in regards to her gender by any of their homies. Sangré and Bloody Money were family who never disrespected their superiors. And on more than a dozen occasions, they proved themselves to be more than loyal. They were family, *till death do they part*.

Red Rum, their most destructive, most dangerous, and most impressive, *when it came to putting in work*, homie was in the middle of the street doing sets of pushups, a hundred a clip. Red Rum was 5' 11" with Timberland tan skin, 270 pounds of injected steroid muscle, and wore red contacts. Whenever he wore a sweatshirt, it looked like he had napkin holders on either sides of his neck. His legs looked like tree trunks, his back looked like he was ready for take off, and his arms looked fake. Red Rum was handsome though, his whole crew was, and every broad that Red Rum brought through the block was from the gym, and appeared to be kin to either Jessica Simpson or Britney Spears. Rum had a mean snow bunny fetish.

Keiser Sozay commanded in a moderate tone. "Yo, Rum, I'm trying to hit the Skate Key up like, right now! Make sure shit is ahight to roll."

Red Rum jumped up after getting in 1700 pushups in forty-five minutes. His goal was two thousand. He pressed the button on his stolen military walkie-talkie and aggressively spoke into the device. "Bttatt! More or less, the boss is ready to make moves. Killer, what's the deal?"

"Bttaatt! Bttaatt!" Lil K.I. blurted out.

Killer turned around, faced his homie and silenced his hyperactive sidekick by whispering, "Lil K.I., ain't nothin' poppin' off right now. Chill wit that *Bttaatt* shit for a minute. The homies are trying to motivate."

Lil K.I. eyed his boss sadly, ejected the clip from his P-89 and unchambered the black Talon, allowing it to fall quietly on the red plush carpet. He and his mentor, Killer, were stationed in a stash house at the corner of the block waiting for anything or anybody that wasn't family, friend or customer to creep through their set.

Killer put his walkie-talkie to his mouth while surveying the ten TV monitors that sat in front of him. Softly, he gave his analysis. "Blood, shit is clear on this end. No homo's (police) and no Erickits (enemy), just a few fiends that Lil K.I. here is going to take care of." Killer looked over at Lil K.I. who was already glued to monitor number seven. He noticed the crew of crackheads entering the abandoned house that was used for transactions. Lil K.I. looked up at Killer, threw up the blood sign and walked out.

"Homicide, what's hood homie?" Red Rum redirected his attention to the other end of the block where Homicide and Lil Hahmo had a silk screening machine in another stash house pressing up red tee shirts that read *Free Danger and B.G.* in big white letters.

Danger was in the Beacon on Riker's Island amongst his other brethren who tagged him as *Zorro* after is first thirty days there due to all the major work he had put in. B.G. was in Spofford, a Juvenile Detention Center in a unit all by himself. All he would do is play Playstation all day long. He was in the segregated unit because when he first arrived, he managed to cut nine other inmates. The staff at the facility considered him *"extremely deadly around other inmates"* and placed him into a dormitory all by himself. He and his fellow comrade and co-defendant were awaiting trial for the quadruple murder of four police officers who were executed gangland style in a housing project off of Laconia Avenue in the Bronx.

Homicide said, "Yo, Lil Hahmo, is shit clear, homie?" he called out to his young'n who was sitting right next to him only moments ago.

There was no answer and Homicide had yelled out loud enough for his companion to hear him even if he was down in the basement. After a few moments went by and no answer, Homicide said, "Hold on," into his walkie-talkie. He picked up his already chambered burgundy A.K. 47 and tiptoed upstairs where he figured Lil Hahmo had wandered off to. *TP3-Reloaded* was playing in the background and as Homicide reached the top step of the two-story row home, a smile eased its way on his grill. He had forgotten that *Chocolate Strawberry*, Lil Hahmo's girlfriend, had stopped by about a half hour earlier.

The scene was definitely something out of a porno movie. Lil Hahmo was sitting on the upstairs sofa with his body sunk down and his ass extended past the pillows. His feet were secured flat on the floor and *Strawberry*, who just *had* to be the vixen from *YaYo's* video, named *Buffie*, was riding the young stallion like it was going out of style.

Lil Hahmo was fourteen, but was hung like he was thirty and his girl was like three years his senior.

Chocolate wasn't yelling, screaming or anything. The only sounds that crept from her mouth were, "Mm, hm, mm, mm, mm, hm."

Homicide was stuck for a minute as he watched *Super Ass* rise up about ten inches *with the magic stick still in her*, and drop it back down like it was hot. Shorty didn't miss a rhythm or a beat.

As soon as Homicide's manhood stretched its eleven inches, he spun around. Not by his own will, but by the force of a bullet that snuck its way into the house.

A blue R-1 with chrome pegs, chrome rims, chrome handle bars and a grey carbon cover, hiding the chrome exhaust pipe, sat right outside of the stash house idling quietly while its occupant, a female in a blue motorcycle suit, blue matching helmet with blue weave hanging freely down her back, was aiming a small caliber handgun at the crib bringing sparks to the wall, window pane and the inside ceiling of the house.

Super Ass was on the floor hiding her face, *ass everywhere*. Lil Hahmo dragged his homie to an adjacent room to check and see if he was okay.

Homicide, holding tightly onto the small hole in his shoulder, looked Lil Hahmo directly in his eyes and said, "I'm good, son," then he looked toward his crimey's mid-section and said, "Your *man*, son. Your *man* is touching me."

Lil Hahmo looked down at his third leg, brought his eyes back to his mentor's, smiled, released his homie and said, "My bad, I'll be right back."

Homicide sighed and thought to himself, *I hope Red Rum handled his business.*

Red Rum was lying on the ground in war zone position eating up the side paneling of every car in his path. The custom painted maroon SK was sneezing at its target. *"Choo, Choo, Choo, Choo, Choo!"*

Red Rum, Killer, Lil K.I.,Sangre', Keiser Sozay and Lil Red Ridin' Hood, who were now standing in the middle of the street with warm, empty burners in their hands, could hear the bike's engine fading away as it disappeared.

"I'm gon' kill Little Miss Muffit's ass," Red Riding Hood murmured.

"No doubt," Sozay smiled at the failed attempt. "We out!" he yelled knowing that the *Rollers* would be through asking questions within the next few minutes.

"Yo," Red Rum tapped the hood of his Prayer Rug red four-door drop top Chrysler 300C, with the red cushion on the row bar that spelled out *Red Rum*. When one looked at it through the rearview mirror, it read *murder*. He continued by saying, "I'm right behind y'all. I'ma check on Hahmo and 'em." He jogged down the block where the blue bandit had put in work just moments before.

Keiser Sozay trotted over to his red convertible, four-door Rolls Royce Phantom with some 24" chrome rims that looked like two Slinkys were chasing each other when the monster was in motion. He pressed a button on his key ring. His space ship chirped and came to life like the *Millennium Falcon*. The digital dash raced to 200 mph then immediately descended back down. The Rolls raised three inches off the ground, the rpm's roared and every light in and around the vehicle blinked as if it were a strobe at a club.

Bloody Money was sixteen and only made moves on his red super charged Yamaha Banshee. After kick starting his quad, it roared to life and up, up and away she went. After the ATV leveled off, Sozay was right behind them with his low beams and fogs on making the hood glow.

Sangré was behind Sozay in his red six-series BMW coupe with the Puerto Rican flag painted on the hard top. Some old red fishnet 22″ BBS rims, served as shoes for the two-door. There were no back seats in the BM, just four 18″ speakers in a box with sixteen tweeters. Sangre' could be heard a mile away, banging some Reggaeton shit from his state of the art sound system.

Little Red Ridin' Hood was in a red 6-4 with the top down. Her beautiful face was painted on the hood of her car *and* on a red floorboard underneath her whip. She kept her Chevy on its two hind wheels, almost all of the time, constantly draining its ten batteries. She would tease Bloody Money every so often telling him that she could wheely her car longer than he could wheely his bike. Every time her vehicle ascended, an airbrushed photo of herself in a red bandana with a Desert Eagle pointing straight ahead could be seen staring hauntingly at all its viewers.

With Bloody Money leading the pack, he stopped at the first light until he noticed Red Rum zooming up in his Chrysler 300. It was on now. The crew left their strip also tagged, *The Red Light District*, hopped on the Bronx River Expressway south, and headed for the Skate Key. A meeting was about to take place and then it would be on and crackin'.

Chapter 2

"Vroooooooommm, uh, uh, uh, uh, uh, uh! Vroom! Vroom! Boop Bop!" The R-1 hummed, ticked, then shut off.

Little Miss Muffit hopped off her bike and hit the alarm system. Standing in her 6" navy blue Manolo Blahnik's, her 5'4" frame now looked like she was damn near six feet tall. With a floppy, loose, Jello, black-chocolate *pretty* ass, titties that looked like the *freak-a-leek* joints on *Esther,* and a face that could double over as the *old* Lil Kim's, Little Miss Muffit, who sat on her two-wheel monster, only moments ago spitting her blue tipped black rhinos at her enemy, had been married to her man, Red Lobsta, through the streets, for eight years already.

Red Lobsta came up with his name to spite his twin brother, *Keiser Sozay,* and their click.

Red Lobsta and Sozay were identical twins except that one *always* wore red, *ate food* like a glut when he was first *brought home*, kept his hands positioned as if each one of them were symbolizing twin scores of 3-0, and always said *Eastside.* The other brother *only* wore blue, *drank milk* like a lush when he first *cuz'd* up, kept his thumb and pointer finger in a partial circle symbolizing a *C,*or some crab claws, and always hung his rag on his left side.

The four-man, one-woman team stayed together and told themselves that it would stay that way until they *laid* together.

Red Lobsta and his brother Sozay had stopped speaking to one another on a *friendly* basis, or rather a *family* basis, four years prior when Keiser came home from Riker's Island after laying up thirty-four months on a *body*. He eventually beat the case at trial, only to come home and find his brother on the opposite team.

"Eastside-031!" Keiser Sozay had his *B* sign up and stared at his brother at first because he had heard the rumors that his brother was crippin'. He never asked him over the phone, in letters *or* on the visits because if it *was* true, then he knew his brother had heard about him too, eating everything in his path that was food when he was in HDM, the 4-building, NIC, West Facility, North Facility, the 3-building, C-95, the Beacon *and* The Pound. Sozay was hoping that if his brother *was* jumping around like a break-dancer, *C-walking* and shit, that he would've taken heed to the havoc *he* was wreaking on dudes on the Island. But after he saluted his brother, Red Lobsta's response confirmed otherwise.

"C's up nigga, 6 alive-5 must die. Slobs get ganked and drank fool, and for really doe,..."

"*Fiifftthh*". Keiser Sozay swung at his brother. He was like a certified barber when it came to a razor.

"Ah, ah, Cuzo." Red Lobsta jerked his head back and plastered a smile on his face. He touched his cheek and felt the crimson liquid. He wiped the outside of his jaw and then stuck his fingers inside of his mouth sucking off all the blood on his hand.

"That's what I do, cuz, I drink you niggaz!" Lobsta laughed evily.

"You know what color it is when it's still in the vein. Ha, Ha! Tell Daddy I said, next time he wanna rape a little boy, that he shouldn't do it and *then* go to sleep."

Red Lobsta pulled out a chrome 44 Magnum with a blue rubber grip and pointed at his kin, his twin.

Keiser Sozay knew that he was about to die; he had just arrived home about forty-five minutes prior to him and his twin's meeting. Thirty-four months fighting a body, beats it, and was now about to *get* bodied was too much for him to fathom. The rumors *were* true. His brother *was* a crip. His brother had put in work, his brother had even killed their pop when they were eleven years old for molesting them from when they were eight up until Red Lobsta killed him in his drunken stupor when they were a month shy of their twelfth birthdays.

Pop Dukes performed the lewd acts on both of his precious little boys one night after guzzling a fifth of Bacardi. After another fifth, Pop Dukes fell out on the sofa in a coma like induced sleep. Lobsta grabbed that *one* kitchen knife. The one used to clean the chicken. The one used to cut the steak. The one used to break down the chitterlings and the same one used to slice their eleventh birthday, matching birthday cakes. That one. Lobsta snatched it up, held it high with both hands gripped tightly on its wooden handle and jammed it into their dad's chest. Pops didn't even move. The first blow killed him, *instantly*. The other fifty-seven blows were for every time they had to taste their nasty old father's private part.

Red Lobsta and Keiser Sozay were taken from their mom, who was out on a crack binge at the time, and brought into Children's Services. After forty-eight months of foster care, abusive foster brothers, mothers and fathers, numerous tests and being told over and over that they weren't shit and that they would never *be* shit, Sozay and Lobsta broke north, and never looked back.

Now, four years later, after Mom Dukes got her shit together, standing in front of her door in the projects, Red Lobsta and Keiser Sozay stood toe to toe. One brother had a dripping *buk fifty*, *phone scar*, on his face while the other brother eyed the bullets in the bulldog that was pointed at his face.

"Kay, my baby, you're home!" The twins' mother heard her *other* son's voice, placed her food back into the oven and opened the door. When the top lock clicked, Lobsta tucked his hammer, covered his bleeding jaw with his blue rag and forced a fake smile. While Mom Dukes and the *red* son played house, Red Lobsta slid off. But before he did, he leaned into his brother and whispered into his ear, "I saved you when we were eleven, now Mommy just saved you. Who's gonna save you next time? Slob!" With his last comment, he plucked his brother on the forehead, something he always did to his twin when they were younger, spun to his left and breezed off.

Now, even four years after that, with nine people dead on both teams, the beef was still on. Drama lords.

• • •

Red Lobsta, who was built just like his brother, rocked a pair of ocean blue contacts and had waves all around his head. He was leaned up against his brand new electric blue H-2 Hummer, chatting with his crew.

Lobsta had his SUV custom designed by 310 Motoring. On the outset of his vehicle, two thin outer fiberglass body kits were installed to give his truck an extraordinarily unusual look. The inner transparent layer had dark blue sand, mixed with navy colored crystals installed in it. The outer most layer had a powder blue watery like solution poured into its panel. On a bright sunny day or even at night when headlights shone on the 4x4 as it moved, the exotic Hummer looked as if it were a body of water driving by on four quarters. The 25″ rims that it sat on were solid chrome plates carved to resemble four twenty-five cent pieces. Red Lobsta's favorite line to anyone who listened was, *"I'm the first nigga to stunt in a Hummer on four quarters / a European fish tank the same color as water."* He would chime those two rap lines to every new chick he'd meet and every new crip that would join his gang.

"What's poppin', Loc?" Red Lobsta said to one of his subordinates whom the streets had birthed as *Blue Steel*.

"Shit, Cuz, you know me," Blue Steel smiled showing off his 75 blue diamonds that he had all throughout his top and bottom eight-tooth bridges. Blue Steel continued fingering his favorite weapon of choice, a blue steel 357 Magnum. "I'm ready to ride on these fools. That nigga, Red Rum, caught me slippin' at my P.O.'s office that one day and slapped the shit out of me in the elevator."

Everyone laughed because they had heard about what had occurred between their 5′7″, dark-skinned, heavyset homeboy and his number one enemy, cock dieseled ass Red Rum.

Monsta Co-Dee, a 5′ 11″, light-skinned crip with no eyebrows, no eyelashes, no mustache, no beard, a bald head, with three scars on his face from a razor taken to his jaw when Keiser Sozay caught him with his girl at a local clinic, wanted a laugh so he asked his brother, by gang affiliation, to tell them *again*, what happened in that elevator.

"Aye, Steel, won't you tell us again how that busta signed his own death certificate?" Monsta tapped their Jamaican affiliate, *Blueberry Dred*, softly on his back indicating that some funny ass shit was about to be said.

Blue Steel was cool with the jokes, so after turning down the volume in his royal blue Excursion, allowing *Back Then* by Mike Jones to barely be heard through his six 18″ woofers, Steel began with his story. "Check it, I goes to see my P.O., right? I slides the nigga the piss with the Visine jumpoff popped off all in it, na mean? So I'm nervous and all that, but ayething is ayething. So I signs the appointment book, I tell Mr. *Smirnoff* that I'll see him in a month and then I hit the elevator. As soon as the elevator door opened, I noticed this big ass, Incredible Hulk looking ass nigga with a red Yankee button up jersey on, with the sleeves cut off of it, and a red Scully. I know Duke is a slob but I ain't tripping'. Plus the nigga had some blonde bitch with him. I thought it was his P.O., so I *stunts*. I get on the vator, move in so the door won't pinch my ass cheeks and I swear I didn't see this nigga swing."

Monsta was already doubled over in laughter. Little Miss Muffit chuckled, looked over at Red Lobsta who was giggling to himself, slapped Lobsta's shoulder softly and mouthed to him, "You better stop."

Blueberry Dred cracked a smile and said, "G'wan mon, Speel it. Speel de beans."

Blue Steel pulled on his clothes like if he were loosening up for a big speech and continued. "So, like I said, I knew something hit me and I knew how these niggas fucked with them razors and shit, so I rubbed the left side of my jaw and *boom*, this nigga smacked me again, on my right side this time. But I'm buggin' 'cause the nigga is mad big. Yo, this nigga's shoulders and guns look like horse legs. So anyway, I'm fuming, 'cause don't know nigga disrespect Blue Steel. I checked my waist and realized that I was heatless. Damn. Why'd I do that?" Blue Steel had his head down, shaking it slowly side to side, smiling. His shoulders jumped twice from a hard giggle, but he went on anyway. "This big ass nigga must've lost his mind. You ever see a clown juggling bowling pins?" Blue Steel was talking to everybody, but he eyed Monsta Co-Dee since it was Monsta who initiated the conversation. "You know how the clown be looking, dippin' low and flinging them pins up and down while moving a little bit side to side? Well, picture my head as those pins. The nigga was knocking me out with one slap, and waking me back up with another slap."

Monsta was on the floor, bawling. Miss Muffit and Red Lobsta joined him.

"Ed's up everybody!" Blueberry Dred yelled out.

At the corner of their block, Bloody Money's little ass was doing spin outs on his 4-wheeler *taunting* his rivals.

Little Miss Muffit went for her bike, but Blueberry stopped her with his hand placed firmly on her shoulder. "Him mine!" Dred hopped in his royal blue Cadillac Escalade EXT and took off after young'n.

When Bloody Money noticed Blueberry headed his way, he discontinued his antics, flipped his middle finger up at the dred and took off with his two front tires in the air.

Two blocks later, Dred hit his Nitro button and caught up to him. "Me ah kill ya, blood clot!" He lowered his window and aimed his Caleco at the enemy. That's when he finally noticed them. Homicide and Lil Hahmo cruising beside him on *their* 4-wheeler. Lil Hahmo had an AK pointed at the dred. "Blood clooooooot!" Blueberry screamed his final insult. He tried to ram Homicide and Lil Hahmo, but their state of the art antilock break system pulled them back. Blueberry's truck slammed into a parked van stopping the heavy 4x4 on the spot.

The third Banshee pulled up. "Where the fuck was y'all at?" Lil Hahmo yelled out to Killer and Lil K.I.

"Nigga, we were right here. But fuck all the small talk, let's punish this bomba clot ass nigga."

The five damu's approached the damaged SUV cautiously. "Yo, I don't see that nigga, homie!" Homicide yelled to his team as he surveyed what carnage was left of the vehicle.

"Ya cyan't stop a mon dat is hallready dead!" Blueberry screamed. His Caleco corroborated his thoughts and peeled some of Bloody Money's scalp off. *Backa. Backa. Backa. Backa!* Then Bloody Money's tiny chest seemed to explode at some point. When he dropped, Homicide, Lil Hahmo, Killer and Lil K.I. lost it.

The quartet turned around and ate food. The choppa's that the four adolescents had, chipped Blueberry Dred to pieces. *Boom, Boom, Boom, Boom, Bung, Bung, Bung, Bung, Pop, Pop, Pop, Pop, Bock, Bock, Bock Bock!* Sirens in the background influenced the youths to disperse.

"It's on, son. Every last one of those fuckin' crabs die tonight!" Homicide stated before lifting his bike on its hind wheels. "Bttaatt, bttaatt, bttaatt!"

The Final Chapter

HERE COMES THE PAIN...

Four hours later...

"Yo, turn that shit up, Blood!" Keiser Sozay barked at his comrade. Keiser Sozay and Red Rum were in a black Crown Victoria with limo tinted windows. They were both draped in red dickies. Red Rum had his scarf covering his nose and mouth while Sozay's scarf dangled loosely around his neck.

Red Rum turned up the volume as Sozay steered the full-size sedan. The heavy piano and strong baseline only added fuel to the duo's super pumped adrenaline.

"Every 'hood we go to / all the gangstas around know my whole crew—nigga what! / We hold it down like we 'spose to / You can stunt if you want we'll be poppin' them thangs..."

• • •

"Stay two car lengths behind them!" Little Red Ridin' Hood spoke firmly into her two-way radio as she trailed two car lengths behind Sangré in her Impala.

"Si Señora." Sangré was in an all black 300Z with a shotgun, two AK 47s and a custom painted auburn colored fully automatic mini-Mac-10. Sangré had on some dark sunglasses and was zoned out off some dro with his arm on the steering wheel with *"Yo, it's the real shit / nuff' to make feel shit / thump 'em in the club shit / have you wildin' out till you pump this, drugs to your eardrums / the raw uncut, have a nigga O.D. 'cause it's never enough..."* pumping in the background. On his forearm, right under his other nine homies' names, a fresh R.I.P. tattoo of Bloody Money's name was etched out in glossy red letters. Sangré looked at it and said, "It's goin' down a la noche para ti, mi amigo. Eastside, Siempre, Sangré. Siempre." He whispered.

• • •

The crips were out deep on their set. A heavy dice game was going down and $11,000 was in the bank.

"I'm taking all bets! Place your bets, cousin," Blue Steel yelled out to his partners who were all huddled in a semi huge circle.

The dice danced in his palm as a stack of hundreds, fifties, and twenties looked like a green brick in his other hand.

"Five hundred dollars you don't four or better, cuz. Five hundred, cuz." A tall dark-skinned crip named Lou from Harlem with a black T-shirt on that said *Gangsta* on it, lifted from the cover of a street novel by some cat named *K'wan*, was placing his bet with the over confident Blue Steel.

Another crip, a skinny brown-skinned cat imported from

Compton a year earlier by his cousin, Monsta Co-Dee, had his hair in pigtails making his skinny face look like a Doberman Pincher.

"Aye, cuz, a gee you don't beat the deuce twice, fool. Matter of fact," Snoopy dropped ten more bills, "make that two gee's, cuz."

"Ooooh, wee, you a big spender, Snoopy. I like that. I'm a show y'all Cali niggas how we put it down on the east coast. And Lou, I done read about the work *you* put in, partner, but you gon' need a lot more dough than that lil nickel you put up to stop the bank. You see this here," Blue Steel fanned the brick-like knot at Lou, "this is dam near fifteen stacks. You wanna impress me, stop the fuckin' bank, nigga!" Blue Steel bellowed as he shook the dice and looked for more bets.

Five other crips from out of Brooklyn had each bet five cent apiece. That left the bank with six thousand to juggle.

"Anybody else wanna gamble their re-up?" Blue Steel questioned the crowd antagonizingly.

"I'll stop it, Crab!" someone said in the background.

Blue Steel looked up and mimicked the same thing everybody else that was present chanted. "What the fuck!"

A black He-Man look alike with a white wife beater on and black jeans that looked like the six guns he had in his waist band, held them up on his ass, and a red fitted Yankee cap turned backwards was standing behind Lou with his arms crossed.

Bong! Red Rum stole Lou in the face. The side that got hit dented inward from the impact of the blow. Although Lou would have been considered brain dead from that one punch, it was when his head cracked into Snoopy's, knocking Snoopy unconscious that sealed the deal. Snoopy was fragile, his head burst right open when he hit the floor. Everybody reached for their weapons and not only was Red Rum built like the father on *The Incredibles*, but he was damn near in the league with *Marion Jones* on the track tip.

Red Rum took off with a school of slugs chasing him. *Pop, pop, pop, pop, pop, pop, pop, pop, pop!* Little Red Ridin' Hood lowered her Impala to the ground, and had John Singleton been present, everyone would've thought that *Set It Off Pt. II* was being filmed. With her Chevy idling in park, Hood waited until all seventy-two bullets were empty from her two Mac 11's before she exited her coupe. She sprayed the dice game up from across the street.

While Red Rum raced around the corner to meet back up with Sozay, his 270 pounds bumped into Blueberry Dred's brother, *Purple*, who was on his way up the block with twin Glocks in his hand. Purple Haze was thrown into some nearby bushes by the collision but he wasn't out cold. Red Rum closed in on the shrubbery only to hear, "True Kingston Killa ah show ahn prove to my yoot!" *Bong! Bong! Bong! Bong! Bong! Bong! Bong!*

Every shot caught Red Rum in his chest. He wouldn't back down though. He felt the burning sensations but he wouldn't get weak. He grabbed Purple Haze from the bushes by his ankles, yanked him from the greenery, and swung him around four hard times as the duo neared a light pole.

Dong! Purple Haze's head collided with the pole and his body went limp. Red Rum released his adversary's leg and slowly slumped up against a nearby car. The footsteps approaching didn't even matter to Red Rum. He felt that he was gonna die anyway, but when he looked up, he smiled, "Eastside."

"All the time!" *Bttattattattattaattaattattat* Keiser Sozay lit Purple's ass up. The dred was on the floor dying while Sozay sang out, "Pon de river, signal de plane, row de boat!" When he looked back over at Rum, he knew his homie was dead. The ceasing of the gunshots up the block told him that Little Red Ridin' Hood had also handled her business.

• • •

Up the block!

Crips were laid out everywhere and some had taken cover behind parked cars and injured row homes.

Whenever a gun battle ended, Hood would always dance at the scene by herself. As she twirled her body seductively to the sweet sounds of *Bobby Valentino*, Little Miss Muffit snuck up behind her with a 50 millimeter. "Pop shit now, bitch!"

Slowly, Hood turned around knowing that her time was up because she had slipped and underestimated the enemy. With the barrel of Muffit's cannon playing chicken with Hood's head, Little Red Ridin' Hood said, *Fuck it* to herself and kept it gangsta. "Fuck you, you crab! I'll meet you in hell, ho!"

Boom! Boom!

The first shot blew the back of her head into her face. The second shot from the pump took what was left of her head off of her shoulders.

Hood smiled at Sangré knowing that he had saved her ass again. "Gracias amigo."

The next sounds were something only heard in the movies. *"Zeeewwwun! Blooomm!"*

Sangré was disintegrated by the grenade launcher that Monsta Co-Dee had in his hand which was now aimed at Hood and her favorite Chevy. Monsta was in the second floor window of a dope house that his crew pumped drugs out of which was located in the middle of the block.

"Zeeewwn! Blaah Blooomm!" The Impala went up in flames just as Little Red Ridin' Hood rolled under an old Cadillac

parked three cars away from her 6-4.

When the first four-wheeler carrying Killer and Lil K.I. came into view, Monsta Co-Dee aimed at them too, but missed, sending Red Lobsta's H-2 to the same automobile heaven that Hood's Impala went just moments before.

The second Banshee pulled up when the Hummer exploded. Lil Hahmo and Lil K.I. were chillin' with Sangré earlier until he came up with a plan. He told them to count to thirty-one, and if he didn't return, to do what they did best. Before you knew it, Killer and Homicide were up in the crip's dope house, hunting down Monsta, killing everything in sight.

Lil K.I. and Lil Hahmo had Sangré's two A.K.'s Amy and Katie, making them bitches choke at everybody else that thought they could hide under cars and behind bushes. *"Caah, caah, caah, caah, caah, caah, caah!"*

Hood opened up her eyes and saw Monsta Co-Dee's severed head sitting in a weed plant pot on the windowsill of the dope house he met his fate in. She smiled, rolled her eyes relievingly, and when she opened them back up, she noticed Blue Steel only inches from where she lay, waving at her. *Blong!* She never even felt the bullet hit her. She died instantly.

Blue Steel got so excited that he clapped his hands and dropped his gun. Instinctively, he looked up and caught eye contact with Lil Hahmo. "Damn!" he mumbled and tried to run.

Lil Hahmo aimed his AK at the fleeing gang banger, but was halted by Lil K.I. saying, "Nah, I got this!"

Lil K.I. ran into the middle of the street and lay on the floor. He leveled his choppa so that he could see his target, who just entered into the street, through the circle that sat on top, but on the tip of his rifle. Closing one eye he said, "Red Rum taught me how to do this."

Just as Blue Steel hit the end of the block, a large police EMS truck barreled around the corner and slammed on its brakes. It stopped just in time as Blue Steel ran into the front bumper with his hands up in the air. When he turned around to point to the ATV riding exterminator's, *"toga"*, his head exploded all over the EMS logo on the hood of the truck. The police driver and his partner, stunned, looked up and saw what appeared to be two children hop on the back of two four-wheelers, driven by two masked men. The four-wheelers then took off and cut through an alley after killing their head and brake lights, and were just missed by the other police EMS truck that entered through the other end of the block.

On the New England Thruway heading towards the Bruckner Expressway, Keiser Sozay was tailing Red Lobsta in Red Rum's Chrysler 300. Sozay peered into the rear view mirror and smiled at what he saw on the row bar. *Murder.* "I love you, Red Rum, R.I.P., homie." Then he stepped on the gas and caught up to his brother who was in Blue Steel's Ford Excursion.

When Sozay pulled up beside Lobsta, Lobsta looked over at him, smiled and sat his blue steeled Desert Eagle on the door pane with the window rolled down. Sozay picked up his Caleco and aimed it at the side of his brother's head. Then, out of nowhere, a helicopter swung low and hovered right in front of both vehicles. The police light on the bottom of the chopper was blinding both drivers. They repositioned their nozzles and dumped on the helicopter. Assisting officers were behind them in Crown Victorias, Chevrolet Caprices, Chevy Suburbans and Mustang 5.0's. The bullets from the Caleco tore up the rear propellers, the bright ass light *and* tore out two of the windows in the chopper. Red Lobsta aimed right under the ghetto bird with his Desert and emptied his clip. The gas tank burst into a fireball and the helicopter started spinning in circles. Sozay and Lobsta floored their vehicles and flew right by the chopper. When the helicopter came down, the three police sedans that were right behind the twins got it the worst. Their bodies were burned beyond recognition. Everything else was like a domino effect. A handful of cop cars that were in the rear of the pack ended their chase and tried to help their fellow officers that survived the wreckage.

Keiser Sozay eased off the exit ramp at Castle Hill Avenue. He had some homies in that area that would put him up for the evening and get rid of his vehicle.

Red Lobsta got off at the next exit, ditched his truck, hopped in a cab and took it back uptown to Bronxwood Avenue where he had another stash crib.

Homicide felt his pager vibrating and reached into his pocket. He and his little team were about two minutes from their crib. He passed his two-way to his homie and said, "Tell me what's poppin', homie."

Lil Hahmo fingered the tiny Motorola, looked at it, closed it, placed it back into his superior's pocket and said, "The big homie said, more or less, for us to fall back until the a.m."

"Aye, Lil Hahmo," Homicide peeked over his shoulder as they rolled into an underground garage.

"Yo," the youngin responded.

"How'd you feel about tonight, lil homie?"

"We had to bring the pain to them niggas. Shit! Death to all those that go against blood. Eastside, homie."

As everyone got off of their bikes, Killer, Lil K.I. and Homicide all simultaneously answered with hugs and hand-shakes and said, "All the time."

THE END

Check out Inch's bio on his website, www.amiayaentertainment.com . E-mail him at <u>tanianunez79@hotmail.com</u>. Also, if you haven't already, check out his other books: *Flower's Bed, No Regrets, Unwilling to Suffer* and a feature in that *Gangsta Sh!t,* vol. one, all by Antoine "Inch" Thomas.

FRIEND OR FOE

by

J. Marcelle

Chapter 1
Scarfaces

A Yo-Yo / what up though / time is runnin' out / it's for real though / let's connect politic ditto / we can trade places gettin' lifted in the staircases / word up, peace incarcerated scarfaces...

"Yo, this jail shit is for the birds. I can't wait to get the fuck outta here. That's my word. I'ma die before I ever get put back in a cage again!" B.K. said with a lung full of smoke as he passed the Black & Mild cigar to his celly, Fresh.

B.K. and Fresh had been tight ever since Fresh arrived at F.C.I. Otisville from Lewisburg Penitentiary and moved into B.K.'s cell. After a few days of talking and feeling each other out and reading each other's P.S.I. reports, both men felt comfortable that the other was a stand up nigga. After a few more conversations, B.K. and Fresh learned that not only did they have a lot in common, but that they were both from different parts of the same Brooklyn neighborhood.

B.K. (who repped Brooklyn to the fullest which was why everybody in Otisville called him B.K.), had been down for five years. Completely maxing out on his sixty-two month sentence for possessing 750 grams of powder cocaine, he was set to be released the next day. When he first arrived at Otisville back in '99, he stood at 5' 11" and weighed 160 pounds soaking wet. After five years of eating peanut butter and oatmeal four times a day, plus the three meals that the feds gave him, and then hitting the weights in the morning and pull-ups, push-ups, and dips at night, he now weighed 198 pounds of solid muscle.

"Yo, how many sticks we got left?" B.K. asked Fresh while nodding his head to the Dip Set song that was blasting out of both of their Koss headphones. Earlier that day, B.K. and Fresh went half on a balloon full of Purple Haze and a quart of white lightning moonshine, which was as strong as any vodka on the streets. Usually, neither B.K. nor Fresh smoked weed or got drunk because there were a lot of *"hot niggas"* running around the compound who would drop a slip on you for a free phone call, but since it was B.K.'s last day, they both figured that they'd break night getting right.

"It's five left and we smoked five already. I'm high as fuck!" Fresh replied. Fresh was a tall, lanky dude with a baby face, corn braids, and a jump shot that would make you think that he could be Carmello Anthony's little brother. Fresh had gotten knocked out of town after he sold an informant fourteen grams of crack. Under the mandatory minimum sentencing guidelines, he was sentenced to eighty-four months. He was down to his last one hundred and eighty days before he was eligible for placement in a halfway house.

"Fuck it, roll up another stick. I'm tryna get high for real for real!" B.K. said passing Fresh a new Black & Mild cigar to roll the weed up with.

"Nigga, you some shit, you outta here tomorrow and I gotta be here for six mu'fuckin mo' months. It'll be just my luck that they call me for a piss test tomorrow," Fresh said, laughing as he split the Black & Mild open and dumped the tobacco out.

"Yeah, I know, a nigga leavin' this bitch tomorrow. Shit feel crazy after being down five." B.K. said. He and Fresh had been cellies for two-and-a-half years and although he couldn't wait to touch the bricks, he hated to leave his homie behind.

"Nigga, you betta not get caught up in no pussy and forget about me, son," Fresh said as he lit the stick of Haze up.

B.K. took a swig off the bottle of white lightning before replying. "Neva dat, son. You my mu'fuckin man. I got 'chu duke. By the time you get out, we gon' be doin big things, ya heard?" It was 12:35, B.K. still had hours to go before he would walk out of the Otisville gates a free man. For the rest of the night, B.K. and Fresh stayed up talking, laughing, and getting lifted. Over the two-and-a-half years that they'd been cellies, they'd become tighter than brothers by a different father, same mother, and they both knew that they would feel incomplete until they were back together again.

• • •

"Sequan Howard, report to R&D." the officer called B.K.'s government name over the loud speaker telling him to report to receiving and discharge. This was the moment that he'd been waiting for, the moment that every inmate dreams about throughout their whole bid; *release day!* Fresh and B.K. had stayed up all night and were the first ones out of their cells as soon as the C.O. opened the doors that morning. Walking up to R&D, B.K. was nervous as shit. Even though he wanted his freedom so bad that his stomach hurt, after standing up for count, walking out for chow, and all the other bullshit that he'd been through as an inmate, it felt funny to know that he was about to be his own man again. Fresh walked with B.K. up to R&D and if you didn't know him, it was hard to tell that he was in his feelings. He had mad love for B.K. and wanted to see him go, but at the same time, he was sad to see his best friend leave.

Once they were at the door to R&D, B.K. turned to Fresh and said, "Hold it down, son. In six months it's your turn and I'ma be here to pick you up, ya heard?"

"No doubt, son, crew love!"

"Yo, make sure you call my crib tonight. You got my numbers on your phone list, right?"

"Yeah, I'ma hit 'chu up right before lock-in."

B.K. felt kind of strange knowing that he wouldn't be amongst those who locked in their cells that night and any other night after. "A'ight, son, I love you, ya heard?" B.K. said as he gave Fresh a dap and a hug.

"I love you more," Fresh shot back.

Forty-five minutes later, B.K. walked out the doors of Otisville a free man. Outfitted in a crisp navy blue Evisu denim jean outfit, a white tee shirt, a blue and white Yankees fitted hat and a pair of retro #9 white and blue Jordans, B.K. ran to the parking lot where his shorty, Kisha, was waiting for him in her '99 325i B.M.W.

Kisha was a pretty chocolate shorty who was about 5' 5" and weighed 135 pounds. Her ass, thighs, hips, and breasts had to weigh at least fifteen or twenty pounds by themselves, shorty was holding! Her teeth were slightly crooked because she still occasionally sucked her thumb, and her pouty lips and dimpled cheeks made her smile seem almost childlike.

Quan had met Kisha while shopping in Kings Plaza mall

one day. They were in the same store. He was looking for a new outfit and she was looking for a birthday present for her brother. As fate would have it, they both reached for the same sweater at the same time. After apologizing and then introducing themselves, Kisha told Quan that he and her brother were about the same size and asked him to try on the sweater so she could see how it would fit. When he came out of the dressing room, Kisha stood there inspecting him up from head to toe. Sizing him up, she saw the strong self-confidence, the borderline arrogance, toasted almond complexion, and heart-melting smile. It didn't hurt that he was styling with his gear, and blinding with his jewelry. She had to admit that she liked what she saw.

Modeling the Coogi sweater for her, Quan said, "I see that they got the dress with the same pattern as this sweater. How about I buy it for you in exchange for your number and a date."

"Sorry, boo, but my number ain't for sale. Thanks for helping me out though."

Quan went back into the dressing room to take the sweater off. Expecting her to still be there when he got out, Quan was surprised to see that she had dipped off. Looking obviously disappointed that she'd gotten away, Quan was about to buy the sweater when a sales clerk handed him a bag. Inside of the bag was the same Coogi sweater already paid for, and Kisha had written her number on the back of the receipt. Quan was intrigued by the thrill of the chase, but ended up being shot by cupid and falling in love.

Jumping out of the driver's seat of the car, Kisha ran up to him and jumped up wrapping her arms around his neck and her legs around his waist, all the while covering his face with kisses and saying, "Damn, I missed you, daddy."

"I missed you too, baby girl," was B.K.'s reply. He buried his face in the side of her neck and deeply inhaled the sweet scent of her body. His dick got hard instantly.

Feeling his manhood poke her through his jeans, Kisha said, "C'mon, daddy, I can't wait to get you out of those clothes."

Chapter 2
You're All That I Need

Shorty, I'm there for you anytime you need me / for real girl it's me and your world, believe me / nothing make a man feel better than a woman / a queen wit a crown that be down for whatever...

B.K. was quiet the whole ride back to the city. It was hard for him to believe that he was actually free. He kept waiting for a federal vehicle to chase down Kisha's car and tell him that it was a mistake, and they released the wrong man, but they never came.

It wasn't until they pulled up in front of Kisha's condo, which was in the back of Canarsie, that B.K. snapped out of his daze. Getting out of the car, Kisha and B.K. held hands as they entered her building.

"Quan, I know that you just came home and you're gonna wanna get out, but for the rest of the week, yo' ass is on lock!

41

I'ma feed you, fuck you and love you one day for each year that you've been away from me. So for the next five days, don't even think of calling anybody 'cuz you ain't goin nowhere and they damn sure ain't comin here to see you."

B.K. almost didn't answer. He was so used to everybody calling him "B.K." that his real nickname, Quan, sounded foreign to his ears. "Nah, boo, you know I ain't tryna leave you home alone to holla at nobody. Right now it's all about you. Fuck da streets."

Stepping into her living room, Quan realized how lucky he was to still have his girl by his side. Kisha had trooped his whole bid with him. Coming to see him twice a month, letters, money orders, pictures, whatever he needed, she held him down. He knew that she probably got her fuck on while he was away, but that was a small thing to him. What really mattered was that she was there whenever he needed her. During his bid, Quan had met plenty of niggas that had chicks leave them for dead, get pregnant by their man's best friends, and all kinds of other bullshit. Quan knew that Kisha was a rider and that made him love her even more.

At 11:15 that night, Quan was knee deep in some pussy working on busting his fourth nut when the phone rang. Not really wanting to, he stopped in mid-stroke and reached over to the nightstand and picked up the phone.

"This call is from a federal prison. This is a pre-paid call. You will not be charged for this call. This call is from "Fresh". Hang up to decline the call, or to accept the call dial "five" now. To block future pre-paid calls from this person, dial 77." Quan let the recording play a second time, giving him a chance to pull out of Kisha's tight love tunnel and catch his breath before pressing five to accept the call.

"Yo, what's really good, nigga?" Quan said into the phone

once Fresh was on the other line.

"Ain't nothing, son, I just got finished hitting the pull-up bar, you know how we do. What's good wit 'chu?"

"Everything's good right now. I'm tryna make up for lost time with baby girl, ya heard?"

"Yeah, I be knowin."

Quan didn't want to say too much. Really, he couldn't say too much because Kisha was giving him some head while he was on the phone and it felt so good that he could hardly talk. Still, he was trying to be considerate towards his homie, knowing that Fresh would soon have to lock in for the night. "Yo I'ma send you some bread by Western Union tomorrow so look out for it, plus I'ma go see your B.M. and hit her with some ones to bring your seed up to see you this weekend. I ain't forgot you, nigga."

"That's what's really hood," Fresh replied knowing that B.K. was the type of nigga who never said he was going to do something unless he really meant it.

Remembering something that happened in the jail that day, Fresh said, "Yo, you remember dat nigga Biz that was in G.B. that you didn't like?"

"Yeah, why? Whassup wit his bitch ass?"

"He was beffin wit dem Jersey niggas and they aired his ass out up in the gym," Fresh replied, putting his homie up on the newest jailhouse news.

"Word?"

"Yeah, they had to shut the compound down and medi-vac his ass outta here. Dem Jersey niggas punished him!"

Quan and Fresh talked for a few more minutes before the phone beeped, letting them know that they would be cut off in sixty seconds. Rather than be disconnected, they both opted to hang up instead.

"I love you, son. Hold it down, ya heard?" Quan said into the phone.

"I love you more, and you know I'ma hold it down, son."

Quan hung up the phone, picked Kisha's 135-pound frame up as if she weighed nothing, and finished right where he left off before the phone rang.

Kisha wasn't bullshitting when she said that she was keeping Quan on lock for the next five days. All he was allowed to do was fuck, eat, and shit for the entire five days that she held him hostage. When it was time to go check in with his P.O., Kisha refused to let him go by himself. It was *she* who dropped the money off to Fresh's baby's mother as well as sent him the money by Western Union. Quan knew that he couldn't complain. Kisha had done a five-year bid with him from the beginning to the end. The least he could do was spend five days with her and her alone. Plus, he knew that she had only taken five days off from her job as a real estate agent and come Monday, it would be back to work for her.

Chapter 3
Can I Live?

While I'm watchin every nigga watchin me closely / my shit is butter for the bread they wanna toast me / I keep my head, both of them where they supposed to be...

"I make 'em wait for you till five in the morning, nigga, I'll put ya' smarts on the side of your garments. This is a warning. Stop fucking wit me..." Quan was in Kisha's house blasting the song *Threats* off of *the Black album* by Jay-Z, but in his mind he was really dealing with *D'evils*. He had been home for two months already and his progress was a slow process. When he got locked up five years ago, he had his own crib, a brand new B.M.W., a hundred and twenty thousand in the stash, and a connect that was hitting him with bricks for 16.5 a piece.

Between his lawyer fees, fines, commissary money and the money that Kisha needed, his stash was looking real light. He'd lost his apartment, he still had the connect, but wasn't trying to go that route, and the only reason that he still had the B.M.W. was because it was in Kisha's name. He gave Kisha his car to keep until he got out, but he knew that he wouldn't take it back once he gave it to her. He'd been through his old neighborhood and bumped into a few of his so-called friends. Everybody appeared to be happy to see him back on the streets, but to Quan, it felt as if everybody was even happier to see him fucked up.

Make no mistake about it, even pushing a five-year-old beamer and rocking the same jewelry that he had before he got locked, Quan was still looking like something, but compared to the level that he was on before his bid, and the way that a few of his friends were shining, pushing ES 55 AMG Benzes, H2 Hummers, and 300c's with twenty inch Sprewells, Quan felt like he was really fucked up and left behind. What really had him in his feelings was that the same niggas that was shining, rocking platinum jewelry, were the same niggas that he used to front bricks to when he was on top.

Chapter 4
I'm a Hustler

Never been a dummy / never did what the dummies do / so I had a 'Mil to burn before I turned 22 / more money, more problems is true / cuz' the more money I make / the more problems for you...

"Damn, I'm playin my fuckin self. I know better than this," Quan said to himself out loud. He was nervous as hell, and he had every right to be. In the trunk of his car was exactly fifty-four ounces of crack along with thirty thousand dollars in cash. Quan had just come from his old neighborhood in Bed-Stuy, and after getting up with a few of his peeps, he collected a brick and a half of cook-up and thirty G's from his mans. A naïve person would think that his peoples had done this out of love, but Quan knew better. He knew that niggas just wanted to be able to say that they were the ones to put him back on his feet.

Quan was leery about taking all of that crack to Kisha's crib, but at the moment, he didn't have anywhere else to stash it. *Fuck I'm supposed to do with all this crack? I'll be damned if I get on a block and sell shit. It's probably a thousand lil' dirty niggas out there with three grams and ten guns, thinking they Nino Brown and shit,* he thought to himself. He was heated that after all the shit he'd done for niggas, this was all he was worth to them in return. "Niggas quick to give a nigga some mu'fuckin crack when he come home, but don't wanna come up off no paper! It's a'ight, I'ma show these niggas how it's done," he said out loud again as he reached Kisha's condo safely.

Stashing the crack and the money in the house, Quan began to put together a plan. He had thirty thousand dollars from his peeps. Another ten thousand from his stash, and he figured that he'd sell the whole fifty-four ounces for forty thousand dollars in one whop. With eighty thousand dollars to play with, he figured that he could invest some of the money into real estate like he'd planned to back when he was in Otisville. While he was locked up, he had read a few books on real estate and did a lot of research on investment and government real estate grants. From what he understood, the shit was simple. He knew that as a high school drop out with no education or marketable skills, he wouldn't be the next Donald Trump, but a few brownstones, a house, and a nice car were enough for him, and he knew exactly who he had to talk to to make all of this happen.

Chapter 5
Brooklyn's Finest

Who shot cha' / mob ties like Sinatra / Peruvians tryna do me in / I ain't paid them yet / I'm tryna push 700's / they ain't made them yet / Rolex and bracelets frostbit / rings too / niggas 'round the way call me igloo / stick who???

"Niggas can't breath when I come through, hung through, some shoes gotta be 20's man, it's not even funny, they can't breath..." Quan sat in the cockpit of his cocaine white Porsche Cayenne boppin his head and singing along with *Fabolous* to the *Just Blaze* track. Sitting in the parking lot of F.C.I. Otisville, he felt good. It was his homie Fresh's release date, and Quan being the real nigga that he was, had come to pick Fresh up and take him to the halfway house. In the back seat was a cute, thick, red-boned shorty who had been on Quan's dick for years. Today she was a welcome home present from Quan to Fresh.

Quan had stepped his game up majorly in the last four months. Armed with a few thousand, his knowledge of the real estate business, the help of a few lawyers, *and* his uncle, Quan opened up *S&K Realty Corp.* Now with a three-man staff of licensed real estate agents and Kisha running the show, S&K Realty now owned four distressed properties, each of which had been renovated into six-family buildings. After the renovations, the realty company applied for, *and* was awarded federal grants for each building to rent apartments to low-income families. Besides the grants, Section-8 paid him six hundred fifty dollars a month for each apartment. Off all four buildings, he collected over fifteen thousand dollars a month in rent.

With the real estate hustle jumping off, it would seem as if Quan would finally be able to leave the streets alone for good, but the streets were in his blood and sometimes old habits die hard.

Quan was back in the game, and back on his grizzly. He had the same connect that he had before he got knocked and even though the price was slightly higher, the work was still fire and he managed to turn a nice profit selling weight while keeping a low profile. His P.O. was a cool ass hood chick who told him that she didn't care if he smoked weed as long as he had a job and didn't catch any new cases. Quan was headed back to the top of the game, but it didn't take a genius to figure out that what goes up eventually must come down.

"Damn, what the fuck is taking this nigga so long?" Quan said to the red-boned short named Myesha, who was in the back seat.

Myesha was a twenty-one-year old 'round the way girl who resembled the R&B singer Faith Evans. The product of drug-addicted parents, Myesha was too cute to be a chicken head or a hood rat, but lacked the self-confidence to carry herself like the dime piece that she was. Years ago, Quan had pistol whipped her boyfriend for talking slick after Quan commented on the black eye that dude had given her. Myesha fell in love with Quan that day and been down to do anything he needed her to ever since. Quan never fucked her though. He made love to her mind by showing her the love that she had been missing her whole life.

It was 9:45 in the morning and Fresh had a three-hour window before having to be at the halfway house on Myrtle Avenue in Brooklyn. Quan had everything planned. He had a room at a nearby hotel where Myesha would take Fresh and give him his first nut in six years, then Quan would put some money in Fresh's pockets and drop him off at the halfway house. The two big shopping bags full of new clothes and sneakers that Quan had in his trunk were also for Fresh, and Quan planned to put him on the payroll at S&K Realty as soon as possible. Quan knew that the faster that Fresh got a job, the faster he could get out of the halfway house. Even though he would be on home confinement for the remainder of his halfway house time, it still would be better than being stuck in a halfway house for six months.

At exactly 10:02, Fresh strolled out the doors and into the parking lot of F.C.I. Otisville. Wearing a royal blue and white Team Roc sweatsuit, a N.Y. Giants wool jacket with the matching fitted hat, and a pair of white on white uptowns, Fresh headed towards Quan's car. Quan got out the car and went to meet Fresh halfway.

"What's really hood nigga?" Quan asked, giving Fresh a hug.

Fresh had the same *"I can't believe I'm home"* look on his face that Quan wore six months ago. "Shit, right now, everything's good! I'm free, it's about to be on B.K., ya heard?"

"Yeah, I feel you, but just so you know, don't nobody call me B.K. out here. It's Quan now, a'ight?"

"A'ight, Quan, but I'm still Fresh, and fuckin' with 'chu that's exactly how a nigga looking too...dead fresh!"

Walking towards the car, Fresh noticed the dubs on the Porsche and the cute shorty in the back seat. His eyes locked onto hers for a second and he hoped that shorty wasn't Quan's wifey because after six years, Fresh was ready to fuck anything moving.

"Damn, son, that's you?" Fresh asked with astonishment in his voice.

"What, the car, or the chick *in* the car?" Quan shot back. When Fresh didn't answer right away, Quan laughed and said, "The car is mines..." Then looking at his iced out Frank Mueller timepiece, he said, "And for the next hour-and-a-half, the chick is yours." Quan got in the driver's seat and Fresh got in the back seat with Myesha to get better acquainted.

"Myesha, this my man Fresh that I was telling you about. Fresh that's my homegirl, Myesha," Quan said, making the introductions.

Licking his lips, Fresh said, "How you doin, ma?"

"I'm fine," Myesha answered, then before fresh could get another word out of his mouth, Myesha leaned over and kissed Fresh, moving her tongue into his mouth. Quan started the car up and tried not to look in the rearview mirror as Fresh and Myesha went at it.

Parked in the parking lot of the small hotel, Quan had just finished smoking a blunt of Haze and watching the movie *State Property* on the TV/DVD in his Porsche. Fresh and Myesha had been in the hotel for an hour and forty-five minutes already and if they didn't hurry up, Quan was going to have to go in there and get them. It wasn't that he wanted to cock-block Fresh's flow, but it was 11:55 and Fresh had to be at the halfway house by 1 o'clock. Just as Quan was about to get out of the car and go into the hotel, Fresh came out followed by Myesha.

Getting into the car, the first thing Fresh noticed was the smell of weed that lingered in the air. "Damn, son, that la-la smell good. I'm sick that I can't smoke right now," Fresh said from the back seat with his arms around Myesha's shoulders.

"Don't sweat the small things, ya heard?" Quan replied while making his way towards the interstate that would take them back to the city.

Doing ninety the whole way there, Quan got Fresh to the halfway house at exactly 1:07. Jumping out of the car, Quan went to the trunk and grabbed the bags of clothes and sneakers and gave them to Fresh. Then he went into his back pocket and pulled out a brick of cash. Not bothering to count it, he shoved it into Fresh's hands and said, "Yo, that's to hold you down for a minute. I got a job and a crib for you, so when it's time for you to get on home confinement, you'll be straight." Then Quan looked at his watch and said, "Go 'head, son, you late!"

Fresh gave Quan a pound and a hug and said, "Yo, I'ma call you tonight. I love you, son."

"I love you more. Be easy kid."

Fresh disappeared through the halfway house doors and Quan got back into the Porsche with Myesha, who had gotten into the front seat, and pulled off.

Chapter 6
Stop Being Greedy

Ya'll been eating long enough now / stop being greedy / let's keep it real partner / ribs is touching / don't make me wait / fuck around and I'm a bite you / and snatch the plate...

Three hours later, Quan was chilling on his block when his cell phone rang. Without bothering to look at the caller I.D., he opened up the flip on the phone and said, "Talk to me."

"Hey, youngster, this is Freeze. What's going on?"

Quan's ears perked up immediately when he heard that it was Freeze on the other end of the phone. Freeze was Quan's surrogate uncle. He'd been getting money throughout Brooklyn and Harlem since the 70s. When Quan had first come home and his peoples had given him all of that crack, it was Freeze who bought it all off of him. Freeze gave Quan forty-five thousand dollars for the fifty-four ounces plus another forty-five for his pocket. Not because he needed the crack. Freeze did that out of love for his nephew. Freeze also was the one who helped Quan get the realty company started. He hired his lawyers and co-signed for any bank loans necessary to make sure that Quan's business venture was a success.

"Freeze, how you doing man?" Quan asked.

"I'm alright. Listen, I got something that I need to see you about. You think that you can meet me at Juniors downtown in about an hour?"

Without hesitating, Quan said, "In an hour? I'm there. Meet me in the back by the bar."

"Alright Q, I'll see you in a minute."

Quan hung up the phone and wondered what could Freeze possibly need to see him about. Freeze wasn't the type of dude that got too close to the streets or street niggas anymore. He was more of a behind the scenes, boss type of dude who rarely ever got his hands dirty. Even when Quan approached Freeze about the fifty-four ounces, Freeze had one of his goons pick up the crack and drop the money off. Then the next day he called Quan and had him go to the promenade downtown. When Quan got there that day, Freeze was waiting alone with a duffel bag slung over his shoulder. Quan watched in astonishment as Freeze opened the duffel bag and showed him all the crack that Quan had sold him.

"Stay away from this garbage. I know you're tired of jail by now. Whoever gave you this shit after you just coming home from a five-year bid is a piece of garbage."

Then Freeze surprised Quan by throwing the bag full of crack into the water and watched it sink to the bottom. Yeah, Quan had to respect his old head's gangsta, Freeze was definitely 'bout it.

Downtown Brooklyn was packed when Quan made it to Juniors. College kids, as well as evening shoppers loitered the area creating the normal hub-bub atmosphere that downtown Brooklyn was famous for. Being that it was 5:30 in the evening, Juniors was full of the people of the workforce who came for their *happy hour*, before returning home to the redundancy of their everyday lives. Not seeing Freeze at the bar, Quan found an empty stool and ordered a shot of Hennesey Paradise on ice. He was taking a sip of his drink, wondering where the hell Freeze was, when a waitress from the dining section tapped him on the shoulder and told him that there was a guest waiting for him at a table and for him to follow her. When Quan got to the table, he wasn't the least bit surprised to see Freeze sitting there sipping on a Martini dry. That was just like Freeze, to arrive early and scope out the scenery. No wonder he had a twenty-plus year run without ever getting caught up. Freeze stayed two steps ahead of the smartest niggas, and ten steps ahead of everybody else.

"Quan, have a seat. I'm so glad you could make it, young-ster." Freeze said with a smile on his face.

"Freeze, what's up? What's going on with you?"

"Nothing much, just taking it easy in my old age."

"Old my ass, what did you just turn, twenty-four?" Quan retorted with a laugh.

"Actually, it's twenty-five, get it right, young'n!" Both Freeze and Quan laughed at that comment, knowing that Freeze was a young looking forty-four. They both went back and forth with a humorous banter for a few more minutes and then Freeze turned the humor off like a light switch.

"Quan, what the fuck is wrong with you? Why you gotta be so hard headed and stubborn?" Freeze asked in a dead serious tone that let Quan know that joke time was over.

Quan was so caught off guard by Freeze's sudden shift in attitude, all he could muster was a feeble, "What you talking 'bout, Freeze?" as a response.

"I'm talking about you pitching stones at the penitentiary walls. Quan, you just came home from a federal prison six months ago, and already you're back out here in the streets slinging coke like its legal. I mean your little real estate cover up is cute, and it might keep your girl and your P.O. off your back, but did you know that once you've been in fed prison and come home, they keep tabs on you for awhile. Chill out before you walk into a conspiracy charge and wind up with a hundred codefendants, and you know that these young punks ain't built to do no jail time so they gonna tell on you and anybody else to save their own asses."

Quan sat there with a dumb look on his face as Freeze pulled him up on all the mistakes that he saw Quan making. Quan had thought that he was doing his thing on the D.L., never serving anybody directly, never talking business over the phone, and never keeping any more than three hundred dollars on him at once. But now, listening to Freeze, Quan had to think that if Freeze knew what Quan was doing, then there was a chance that the feds also knew exactly what he was doing out there in the streets.

"Quan, listen to me. You're like a son to me. I've watched you grow from a snotty nosed lil' kid into one of the smoothest hustlers that I've seen come out of this generation. You're father was my right hand man. After he got killed, I made it my business to look out for you and your mother. When you turned seventeen and wanted to start hustling, I was against it, but I knew you, and I knew that if that's what you wanted to do then there was nothing that I could say *or* do to talk you out of it, so I hooked you up with one of my associates and made sure that he took care of you. I know that you don't like taking handouts, but before you turn to the streets, come to me. If there's anything that you want or need, please, just ask me, okay? Take my advice and leave the drugs alone, at least for a little while. Do that for an old man, a'ight?" Freeze said the last line with a laugh. He was trying to take the sting out of his words and ease some of the pain that he had caused Quan by mentioning his parents. Quan's skin was thick, but when it came to talking about his mother and father, the emotional side broke through his thuggish façade.

Quan's father was Freeze's best friend and right hand man. The two of them had come up through the slums of East New York, Brooklyn, together, and were as close as street niggas could get without being born of the same mother. Freeze had been Quan's uncle for as long as Quan could remember. Quan's father and Freeze had made their first piece of real change together robbing banks back in the day. From there they muscled their way into the cocaine business almost right in time for the crack epidemic that exploded in New York throughout the decade that was the 80s. By the year 1991, Freeze and Quan's father had an empire that stretched throughout Brooklyn and into parts of Queens as well as Harlem. Then Quan's father had gotten killed by a stray bullet in a drive-by shooting and Quan was left with a surrogate uncle, but without a father.

Freeze made it his business to see to it that neither Quan nor his mother ever had a need or want that went unfulfilled. Quiet as kept, Quan's mother had been the object of Freeze's affection for many years. It was out of respect for his dead other half, that Freeze never tried to take advantage of her in her times of loneliness. Five years after Quan's father died, his mother lost her battle with ovarian cancer and went on to join her husband. Quan and Freeze were left alone. With no one but Freeze to console him, Quan turned to the streets for the love that he no longer had in his life. He found that love in the form of a pretty chocolate shorty with brown eyes, whose name was Kisha.

Quan knew that Freeze was right about leaving the streets alone, but now wasn't the time when Quan was ready to quit just yet. His goal was to stack a mil' between the real estate and the drugs, then retire down south in the Carolinas with Kisha. So far, between the equity in the buildings that he had on paper and the few bricks that he was moving in the streets on the grind, Quan was worth close to four hundred thousand dollars. All this in just six months. He figured that if things stayed the same, it would take him at least another six to eight months before he reached his goal and then he was out. But sometimes things don't always go as planned. Still, Quan's heart and mind were set on reaching his goal.

After assuring Freeze that he would leave the drugs alone soon enough, their conversation shifted back to more jovial topics as Quan and Freeze laughed over drinks. Freeze said that he had some important business to take care of and Quan stood to bid his uncle farewell. Walking Freeze outside to his triple black Maserati Quattroporte, Quan watched as Freeze's driver/bodyguard opened the car's rear door with one hand, while the other hand was on his gun. Freeze's name fit him to a tee, because he was one cool dude.

Chapter 7
Give up the Goods

I got my mind on a stick up now it's time to get paid / thinking of ways to take loot already made / it's crime in the air ain't no time to be afraid / gimme yours or get laid...

Later that night while sitting in his Porsche with the seat laid back, Quan was smoking a blunt and plotting. He wasn't really into robbing niggas, especially niggas that he knew, but he reasoned that not only would this jux bring him closer to his goal, but he never really liked the nigga that he was plotting on anyway. Quan had been following the dude for two weeks. He knew that the dude had the dope flow locked in Brownsville and he was getting major paper. Quan didn't like the dude because he was Myesha's cousin and when her boyfriend had given her those black eyes, he didn't do shit about it because her boyfriend was his homie. What really made Quan not like the dude was when he heard that Quan had pistol whipped Myesha's man, he had the nerve to call Quan a bird ass nigga and then give the dude a gun to get at Quan with. When the word got back to Quan, he didn't react right away. He let the shit slide since nothing ever happened, but since then, Myesha's cousin had gotten his weight up big time, and Quan chose *now* to show him exactly who was the bird ass nigga.

Quan knew that the dude could get it, but he wasn't about to rob him that evening. He just wanted to watch his mark go about his business and then follow him home like he'd done so many nights before. Quan figured that, being that dude was a major supplier, the jux would be good for at least two hundred thousand dollars in cash, drugs, jewelry, and whatever else dude had in his house that Quan thought was valuable. Quan followed dude to his Park Slope brownstone and parked on the corner of the block. He watched as dude entered the building with a dark skinned chick on his arm. Dude never saw Quan parked on the corner of his block as he closed the house door behind his company.

"I got your bird ass nigga right here," Quan said to himself as he patted the sixteen-shot Glock that was tucked in his waistline.

Three weeks later, Fresh was on a 24-hour furlough. If he completed the furlough successfully, then he would be released from the halfway house and placed on home confinement the following week. After waiting for the halfway house to call and check up on him, he decided to call Quan and see what was popping. He was trying to get out of the house and convinced Quan to come and scoop him up. Quan had other plans and chilling wasn't one of them. He planned to rob Myesha's cousin that night. Quan didn't tell Fresh what he had planned. He figured that now was the time to see exactly how thorough Fresh actually was.

Quan was dressed in all black with a pair of black Chukkas, a pair of black Nike batting gloves, and a black White Sox baseball cap when he picked Fresh up that night. On the back seat he had a black sweatsuit, mask, and gloves for Fresh, just in case Fresh said that he was down for the jux.

"Yo, what up, nigga?" Fresh said as he jumped in the rented Dodge Intrepid that Quan was pushing. Quan had stolen license plates on the rental in case somebody saw the vehicle while he was making a getaway.

"Ain't nothing son, what 'chu tryna get into tonight?"

"Whatever's good."

"I got some shit I need to handle and since you're here, you can help me get right."

"What's really hood?" Fresh asked curiously.

"Let me put you on." Quan started the car up and pulled off.

Chapter 8
Gimme the Loot

Goodness gracious the papers / where the cash at? / where the stash at? / Nigga pass that / before you get your brains blown / from the main thug / 357 slug...

It wasn't until Quan got on the corner of Myesha's cousin's block that he told Fresh what he had planned. He did this purposely because he figured that even if Fresh said that he wasn't down with the actual robbery, then he could stay in the car and play the look-out role. When Fresh heard what Quan was up to, he immediately wanted in. This would be his first crime in six years and he welcomed the opportunity to be back in the streets doing dirt. Quan reached over onto the back seat and passed Fresh the black sweatsuit, mask and gloves, and let him get dressed in the car. Next, Quan passed him a chrome Colt .45 and told him to get ready because as soon as their vic showed up, it was on.

Twenty-five minutes later, both Quan and Fresh sat with their seats reclined and their guns on their laps. Less than a year ago, they were cellies locking down for count, and now here they were, suited up, ready to lay their robbery game down. When a red Navigator pulled up and parked behind Quan's car, he tapped Fresh and let him know that their mark was there. Pulling their masks over their faces, they waited until Myesha's cousin got out of the truck and walked towards his house before making their move.

Quan and Fresh let their mark get a few feet in front of their car before hopping out of the Intrepid with their guns up. Myesha's cousin turned around when he heard car doors slamming, but by that time, both Quan and Fresh were right up on him. Quan spoke first saying, "You know what time it is. Make a move and I'ma burn you, duke! Let's go inside the crib. Do the right thing and you might live to tell ya homies what happened." They walked him to the front door of his building and with both guns aimed at his head, let him lead the way into his apartment.

As soon as they all got inside the apartment and locked the door behind them, Quan told Fresh to check duke thoroughly. Fresh patted duke down and found a few G's in his pocket, a Taurus 9mm on his waist, a T-Mobile sidekick, and a cell phone on his waist. After Fresh said that he had everything, Quan went into his own pocket and pulled out two sets of handcuffs. "Cuff him to the radiator," Quan told Fresh while keeping the gun pointed at dude. Once dude was secured, Quan told Fresh, "Tear this muthafuckin' house up! Take everything that's worth something, drugs, jewels, whatever."

While Fresh was ransacking the house, Quan went over to dude and knelt beside him. "Where the safe at, son? Tell me and

I'll let 'chu live," Quan said calmly but menacingly at the same time.

"I ain't got no safe. It's a few G's under my mattress and that's it. That's my word," dude said lying. He figured Quan and Fresh to be a couple of young, dumb niggas who would grab the few thousand that he threw at them, take his jewelry and break out.

Upset that dude was lying to him, Quan slapped him with the gun he was holding. "You think I'm fuckin' stupid, nigga? This is ya last chance, then it's gonna get real ugly in here!"

"Son, I swear, I ain't lying. I ain't got no safe. I ain't getting money like that."

Quan knew that dude was lying, but he wasn't worried. He had a way to make sure dude would tell him exactly what he wanted to know.

Ripping a pillowcase off one of the sofa's pillows, Quan gagged dude's mouth and tied his legs to the radiator. Then he left him there for a second while he went into the kitchen. He came back minutes later with a sharp knife that was so hot it was glowing, and Fresh was following right behind him. "Pull dat nigga's pants down. We gon' make his bitch ass talk!"

When Fresh had dude's pants down, Quan wasted no time before shoving the red hot knife up dude's asshole. Fresh watched in amazement as Quan shoved the knife deeper into dude's ass, twisting it as he went. This was a side of Quan that he'd never seen before. Dude's screams were useless because of the gag that Quan had over his mouth. "This is just the beginning. It's gonna get a lot worse if you don't tell me where the safe at, son!" Quan said, as he pulled the bloody knife out of dude's rectum. Myesha's cousin knew now that he'd underestimated these two niggas, especially the one with the knife.

"What 'chu say? You ready to talk now? A'ight, I'ma take the gag off and if you scream or make too much noise, I got some shit worse than a knife for yo' ass!" Quan put his gun to dude's head and pulled the gag down off of his mouth.

"A'ight ch-chill, dawg. The safe is in the floor of the bedroom closet. Move the sneaker boxes out of the way, then pull the carpet up and it's right there. The combination is 22-32-42."

Quan told Fresh to watch dude while he went and checked for the safe. Fresh pointed his gun at dude while Quan left the room.

Quan followed dude's instructions and sho 'nuff, the safe was where he said it was. Using the combination that he'd been given, Quan opened the safe door and immediately knew that he'd chosen the right nigga to rob. Grabbing a pillow off the bed, Quan took the pillowcase off of it and used the pillowcase as a make shift duffel bag. Inside the safe was at least a hundred fifty thousand in cash, two Llamma 9mm pistols, a jewelry box containing two platinum link chains; four different diamond rings; a platinum Masterpiece Rolex; an iced out Jacob; and three different sets of diamond earrings. At the bottom of the safe, Quan found a brick and a half of china white heroin. Quan filled up the pillowcase and went back into the living room.

When Fresh saw Quan carrying the pillowcase full of goodies, his greed and stupidity made him make a mistake. With his eyes on the pillowcase, Fresh said, "Damn, Quan, if all of that is cash, we came the fuck up!" Fresh realized his mistake at the same time Myesha's cousin realized what was just said.

"Oh, shit, Quan, that's you? Damn, son, you know my family and you gon' do me dirty like that, stickin shit up my ass-n-shit?"

Quan hadn't planned on killing dude, just robbing him, but now that dude knew it was Quan that robbed him, there was no way that he could be left alive. Without hesitating, Quan dropped the pillowcase, grabbed a pillow off the couch, then he put the pillow on the back of dude's head. He put the gun to the pillow and pulled the trigger. It all happened so quickly that Fresh didn't even have time to blink.

If Quan had been following the code to the streets, he would have shot Fresh dead where he stood that night, but he had his own reasons for giving Fresh a pass that time around. For one, he'd just spent two-and-a-half years in the same cell with Fresh and he took a liking to him. Quan knew that Fresh wasn't used to seeing major paper. Fresh was a petty half ounce, sneaker and weed money type of hustler. When they were locked up, it was Quan who spent two hundred and ninety dollars every month to make sure that he and his celly ate every night. Another reason Quan didn't kill Fresh was because of Myesha. He knew that Fresh was still fucking her whenever he got the chance, and if Quan would have killed Fresh in that apartment, then Myesha could finger him as the only person she knew that knew both *Fresh and* her cousin.

Quan took the Colt .45 from Fresh, threw it in the pillowcase and made his way towards the front door. Fresh was kind of shook. He'd just saw Quan sodomize, then kill a nigga right in front of his eyes. Going out of the door with the pillowcase slung over his shoulder, Quan looked like a black Santa Clause. But it wasn't Christmas, and the only presents that Quan was giving out were first class trips back to the essence.

Chapter 9
Story to Tell

Now I'm like bitch you better talk to him / before the fifth put a spark to him ; fuck around shit get dark to him / put a part through him / lose a major part to him / arm, leg...

"Don't tell nobody 'bout this shit, son, not Myesha, ya' baby moms, none of them halfway house niggas...nobody!" Quan was barking on Fresh. It wasn't that he was mad about the mistake that Fresh had made that made him lose respect for Fresh. What had him upset was the excitement that Fresh had shown about catching the jewels off of Myesha's cousin's neck and the few thousands that dude threw at them. Fresh's actions really spoke volumes about his character to Quan. "Yo, we gon split the money down the middle. You keep the jewelry and I keep the drugs, a'ight?" Quan said to Fresh.

Even though the statement was posed as a question, Quan's

tone of voice let Fresh know that it was not up for negotiation. "It's all good wit me, son. I came up tonight. Good looking for putting me down," Fresh replied.

"Well, if you do the right thing, you'll be able to get a lot more money with me than that."

"That's what's up."

They sat in Quan's Porsche after switching plates on the rental and then parking it up. The pillowcase full of Myesha's cousin's possessions sat in Quan's trunk and Quan wouldn't even think about counting the jux money in front of Fresh. Instead, Quan promised Fresh forty thousand dollars and the jewelry as his half of the profit. Thinking more about it, Quan knew that he couldn't let Fresh keep the jewelry simply because Fresh didn't know that it was Myesha's cousin that they had just robbed and killed, and if Fresh wore any of the jewelry around her, then shit would be a wrap.

"Yo, matter of fact, I'll give you your forty plus and I'll keep the jewelry," Quan said as he and Fresh shared a Black & Mild just like they used to do back in Otisville.

Fresh knew that eighty thousand was a major come up after just being home for two weeks, but he really wasn't feeling coming up off of all that jewelry so he said, "Damn, son, why you wanna take the jewels? I was about to get my shine on sumpthin vicious."

To this, Quan replied with half of the truth and half lies. "Cuz', most of the jewels are custom made pieces and the nigga we bodied knows a lot of people in the hood, so if you running around rockin' his shit the day after he got killed, then only two things can happen: one, somebody that he knew might see you and try to pop your top, or two, they might get on some bitch shit and go to the cops on you. Either way, it won't be a good look for you. Now I know a dude who owns a jewelry store and he'll probably give me thirty or thirty-five G's for everything. That way, the jewels are off us and that's one less thing we got to worry about."

Fresh didn't want to give up all that platinum and ice, but he was scared that if he refused then Quan would just dead him on everything, so he reluctantly agreed.

It was close to three in the morning by the time Quan dropped Fresh off in front of his building. Before Quan broke out, he decided to drop a jewel on Fresh. "Yo, 80 G's ain't chump change, kid. If I were you, I'd be thinking of a plan to clean that money up because the minute you run out and try to buy a fifty thousand dollar car, the feds and the I.R.S. gon' be on yo ass. If you want, I'll show you how to use your job to secure a small business loan and start up a business. That way you can use your credit to cover your ass on your street money."

Fresh felt like Quan had read his mind because he was already thinking about trying to cop an Escalade with some of the eighty thousand. "That's what's up. I need a plan like that in my life. A-yo, I'm sorry about the fuck up I did earlier. It just slipped out," Fresh said apologetically.

"It ain't nothing big. What's done is done. Don't sweat the small stuff," Quan replied. Then he gave Fresh a dap and told him that he would be there to take him back to the halfway house in the morning.

After leaving Fresh, Quan headed home to be with his wifey. He felt that with all the 'hood hopping that he'd been doing lately, he was neglecting the woman who had been with him through thick and thin. Quan's mind drifted to the pillow in his trunk. He knew that there was at least a hundred fifty thousand dollars in cash and at least the same amount worth of jewelry and depending on how pure the dope was, he knew that he could sell ounces for fifteen hundred easy. At sixty dollars a gram, niggas would be lined up trying to see him. All in all, he calculated that with everything in the pillowcase, after he paid Fresh, he still would have about three hundred thousand dollars, maybe more, maybe less. That plus his net worth put him at three quarters of a million. He was so close to his goal that he could smell the country air.

Chapter 10
Grinding

Especially when them 20's is spinning like windmills / and the ice 32 below minus the windchill / filthy's the word that best describes me / I'm just grinding man / ya'll never mind me...

Fresh pulled up to a corner store in his hood and rolled down the window of his burgundy Cadillac Escalade EXT pickup. True to his word, Quan had blessed him with the eighty G's from the jux that night. When Fresh told Quan that he wanted to cop some wheels, Quan leased the Cadillac with the option to buy as a company car. Fresh put down ninety-five hundred dollars and his payments were two hundred ninety-nine dollars a month. Having gotten out of the halfway house three weeks ago, Fresh was now on home confinement. Being that he was employed by S&K Realty as a property scout/appraiser, his job required that he be in the field all day and keep a Nextel cell phone for instantaneous contact with his employer. The halfway house administration could care less what Fresh's job description included. As long as he could show recent pay stubs, pay twenty-five percent of his gross income from every check, and submit to random drug screening, property and housing searches, then he was all right with them.

"A-yo, ma, let me holla at you for a second," Fresh said to a brown-skinned shorty who was in front of the store.

"What's good, boo?" shorty replied as she approached the passenger's side window.

"A lotta you and a lil' bit of me," Fresh shot back. Then while shorty was laughing at his comment, he asked, "What's your name, cutie?"

"Kianna, but my friends call me Kia."

"A'ight, Kia. I'm Fresh. So whassup? You tryna ride wit a nigga like me?"

"Where you going?"

"Nowhere special, just cruising the hood."

"I'on care, I'm down." Kia hopped in the passenger's seat of Fresh's truck and he pulled off real slow while looking at her thick ass and thighs and just like that, Fresh had a *jumpoff* for the day.

Fresh was feeling his new found swagger. Out of the eighty thousand dollars, he spent at least fifteen on clothes and another fifteen on jewelry. The lifestyle of a baller was new to him and he was enjoying every minute of it. Quan was in his ear talking about investing some of the money, but the only investing that Fresh was into was the weight that he was copping and slinging on the low. Fresh got a taste of what it was like to be a big dawg and now he was willing to do whatever it took to stay on top. He was loving his new-found wealth, as well as the new respect that he was getting in his hood, so if he had to sling a few birds behind Quan's back to stay afloat, then so be it.

Cruising down Fulton Street two hours later, Fresh's cell phone rang. To anybody outside the vehicle, it would look as if he was riding solo, but that was because Kianna was stretched across the seat with her face in his lap giving him some brains. "H-Hello, who dis?" he asked, trying to concentrate on the road, and the phone call, while Kianna laid her head game down.

"Yo, Fresh, whaddup? Dis Jazz-o, I got cha' number from my man, Blitz. He told me dat you was the nigga to see about dem birds."

Fresh knew Blitz, but he didn't know Jazz-o. At that moment, it didn't matter. He just wanted to get off the phone so he could bust off in Kianna's mouth. "Yeah, I got 'em. What 'chu need?"

"I need two of dem thangs in an hour, can you handle that?"

"Yeah, it's nothing. They twenty-five a piece, straight money. Meet me at the funeral home on Pitkin Avenue and North Conduit in an hour and a half, a'ight?"

The funeral home request caught Jazz-o off guard. "Why the fuck you wanna meet in a funeral home, homie?"

"Cuz, if you short on that bread or you try some funny shit, then dat's where you gonna end up at, homie! See you in an hour and a half," Fresh said as he hung up the phone. Putting the phone on top of the dashboard, Fresh grabbed a handful of Kianna's hair and pushed her head down on his pipe as he let off a super nut in her mouth.

One hour and fifteen minutes later, Fresh was in the funeral home's parking lot waiting for Jazz-o to show up. In his glove box was two kilos of compressed coke, on his chest was a bullet-proof vest, and in his lap was a Tec-9 that had been converted to fully automatic. It was obvious that he was new to this level of the game. For one, nobody makes a deal over the phone for two keys of coke with somebody that they don't know, regardless of which one of your homies they say that they got your number from. They could be police, or stick up kids trying to set you up. Either way, it's a bad look.

Laid back in his seat with his engine running, lights off and his hands on the Tec, Fresh noticed a black Dodge Magnum with chrome rims pull up into the parking lot. He flashed his lights on once and the Dodge pulled up beside him. Looking through the Dodge's windshield he saw that the driver was alone. *So far so good.*

"What's poppin', pimpin?" Jazz-o asked as he slid his window down.

"Ain't nothing. Check it, turn your car off, grab ya scrilla and come get in my truck."

Jazzo-o did as he was told. When he got in the truck, the first thing he noticed was the Tec sitting on Fresh's lap. "What's good, son? Blitz told me that you played fair, so what's the hammer for?"

"As long as this deal is on the up and up, you ain't got nothing to worry about."

"All my money is on time, pimpin," Jazz-o said passing Fresh a Jansport full of cash.

After searching the bag and making sure that the money was right, Fresh told Jazz-o to look in the glove box. Jazz-o opened the compartment and grabbed both kilos of coke. "Dis what I'm talking about," Jazz-o said excitedly after he'd slit one of the kilos open and sniffed some of the coke up his right nostril.

Fresh threw the Jansport on the back seat and told Jazz-o,

"Yo, I gotta roll out, son."

"A'ight, pimpin, but yo, check it, I'm out of town wit these right here and they gon go real fast. I need a constant connect who got dat raw. Can I holla at 'chu when I get back?"

Instantly, Fresh thought back to his own out of town days before he got locked up. Depending on where Jazz-o was at, Fresh knew that he was probably going to make close to a hundred and ten G's off of one brick. "Yeah, yo, you do that and depending on how many you coppin', I might be able to drop the price for you," Fresh said sounding like a real hustler when the truth was he was just a front man. The coke that he was moving wasn't his, it was his cousin's. Whatever the amount of coke Fresh copped, his cousin would front him the same amount on consignment.

"A'ight, pimpin, dat's what's up," Jazz-o said as he slid out of Fresh's truck with the kilos in plain view.

Fresh pulled out of the parking lot first, driving past a white van that was parked right across the street from the funeral home's parking lot.

"Agent Reynolds, did you get everything?" Special Agent in charge Jefferson asked.

"That's affirmative. The conversation came in crystal clear. I got pictures of our guy entering the vehicle with a bag and leaving with the drugs in hand. The video camera that our guy wore caught everything that we might have missed. You wanna pull the perp's vehicle over now?"

"Hell no! You heard that idiot. He's good for at least three or four more buys. That way when we grab him, we'll have enough evidence to either make him give up his supplier, or do a hundred years in jail."

Just then, Agent Reynolds looked up from his computer and said, "Sir, I've got the feedback from the vehicle's tags.

According to DMV, that Escalade is registered to a S&K Realty Corp."

"Run a check on the company. Find out what year it was started and who's listed as chairman. I need that dope A-sap!"

Jazz-o, AKA Agent Mitchell, pulled over the Dodge Magnum on a side block and cut the car's interior lights on. Grabbing the kilo that he'd slit open inside of Fresh's truck, he pulled out a dollar bill and rolled it into a quill. Stuffing the bill into the slit, he inhaled deeply letting the raw coke rush his brain. Next, he grabbed a Ziplock bag from under his seat and opened the slit wider. Filling the bag halfway up, he taped the kilo closed before grabbing the next brick and doing the same thing. Satisfied that he had at least eight to ten ounces, he stuffed the kilos into his glove compartment and put the Ziplock bag into his jacket pocket. Riding back to headquarters, he thought to himself, *I love my fuckin job.* With the way he operated, it was easy to see why. Where else could he get high for free, then bust petty street niggas, get them to tell on the bigger fish, then turn right around after he busted the big man, and sell them the information on who told on them in the first place. Living like this kept his kids in private school, his wife in a new Benz, and him with a nest egg in an off-short account. Who said crime doesn't pay?

Later on that evening, Fresh was back in da 'hood chillin with Blitz and a few of his other so-called friends. Little did Fresh know, Blitz had gotten snatched by the feds a few days ago and instead of locking him up, they put him back on the streets to bring in more people in exchange for a lesser sentence. Blitz was working for them people, ha! At that moment while Fresh was running his mouth, an unmarked federal vehicle was parked around the corner listening to everything that Fresh had to say, courtesy of the wire that Blitz wore under his shirt.

Even though Fresh wasn't talking about much at that time, Blitz knew that his freedom depended on getting Fresh to open up to him.

Blitz had known Fresh since they were both petty, seven gram hustlers, and he knew that Fresh was a braggart, so it wouldn't be a problem getting Fresh to start bragging about how he'd come up so fast, but he had to get Fresh alone first, maybe get him high or drunk and then ask the right questions. Blitz didn't feel any remorse for what he was doing. He had the game twisted. To him, what he was doing was survival of the fittest, but what he was really doing was prostituting himself for the government, being the hoe ass nigga that he was!

While Fresh was being set up, Quan was sitting in a restaurant with Kisha sitting across from him. Over the last past month, Quan had been taking it real easy in the streets. After the robbery, he made a few moves to get rid of everything and ended up with three hundred twenty thousand dollars after selling the jewelry and moving the dope to some niggas that he knew uptown. Once that was done, he got real low. He was less than three hundred thousand dollars from his goal, but the more time he spent with Kisha, the more he realized that having a million dollars wouldn't keep him happy. It was the woman whom he wanted to mother his children, the woman whose eyes he was staring into at that very moment that would make him happy for the rest of his life.

Quan had a surprise for Kisha that night. He'd been to the restaurant earlier that day getting everything ready for the big moment. When ordering the food, Quan ordered a rack of lamb, flambé for the two of them. That was the secret code to the waiter to bring out Kisha's surprise. When the waiter returned, he carried an exquisite looking dish containing the rack of lamb. As he set the dish on the table, the lights in the dining area were dimmed to accent the mood. Both Quan and the waiter reached into their pockets at the same time; the waiter to get the matches he needed to flambé the food, and Quan to retrieve the velvet box containing the pink, pear shaped, VVS1, five carat Bellataire diamond engagement ring that he'd ordered from Lester Lampert's in Chicago.

At the same time as the waiter struck the match and ignited the food, Quan was on bended knee in front of Kisha. By the flame of the food, Quan looked into her eyes and said, "You are my sunshine when my days look cloudy, my shelter when life tries to rain on me, and my warmth when the world treats me cold. You complete me, and I want to spend the rest of my life in your arms. Kisha Monique Scott, will you marry me?"

Kisha had tears in her eyes as Quan slid the ring on her finger. She often dreamed of what the exact moment would feel like when she'd be asked to marry. Never did she imagine that Quan would get on one knee in a restaurant full of people. But he did, and he'd done everything so romantically that her heart was fluttering in her chest. Looking at the sparkle of the Bellataire diamond, and then the sparkle in Quan's eyes, Kisha knew that she was going to say yes. Quan was her Prince Charming and she'd been waiting for him to rescue her for years.

"Oh, Quan, I've waited forever for you to ask me that question. Of course, I'll marry you," Kisha said as she hugged Quan and cried tears of joy. The waiter covered the fire until it smothered out, and all that was left was a beautifully flambéed rack of lamb. The lights were restored and all the patrons in the vicinity clapped and cheered as Quan and Kisha kissed passionately. For the rest of the evening, the newly engaged couple enjoyed each other's company, and planned their future together, but Quan's life was about to take an unexpected detour.

Chapter 11
Just a Week Ago

*It was cool when you had hella weed to smoke / and you bought
a new hooptie just to keep ya' coke / I don't see how this side of you
can be provoked / it was all good just a week ago...*

Two weeks later...

Fresh was sitting in his Escalade, in the parking lot of the
Albee Square Mall in downtown Brooklyn. In a Macy's bag on
the backseat were three kilos of coke. He was waiting for Jazz-
o to show up with the seventy thousand, five hundred dollars
that he was charging for the product. After getting the word
from Blitz that Jazz-o was getting major coke down in Virginia,
Fresh decided to drop the price down to twenty-three point
five in hopes of keeping Jazz-o copping from him exclusively.
Fresh had gotten a call from Jazz-o that morning saying that he
was back in town and that he needed three of *dem thangs*. Fresh

gave him the price and the meeting spot over the phone.

As Fresh sat back in his truck, you would be hard pressed to find a nigga on his own dick more than Fresh was. With the type of money that he was seeing, jewelry and clothes that he was rocking, bitches were throwing the pussy at him, and Fresh found himself getting head from girls that used to hardly speak to him before he got on. He wished that he could show Quan how he was doing the damn thang, but to Fresh, Quan was on some hide out shit. Ever since the robbery, Quan rarely played the streets like that. He thought that Quan was shook, but Quan had bigger plans and flossing for the hood wasn't one of them.

Jazz-o pulled into the parking lot while Fresh was day dreaming. Fresh didn't notice him right away because he was looking for the Dodge Magnum that Jazz-o drove last time. This time Jazz-o was pushing a midnight blue 645i BMW with Virginia plates on it. It wasn't until Jazz-o pulled along side of Fresh's truck that Fresh noticed the beamer coupe with VA plates on it.

"What's poppin, pimpin?" Jazz-o asked as he let the window down on the coupe.

"Same shit, different toilet. I see you got a new whip," Fresh said, admiring the car.

"Yeah, dis my outta state car. So what's good? You ready for me?"

"Yeah, get in the truck."

Jazz-o got out of the BMW and got into the front seat of Fresh's Escalade. The BMW, platinum bracelet, Rolex and chain were all given to Jazz-o to help him look the part of a successful hustler, courtesy of the F.B.I. The sunshine glared off of the iced out lion's head pendant that Jazz-o wore on his chain. That particular pendant had been altered and now held a tiny camera in one of the lion's eyes, and a microphone in the other. Fresh had the starring role in the movie without even knowing it.

"I see you got the jewels on today. Virginia must be treatin' you real good."

"Yeah, you know, it's like Hova said, '*I got it dirt cheap for them, and if they short wit cheese, I'ma work with them!*'" Jazz-o said with a laugh.

"Damn, that lion's head is sick. I know you had to pay at least twenty G's for the piece by itself!"

"Really, twenty-four, but what's the sense of hustlin' if you don't splurge on yourself?" Jazz-o countered, trying to take the focus off of his jewelry and onto the drugs.

"Yeah, you right. So what 'chu got for me?" Fresh asked as he pointed towards the book bag on the floor between Jazz-o's legs.

"You said twenty-three point five a piece right? So here's seventy point five for three. I hope this shit is as good as the last two. Dem shits was fire!"

Fresh looked into the book bag and checked out his money. It was impossible for him to know that the serial numbers of half of the crispy hundred dollar bills had been previously recorded, and that he was now in possession of marked money. The F.B.I.'s plan was that as soon as the deal was done, and Fresh pulled out of the parking lot, both his car and the car that Agent Mitchell was driving would be surrounded. To keep Agent Mitchell's cover intact, he would be arrested right along with Fresh. Agent Mitchell's only gripe about the whole situation was that he wouldn't have the time to tap the product before turning it over to the lab for testing.

Fresh put the book bag on the floor between his legs and reached onto the back seat to retrieve the Macy's bag with the three bricks in it. Passing it to Jazz-o he said, "This is better than the two I gave you last time; it got less cut in it."

Just like last time, Jazz-o slit one open and took a quick snort up both nostrils. The drip that he felt at the back of his throat let him know that the coke was on point, and made him sorry that he was going to get busted with it all. "Yeah, this is the truth right here. Dem Virginia niggas gon' go crazy once this shit hit the town," Jazz-o said, trying to sound like an authentic hustler. Putting the coke back into the Macy's bag, it was Jazz-o who was in a rush this time. "Yo, I gotta breeze. That lil' one-on-one got me geekin. I'm ready to put these shits on the bus tonight and head right back O.T."

"Yeah, I got this big butt freak that I'm bout to holla at anyway, but yo, when you get back in town, holla at me, ya heard?" Little did Fresh know, he would never make it to shorty's house that day.

Fresh pulled out of the parking lot with the windows on his truck down and the music blasting. He was feeling really good, but all that was soon about to come to an end. Jazz-o pulled out the lot two minutes behind Fresh and was two cars behind him when they stopped at the red light on the corner.

Suddenly, two black Crown Victorias pulled in front of Fresh's truck blocking the street off. "Freeze, F.B.I. Don't you fucking move!" Agent Reynolds said, as the swarm of F.B.I. agents converged on Fresh's vehicle from all sides. It all happened so fast that Fresh had no time to react. He was boxed in and even if he floored the Escalade, he wouldn't have the speed to do anything but crash the front of the truck up. He sat motionless as three agents snatched him out of the truck and put him on the ground, face first. Looking over his shoulder, he saw Jazz-o getting the same treatment at the hands of the F.B.I. Fresh closed his eyes and sighed. He knew that this was the beginning of the end.

Chapter 12
Verbal Intercourse

Live on the run / police paying me to give in my gun / trick my wisdom / with the system / that imprisoned my son...

Quan was putting his plan together to get out of New York for good. Months ago, he'd put in for a transfer of his supervised release. His P.O. okay'd the move, and the paperwork was almost complete. Due to the federal grants that he'd gotten to acquire most of the property owned by S&K Realty, he couldn't sell any of the buildings until he'd owned them for three years. Considering where he was planning to relocate, owning property in New York was an asset, not a liability. As the CO-CEO and chief shareholder of S&K Realty, he would be able to use the property in New York as collateral when making acquisitions in the Carolinas. Already he had a seven-room estate being built on ten acres of land in Raleigh, North

Carolina, and as soon as the house was built, his affairs in order, and his transfer paperwork complete, he and his wife-to-be were both out of town for good.

As soon as Fresh and Jazz-o got to the F.B.I.'s drug task force command center, they were immediately separated. Fresh was taken to an interrogation room and cuffed to a chair which was bolted to the floor. Jazz-o, AKA Agent Mitchell, was taken to a back office, uncuffed, handed a pack of Newports and a lighter, and was told that he'd done a great job by both Special Agent in Charge Jefferson and Agent Reynolds.

"Now it's up to you guys. Go in there and scare that young punk with the chance of doing fifteen to life, then see if he'll go back on the street for us like his friend Blitz did. Blitz gave us him, so let's see who he'll give us..." Agent Mitchell paused and took a deep drag off his Newport, then he rubbed his wrist where the handcuffs had been less than five minutes ago and said, "And tell Agent Gibson I'ma kick his ass for putting the cuffs on so tight!"

Fresh was sitting in the chair with his head down. He knew that it was over for him. Here he was with two previous drug charges on his record, and a brand new charge, all while he was supposed to be on home confinement. He knew that just the amount of coke that he sold by itself was a five-year minimum; then, if convicted, he was guaranteed to be a career criminal. That was an automatic fifteen years, plus he had a 9mm under his car seat, and to top it all off, he still had sixteen months left before his max date on his last charge. He knew that he was looking at a twenty piece if not more.

Just as Fresh was wallowing deeper into self pity, Special Agent in Charge Jefferson and Agent Reynolds burst into the room. Sitting down at the table across from Fresh, both agents looked him in the eyes, as if trying to determine whether he would play ball or not. Agent Reynolds broke the silence by offering Fresh a Newport. Fresh didn't usually smoke cigarettes, but at the time, he needed something to calm his nerves. Accepting the cigarette, Fresh leaned forward as Agent Reynolds lit it with his lighter.

"You know that you're facing some serious charges, don't you?" Agent Reynolds asked, hoping to draw Fresh in with kindness before lowering the boom on him.

"I guess," Fresh answered nervously.

Then Special Agent Jefferson broke in saying, "Oh, there's no need to guess. The amount of drugs that you sold, and the gun that we found in your car, that alone carries at least ten years. And we haven't even run your prints through NCIC yet..."

It was at that moment that Fresh knew that there was something that the agents weren't telling him. He figured that this was an open and shut case, so why wasn't he at the federal building getting booked and printed yet?

"There is a way to help yourself out, you know." Agent Reynolds threw that out there and let it hang in the air, hoping that Fresh would bite the bait.

"Oh, yeah? How is that?"

"It's simple. You can either be a hard ass and get twenty-five years or you can go back on the streets and set up your supplier. Depending on how well you do, you may end up getting thirty-six months, *if that*. The choice is yours, but if I were you, I'd be thinking of myself on this one."

Fresh thought about it. He was twenty-four. He'd been locked up since he was eighteen. He couldn't see himself doing twenty-five years and coming back home when he was forty-nine. That was beyond his imagination. He already knew that if they came at him with an offer like that, he would cooperate, but the question was: *could he tell on his own cousin,* and if he did, *would that be enough? What if they wanted more? Who else could he turn in?* He thought about Quan, and hoped that it wouldn't come to that. He had mad love for Quan, but if he was forced to choose between his freedom and his love for Quan, well...

"Okay, say I do decide to help y'all, explain to me exactly what do I need to do."

Once Fresh said that, both agents knew they had him. They would squeeze him for every connect, every name, and anything else he knew, before they would intercede with the prosecutor for a downward departure for him.

"Well, first we need to get you to the federal building and go through the proper arrest procedures. Then we'll get you in front of a judge for arraignment, and once that's done, at our request, the judge will release you into our custody and we'll take it from there," Special Agent Jefferson said with a smile. He loved arresting dumb young blacks, scaring them with outrageous numbers, and watching as they prepared to sell their mama's ass in exchange for their freedom.

Six hours later, Giovanni "Fresh" Bryant was fingerprinted, photographed, arraigned, and formally charged with unlawful distribution of cocaine, a level two controlled substance. As promised, the federal magistrate released fresh into the F.B.I.'s custody, pending his cooperation in an ongoing federal investigation.

After a thorough interrogation, Fresh gave up his cousin, the names of some of the people to whom he sold, and when that wasn't enough, he gave them everything illegal that he knew Quan had done except for the robbery/ homicide in which he participated. After signing a sworn affidavit, Fresh agreed to wear a wire and complete illegal drug transactions with all the above named people. He hated that it'd come down to this, but twenty-five years was too much time for him to contemplate doing.

Later that night, Fresh pulled his Escalade out of the federal impound lot. He'd been arrested, arraigned, charged, and recruited by the feds all in the same day. Suddenly, a baller's life was moving way too fast for him. On his wrist was a special Rolex made of titanium that couldn't be broken or welded off, and could only be removed by using a special key that the feds had. Inside of the watch was a tracking device that would allow the agents to monitor his whereabouts twenty-four/seven. He'd been given back all of his property including all of his jewelry and cell phone. Accidentally on purpose, the feds gave him Jazz-o's chain. When Fresh commented on the chain, the agents told him that he should consider it a gift, and accident in his favor. The feds gave him the same marked money that Jazz-o had used on him, then sent him to make a buy from his cousin that night. Fresh was on his way to sell his soul to the devil for a discount price.

Chapter 13
Deep Cover

Let's go straight to the undercover source / and see what we can find / crooked cops that pop us / and give us a gang of time...

One month later...

Fresh's cocaine connect, a few hood niggas that were getting money, a couple of niggas who had caught a body or two...more than a few people were sitting in MDC because of the shit that Fresh was doing on the streets. With just the bodies and his connect alone, the agents told him that he'd knocked his time down to about sixty months, but he knew that he'd be lying to himself if he said he could do another five years right then, especially after just doing six, and only being home for a few months. He tried to get Quan on tape talking about making a sale, or anything drug related, but Quan had left the drugs alone awhile ago. Fresh didn't want to turn Quan in on the robbery/homicide because he knew that he was an accomplice and he wasn't trying to tell on himself, nor was he trying to let all the snitching he'd done go down the drain.

Eight federal vehicles surrounded the little office building that Quan and Kisha had rented to serve as the S&K Realty headquarters. Quan was behind his desk wearing a suit and tie, while on the phone discussing property acquisitions, when federal agents and U.S. marshals stormed his office as if they'd found *Osama Bin Laden*. Flashing a warrant signed by a federal magistrate, they cuffed Quan and rushed him out of the building. Kisha just happened to be coming into the office at the same time as the marshals were rushing Quan out of the building. It took three agents to restrain Kisha as they escorted Quan past her, and into a waiting vehicle. The only thing Quan screamed to her was that he loved her and for her to call his Uncle Freeze.

Downtown, in the federal building, the agents tried the same interrogation tactics on Quan that had worked on Fresh, but the only thing Quan had to say was, "I wish to speak with my lawyer, and until then, I exercise my right to remain silent." The agents still didn't tell Quan why he was being arrested and detained, and left him in the interrogation room hoping that he would break.

Quan had been sitting in MDC for a week now, without seeing a judge or being arraigned. He didn't know much about law, but figured that what was going down had to be a violation of his due process rights. Freeze had retained a reputable criminal attorney for him, but even the lawyer couldn't get an indictment number, or even a copy of the indictment, which led Freeze, Quan, *and* the lawyer to believe that Quan hadn't actually been indicted yet.

Quan was laid up on his bunk when the C.O. called him

for a legal visit. As he was being escorted to the part of the jail where the legal visits took place, he was hoping that it was his lawyer with some good news. Getting into the conference room, Quan was surprised to see a young, black dude with a familiar face sitting there.

Jazz-o, AKA Agent Mitchell, watched as the C.O. escorted Quan into the conference room. Looking into Quan's face he could tell that Quan was trying to figure out why Jazz-o looked so familiar. Jazz-o knew everything about Quan. From his mother and father, to his cover up realty corporation, to his relationship with Freeze. Jazz-o had been on Freeze's payroll ever since he'd passed the F.B.I. academy and became a field agent. By providing Freeze with valuable information about the F.B.I.'s informants, and drug raids, he was handsomely rewarded with a monthly payment that was triple the amount he made as an agent. When Freeze contacted him and told him his nephew had been arrested by federal agents, Jazz-o told him not to worry, he would find out exactly what evidence the feds had on him, and do his best to make it disappear. Jazz-o was shocked to find out that the informant in Quan's case was none other than Giovanni *Fresh* Bryant. Jazz-o had no idea that the *Quan* that Fresh was talking about was the same Quan that Freeze asked him to look out for.

As soon as Quan sat down, Jazz-o flashed his federal shield. Quan was caught off guard because he thought that he knew Jazz-o from somewhere else. Jazz-o's next few statements shocked Fresh, but cleared things up at the same time.

"My name is Agent Mitchell. I've been with the bureau for seven years and I've worked for your uncle for six of those years. Oh, he said to tell you that he bets you wish you would have listened to what he told you when the two of you met at Juniors that day." That was supposed to be a confirmation that

Jazz-o was who he said he was, but Quan was still leery.

"Quan, listen, I'm here to help you. I know the fact that I work for the F.B.I. may throw you off, but if I can give you a date at a particular event where you saw me and your uncle together, laughing and having a good time, will you believe me?"

After Quan agreed, Jazz-o reminded him of a time when Freeze had thrown a party, and not only was Jazz-o a guest, but he and Freeze had gotten drunk and sang karaoke together. Quan remembered that party because it was at that same party where Freeze plugged him into a coke connect. Now that Jazz-o was sure that Quan believed him, it was time to get down to business.

"Now here's what it is. You haven't actually been indicted or charged yet. You're being held as a suspect because of information given by an informant about an unsolved homicide."

At the mentioning of the words *informant* and *homicide*, Quan already knew the deal. He figured that Fresh was the informant and the homicide was Myesha's cousin.

"So what evidence do they have besides the informant?" Quan asked, knowing that there could be none unless Fresh made some up.

"Well, that's the good news. There is no physical evidence linking you to the crime scene. No prints, no saliva, no DNA, not even a strand of hair. There are no witness statements, nothing. Because of the lack of sufficient evidence, we were hesitant to pick you up. Without mentioning any names, I'm sure you already know who the informant is. In two days, he is scheduled to testify in front of a grand jury about your involvement in this crime. Should he make it to testify, I'm sure that the grand jury would hand down an indictment. Now if for some reason beyond our control he doesn't show up, then I can almost guarantee that you won't be indicted on his affidavit alone. As of now, he is still on the street, working for the bureau. My involvement in his disappearance has to be kept to a minimum for all of our sakes, but your uncle is willing to take full responsibility in solving this problem. What he needs from you is the name, phone number or address of a female that he stays in contact with or has frequent sexual relations with, that would be willing to help us out. Do you have anyone in particular in mind?"

Quan thought of Myesha. He knew that she was still fucking Fresh because she told him so. The irony of the situation made him laugh. He killed her cousin, and now he needed her to help him kill the one nigga who could place him at the scene of the crime. How real was that?

Quan gave up Myesha's phone number and told Agent Mitchell to have Freeze call her, and they could take it from there. After the visit was over, Quan was escorted back to the elevator which would take him back up to his temporary home, and Jazz-o left to go get the damn thang popping.

That night, while he was laid up on his bunk, Quan didn't know what was more unbelievable, the fact that Fresh had turned on him after all that he'd done for the nigga, or that Freeze had the F.B.I. on his payroll. Quan always knew that Freeze was a boss type nigga, but now Freeze seemed so much larger than that, something like the Don of all Dons.

Chapter 14
Long Kiss Goodnight

I'm flaming gats / aiming at / you fuckin' maniacs put my name in raps / what part of the / game is that? / like they hustle backwards...

Freeze smiled as he hung up the phone with Myesha. When he first told her that Quan was locked up, she broke down in tears. When he told her who was the snitch and what was the plan, she didn't hesitate to say that she loved Quan and would be down for whatever it took to get him out. *Yeah*, Freeze thought, *Quan sure knows how to pick a ride or die chick.*

Fresh was riding around the 'hood in his truck, smoking a blunt of Hydro. So far, nobody knew that he was working with the feds. He'd been promised that he not only wouldn't have to do any jail time, but after he testified at everybody's trial and they were convicted, he'd be taken off of his supervised release all together. He knew that once the word got out that he was snitching, he would have to move out of town, but the only thing that mattered to him was that he would be free.

Pulling up to the drive-thru window of a McDonalds, Fresh was about to order his food when his cell phone rang. "Hello, who dis?" he asked before screaming his order into the McDonalds speaker.

"This is Myesha. Whassup, boo?"

Fresh hadn't spoken to Myesha since he'd set Quan up. He was trying to avoid her, but he found himself missing her and her killer head game. "Ain't nothing, ma. What's really hood?"

"You. Where you been? I'm tryna see you tonight. I miss you."

When she said that she missed him, he got gassed up. His ego had been fucking with him before. He wanted a dime chick like her to be on his dick because of him, not because Quan told her to be. "I'm saying, what 'chu tryna get into tonight, ma?"

"Let me paint a picture, and you tell me if you like it. I got on a Vicky's Secret negligee, a bottle of Cristal on chill, some Dro, and a few porno flicks. The only thing that's missing is you."

Fresh's dick was hard already as he drove to the second window to pay for and pick up his food. Myesha's sex game was on one million and Fresh knew that he wanted to be the one to get her hot and wet. "I like how that sounds. What do I gotta do to get down with that picture?" Fresh asked seductively.

"All you gotta do is show up."

"What time?"

"The sooner the better," she cooed into the phone.

"I got some shit I need to do real quick, but I'ma be there by 8 o'clock definitely."

"I'll be waiting. Don't take too long or I might start without 'chu," Myesha said before hanging up the phone. "How did I do?" she asked, turning to face Freeze.

"Fine, baby girl. You did just fine," he answered with a sinister smile.

By 7:30 that night, Fresh was parking his truck on Myesha's block. The shit that he'd been into for the last past few weeks had him tightly wound up, and a night with Myesha was just what the doctor ordered. When he knocked on her front door, she answered it wearing a see-through Vicky's Secret teddy and holding a bottle of Cristal.

"Hey, handsome, you're right on time," she said as she let Fresh into her apartment and locked the door behind him.

Fresh hugged her, grinding his manhood on her butt.

"Ooh, it feels like you've missed me as much as I've missed you," she said with a laugh. Then she said, "Go in the bedroom. The DVD player is on. Don't start it yet, I got a surprise for you that I can't wait for you to see."

Fresh did as he was asked, watching her as she switched her hips to the kitchen to get some glasses for the champagne.

Freeze had left not too long ago. Two of his goons were waiting inside of her bedroom on the inside of the door. One was holding a .40 caliber handgun and the other was holding a chloroform soaked rag. When Fresh walked into the bedroom, the door slammed shut behind him. Turning around, he stared down the barrel of the .40 cal and knew that there was no way out of this one.

"Quan sends his regards," the one with the chloroform rag said before covering Fresh's nose and mouth with the potent anesthetic that rendered him unconscious in less than ninety seconds.

Fresh never made it to the grand jury to testify against

Quan, and somehow, the affidavit that he gave against Quan mysteriously disappeared. Quan's lawyer filed a motion to either have his client indicted and charged or immediately released. As much as they hated to, the F.B.I. had to concede with the motion due to their lack of sufficient evidence or a witness.

When Quan was released from court the following week, he saw the last two people he expected to be together waiting for him in the back of the courtroom. Kisha and Myesha were all smiles as the judge ordered Quan's immediate release. They had met the night when Freeze made Fresh disappear. Freeze had called Kisha and told her to go pick up Myesha so that she could personally thank her for making things happen for Quan. After talking, hugging, laughing, and crying with each other that night, Kisha and Myesha found out two things: One, they both loved Quan to death; and two, they were both curious about having sex with another woman. They decided to wait until Quan came home and surprise him with his fantasy, while satisfying their own curiosity at the same time.

It took another three months for Quan's transfer to be completed. His home had just been finished and he and Kisha were making wedding plans for the following year. Strangely, Kisha had fallen in love with Myesha and now she was planning to make the trip down south with Quan and Kisha.

Set to leave in three days, Quan was having dinner with Freeze at *Justin's* in Manhattan. Quan wanted to thank Freeze for all that he'd done for him, but Freeze said, "There's no need to thank me. I owe you more, so much more. Let me tell you a story...."

"Once, me and my best friend were competing for the same woman's affection. He had all the smooth moves, and knew all the right things to say, so obviously he won her over. Over the course of

time, I learned to accept their relationship, but I never stopped loving her. They eventually got married, and I was the best man at their wedding. Then things started to go bad, and he started to cheat on her and physically abuse her. She turned to me for support, and in the midst of me consoling her, we ended up making love. She ended up pregnant by me, just as her marriage was getting better. Out of love and respect for her, I put my feelings aside and let her and her husband raise my child as if it were theirs. Years later, her husband died and my child was almost a teenager by then. She thought it best that we not confuse the child with the truth. I stayed in my child's life and it hurt me to watch my child grow up thinking that I was his uncle."

"What I'm trying to say, Quan, is that I am your true father. I don't expect you to understand why things had to be this way, but I just want you to know that I really loved your mother, and I have loved you since the day you were born."

Quan sat in utter shock and disbelief. *How does one react after hearing that the man who was believed to be your cool ass uncle was actually your father?*

"Damn, Freeze, you could have told me way before now. I don't even know how to react now, after hearing that. I'm happy *and* angry at the same time. The funny thing is, I always used to wish that you were my father when I was little. How ironic is it that it would turn out to be the truth?"

"Quan, listen, I know that you're hurt and angry, and you have every right to be, but try to understand, when your mother died, her last request of me was that I protect you and protect your memory of her by not divulging the truth. Do you know how much it hurt me to have to live with that secret? To not be able to call you son and hear you call me dad? Now that you're leaving, it's like losing your mother all over again. All I can think about is what *could have been* but never was."

The rest of the dinner was filled with emotion from both Quan and Freeze, and in the end, Quan's happiness took precedence over his hurt and anger. After all, Freeze had been there for him since day one, and it wasn't every day that you find out that the one person you respected above all turned out to be your father.

• • •

Epilogue

One year later...

Quan and Kisha were married in an exclusive ceremony with Myesha as the only bridesmaid, and Freeze as the best man. Myesha happily played her part as Quan's mistress, although really, she was more Kisha's lover than anything.

The chain that Fresh had inherited from Jazz-o was shipped back to Special Agent Reynold's office, along with the special Rolex which was still attached to Fresh's amputated hand and wrist. That was Freeze's idea. He wanted to show the feds what type of time he was on...*That Gangsta Shit!*

THE END

Be on the lookout for J-Marcelle's highly anticipated release "Here Today, Gone Tomorrow" on Amiaya Entertainment, LLC this summer. For any questions, comments, or concerns regarding the self-proclaimed "J-Hova" of the book game, e-mail him at tanianunez79@hotmail.com.

DETERMINATION

by

Derrick "Blue Gambino" Phillips

Chapter 1

"Yo, that shit is just a bigger circle to swing in."

"A bigger circle?" Leem asked.

"Yeah, a bigger circle, cuz. You now how when you out there pushing ballgames and quarters, it's a certain circle you fuck with, right?"

"Right."

"Then, when you get on ya feet and you pushing quarter bricks and half bricks, you start fuckin' with another circle because you got money."

Leem nodded. "Yeah, I feel you."

"Well, that's all that rap shit is. It's just a circle full of entertainers that got money. They people just like you and me, dawg. They just sitting on some heavy change, so they fuck with people that got the same type of change they got, feel me?"

"Yeah, I feel you," Leem said. "But how do you make shit happen? I gotta hear this story." Leem chuckled the words out of his last sentence, crossed his arms and waited to hear what I had to say.

I really hated telling the story because I didn't like to brag. Plus, I never liked to be seen above my peers because that was sure to make a nigga feel jealous and cause contempt and hatred. But this is my right hand man, so I decided to tell him what it was hitting for.

"I guess I was just focused. In life, all it takes is sincere determination, a little bit of devotion, and a strong will. That's all I had. That, along with putting myself at the right place at the right time."

Honestly, I always knew I had the potential. This was a talent I realized I had since I was twelve years old. The only problem was that I never took it seriously. Of course I always wanted to take it serious, but my circumstances always hindered me from pursuing it full time. How could I? Every day in the concrete jungle was a struggle. We had to survive growing up. But finally the day came when I was tired of being separated from my life and the people I loved. A day when I was tired of settling for less and bullshitting. I came up with a plan to make it happen.

For real, for real, the cards were stacked against me and nobody truly believed in me. But instead of that continuing to discourage me, that became my motivation. That became the boost I needed to push me to conquer the world. But that was also the price of my demise.

"Yard in for A, E, and C...Alpha, Echo, and Charlie—Charlie through the rear!" the yard's P.A. system blared.

After shaking my two homies' hands and hugging them, I followed the crowd back into the prison.

"Yo," Leem exclaimed, "I want you to finish that story when we come out tonight."

"Ahight. I'll holla at you, Rumsfield," I said to him.

"That's what's up. See you tonight, Mr. President!" Leem

threw me a peace sign and spun off.

With that said, I headed to my cell, hoping that maybe there was some mail on my floor. But I'm thinking, *Here I am, a certified star, walking the prison yard, telling my story like on E! True Hollywood Story.*

But it's something I've got to do, because my man is on his way out and I want to be sure he doesn't make the same mistakes I did. That's why while we walked around the track ninety-nine times, I told him stories about the various entertainers I met and the places I've been, so he'd understand how I made my big mistake.

• • •

"You're gonna be late, baby. Come on!" my mom yelled.

I really didn't want my mom to take me to the interview, but she was the only reliable transportation I had. After I got the deal, I planned on buying a car immediately. Even though this was only my second week home, I already knew how *inconvenient* it was *not* having a car.

I took a look in the mirror once again and smiled. *I'm a sharp-ass nigga,* I thought to myself, flipping the collar up on my button-down Sean Jean shirt. I grabbed the matching blazer that came with my slacks and rushed down the steps.

"Why you didn't put the blazer on?" my mom questioned, as if she was telling me to put it on, but I *damn* sure wasn't wearing that nut-ass jacket. That was dead.

I was only going to a book publishing company. And being as though they already read my book, they should know that I was a street nigga. Honestly, wearing all of that was too much for me—slacks and shoes. Even though it was Sean John and the shoes were Ferragamo, I still wasn't feeling the whole lay. I would have rather been wearing jeans, Timbs, a bright-ass shirt, and a leather jacket. But I was doing all this for my mom, the only person who stood by me when I was down and out. I owed her this much, to at least try and do something positive and productive in life. For her, it was a dream come true.

When we pulled up at the publishing company, I was kinda nervous. It looked more professional than I assumed it would, like one of those downtown buildings near City Hall. It took us almost five minutes to find a parking space nearly a block away. But I threw on the fake smile and tried to be optimistic. This was a suburban area in Jersey that I had never been to, so I wasn't sure what the people would be like, whether they would accept me or not.

Omar, my business manager, was the person responsible for the interview. So I was kinda upset that he had prior obligations because I knew he would know how to handle these people with ease.

After giving my name to the receptionist, I took a seat in the waiting area and browsed through some magazines that were sitting out. Five minutes later, and just when I was getting into this one article, I was called into the meeting.

The woman in front of me, on a scale from one to ten, was like a twenty-five. She was definitely wifey material. Just the way I like 'em: light skin with beautiful eyes that were softer than a salt water taffy. Pretty lips that screamed *kiss me*, long jet-black hair bouncing with life, and a body that could cause a ten-car pile up. She extended a perfectly manicured hand for me to shake, and it was so soft that my penis started swelling.

"Hi, my name is Betty Hampton," she said with a wind chime voice, giving one more on top of the ninety-nine reasons I already had for wanting to be signed to Hampton House. "There's no point dragging this out. We are very interested in your manuscript, however, there is a lot of work that needs to be done before it will be ready to be published," she informed as she sat down and opened up a file folder of notes.

"A lot of work," I said to myself.

I immediately thought of all the work I had put into the book. I didn't say anything, but I damn sure was mad I paid all that money in jail to have it edited.

"First of all," Ms. Hampton went on, "we need to change all of these ghetto names. Sasha, Shawanna, Ta'quana.... We like using more conventional names like Cindy, Nicole, Mary, and Susan."

Of course I wanted to tell her how good Sasha's pussy was in real life, and how sexy Shawanna looked, or how Ta'quana was really a stuck-up hood rat. But I let her talk.

"Then, after we change the names, we want to diversify the characters. They need to have socially acceptable jobs, and they need to think with ambition and have priorities, especially these guys *Skate* and *New York*. They seem like intelligent characters, but they don't think with the level of sophistication that they need to."

Little did she know that Skate and New York were both doing life in jail, and if I were to make their characters more sophisticated, I would have been assassinating their characters. These dudes rode by the code of the streets, and ultimately it was the code that got my niggas booked.

"Finally, I think that we need to change the setting of the book and focus on a more major metropolitan city like New York, Los Angeles, or Atlanta."

Because they have bigger markets, I figured.

"We also can tone down some of the violence and give it a more reality-centered plot."

Whose reality was this chick talking about? In my reality, niggas die every day. This wasn't no fiction hip-hop lit I made up, like some kid from the suburbs did. This was the shit I really saw with my own eyes. I told a fictitious story and all, but where I'm from, everybody knows these characters and what they stand for. Furthermore, writing about another city was out of the question. Still, to make my mom happy, I decided to keep my mouth shut because ultimately, I was doing this for her. To buy her a house and get her the proper treatment she needed to take care of her Lyme disease.

I asked Ms. Hampton, "So who's gonna make the changes, you or me?"

"Well, I can have someone make the changes, but it will take some time and your book won't be ready until maybe a year or two from now."

I thought, *A year or two!*

I guess she could tell by the look on my face that I wasn't feeling the idea, because she shot some more drag at me.

"Well, you're more than welcome to look somewhere else if you want, but right now we have over a dozen books ready to go to press. And for us to stop working on them to rewrite your book would be a total waste of time. Rewriting is a very time-consuming process in which we try to get to whenever we find time. But I assure you that you will get everything your book is worth on the streets when the process is complete."

"So does that mean you're gonna cut me a check?"

"Oh, no! We do not give out advances. We don't work like that," Ms. Hampton was hasty to inform me. "After your novel is pressed up and in the stores, we will provide you a quarterly royalty check, after production costs are recouped, of course."

Okay, now I was mad. And even though Ms. Hampton could probably fart on my face under different circumstances and I wouldn't mind, business was business. So what I was in a fucked up situation? I still refused to let someone take my pride from me. Because point blank, I was a broke millionaire. In my little thirty years of existence, I done run through more money than P. Diddy does on a White Party.

Plus, on a broke day, I had chicks that looked as good as *Ms. Snobby Dime*, eat my dick while I drove from Chester to New York and back when I grabbed birds, and not miss a beat with her neck.

Momentarily I considered keeping quiet and going along with what she was saying. Something even told me to let my business lawyer handle it. But I got pride like Rosa Parks, so I let her have it...professionally.

"Ms. Hampton, I know you probably know ten times more than I do. I respect that and all, but when it comes to my work, I don't think we see eye to eye. Why? Because where I'm from, ain't nobody make it in the literary world. So a book about where I live and what's going on in *my* hood is going to sell through the roof. People gonna buy my book as is just because of who I be and the people I talk about.

"Now, I'm quite sure it needs editing, but do you know how many books I read that need editing? Every *Triple Crown* book I ever bought needed editing, desperately. Their editor must still be in elementary school. The princess of the urban literature world, Ms. Nikki Turner, needs editing on everything she puts out. And, Ms. Hampton, every book you have put out still needs editing—has typos *and* could be written better.

"I understand this is a woman's world, meaning, that it is much easier for a woman's work to be accepted because more women *than men* buy books, and in society in general, it's just easier for women to make it than men.

"So I can see why you feel the way you feel. But on this situation, I know what I know. Just like A&Rs knew that Nelly was gonna sell before St. Louis blew up and that David Banner was gonna sell before a Mississippi rapper was accepted, *I'm* gonna blow up. My whole city is gonna buy this book *as is*. So if you feel as though you don't wanna put it out, then don't. But somebody *will*."

On my way out the office, with my manuscript in my hand, I felt like shit. I held onto my dignity, but just seeing the look on my mother's face crushed me.

On the ride home I tried to justify why things went the way they did. I thought about all the women who claimed they couldn't find a good man.

I wanted to do something positive. I was intelligent, determined, humble, and considerate. I even had morals and values, otherwise, I would have never ended up in jail for as long as I did, because I would have just rolled over and snitched. But in society, it's just harder for a black man to make it. Men make up eighty-five percent of the jail population, and eighty-five percent of *them* are black. We make up eighty-five percent of the yearly homicide rates, on top of a large percentage of the homeless and unemployed. Statistically, it's dam near impossible for a black man to succeed. But do you think intelligent women that run companies think about that? *Fuck no!*

They don't understand the struggle we face. A woman can come out the house in a 3-5-9 outfit that cost ten bucks, a pair of Keds, pull her hair back in a ponytail, and guess what? Niggas'll *still* holla. But if a man is wearing a plain *Russel* sweatsuit and some Chuck Taylors with a nappy head...*man*. Chicks are gonna clown that nigga, especially if he ain't got a name for himself. Point black, don't no chick want a broke nigga, *or* a nigga that ain't nobody. I don't care how smart he is or what kind of morals and values he stands by. If that paper ain't right and he ain't got no respect, he's just a useless-ass nigga born to fail.

When I got back home, I convinced my mom to let me use

her car because something inside me wanted to know what was going on out in the streets. Now, mind you, I'd been home for a minute, but I hadn't been fucking with the streets because I knew going back into the streets would open up doors I wasn't prepared to walk through. But I was frustrated, so I had to go back to the place I knew would show me unconditional love.

First I changed my clothes and put on a black dickie and some black Chukkas and then I rode down Third Street. When I pulled up in front of my old head Jerv's house, the block was packed. Before I even got out of my mom's Honda Accord, I noticed the smiles and frowns on the faces of my *so-called* friends.

"When you get home?" my old head asked me while giving me a firm shake and hug.

"I just came home," I replied, knowing that if I told him two weeks ago he'd be mad I hadn't gotten in touch with him sooner.

"That's what's up. What you tryna do?" Jerv inquired while I greeted Jamir and a few others.

I knew what the question entailed, but I still played dumb.

"Do about what?"

"What you tryna do, nigga? You know I got this shit on smash."

Oh, well, I knew it was only a matter of time before I got back at it, so now it was a matter of what my old head was tryna drop on me. I followed him, Jamir, and Pooter up into his house and we sat down to bullshit.

Jerv's room was like the hangout headquarters. This was a place everyone on the block wanted to be, if only to sit around and listen to his thousands of CDs, or play his PS2 with hundreds of games, or watch DVDs or his camcorder tapes with all the hottest smuts. He had everything.

Big Jerv was just that, an easy six-three and about two hundred seventy pounds. He didn't look fat; he looked like Biz Markie on Celebrity Fit Club. There was no way to tell he was fat unless he took his shirt off, *then* you could see the stomach protruding from his beltline. But he carried himself well in clothes.

Jamir was the opposite. He was a solid football playing muthafucka. He was supposed to play professional ball, but an injury to his elbow ended his dreams of advancing to the NFL, so he dropped out of college.

Pooter was also in excellent condition. Just like Jamir, he also was a football playing muthafucka, but he never wasted his time with college because he vowed dedication to the streets earlier than his friends.

Out of the three, Jamir was really the high man on the totem pole, but he was also the most discreet. So if you didn't know him personally, you would assume he was broke, and that was just fine with him.

Jerv was the most flamboyant. He was the nigga that I wanted to be like before I went to jail, because even if he was broke, people would still assume he had money. On his bad days, he was still worth a quarter mil. With three dollars in his pocket, he still got the respect of a nigga that just sold ten bricks.

Pooter was a stunter too, and even though I never seen him with a mil, I knew he probably saw one before if he didn't have one.

Once we sat down, Jerv threw his CD player on and started playing the latest Nelly cut. At first I was wondering how he had the disc when I just heard that it wasn't even in stores yet. But, knowing who *he* was, I didn't waste time asking.

"You got any money?" Jamir inquired, picking up one of the

joysticks to Jerv's PS2.

"Naw, I'm broke as shit," I replied somberly.

Jamir looked from the game to me. He shook his head before digging into a pocket of his dingy, old-looking sweatpants and pulling out the biggest knot I ever saw. He peeled off a nice amount of bills and tossed them to me.

"Don't spend it all in one place," he suggested with a smile.

I grabbed the money and counted it. It was twenty-five hundred dollars. *Yeah, now this a starter kit,* I thought, making a mental list of the things I needed to get. Pooter peeled off a stack for me before picking up the other joystick to join Jamir in a game of NBA LIVE.

Jerv just sat back on the bed, watching me. I knew he had something nice for me, but he was the type that wanted to see where a nigga's head was.

After I stuffed the money in my pocket, I sat back on the king-sized bed to holla at him.

"So, what's good?" I asked him, wondering what he had on his mind.

"You tell me. What kind of plan you got?"

"Well, actually," I said, "I just came from a book company today. I really wanna publish these books I wrote."

He gave me a look that said, *Are you serious?* Before smiling at me.

I couldn't read minds, but I could only assume that he thought I was still giving him jail talk.

Before the night was over, my old head dropped nine ounces on me. That was my first mistake. Something told me not to take no coke, but then again, something told me that this was my destiny.

Chapter 2

When I finally got to my cell, I was happy to see that the mailman *did* stop through and drop off a little love for me. I was so eager to see who wrote me that I didn't even take off my jacket or boots before I checked the names. Two letters were from my chick, Chareen, and one was from my moms. I was disappointed that nobody I was running with wrote me, but that's jail: *out of sight, out of mind.*

Not even a month ago I was sending my squad pictures from video shoots with 50 Cent, and here I was, now sitting in a 6 x 9 cell looking at a 13″ TV, rolling a cigarette.

My cell is so small. Especially with two of us in it. There's about a two-foot space between the bunk bed and the desk. Plus, I have a trunk and two boxes. In one box I've got my draws, tee shirts, and socks. You're only supposed to have six of each, but I have double the legal amount. In my other box is commissary: soups, chips, cookies, candy, and juice. That's all commissary sells outside of cosmetics and stationery and shit like that.

A good meal in this jail is tuna fish and summer sausage chopped up inside of an empty potato chip bag, mixed up with Oodles of Noodles and Cheese Squeeze. If you're doing it real big, then you toss in some chopped green and white (green peppers and onions). Can you imagine eating this same bullshit every day for years at a time? Or even worse, being without and having to eat chow hall food: grade F beef that ain't fit for a dog, processed chicken patties three times a week, turkey tettrazinni and rice, or spaghetti. That's the basic menu right there, *on good days*. The bad days were pork, chili, veal, turkeyburgers, pot pie, and hoagies. Everything is cooked without seasoning and baked because they were implementing some sort of healthy diet. *So they said*. At breakfast, they don't even give you enough sugar for a cup of coffee. But since nobody complains, it just keeps getting worse.

My trunk is filled with my entire life: my mail, my books, my raps, and anything else that I've managed to accumulate while in jail. Usually I keep my shit locked up because I really don't trust my cellie. Even though I've been back in jail for almost nine months on a parole violation, I've only been back in *my* jail for two days. SCI Huntingdon, *my home jail*—as they call it, is the prison I'm assigned to. This state correctional institution is the only thing that keeps Huntingdon County from going bankrupt. Without this prison, this little county would be poor as shit, and this is information I've obtained from the guards. The jail should've *been* condemned, as old as it is. It was built back in the 1890s, and all they do to keep it from looking raggedy is paint it over, and over, and over again.

Once I got comfortable, I opened my mail and read my letters. The first one was accompanied by a picture of me and my chick, Chareen.

I had on a Gucci ensemble. Shirt, slacks, boots, glasses,

belt...the whole shebang. I looked damn good, if you ask me. Good enough to give Shemar Moore a run for his money, but I was a light brown with a cut sharper than Steve Harvey's. I resemble the Game, facial features-wise. He could easily pass for a sibling, but I don't have all the tattoos.

Chareen was wearing Christian Dior from head to toe. She's naturally beautiful, like Amerie without all the makeup and whatnot.

The picture is from my album release party. On the back, it reads: "To Castro. You still a star in my eyes." That's my rap name. My real name is Fidell Williams. So naturally people started calling me Castro since forever. My close friends call me the President, because I've always been the guy who calls the shots.

After reading Chareen's letters, I felt good that she's the one I chose to build my life around. She's loyal, sincere, gorgeous, and she don't get jealous when it's time for me to go to work. She probably knows I was cheating on her when I was running around, touring with my label and doing what I do. But for the most part, she's never made unsupported accusations or complained about the life I chose, because I treat her like a queen.

I got signed to Blockwork about a month after I came home. My old head, Jerv, had backstage passes to one of their shows, and that's when I hollered at Blue and Black.

Being as though I knew them already, it was reasonably easy for me to get signed. All I had to do was spit for them. I killed that shit when Blue threw on a beat for me. It was that Dynasty shit; the jawn when Jay be like, *"Knock the man off ya Polo sweater."* Yeah, well, I free-styled to that, and it was so hot that they made it a Blockwork mix-tape. I said some shit like:

Worst Muslim of all, because I swear by Allah/

I'll stab you in jummah after the khutbah...
Astafarallah! That's just the way I ball/
I don't talk, I ride. Y'all niggas'll stall...
So act tough and stand tall so I can break ya jaw/
I got star quality without a flaw at all...
Castro! Just the name let you know I got dough...

After that, Blue had Tariq bring a contract to me and a chain and I was signed. I ended up in the studio two days later and had my album done in two months; from there it was history.

As I got caught up in my thoughts, the P.A. barked: "Four o'clock standing count!"

My cellie, Li'l Homi, was the first to move. He slid down to the end of his bunk and hopped down on the sink and toilet to get to the floor, which was an easier move than climbing down the ladder. He flipped the light on as I got out of the bed to adhere to the prison rules and regulations.

After standing for what seemed like an eternity, a dorky-looking correctional officer came along with a clipboard and marked us both present. When the C.O. walked past us, I grabbed a pair of boxers off my clothesline, along with my towel, and prepared for the showers.

It's a common practice for a lot of inmates to wear two pairs of boxers to the showers to conceal themselves from the wandering eyes of fruity inmates. But it's also common practice for some to shower ass-naked, or with only one pair of boxers, barely protecting their private parts.

It takes about fifteen minutes for the guards to call showers, and like always, everyone rushes from their cells to get to their favorite shower spots. I, however, never rush, because I'm one of the few fortunate individuals who has their own shower.

The shower room has about eighty showerheads, and two handicapped showers. One tier houses sixty-eight people. I'm housed on the top tier on the right side of the cellblock (normally called the low side), which only has single cells, so that's another thirty-four people. Which in total means that if everybody were to shower, there would be a hundred and four people to eighty showerheads. On the first and second tiers, there are a hundred thirty-six per level, meaning somebody somewhere has to share. *Can you imagine being forced to share a shower with a man in a pair of wet drawers?* That's something I don't tolerate at all, unless it's one of my good friends who I *know* doesn't have homosexual tendencies. Other than that, I ain't doing nothing. After the five-minute shower, which always seems like two minutes, I walk damn near a street block to get back to my cell, past open windows and all. The C.O.s always open the windows, claiming it's hot, in an attempt to get inmates sick so we have to pay that two dollars for sick call.

That's just how cruel and insensitive the opposition is. To them, it's simply part of the job description, making us inmates miserable because, technically, we're the lowest of the low. *Society's worst.*

Back in my cell I quickly take off my wet drawers under my towel and slip on my dry ones, careful not to expose my privates in *any* type of way. I lotion up and put powder and deodorant on before getting dressed. After making Salaat, like clockwork, they call chow. Everything in jail is on a schedule, so you can easily calculate when everything is about to happen.

I wait for my man Peasey to walk to chow. After standing in line for almost forever, I get a tray full of bullshit that I can't fix my stomach to eat.

For a lot of people, it takes some time to get adjusted to eating jail food. Being as though I just came back, I don't hardly want to eat no meat sauce casserole. I damn near don't eat no state meat at all, because that shit ain't good for you. I ain't no health and fitness nut, but I try my best to eat right and stay in shape. This is still the penitentiary, and even though it's lax at times, shit can jump off at any given moment. So I try to always be prepared, in case I gotta split a nigga's shit.

When me and Peasey sat down, we got into a light conversation, and he asked me a question that I didn't know how to answer.

"So, what's Biggs out there doing?"

Chapter 3

That night when I got home, I just looked at the coke Jerv gave me for about fifteen minutes. I really didn't want to sell no coke, but I needed to do something to publish my book.

I thought about it long and hard and finally decided to flip the coke once and use the proceeds on my book.

Since I knew I could be going out of town, I had to cook the coke up. I waited until my mom and sister were in the bed, asleep, preparing for work and school, and that's when I went to work.

My moms kept baking soda in the fridge to keep the refrigerator smelling fresh. Since it was a new box, I knew it would be enough to do what I had to do.

I had never cooked up nine ounces at one time, so I dropped two ounces into a mayonnaise jar that I found in the cabinet, then added about half an ounce of bake on them. I poured some water in before setting the jar inside a pan full of water. After an hour, I was done cooking up the whole nine ounces. I didn't have any bags to bag it up in, so after I was

120

sure it dried, I split it up into individual ounces and put each ounce into a sandwich bag.

The next day I got up bright and early and got a ride over town. Over town was a little spot in Chester where people went shopping. I had to leave at eight o'clock with my mom, but it was cool because I really needed to buy a beeper, cell phone, and some baggies. I also wanted to buy a car from down Ninth Street. I knew the Spanish niggas that worked there would give me some temporary tags to drive around with until my insurance was right. I didn't have a license, but they didn't care.

After grabbing a phone, a two-way, and a gang of bags, I was about to catch the bus to the used car lot when I saw Biggs coming out of a sneaker store.

Biggs was one of my favorite young bulls. Besides having major potential as a hustler, he fucked a lot of chicks. Biggs was light-skinned, tall, and husky. He looked in shape, but was just naturally built like that. That young nigga ain't know what the word *workout* meant. He was a nice looking dude, *so the chicks would say*, but he had a cocked eye that me and a few of his other friend teased him about.

In jail, we even made up a song to tease the nigga:

"Crooked-eye Biggs...keep him away from ya girl, 'cause he swear he a pimp."

Initially he didn't like the song, but after a while he started to dig it, even told us to change it from *"swear he a pimp"* to *"know he a pimp."*

"Castro, what's the deal, my nigga?" he called out to me.

"Crooked-eye Biggs, my favorite young bull! What's good, pimp?"

After we greeted each other, we conversated lightly before he asked me what I was about to do.

"I was about to catch the bus down Ninth Street to buy a

bucket so I can get around."

"Man, ain't no need for you to catch no bus; I'll shoot you down there."

On the walk to his car, he asked me a question that I knew was coming.

"So, what you out here doing for 'em?"

I tried to be nonchalant, because I was hoping he might drop something on me. I knew he wasn't fucked up. He was pushing a '99 Lumina with Giovanni rims and a banger, and he had a nice piece of ice on his neck. Plus, his cell phone rang a good ninety-nine times while we were together.

"I ain't doing much," I casually replied. "I only been out for a minute, so I'm just trying to get back."

"Man, well, listen, I ain't got much, but I'll break off what I do got if you need some help."

"Damn," I said, "what, you fucked up?"

"You know me, I like to gamble and trick, so I just spent a stack over AC, and lost like six stacks in the casino. But at least the pussy was good," he finished with a smile only he could give me.

"Listen," I said, "I just got something light and I'm shooting out my spot tonight. You know where I'm at. We bagging triple on the flip."

"Well, I got an ounce to my name."

An ounce? I thought. *Damn, you just lost nine-ounce money, and that's all you working with?*

But that was the streets: a nigga might be balling one day and broke the next. But a broke hustler still looked like he was on top, which I'm sure Biggs was doing, because he just bought a brand new pair of Timbs and a Rocawear sweatsuit.

Once I started laying the plan down, he was sold. It didn't take long to convince him. I was Castro, the name spoke for itself. So I planned on taking him with me. He tried to talk me out of buying my car, but I knew that was a bad idea, because anything could happen and I had no intentions of being stuck if something came up and he had to hurry back.

I bought an '88 Cutlass for seven hundred dollars, slipped the dude an extra two hundred for the temporary tags, and I was out.

First I drove home and grabbed the work, then I met Biggs on McDowell to drive down my spot.

An hour later, we pulled up in Williamsport, two cars deep. I shot straight to my people's house and set up shop. It took me a whole week to get rid of the nine ounces. Mainly because I didn't have clientele like I used to, but after I dumped the nine ounces, I grossed twenty thousand. I used ten to buy a half a brick from Jerv, which I bagged up and dropped off to my nigga Biggs. I took the other ten thousand and invested it in my book company. I registered my trademark so I could do business under my company's name. I got my ISBN number, and I paid a company to typeset my book so I could have it printed. It took me three weeks to get the *Homicide Division* up and running.

But I made one crucial mistake.

I didn't do anything to promote the book. I basically printed it, only to end up frontlining it as if it was coke. And being as though I was a new company, I lacked the necessary connections with stores to push it.

Don't get me wrong. It sold like crazy in my city. But that's all it did. I never pursued it fully to give it the opportunity to blow up. I gave up on it after about a month and started hustling again.

During the time that I bullshitted around, wasting time publishing my book, Biggs sold damn near two bricks. Even though I was making a nice cut off the coke, for real, Biggs was making the most profit. He was bagging up three thousand dollars off each ounce, and making damn near twenty-five hundred off each one. Which was coming out to ninety thousand dollars a brick. Despite us splitting the money, I wasn't coming up the way I should have because I was buying the coke. Plus I was paying twenty thousand dollars a brick, so I was only making twenty-five thousand dollars profit.

My first profit, I didn't even see because I was tryna get my book out. Plus I had to upgrade. Being as though I had the book money coming in, I had legitimate money to spend. So I got a brand new car (something small, a 2000 Maxima). I furnished my crib, and got my wardrobe up. I don't know how much I ran through exactly, but it had to be at least thirty thousand. My note on my car was low because I dropped eight stacks.

So I was up, but I was fucked up. That's when I got my break. It happened one day when I went to score.

I showed up at Jerv's house and dropped twenty stacks on him for a brick. Instead of rushing out like I usually did after I copped, I sat around bullshitting; playing the PlayStation and conversating.

My old head was proud of me for putting my book out. He never said it, but I knew he was. After about a half hour, one of his young bulls, Blue, called him and asked him if he wanted tickets to a show. Of course Jerv said yeah. When he hung up, he asked me if I wanted to go.

"You still rapping, nigga?" Jerv asked me.

"Yeah, I got some fire. Why, what's up?"

"My young bull just told me he got me some tickets for the *Blue and Black* concert."

"That's what's up," I said. "Let me call my young bull and

give'm this work and we out."

"All right, make it happen, because I wanna go buy something to wear."

So I picked up the phone and called Biggs and told him to meet me to grab the coke. Since this was the first time he gave me half of the re-up money, he shot to grab the coke. He wanted to make his ten stacks back immediately. Which I could understand.

No soon as Biggs picked the coke up, me and Jerv shot to the mall, grabbed something to wear, and got ready to shoot to the concert.

• • •

"Yeah, that was my main man, Peasey. I was fucking with Biggs out there. He made one big mistake, and that was the mistake that got us booked."

"That's crazy!" Peasey exclaimed.

"You ready?" I asked.

We got up from the table and dumped our trays. I dropped off my plastic utensils in the containers by the exit and walked past the C.O. who monitored the containers to make sure nobody stole flatware. On the way back to the block, I got randomly searched by a C.O. on center, trying to make sure no inmates stole from the kitchen.

When I got back to the block, I went to my cell thinking about the opportunity I had and how I blew it. There were so many things I could have done differently. But I try to never get caught up in the shoulda, coulda, wouldas. I just make the best of the situation and roll with the punches.

Chapter 4

No soon as my favorite video of the week comes on, *1 Thing* by *Amerie*, evening yard is called. My cellie doesn't move, but then again, he rarely does. For some people, yard just ain't the place to be. For me, it's the only place to be.

I slide into my sweatsuit and fresh butter Timbs and I'm ready to go. Before I make my exit, I grab my Newports off the table and a stack of pictures for my mans *Geez* and *Alim* to see.

On my way down the tier, I wait on two of my other homies, *Bird* and *Calhoun* so I can have someone to conversate with, otherwise I really don't do too much rapping. There's plenty of dudes I'm cool with, but not enough to disclose my personal business. I'm the type that's respected by everybody, so I speak to a lot of dudes, but in all actuality, I really don't fuck with them.

In the yard I run into the *Cabinet*, Geez and Leem, posted by the weight pit. I call them the Cabinet because these two dudes are undoubtedly the only real friends I got.

Geez is my best friend, the Vice President. He's from North

Philly. A brown-skin, skinny, apple-head nigga. He probably weighs about a buck-sixty, stands five-eleven, so he isn't really skinny. He just looks that way from carrying that big-ass head. But he's the most sincere, genuine, trustworthy nigga I know.

Leem is a short, stubby nigga. Built like a *He-Man* action figure or something. He's brown-skin, five foot, eight, and a solid one hundred and eighty pounds. His nickname is Rumsfield because he's always ready to go to war or fuck some niggas up—the type of nigga that'll haul off and smack a muhfucka instead of punching him, just to totally disrespect him.

Both of my boys got chicks coming through to holla, so I guess they good-looking, but personally, I wouldn't know, dig me?

"Mr. President," greeted Geez, "what the deal with you? Pimping?"

"Awl, man, I'm just lounging. I almost ain't make it, fucking around with that Amerie video."

"Yo, didn't she show her ass?" Leem said, referring to how sexy she was in the video.

"Yeah, she doing the damn thing," I agreed.

Geez, hoping I had a story to tell them about her asked, "Did you meet her out there?"

"Yeah, but it was on some '*Hey, what's up? I like ya work*' shit. I ain't really get a chance to holla at shorty because we was moving in two different directions," I explained, never one to exaggerate or falsify information.

Geez just smiled.

Geez was the laid-back nigga out of the three of us. The smooth, cool nigga that didn't have a lot of frivolous things to say out of his mouth. Plus, he wasn't impressed by the bullshit like a lot of niggas because he was getting some serious change in the streets.

While Geez and Leem looked through the flicks I brought out, Geez said, "Yo, here come Lame-ass Joe."

"Castro, what's up, playboy...or should I call you *Mr. President?*" The drawing-ass nigga greeted, extending his hand for me to shake. I, of course, opted for a pound and gave him a closed-fist dap.

"What's up, y'all?" Joe said to Geez and Leem, getting barely a head nod in return.

"Yo, they ya pictures?" he asked me with a stupid smile on his face.

Of course by now this nigga has gotten on my nerves. I'm ready to let him look at the pictures, because that shit ain't about nuttin. But before I can answer, Rumsfield goes right into his bag.

"Get ya lame-ass outta here. You making me itch, *flea*. Can't you see I got my flea collar on?"

Lame-ass Joe was stuck, as he looked at Leem, then back at me, thinking of what he could say to regain his pride. "Yo, you stay fronting for Castro, you nut-ass nigga," was what ended up coming out of his mouth.

"Yeah, yeah. Speed on before you get peed on, dickhead," Leem ordered, shooing Joe away like a stray dog.

Instead of continuing to humiliate himself, Lame-ass Joe stepped off, talking shit and hollering useless, playful threats.

"Wait till I catch you without the President. Watch what I do, nut-ass nigga."

"Ya mother sure don't think so. That's why my name tattooed on her ass! Now, fucking dickhead!"

Joe just kept it moving. He didn't want no trouble. He just wanted to be accepted and treated with some type of respect. His only problem was that he tried too hard. Some niggas just don't have a cool bone in their body, and Lame-ass Joe is the perfect example. He's nosey, talks too much, and don't know to stop playing. All the characteristics of a total lame.

After Leem and Geez finished looking through the pictures, the three of us headed out to the baseball field to watch the softball game. As soon as we sat down, I pulled out a cigarette and lit up. Whenever I had things on my mind, I enjoy smoking or talking. Luckily, I got somebody to talk to or I'd probably run through the half a pack I had left.

"So, what the rap game was like?" my nigga Geez inquired.

How can I even begin to explain the rap game? Whenever you're doing something that you love to do, there's always an exhilarating feeling. For me, the rap game gave me a sense of self-worth, a sense of pride. It's what I truly loved to do.

"I can't explain it, Geez. That shit was like a crackhead finding a brick."

They both chuckled at the analogy, but I was serious. As I began telling my homies about the rap game, it led me straight back to the night I got signed to Blockwork. The best day of my life.

• • •

Jerv pulled up into the First Union parking lot. And with the greatest of ease, we slid through a back entrance by showing our VIP passes that Jerv got for us.

We were five deep. Me, Jerv, Jamir, Pooter, and Jerv's man, Shaheer.

After we slid through the back entrance, security ushered us to a dressing room. When they opened the door to let us in, I swear to God, it was like walking into the biggest party of the year. I'm talking wall-to-wall women, drinks flowing, and the music was banging. We walked through the mass of people and found *Blue* and *Black* in a heated crap game against a back wall.

"What's the deal, y'all?" Blue greeted happily, before whispering to all of us. "Go with the young bull, *Shot*. He can't miss."

At first I didn't know what he was talking about, until I noticed the young bull. His name was Hotshot, or at least that's what they called him. He was rumored to be the best dice shooter in the country, but I couldn't tell. The last time I saw the nigga he was missing every shot. Allegedly some mob bulls over Atlantic City broke his arm or some shit for trying to take the casino for a couple mil. But niggas like me ain't believe a lot of street stories, because I knew people always blew that shit up.

I wasn't sure how old Hotshot was, but I had assumed he was at least seventeen or eighteen. I knew he was ahead of his time though, since his name had been ringing in the street for like five years. Plus the platinum chain he was wearing looked like it cost too much for me. He was a little pretty-boy; *too*-curly-ass hair, with them girly hazel eyes. He even looked like he had a manicure or some shit.

Whatever, though, because I ain't no hater. My opinion quickly changed when I noticed he was hitting every number straight. I started betting everybody that would take a bet. I noticed he had *Little Easy* and *Lotchy* with him, so I completely understood why nobody was trying to rob his little ass.

Easy was a little light-skinned nigga. On the low, he was supposed to have a couple of bodies.

His partner, Lotchy, was a certified gangsta as well. He had just got shot up like three times, and was surviving everything. Niggas had hit him in the leg, the chest, and even in the head. This young nigga was a machine! His body count was rumored to be in the dozens, but it was something you would never hear him brag about or condone by putting numerous teardrops on his eye like his right-hand man Easy did. This young nigga was more discreet.

An hour after I walked into the dressing room, the crap game was finally over, and niggas were far from broke. They simply had sense enough to know when to quit. Since I joined in the crap game, I believe Hotshot only missed three numbers, so that was almost an hour's worth of winning. And I was almost sure they were there an hour or so before I got there. Which meant if I won a little over twenty-five grand or so, I know they won a couple hundred. Their victims were all celebrities. This was the *Blue and Black Tour,* and they had so many celebrities performing it was ridiculous. It was equivalent to the *Jay Z and Friends Tour* that Jay put together after R. Kelly snitched on Ty-Ty.

It was a who's who of the rap industry. This was also the night I got signed.

From that day on, my life changed. No soon as Amir, the CEO of Blockwork, put that chain around my neck and they gave me that check, I knew my drug dealing days were over.

Or so I thought.

For the next couple of days I started going to the studio real heavy with the bull Black. Black was a dark-skinned, husky nigga, with a raspy-ass voice. He conducted himself like he wasn't even a star, even though the radio was playing his song a hundred times a day. That's what I liked most about the nigga. He didn't try to be real, he *was* real.

On my third day in the studio, Biggs hit my cell phone up and left an urgent message on my voice mail. I immediately called him right back to make sure my mans was cool. When I got on the phone, I'm thinking anything but the obvious.

"What's up? Everything cool?" I inquired.

"Yeah, I'm cool. I just need four of 'em real quick."

Four of them, I thought. Something told me to find out exactly how he managed to double his number in a matter of days. But then again, I didn't really want to hustle.

"Listen, man," I told Biggs, "I ain't really trying to do the hustle thing. I just got signed to Blockwork."

"*Blockwork?*" Biggs said incredulously. "Yo, them niggas is hot, dawg! They got more beef than a slaughterhouse. They going to war with the bull *Reckless* from the westside, and they got some eastside niggas they going through it with. On some real shit, it ain't safe to be with them niggas," he warned me.

"How you know?" I asked, not believing he knew what he was talking about.

"I used to be a hype man for them niggas. I met the bull Blue one day coming out my chick crib. We clicked, and he put me on. I used to get me a check just for doing shows with him. That shit was fun, but after one of their artists got killed, I had to fall back. Plus, they was getting questioned by the feds and all that shit.

"Then," Biggs went on, "they had a celebrity boxing match. After Blue won the fight, he got shot that day. Man, I love my life too much to be getting shot at and all that. Fuck that. I'd rather take my chances hustling."

For me, it just seemed like it couldn't be true. But I decided to ask Black when I hung up, because I knew he would tell me the real deal. To me, this shit sounded like some *50 Cent* shit, and I wasn't trying to be getting shot at. Don't get me wrong, I'm a certified gangsta; if I got beef, I got beef. But I'm not no fucking pawn a nigga gonna push to have me all out there fighting a war for him. Furthermore, the idea of the feds watching was way too much for me to handle as well.

However, this was also an opportunity for me to do something positive and legit in life, so, like any rational person with good sense, I didn't wanna back away from it. But instead of making hasty decisions, I hollered at Black while I was in the studio that night. That's when I found out the whole story. Which, of course, confirmed everything that Biggs told me.

Yes, they *were* beefing with Doomsday Records. And, *yes,* the feds *had* questioned them on several occasions.

That left me in an awkward situation. Why? Because I was still on parole. Beef and feds were something I really didn't need to be caught up in the middle of. But then again, neither were drugs.

So I was stuck in between a rock and a hard place. Instead of stepping back to evaluate the situation, I decided to go get the four bricks for Biggs and holla at Black the following day.

When I got out Williamsport, Biggs was in a bar called *The Shamrock*, a little joint that was half-ass jumping in the town where anybody and everybody that was half-ass thorough hung.

I parked around on the side of the bar and quickly walked in. Inside, I wanted to find Biggs so I could handle my business, grab the dough, and be on my way. I was paying twenty thousand dollars a piece for each jawn, and I was charging Biggs twenty-two, five. That meant I was making a whole extra ten thousand off the flip.

Being as though me and Biggs usually scored together, I was wondering where and how he got the money to buy four so fast, but I just figured he flipped the coke I gave him and finally got smart enough to invest all the money back into the flip.

But I was sadly mistaken.

When I walked up on this nigga, he had some bull named P-nut with him from out there that I never saw before in life. I immediately got butterflies in my stomach. Something told me not to serve the nigga, but Biggs pulled me to the side and said that the nigga was cool. So I decided to trust his judgment.

Fuck it, if Biggs said he was cool, then he was cool. He also told me he was charging dude twenty-five thousand dollars a key. So *he* was making an extra ten grand, of which he said he'd give me three. So that was thirteen thousand dollars I was making off the move. Besides, I wasn't giving it to the bull Nut; I was giving it directly to Biggs. Fine by me, because there was no way I was driving back with all that coke in the trunk. Feel me?

I told Biggs to walk me to the car. But instead of this nigga handling his business discreetly, he pulled the nigga Nut's coat and told him to meet him at his car.

I was mad, because I didn't want the nigga to see me give Biggs the coke, but I guessed I would have to wait around for the money anyway, so I went along with it.

As we were walking out, I noticed *Salinni* coming in the door. He gave me a warm smile as we embraced and shook hands.

"What's up with you?" he asked, looking up, noticing Biggs and Nut following me.

"Ain't shit. I'm about to handle some business right quick. What's up with you?"

"Same shit, but I'ma holla at you later. Keep ya grass cut," he said before going about his business.

Now I heard what he said, but I was so caught up in making the transaction so I could keep it moving that it didn't register right away.

I popped my trunk and handed Biggs a duffel bag while his man P-nut walked down to his car to get the money.

When Biggs walked over to P-nut's car to grab the money, I hopped into my car, started it up, and turned on my CD player. I flipped through my thirty-disc CD changer to listen to *The Dynasty* by Jay-Z, but when I pushed *Play*, the Lox's *We Are the Streets* came on. Now that I think about it, in hindsight, I believe this was a sign.

I shoulda caught it right away, but I didn't. Just the fact that Salinni wasn't serving the bull Nut shoulda said something because, for real, for real, he was one of the main suppliers in Williamsport. He wasn't from Williamsport, but had been there so long that you might think he was. Majority of the coke that was flooded through the town came from him. Quiet as kept, Salinni was a real boss, and most of the niggas from the small town were intimidated by his capabilities. Salinni kept his hands pretty clean, but it wasn't hard to tell what work he had put in, because if you disrespected him or had a run-in with him, something happened to you shortly thereafter, cut and dry.

It took Biggs about three minutes to make the drop. And the smartest thing he did was hop in his own car with the money and told me to follow him to his spot.

That night was the first time the feds took my picture.

After grabbing the cash from Biggs, I felt them butterflies again. And when I got in the car and drove back to the city, what Salinni said to me finally hit me. It jumped right out of my car's speakers and slapped me in the face while I was listening to *Fuck You* by The Lox:

Everybody's a snake, that's why I keep the grass cut
So I can see them when they coming and heat they ass up.

Chapter 5

After that, I decided it was in my best interest to leave the drug game alone. I began going to the studio every day. I would sit in that jawn from sun up to sundown, writing raps. At that time, I think I had the work ethics of the late great *Tupac Shakur*.

One of the producers I was working with, *Sheem*—a humble, brown-skin, skinny bull who reminded me of *Antoine Fisher*—was making all my beats. He quickly took notice of how hard I was working and began flooding me with CDs full of beats. That way, if something came to me while I was driving my car, I could spit that shit on this little pocket recorder I carried around. That's how I came up with my hit single.

I had a sit-in with Amir and Blue one day. After listening to my CD, they told me I needed a more powerful hook. They said my album was good as is, but I needed something that would touch the world. They wanted me to dig deeper and give them greatness. So I had to go back to work.

About a month later, I finally wrote the song they were looking for. It came to me while I was out barhopping one night. By now, I was done selling drugs, period, and Biggs had been scoring off Rudy for the past month, so I hadn't seen him.

Anyway, I was down Third with Black, bullshitting around. That's when Biggs pulled up on me in an SC-500 hardtop. That jawn shut shit down. Candy apple-red, with them Giovannis on it, system pounding. Man, if there was ever a day I regretted not hustling, that was the day.

That nigga jumped out with one of them NBA leathers on with all the patches and shook my hand and hugged me. He told me that he had shit on smash, and he had some young bulls hustling for him who were giving him seventy percent off a 70/30 split. The nigga was always tight, so that was to be expected. Anyway, he hung out with me for a while and gave me like five stacks before he rolled out.

Oh yeah, I was fucked up by now, still waiting for my album to drop. I wasn't broke, but I had spent most of my money buying my moms a house. I might've had about ten thousand to my name.

After Biggs left, I decided to go to the studio and work on my album. As is, it was done, but I needed two hot singles that would get me some heavy radio rotation.

When I hopped in my car, I popped in a compact disc Sheem gave me and pulled off. The beat sounded like that R. Kelly and Jay-Z *Best of Both Worlds* jawn...with all the hollering and shit. Black opted to hit the hotel with some chick he was trying to get at, so I had plenty of time to think.

As I was driving to the studio, the song came to me from deep in my soul. I grabbed my little handheld recorder and spit that shit in one take. I just let it flow:

My name still ring bells like Jack and Jills,/ on the hottest day of

the summertime
> *Frontline...*
I'm the eyes for the blind, lost doing time./ stuck on the grind,
that ain't afraid of dying...
> *What?*
I'm the voice from the front of the line/
the choice you still got if you kept on trying...
Not only speaking for the niggas riding, that's still grinding,/
But I'm speaking for them mothers that's crying,
> *That's still trying...*
To help they babies that's out there dying
That think we crazy for being so violent
> *You got to feel me...*
They still out here plotting to kill me/
Wanna put me in a box and conceal me/
> *These niggas hate me...*
They wanna break me, saying I'm too arrogant,/
Confident swag, niggas calling me the President...
My flow too elegant, words too relevant/
I'm here to show you niggas how to make it through the extra
shit...
And find a purpose in life./Come on!
Let's get together and find a purpose in life...
Hook: I know you struggle between wrong and right, but you
gotta be easy./So you don't lose ya life./
Let me be the light, give you the will to fight
Because you can blink too many times and lose your purpose in
life...

After I laid the hook, I knew that was the song. I was on my own dick. I stopped the tape and listened to it. Yo, I swear I thought I was *X* or *Mystikal*. This shit was fire!

Once I had let it play through a few times, I felt like there was something about the hook I didn't like. Probably because it wasn't street enough, and all of Blue and Black's hits were street. So I compared my song to theirs. That night I went to the studio to lay it down. I think if I woulda never stopped recording, my second verse would've been so much better. But when I laid it down, it was definitely hot.

The next day I woke up early in the morning and took it straight to the record label. At that time I really thought *Just for Me* was the better song. It was geared toward the women and it was sweet. But Amir said it could be the second single and went with *Purpose in Life*, which he took to the radio stations immediately.

From that day on, I had a lot of work to do. My promotions schedule was crazy. I had to travel to a thousand radio stations (at the company's expense, thank God). But I was on the road all the way up to my album release party. I did *106 & Park*, *T.R.L.*, and *Jay Leno*. *Access Granted* even came for my video shoot.

After the video shoot is when the situation got ugly for me. Not only did I run into some beef I didn't have shit to do with, but that's when my past came haunting me.

• • •

"The new yard is now closed!" blared the announcement over the P.A. When I looked up from the conversation I was engulfed in, I noticed the softball game was over and it was time to go into the main yard.

As me, Geez, and Alim strolled into the main yard, the two of them began badgering me about finishing my story. At the most we probably had about a half hour left in the yard, and I just reached the climax to the story. Nobody likes to hear half a story, so when we walked into the yard and posted up, I told them what happened to lead up to my parole violation.

• • •

After my video shoot, my label had an album release party for me at *Palmer's*, one of the hottest clubs in Philly. I showed up dressed to impress, Gucci from head to toe. The night was going great. I was spending time with my wifey and I had just received my second advance check, so I was on top.

My young bull Biggs showed up fashionably late in a white, tailor-made suit looking like P fucking Diddy. Canary diamonds in his bracelet and platinum chain, and a rose-gold, iced-out Rolex. He had on so many different colored diamonds he looked like a pack of Skittles...he was definitely doing it.

Biggs conversated with me, Blue and Black, and not long afterwards, he cracked on us for a connect. He knew that since we were in the industry, we knew somebody who had to have some major coke.

I, however, wasn't fucking with the coke.

That's when his homey Nut walked up, and Biggs introduced him to me, Blue and Black. When I saw him, my mind raced back to what Salinni had said. And as I attempted to pull Blue and Black to the side, a bottle came crashing across Blue's head. Before I could react, a punch caught me square in the mouth.

Biggs and P-nut jumped right into the mix, throwing punches to defend us. I regrouped quickly and got back into the mix of the brawl.

That's when I noticed *Reckless*. Him and two of his homies were jumping Black.

Altogether it had to be like ten of them niggas and five of us, and Blue and Black were already fucked up.

"Here, baby! Here!" Chareen exclaimed, handing me a box cutter that she always kept for protection.

I turned around like I was *Zorro*...on some karate shit. I'm literally spinning through the crowd slicing these niggas up.

"Huh, huh, huh...," I was grunting and swinging, and niggas were bleeding and screaming.

I must've sliced like six dudes—I'm talking faces hanging open and shit—by the time Reckless saw I was coming for him. He tried to run, but my girl blind-sided that pussy with a Cristal bottle.

The nigga went straight down, and we stomped his ass till the lights came on. The few friends he had practically abandoned him. All except his cousins. His artists took off running like the building was on fire when that razor hit their faces.

When the lights came on, the deejay gave us a heads up.

"The police are in the building!" dude hollered.

I helped Blue up off the floor, and Biggs and Nut helped Black, and we were out. Chareen, being the soldier that she was, picked up the razor I dropped and a few platinum chains that got torn off people's necks in the frenzy and brought up my rear. Then she shot past me like a bat out of hell, barefooted, and ran to the car.

When we got to the street in front of Palmer's, she was pulling up in my Max. Biggs and Nut helped Blue and Black into the car and I pulled off.

I drove straight to the hospital because Blue needed stitches in his head *bad*. After we dropped off Blue, I took my girl home and tore her ass up. If I had ever been unsure about how much she loved me, her actions confirmed everything for me that night.

The next day it was plastered across all the newspapers: *Rap War Goes Down at Album Release Party*.

This was the first time my name appeared in the papers. They even had pictures of the brawl and us jumping in my car.

They also had photos of Reckless and a few others being dragged out on stretchers. The paper said Reckless was in critical condition at Hahnemann Hospital, and that the cops were seeking the suspects for questioning.

Amir called me that next afternoon and told me that the Blockwork attorneys would represent me and not to say anything if the police picked me up.

I decided to be a man about the situation and turn myself in. I figured since Blockwork was paying for my lawyer, I would be okay. When I called Amir to tell him my plan, he said cool, because Blue and Black were planning on doing the same thing.

Later that night, me, Blue and Black turned ourselves in. Since no one had pressed charges from Reckless' camp, we got out that night; however, we were still under investigation. So we had to move with caution. I had to go see my parole man after the incident, and I escaped being violated that time by the skin of my teeth.

The good side about the publicity was that it shot my record sales through the roof. That first week I went gold. All the news made people want to see what I was talking about, I guess. I don't know, but what I do know is, just when everything seemed like it was going my way, I got hit with the indictment.

Chapter 6

Everything was going great for me. My album sales were up, and I was scheduled to do a video shoot for my second single, *Just for Me*.

I woke up early that morning and called my label to make sure everything was still a go. Then I got dressed and headed out early that morning to go take care of business.

When I got to the label, no soon as I parked and got out, the feds gripped me up. After flashing an indictment in my face, they handcuffed me and threw me in the back of a Crown Victoria.

When they got in the car, an agent who looked like *Tom Cruise* began to read me my rights. His partner, a skinny, freckled-face agent who resembled *Carrot Top* from the *1-800-Collect* commercials, tossed a newspaper into my lap. I gazed at the nerdy-looking kid with a deep scorn and hatred in my eyes. Not only because he looked like he didn't even deserve to be a fed, but because he had a dorky-ass smile on his face as if this was the highlight of his day. I was surprised he didn't ask me for an autograph.

When I finally looked down at the paper, I saw Bigg's picture on the cover, big as day. The headline read: *Feds Nab Drug Kingpin of Multimillion-Dollar Drug Ring.*

The story alleged that Biggs, a.k.a. Shaleer Henderson, sold over fifty bricks to a federal informant. They even had a long-ass list of codefendants, of which me and Rudy made the top.

I automatically flashed back to the night I saw Salinni at the bar. That was the sign that made me stop selling coke, but, still, my greedy ass had to sell those four birds.

Right then and there I assumed I was booked solid for the long ride to the Federal Building. All the shoulda, coulda, wouldas flashed through my head as I mentally scolded myself for making such a careless decision. I knew better. I was from Chester; a city where the snakes crawl freely and best friends become worst enemies quicker than a dirty cop pockets drug money.

When we got to the Federal Building, the feds tried to run a bunch of bullshit on me, claiming that Biggs and the rest of my codees were going to testify that I was their supplier. Once he said that, I knew I was cool, because I didn't' even *know* the rest of my codefendants, let alone sell them some coke.

They wasted their time for about an hour, running bull-shit game on me, trying to manipulate me to save myself. But ya boy Castro held water like a cup. So eventually they arraigned me in front of a magistrate and detained me without bail.

That night, I made a phone call and told my chick to go to my label and get me a lawyer. Two days later, Riley Patterson, the best lawyer money could buy, summoned me out for an attorney visit. Since I didn't trust anybody, I lied to him straight-faced when he asked me to tell him what happened.

Confess? To this old gray-haired conservative, Republicanlooking mothafucka just because he was paid to represent me? Yeah, right. That mothafucka eats lunch and plays golf with them D.A.s and judges every day. His kids go to school with their kids, and they run in the same circles. They're his colleagues. No matter what side he's playing on, I wasn't gonna trust him either.

So I threw on my Academy Award-winning, *I'm innocent* face, forced a couple of tears, and told the best lie I ever told in my life. Because, ultimately, if he was convinced, I knew Patterson would fight for me ten times as hard.

"Man, me and Biggs were together the night before with these chicks he knew, and we went to the hotel and had sex with them, got high and drunk, and fell asleep.

"The next day we had to wake up at eleven o'clock and leave, so we were all tired. I ended up dropping everybody off and then I went home to my girl, Chareen. Well, he called me later on that night, nine-one-one, and when I called him back he told me he left some clothes in my car. Being as though he changed his clothes at the hotel, I thought nothing of it. I just asked him where he was and took him his bag. I didn't bother looking in it because I thought it was clothes.

"When I got to the bar, he told me where to meet him at, we had a couple drinks, I gave him his bag, and I jumped in my car and left. We didn't exchange any money or no shit like that."

That's when I started the tears rolling, rolling, rolling like a river.

"Mr. Patterson," I sobbed, "I don't know how I got caught up in this shit. I don't sell no drugs. I got a hit song on the radio. My days of running the streets are over. I got a fiancée and she's pregnant with my first child; I'm a family man now."

He was still on the fence by now. I guess this wasn't the

first time he's seen this type of performance. He was buying the story, but not a hundred percent. And without him buying it a hundred percent, I wouldn't get his best results. So I went in for the kill...

"You gotta do something, talk to my codefendants and ask 'em. I don't know them. I know Biggs, but that's it. Please, Mr. Patterson, because if I lose this case, I might, I might...kill myself."

That was the one. If you coulda seen his face.... I almost laughed, but I knew that my life was riding on this show. And if it's one thing I can do, it was perform. That's what I got paid to do.

Once I buried my face into my hands, he began to console me. He told me that the case wasn't that solid because I didn't have any superceding indictments. The indictment I had only charged me with one count of conspiracy to possess with intent to distribute in excess of two kilograms of cocaine, in violation of 21 U.S.C. §846. The other charge was the same thing, it just read: Attempt to distribute in violation of 21 U.S.A. §841(A)(1). Besides that, I was basically straight. The lawyer told me as long as the prosecutors didn't get Biggs or my other codees to flip on me, *and* everything that I told him was true, I was cool.

So I felt good, confident, that Biggs wasn't gonna snitch. And his codefendants probably didn't know my name, let alone what I looked like. But I wasn't sleeping; I was well aware how slimy them D.A.s were. So if they did mention my name, I had a hell of a backup plan.

It took my lawyer about six months to get the indictment dropped. Biggs told my lawyer the same story I did, since I had Chareen go tell him what to say the same day Patterson visited me. And like I said, the other codees didn't know my name. But that didn't mean the D.A. couldn't have manipulated them. So I had my girl pass their names off to my label to put some niggas on they heads. You know, just in case.

Meanwhile, my CD was selling like crazy. All the media coverage and controversy was making everybody and their mom buy my CD.

Just when everything started to look good for me, things went from sugar to shit....

First, the lead artist on my label got shot. Blue was just leaving a radio station, making the rounds to promote his second release, *Harsh Reality*, when he got drive-byed. He was hit three times. And even though it was touch and go, the doctors said he would survive.

But that wasn't the worst part.

The worst part was, six months after I'd already been in jail and the feds dropped their indictment, the state re-arrested me on an aggravated assault charge for the Palmer's incident. Somebody from the club allegedly came forward to testify on me.

To make a long story short, not long after I got the witness' name from the Discovery, I passed it along to my girl, who just happened to bump into him.

They found the joker in a hole-in-the-wall motel the next day, deader than mackerel.

So I sat for three months waiting on a preliminary hearing for the agg/assault before, finally, *that* case got dropped. But that same day, my parole officer hit me with a detainer for a violation of parole.

The shit just don't stop, right?

At my parole hearing, my P.O., Austin Goldstein—a fat *Danny DeVito*-looking mothafucka with *Steve Urkel* glasses— slandered me something serious. He presented pictures from

Palmer's and said that I was a menace to society hiding behind a rap career.

Well, that was more than enough to get me violated. So the board gave me an eighteen month hit. Being as though I ain't got much time to my max, I'm assuming I'll be out there in a deuce, three years at the most, and when I get there this time, it's going down.

• • •

"Yo," commented Geez, "you was going through a whole lot out there."

"Yeah, plus after you came up, you fucked around and almost got booked up on some bullshit," Alim interjected.

"Yeah, who you telling?" I agreed. "But you know what? There was something good that came from all of this," I told my two friends. "The good part was, my album went platinum, and I finally got one of my books published. It wasn't the book I initially began shopping, *Whatever Start on the Streets, Stay on the Streets...,* it was the story of my struggle to make it; how my label was formed, the beef they went through, and how they still succeeded even though a lot of people doubted them. I sat on visits with my labelmates for months to get the facts behind this book, and now it's finally ready to be released."

"So, what's it called?" asked Geez.

I smiled as I prepared to tell him the title. It explains so much about the lives of so many people.

"When Dreams Become Nightmares," I said with a sense of pride.

Alim asked, "Why you name it that?"

"Well," I explained, "when you become blessed with the opportunity to actually accomplish things in life above the so-called *norm,* you become a star—you're basically living your dreams. But when you go from living your dreams to facing situations like the current situation I'm facing, it's like living a nightmare. But the reality of it all is life. So when you're living a life of such magnitude, that's when your dreams become nightmares.... I actually got the title from Blue and Black, but that's basically what it means."

"Yard in for A, E, and C blocks—C through the rear!"

After a quick handshake and hug, me and my squad make our way back into the jail and back to our individual cells. When I get to the cell, I start working on my next album, jot a few things down in my journal for my next book, and focus on putting my life back together after jail. Believe you me, this ain't the last you gonna hear from me. My will to succeed is too strong. I got too much determination...

That's my story, and I'm sticking to it.

THE END

Derrick "Blue Gambino" Phillips is an awesome writer. Hailing from Chester, PA, this talented young man is destined to make a mark in the literary world. Be on the lookout for what will undoubtedly be one of the best releases this summer from Amiaya Entertainment L.L.C. "Whatever Start On the Streets, Stay On the Streets," is only the beginning of what "Blue" and "H.D." have in store for their readers. For further questions, comments or concerns, e-mail Derrick Phillips at tanianunez79@hotmail.com.

EAST SIDE

by

Eric "E-Boogie" Ferrer

East Side

"Damn baby boy, I've been calling you out the window for about fifteen minutes, yo," Frank Nitty said to his man Ezo who was lying on his bed partially covered by his off-white Nautica comforter.

"Ayo, I was fuckin' sleeping until your dumb ass came and woke me up," Ezo remarked. He tried to slide his 44 Bulldog back under his pillow. Nitty peeped him and smiled at how on point his right hand man was. Then he continued, "How the fuck you get in my crib anyway?"

Nitty reached for the stumped out blunt in the ashtray on Ezo's dresser that Ezo was saving for when he woke up. When Nitty turned around, Ezo nodded his head upwards telling his man to return his gaze back to the dresser. When Nitty did, he noticed what Ezo was referring to. Nitty grabbed the half empty book of matches, lit the blunt, took the ill drag and passed it to his homie. As the smoke from the *Sticky Icky* seeped from Nitty's mouth, he coughed once, tapped his chest and said, "Your lil brother, *Strange*, let me in."

Ezo passed the blunt back to Nitty, exhaled what he inhaled, through his nose and said, "I'm a fuck that lil nigga up. He always letting your bum ass in the house like you family or something." Ezo's pants were halfway on so he stood up and pulled his *Sean John* jeans around his waist. He had a lil bulge in his pocket indicating that the night before was on and popping with the fiends.

Frank Nitty and Ezo were like brothers. They even resembled one another. Frank Nitty was from Taft Projects on 115th Street and Madison Avenue and Ezo was from Johnson Projects on 112th Street between Park Avenue and Lexington Avenue in Spanish Harlem. Nitty was about 5'10", 145 pounds. He was brown skinned and rocked a low haircut with waves.

Ezo had an Indian complexion. E stood about 5'4" and weighed about 130 pounds. He rocked his straight hair in long cornrolls that reached halfway down his back. Ezo was Puerto Rican but you wouldn't know it unless he told you so. He fucked a lot of people's heads up, having people think that he was black, especially the females. The broads loved his Native American look and everyone thought that son was African American from the way that he carried himself.

"Ayo, Nitty, what the fuck you waking me up for anyway?" Ezo had a sandwich bag full of weed on one side of him as he sat on the edge of his bed while the nine hundred dollars and change he made five hours prior rested on his other side.

Nitty leaned up off the dresser, plopped down next to his man, turned on Ezo's Play Station, inserted *Mortal Kombat 3* and started getting busy against the computer. Biting on his bottom lip, he answered his road dawg, "What the fuck nigga, you act like you been up all night fucking. ... You know you still a mothafuckin' virgin, nigga." Nitty placed the joystick flat on the bed and punched one of the buttons like a mad man. Three seconds later, his opponents' head exploded, then his torso, then his legs wiggled and blew all across the screen.

"Yeah, right, Nitty, you know them hoes be loving this Puerto Rican dick." Ezo smiled as he thought about the lil shorty he met the other day that he had yet to run up in.

Nitty sighed, dropped the control pad, stood up, turned around, looked at his partner and said, "Anyway, Ezo, I'm about to hit the block and get this paper. I just shot through to see if you wanted to come flip some packs with me." He looked at Ezo for a facial expression that would indicate whether or not he was feeling the idea of hitting the streets. Then he said, "You trying to get this paper or what?"

"Yeah, I'm wit' that, dogs. Just give me a minute to wash up and get dressed." Ezo grabbed a washcloth from a hanger behind his door and asked, "Nitty, is it real cold outside?" He paused and squeezed some Colgate onto his toothbrush.

Blocka!

Ezo and Nitty heard the gunshot that came from outside at the same time. They both ran to the window to see what was going down.

Outside, two dudes were roughing up some cat on the hood of a car!

One dude with reddish colored hair had the victim hemmed up. He was trying to put the dude to sleep by tightening up the grip he had on him.

"Fiend that nigga out yo, fiend that nigga out!" the red haired one's accomplice yelled.

Red's partner went to punch the dude in the face but was caught with a vicious kick to the stomach. The victim was going hard because he knew that as soon as his lights went out from the sleeper hold, that they were never coming back on again.

"Yo, that's son and them!" Nitty said excitedly to Ezo.

Without moving from the window, Ezo said, "I know."

"Let that nigga go!" Redhead's crimey yelled.

Redhead looked up and understood why. He unleashed his victim and immediately his man let off a second shot. The first shot that Nitty and Ezo heard was supposed to be in dudes head, but homeboy had the mean feet game and kicked the toast out of the gunman's hand. Then redhead grabbed him up in the chokehold. Now, the second shot was released and as the shell exited the weapon, it danced through the air looking like it was doing the *Harlem Shake*. That one shot was all it took. The bullet pierced their victim's skull and left his brains sitting across the street about twenty feet away from his body. The perps took off and Ezo and Nitty stayed upstairs until the cops came and left.

• • •

"Ayo, Nitty, next week is my birthday, dogz, and I'm trying to get crazy blitzed." Ezo was counting and straightening out the money he just collected from a sale that he just made to a fiend. The duo had already gotten over the incident that took place earlier that day.

Nitty placed his hand on his chin and as he watched his man fix every single bill and face them all in the same direction, he said, "I feel you, dogz, that ain't about nuthin' cause we do that everyday, feel me?" When Ezo looked up and caught eye contact with Nitty, Nitty said, "Ayo, we got three packs left before we can even think about bouncing, dogz."

Ezo shrugged his shoulders, looked over Nitty's head, spotted a fiend and walked over to handle his business.

Ezo and Nitty were selling packs hand to hand for some older dudes that were from their projects.

"Ayo, Nitty, I'm tired of doing this hand to hand shit, dogz, word up," Ezo informed.

156

"I feel you, Ezo. I've been thinking and saying to myself the same thing, yo."

"I'm saying, we can save this money, go uptown and buy some weight from them Dominican niggas, dogz." Ezo was returning from making the transaction with the crackhead.

"I'm wit that, Ezo. We gonna go up there tomorrow and cop an ounce of coke and get that basehead, *Cook-up-Country*, to cook it up for us. That's the best cooker around this motha-fucka. But right now, let's call a cab and hop over to 174th and Autobon, cop some of that Dro, snatch up a bottle of Henn-Rock and shoot to my crib and chill." Nitty summed up.

"Aiight, dogz, you call a cab while I finish these last few bottles out the last pack." With that said, Ezo spotted yet another fiend, trotted over to the frail young lady and *did him.*

• • •

"Skee-yo," called Chuleta from across the street to where Ezo and Nitty were. Chuleta was from Nitty's projects too. He was about five years older than Nitty and E but that didn't matter because the two youngsters hung around older dudes all the time.

"What up, y'all?" Chuleta said after making his way across the street to where the duo took refuge.

Ezo extended his arm, gave Chuleta a pound and said, "Ain't nuthin', dogz, we about to go uptown and cop some Dro from Autobon, then go to Nitty' crib and chill. Why, what up?" Ezo asked him. Nitty and Ezo weren't really looking for any stragglers for their two-man team, but Chuleta was cool so they said fuck it.

"I'm coming with y'all, yo. I got twenty dollars for the smoke and I got a nickel for that bottle." Chuleta had his hands out looking like a *B-Boy* from the early eighties.

Ezo was smiling hard because he didn't want to bust out

laughing. The nigga Chuleta was a funny nigga and looked even funnier, so instead of letting out his chuckle, E just said, "What about the cab, you big-head bastard?"

Back in animation mode with the mean *Beastie Boys* smile, Chuleta once again covered his tracks and said, "I got ten dollars on that too."

"Ayo, we might as well rent the cab for like two hours and just get blowed in the back seat of the whip," Ezo suggested.

"Nah, Ezo, we got some shit to take care of tomorrow, dogz. Or did you forget?" Nitty was looking at his homie like, "Duh."

All the weed that E done smoked in his short life had him fucked up. Brain cells were evaporating left and right. When his memory came off its lunch break, Ezo thought to himself, *Damn, I almost forgot, I'm buggin'.* Then he looked at his crimey and said, "Oh, yea, my bad, I almost forgot, dogz."

Ezo walked to the pay phone a few yards from where they peddled their product, inserted a quarter and dialed the cabstand's telephone number.

Ezo spoke to someone, hung up, then walked back over to where his crimey and other homeboy stood.

• • •

"Anyway, Nitty, the cab said that he'll be here in twenty minutes. That's good though, 'cause by that time we should be finished with these last six jump offs. Feel me?"

Ezo reached in his waistband, removed a sandwich bag that held his six remaining slabs of five dollar cracks, played with them in his hands and when a car drove by doing a hundred miles an hour, the shit scared Ezo and made him re-tuck his work.

Nitty had just received a page, looked down at his hip, observed the number, noticed that it was a broad that he was trying his best to avoid, looked back over at his man and said,

"Yeah, I feel you, dogz!!! On some other shit though, Ezo, what happened to them Spanish broads from Douglas projects on the West Side that you and Chuleta were fucking with?"

Ezo racked his brain for a quick second and the chick that Nitty was referring to registered in his brain. "I still be fucking with shorty every now and then, why, what up? All I have to do is call that bitch and everything's a go." Ezo smiled."

Nitty waved him off. "Fuck out of here, you fake ass Rico Suave...peep game though, call shorty and see what's really good?" Nitty laughed after making his request. When it came to the females, Ezo *did* think he was all that.

"Ayo, what I'm a do is beep her and put my beeper number in just in case the cab come...feel me? That way, all we have to do is tell the cab driver to pull over at the nearest pay phone. Anyway, where the fuck did that blockhead nigga Chuleta go?" Ezo started looking around which caused Nitty to follow his lead.

"I think he went into the pizza shop to play a game or buy a slice or something."

"Tell that nigga to buy a box of Dutchs, dogz, while I make this last sale." Ezo approached a scroungy looking dude who was trying to copy five nickels for twenty dollars.

"Oh shit, ayo, Chuleta, Teddy up. They just went up the block and Ezo is over there making a sale. I hope he see them dogz..." *Teddy up* was the signal that meant the police were around.

"Why the fuck you ain't watching that nigga back anyway?" Chuleta barked as he headed in E's direction.

"'Cause nigga, he told me to go and get you and tell you to buy them Dutchs. If not, I would've been out here holding my nigga down."

Chuleta paused and looked up the block. "I think I see him coming up the block now with that lil bad bitch from

First Avenue."

"Ayo, I've been trying to bag shorty for a minute," Nitty informed. "But every time I holla, she always asking about my brother Ezo. That bitch is on that nigga dick so I know he tricking," Nitty assumed.

When Ezo approached the duo, he said, "Damn, yo, I almost got knocked just now. Them housing police pulled up a few seconds after I made that last sale. Luckily my shining star was coming up the block. Plus, you know I got my motha fuckin' .44 Bulldog on my hip. If I would've got knocked, they would've knocked my dick in the dirt." That gangsta shit E was kicking sounded real sweet, but the way his face looked told everybody that the police cruiser had him on *shook* status.

"Yo, you be carrying that shit like you got beef or something, dogz. You should keep that shit in the house and only bring it out if you need to!" Chuleta advised.

Ezo was hard headed. He had the Napoleon complex and he was type paranoid after his recent shootout. Naturally, his response was "Fuck that nigga. I'ma always carry my heat out this motha fucka. Ever since my brother Boo got into that beef with them fake ass niggas from *mad Madison* and got knocked, I have to stay on point. Them niggas are about they B.I. and so am I. I got to rep for my brother however way it goes, feel me? Anyway, yo, here comes the cab now. I'll be right there, just let me holla at shorty real quick. At least I'ma have a set up in case them broads don't beep me back. All I need is five minutes and I'll be wit y'all." Ezo trotted over to his little shorty walking zig-zag on the sidewalk like if he were dodging some incoming bullets in slow motion. When he got close enough to Niesha, he licked his lips in case they were dry and chapped. He folded his arms across his chest, removed all smiles from his face, deepended his voice and said, "Ayo, Niesha, I'ma have to holla at you later, aight, I'ma go and get some smoke from uptown with my peoples. I'll holla at you as soon as I get back, if that's cool with you?" Ezo licked his lips again and waited for Niesha's response.

"Call me whenever you want to, but if you don't call, that will be your loss, not mine. Check this, Ezo, I'm really feeling you, but you be playing a lot of games." Niesha folded her arms, then uncrossed them. She leaned all of her weight to one side of her body, rolled her eyes, then looked towards the sky preparing herself for whatever it was that Ezo was going to hit her with.

"Look, ma, I ain't about no games. I'm just trying to do me and come up. Feel me? But check it, I'ma call you tomorrow and take you out to the movies and hit the steakhouse on 86th. Are you with that, ma?" Ezo gently raised her head by softly gripping her chin, and positioned her face so that they were peering into each other's eyes. When he first started talking, Niesha expected to hear some lame ass excuse so she lowered her head, but the thought of being at a movie or sitting beside her man at a restaurant humbled her and made her submit to his words.

She smiled, "Yeah, I'm with that."

"If it's all good, can I get a lil kiss to hold me over until tomorrow?"

"Of course you can, baby-boy."

The two kissed. The car horn from the cab blew and Nitty screamed to Ezo to hurry up and stop making love.

Ezo faced the cab. "Here I come, you hating ass nigga. I know you want my lil boobie, but you can't have her."

"Whatever, you fake ass Puerto Rican pimp. As long as you got *her*, I'm good. 'Cause now I can fuck her sister or moms or something." Nitty giggled.

When Ezo entered into the vehicle, the cab driver gave him a pound.

"What up, E?" the cab driver greeted him by turning around and shaking his hand. Ezo and Nitty had befriended the cabdriver after an incident where one day they had gotten pulled over by the police and Ezo had his gun on him. The cabdriver had only known the duo from two previous trips. Assuming that Nitty and E were dirty, the cabbie caught eye contact with Ezo through the rearview mirror, noticed how quickly sweat had formed on his brow and without making any sudden movements asked, "Ayo, Poppi, you dirty, yo?" Ezo replied in the affirmative. "Slide me whatever it is that you have. Look at my hand. You see it?" The driver still had E's attention in the mirror. Nitty noticed the man's hand wiggling near the center console, tapped Ezo to get his attention and when he did, he motioned for Ezo to pass his hammer to the cab man. E slid it to dude real smooth like. When the cops approached, Ezo and Nitty were searched. Nothing was found and they were allowed to continue on their way. They had set up their appointment with the cab company to rent the guy for two hours which would've ran them about seventy dollars. At the time, they had only occupied forty-five minutes of that time. Ezo and Nitty decided to call it a night. They paid the dude a hundred dollars and ever since then, homeboy was their chauffeur every time they needed a ride.

"Ain't nothing yo, just chilling. Ayo, take us to Autobon and back and put that DMX shit on, yo...*Flesh of my Flesh, Blood of my Blood*...that whole CD is popping."

On the way to Autobon, all three of the passengers sang song after song, word for word. When the cab pulled up to the smoke spot, Nitty and Chuleta got out to get the smoke.

Ezo's beeper went off and to his surprise, it was Sadie and them from Douglas Projects. Ezo walked over to the phone to see what those silly bitches wanted to rap about. He popped a quarter into the phone and dialed their number.

Ring, ring, ring. "Hello," Sadie answered. "Who is this?" she asked as if she had an attitude.

"Ayo, it's me, Ezo..."

"Oh, what's popping, E?" When Sadie realized it was the cat she called her *cutie*, she immediately jumped into her act. Sadie had beeped like four niggaz and out of the four, two were liable to call back. Whichever two it would be, hopefully one of them had some paper. As soon as Ezo's voice sang through the receiver, Sadie thought, *Bingo*, and her nipples instantly got hard.

"Ain't nothing. I'm just chilling with Nitty and Chuleta. I'm uptown right now at Autobon getting some smoke. What's good? We trying to come through and chill? Who's there?" Ezo questioned.

"Nobody now, but Nicole and Damarus are on their way."

"Aight, tell them we coming through, to chill for a lil while. As a matter of fact, tell them to be ready to smash 'cause it's not a game. Feel me?" The thought of Sadie being home alone made Ezo's dick get hard. He grabbed his meat, adjusted it so that it wouldn't be poking out and smiled as he waited for her response.

"Aight, I'll tell them, but that don't mean that everything's a go." Sadie was trying to *go*, but whatever Damarus and Nicole were going to do was totally up to them.

"Aight, one. See you when I get there."

When Nitty and Chuleta got back in the cab, Ezo told them the good news and they got open. They started talking about who was gonna get whom and how they were going to beat the pussy up...

"Yo, my nigga, drop us off on 103rd Street and Amsterdam on the right hand side," Ezo told the cab driver.

"Aight," the cab driver agreed.

The car they were in was a Lexus GS300. Some rich Africans

owned a cab service that had nothing but luxury cars and SUVs that were laced to the T. The driver was cool with them and he even broke night with them the couple of times that they rented him.

"Ayo, Ezo," Nitty called, "let's go and get that bottle of Henn Rock so we can get it popping," Nitty suggested as he exited the whip.

"Word life son, and make sure you get some condoms," Chuleta added, "'cause I ain't going raw in those West Side broads."

When they got out of the cab, they spotted some dudes from the project ice grilling them.

Ezo spoke first. "Ayo, Nitty, that's my word, I'ma put a hot one in one of those bitch ass niggas if they stunt on us. See Chuleta, that's why I always got my 44 with me, 'cause you never know when shit is going to pop off out this bitch." Ezo clutched the handle on his ratchet and adjusted it a little bit.

Nitty glanced at his homie and said to himself, *My lil man is trained to go at all times and I'm with that nigga a hundred percent.* "Ayo, Ezo, do you homie 'cause it's whatever with me." Nitty had his *fitted* pulled real low concealing the top half of his face.

When they entered the building, one of the cats in the front said something slick out loud, referring it to the trio. Ezo turned around and asked the dude who he was talking to. "Fuck you talking to, Duke?"

The guy was a Spanish cat by the name of Papito that was well known for starting a lot of trouble in the projects, but that didn't matter to the threesome because they weren't trying to hear nothing at all.

Before Papito could respond, Chuleta chimed in. "Ayo, dig this here, my man, we don't want any problems. We just came to see somebody. We tryna go about our B.I. Feel me?"

"Nah, fuck that. Y'all niggas from the East Side think shit is sweet out this way." Papito started waving his hands recklessly like if he were a rapper performing in a video. To make matters worse, he started to slowly approach Ezo, Nitty and Chuleta.

"Yo, Chuleta, fuck that yo, these niggas want problems so we gonna give them some problems," Ezo stated.

"Word life, dogs, y'all niggas got us fucked up thinking that we soft or something." Nitty added his two cents.

While Nitty was talking, Ezo pulled out his 44 Bulldog and aimed it at Papito and his crew. "I'm saying, what y'all trying to do? As a matter of fact, do me a favor and hold this for me." *Pop, pop, pop, pop.* Ezo let off four shots. When the slugs exited the barrel of the tiny cannon, they soared through the air like miniature rockets.

Papito was hit twice in the stomach and once in the leg. The fourth bullet hit one of Papito's boys in the shoulder. Ezo and them tore ass out the building. Running behind one another, they ran toward Columbus Avenue and slowed down after a while so that they didn't look obvious to other patrons on the street.

Nervously, Ezo said, "Ayo, Chuleta, try to stop a cab." He was out of breath from running. "I'm a fall back because I got the burner on me, feel me?"

"Damn, Ezo, you just like your fucking brother, Boo," Chuleta reminded him. "Y'all niggas are trigger happy. If he could see you now, he'd be bugging. I'm going to write that nigga and let him know how you be wilding."

"Nigga, shut the fuck up. Them niggas was talking crazy shit, plus they thought shit was sweet. But guess what, they were wrong 'cause ain't shit sweet on the East Side," proclaimed Nitty.

"Ayo, I think I hit that cat Papito about three times and I

think I got one of his peoples too. And yo, Chuleta, I don't give a fuck what you tell my brother, I'm doing me just like he was doing him. Plus, them niggas probably would've did the same thing to us if we wouldn't of reacted first."

As Chuleta stood on the street trying to stop a cab, he looked back at Nitty and Ezo and told them that no cab was going to stop for them. They decided to walk up 110th then back down towards the East Side by Central Park, that way they could toss the burner in the park if *popo* pulled up. Ezo wasn't trying to lose his baby rocket launcher. He loved that burner. It was his first, plus his brother Boo had given it to him a couple of weeks before he got knocked for laying a nigga down on Madison Avenue.

Ezo's brother Boo was a year older than Ezo and looked just like him. Everyone thought they were twins. They also had three younger brothers. Strange was about six years their junior and already wilding out. The other two were small children, four and six years old.

Boo was bidding up north in Clinton for hitting the clown nigga up. The dude didn't die. He was struck twice in the back. When Boo pulled out, *Bozo* started running. Boo banged off and Dude got hit in the back. Boo ended up receiving a seven-and-a-half to fifteen for the incident. He continued wilding up north too. Ezo would always talk about how his brother was in the hole for cutting somebody.

Out of nowhere, Ezo started laughing out loud. This caught Chuleta and Nitty off guard.

"Ayo, what the fuck you laughing at, nigga?" Chuleta asked him.

"I'm laughing at what just popped off, you fat bucket head motha fucka. You was running like you was scared to death or something. I wish I had a camera so that I could've video taped your ass." Ezo laughed harder which had begun to slowly force him on one knee while he held his stomach.

Nitty started laughing at what Ezo had just said and while doing so, Ezo cut him off and said, "I don't know why you laughing 'cause you was right in front of that nigga." Ezo had tears in his eyes from laughing so hard.

"Word up, nigga, now you think you untouchable or something," Chuleta rubbed in.

"Nah, I'm just fuckin' with y'all. I ain't going to front, I was a lil shook, dogs. Especially when I let off the first shot and that nigga Papito fell. I thought I caught a body," Ezo clarified his position.

After the trio reached their block, they walked into Ezo's projects so that he could put the burner away. Afterward, they started to roll up the dro they didn't get to roll because of the situation that just popped off.

Buzz, buzz, buzz. Ezo's beeper was going off crazy.

"Damn, nigga, I bet you that's them bitches from Douglas projects trying to find out what happened," Nitty figured.

"I'm going to go and grab my mom's cordless phone and call them bitches back to see what they know."

Ezo ran up the stairs to the second floor to get the phone while Nitty and Chuleta waited impatiently for him to come back so that they could light up the smoke.

Ezo returned with the phone and started dialing the number from his pager.

Ring, ring. "Hello," Sadie answered.

"Ayo, what up, yo?" Ezo spoke slowly.

"I don't know, you tell me." On the other end of the phone, Sadie had one hand on her hip, the other gripped her phone and every time she spoke, her eyes would roll into her head while she'd flutter her eyelids.

"What you mean, *tell you*?" Ezo had hardly any patience. So by Sadie seeming as if there was something that she wasn't telling him, Ezo got angrier by the second.

Sadie raised her voice. "Stop playing fuckin' games, you know what the fuck I'm talking about. You and your bitch ass friends shot my cousin and his man in the lobby about an hour ago."

Sadie was furious, but Ezo didn't give a fuck. "What the fuck are you talking about, bitch? As a matter of fact, fuck you, you baby guzzler. That's good for them niggas...they got what they had coming. Ain't nothing sweet on the East Side, bitch."

"It's all good, nigga, 'cause you going to get yours, you'll see," Sadie threatened.

"Tell them niggas that ain't shit sweet, and it's whatever with me and my peoples." Ezo slammed the phone down on Sadie.

Click!

"Ayo, Nicole, them niggas *are* the ones that shot Papito and them in the lobby. That nigga was talking greasy to me on the phone just now too," Sadie explained to her friend.

"Ayo, Sadie, you know your cousin and them always be starting some shit, yo," Nicole reminded her.

• • •

"We stay strapped," said Ganga, tapping his waist. He was referring to his partner Cano, but was looking at Ezo who was standing in front of their building with Chuleta and Nitty. The remark came after Ezo had asked them if they needed him to hold them down.

Cano and Ganga were getting money on 111th Street and Park Avenue. They were the best of friends just like Ezo and Nitty. The only difference was that they were getting a lot more paper selling weight uptown *and* selling five dollar slabs on 111th Street.

Cano was a Puerto Rican cat from the West Side of Manhattan but grew up in foster projects on 115th and Fifth Avenue. He was about 5′ 11″ and 190 pounds with red hair and green eyes. He was a wild nigga and dudes respected him not only for the paper he was getting, but for the way he banged his gun.

Ganga was from Ezo's building on the third floor. He and Ezo grew up together, but they did their own thing. Ganga was also getting paper. He was Cano's partner. Together, they were like rice and beans. They never left each other's side. Ganga and Cano were the same height and size, but Ganga was a little darker and sported a skin fade while Cano sported a low Cezar.

"Ayo, Ezo, when you get back from walking Chuleta home, holla at me, aight?" Ganga told him.

"Aight, dogz, I'ma call you out the window when I get back," Ezo replied.

"Aight, one," said Ganga.

• • •

"Damn, Ezo, I thought shit was about to pop off just now." Chuleta spoke to Ezo as they walked.

Chuleta didn't trust Ganga and Cano. He'd heard about what they did to that one cat outside of Ezo's window a day prior.

"Yeah, I thought so too, Chuleta. That's enough shit for one night. What you think, y'all?" Ezo asked.

"Hell, yeah, that's enough shit, dogz," they both said laughing out loud as they reached Chuleta's building.

"Aight, y'all, I'll see y'all tomorrow." Chuleta gave Ezo and Nitty some dap.

Nitty and Ezo walked across the street and entered into Nitty's building to get a change of clothing for the next day for Nitty.

"Ayo, come on, dogz, what the fuck, dogz. You taking forever just to get some clothes," Ezo complained.

"My bad, dogz, and stop fucking cursing in my crib before my moms start flipping out, dogz," Nitty responded.

"True, true, my bad," said Ezo.

As Nitty and Ezo were exiting the apartment, Nitty told Ezo that he loved him and that he'd go all out for him no matter what.

"Nah, nigga, I know you ain't getting all sentimental on me, yo, but on some real shit, I love you too, kid." Ezo smiled at his comrade. The duo embraced for a hot second, but immediately separated. Then Nitty spoke.

"Ezo, are we still going to get that work tomorrow or what?"

"Yeah, dogz, ain't nothing change, but the rounds in my burner, feel me? But when we get to my building, I'ma holla at my man Ganga and see what he talking about. If anything, we can probably cop some weight off of him and his man when we go uptown, plus he might even smash us."

As the duo crossed the street on Park Avenue and strode into Taft projects, they noticed two dudes walking in their direction with hoodies on.

"Ayo, who the fuck is that coming our way with them hoodies on?" asked Ezo. He and Nitty were already paranoid from earlier.

"I don't known," Nitty responded.

"Peep game, yo, I'ma pull out as soon as we get close 'cause I ain't going to let them rock me to sleep," Ezo said cautiously.

When the two dudes got closer, Ezo pulled out his burner and told them to remove their hands from their coat pockets and to take their hoodies off.

Cano and Ganga raised their hands above their head. Cano spoke up, "Ayo, E, chill, nigga, it's me."

"Stop fucking playing, nigga," said Nitty. "Shit ain't a game out this motha fucka." Nitty was stunting like he had a gun on him as well. His hand was in his pocket with his index finger extended straight out, hoping that his pointer looked like an imprint from a gun.

Cano and Ganga dropped their hands. They both smiled at Ezo and Nitty. Cano grabbed Ezo and gave him some dap while Ganga followed up and did the same with Nitty. Cano released Ezo's hand, snapped his fingers and said, "My bad, son, it ain't that serious. We was just fucking with y'all."

"Ayo, Cano, I was about to lay you and Ganga down. I thought y'all was some of them niggas that we had to pop off on earlier," Ezo boasted.

"My bad, son, I ain't know. You know how I get down, dogz. I'm about this paper, but I *will* lay a nigga down." Cano pulled out his 357 snub nose. They examined their weapons like if it was the first time they had seen them.

• • •

"I don't give a fuck, yo. That's still my family,. All that nigga Ezo is, is a piece of dick, feel me?"

Sadie spoke with much attitude. Damarus agreed with everything that came out of Sadie's mouth. She let Sadie vent while pacing back and forth in her living room, while *she*, herself, sat back on the sofa and played her position.

"Yeah, I feel you, Sadie. Regardless, ma, I'm riding with you 'cause you my girl," Damarus assured her.

• • •

Back in the lobby of Ezo's building, Ezo was explaining to his peoples what Sadie had said on the phone. They were all high and really didn't care too much of what Ezo was saying. Ezo was their man so they were going to ride with him no matter what. Chuleta had strolled back over to Ezo's spot to smoke a little bit more.

After two blunts of dro, Ezo finally broke the silence and said that he was going up to his crib to get some sleep. Nitty said that he would be staying the night in Ezo's crib because they had some small business to take care of the following day.

"Ayo, y'all niggas better walk me home, yo, fuck is wring with y'all? Did y'all forget what the fuck just popped off? I ain't walking home dolo, yo," Chuleta frowned.

"Come on, Nitty, let's walk this nervous ass nigga home. First, let me go and grab my burner before we bounce." Ezo hopped on the elevator and rode to his crib. Ezo and Nitty walked Chuleta home, then made their way back to Ezo's building without incident.

They walked through the back door of Ezo's building that led them to Park Avenue. Ezo received another beep.

"Ayo, E, is that them bitches again?" asked Nitty.

"Yeah, I'ma call them when we get back with something, feel me?"

"Yeah, that might be a good look for us both, dogz," said Nitty.

When they arrived in front of the building, Ezo called his man Ganga out of the window. "Skee-yo, Ganga...skee-yo."

"Ayo, what up, E. Meet me in the hallway, aight?" Ganga yelled.

"Ayo, Nitty, meet me in my crib while I go holla at this nigga Ganga." Ezo looked over at Nitty.

"Aight, dogz, I'ma be in your room rolling up some smoke until you get back."

"Aight, just don't spark up until I get back you Hoover," Ezo joked.

"Whatever, nigga, just hurry up."

"Yo, E, come on, yo. You got a nigga up here waiting," Ganga yelled form the lobby of the building.

Ezo trotted over. "Oh, yeah, here I come, nigga. What's good, Ganga? What you had to talk to me about?" Ezo gave Ganga a hug and entered the building behind him.

"Dig this here. You know I'm doing my thing with my man Cano and all that, right?" Ganga was making more of a statement as opposed to asking a question.

Ezo nodded. "Yeah, I be knowing, dogz. Check this though. I was going uptown tomorrow to buy some shorts with Nitty so that we could do us and all that." Ezo looked at Ganga hoping that Ganga could help him out.

Ganga sighed, placed his hand on his chin, looked at Ezo and said, "I'm feeling that yo..., but since you going all the way uptown, y'all might as well come and see me and Cano."

"That's what's up, but what you gonna do for the kid?"

"I'm going to front y'all whatever y'all cop."

"That's peace yo, but we only buying some shorts like I told you."

"It's whatever, yo...it don't even matter."

"Aight then, yo, I'ma see you tomorrow then, but I'ma hit you on the hip when I'm on my way up with Nitty, aight?" Ezo concluded.

"Aight, E, one."

On the way down to Ezo's crib, his pager went off again. This time it was Niesha beeping him. He looked at the number, but before that he remembered that he forgot to call that bitch Sadie back when she beeped him on his way to walk Chuleta home. So his first priority was to call Niesha and try to get her to come to his crib, then call Sadie to see what else that bitch had to say.

When Ezo entered his room, Nitty already had the blunt lit up.

"Damn, nigga, you couldn't wait for me to get back?" Nitty tossed the extra T-shirt that he had hanging over his shoulder onto the bed next to his homie.

"Nah, nigga, you took crazy long."

"Ayo, pass me that phone and be quiet. I'ma try and set some ass up."

"That bitch better have a friend," Nitty added.

"Watch your mouth, nigga, I'm calling my future wifey," Ezo smiled.

"You must be talking about Niesha."

"That's right, nigga. Ayo, if she dolo, you just got to fall back and go sleep in Boo's room, aight?"

"Whatever, you sucker for love ass nigga," Nitty joked.

Ring, ring, ring. "Hello," Niesha answered.

"What's good, Niesha?" Ezo inquired.

Niesha recognized Ezo's voice. "Hey, baby-boy, I was just checking to see if you was alright," she said seductively.

"I'm good, ma. Thanks for asking though. What you doing right now, Niesha?"

"Nothing. I was just watching videos on the box."

"Why don't you come through and chill with the kid?"

"Aight, I'll be there in about twenty minutes. Let me just put some sweat pants or something on."

"Aight, then, I'll see you when you get here, baby-girl, one."

Ezo turned to Nitty. "Ayo, Nitty, she was dolo and she on her way, so you know the drill, nigga. Go over to my brother's room. Oh yeah, let me call them bitches from the West. You know they probably got some slick shit to say," Ezo laughed.

Ring, ring, ring, ring. "Hello," answered a male voice. "Who's this?" he questioned.

"This is Ezo, let me speak to Sadie."

"Nah, nigga, I paged you. I just want you to know that it's

on and popping, nigga. We know where ya rest at *and* who you be. In case you forgot, bitches talk a lot," the kid spoke with confidence.

"Nigga, I ain't worried about y'all. Ask your man that got the hot ones in him." *Click.* Ezo hung up.

"Ayo, Nitty, them bitches gave them faggots my beeper number *and* told them where we live and all that. We got to be on point, dogz. It's on and popping," Ezo figured.

"Damn, the crazy shit is we only got one burner, dogz, and you always got it," Nitty stressed.

"Don't worry, dogz, I ain't gonna let nothing happen to you *or* me and if it do, it's an all-out gun war."

Knock, knock, knock. "Who is it?" Ezo barked.

"Niesha."

"Ayo, dogz, you know what it is. My baby-girl is here."

Nitty was raising up from the couch. "Damn, you claiming shorty already?"

"No doubt. She official, dogz. You know that."

Niesha was the same complexion as Ezo, with shoulder length hair and a fat ass. She was very pretty too. A lot of niggas wanted to get with her all around Spanish Harlem. She was also well-known for beating bitches down and she even gave a few bitches *buck fifties* on their faces. It's what attracted Ezo to her, besides the good sex they would have every now and then. Niesha loved Ezo but never told him because she was scared that he didn't love her back. But little did she know, Ezo loved her too and didn't know how to come straight forward either. However, before the night was over, it would definitely be known that they were going to be together *and* loved each other.

"Coming," yelled E at the door. "What up, baby-girl? Come in." He escorted her into his crib.

"What took you so long, nigga?" she snarled playfully.

"I was talking to Nitty. He's in my brother's room. My bad. Meet me in my room, Niesha. I'ma get something to drink. You want something?" he asked nicely.

"Yeah, get me some water with ice."

"Aight, I'll be right there in a minute." While Ezo approached his room with the drinks, he thought about what was about to go down. "Here you go, Niesha. You know what it is, get comfortable, baby-girl," he told her while he passed the glass of water to her.

Niesha accepted the drink, took a sip, patted a spot on the bed next to her, telling Ezo to sit beside her and sincerely spoke. "We've been seeing each other for a while now and I'm getting tired of this friend shit. I'm trying to be your baby-girl for real."

"What do you mean? You are my baby-girl for real," Ezo smiled at her.

"Nah, nigga, I mean, your *main* girl, *wifey*, that's what I mean."

"You know what? I've been thinking the same thing, yo. I just didn't know how to come at you. I fall deeper and deeper in love with you every time I'm with you. I didn't want to say the wrong thing to you and scare you away, feel me?"

"I feel you, E, but I love you too and I worry about you all the time. That's why I called you tonight, to check on you. I even told my moms how I feel about you, E." A tear had formed in Niesha's eye and fell when she blinked.

"Come here, Niesha." Ezo grabbed her hand and with his other hand, he rubbed her face with the back of it.

"Look, Niesha, on some real shit, I love you. I just didn't now how to come clean, like I said, feel me?"

"Yeah, I feel you."

Ezo moved closer and kissed Niesha's forehead, but before

doing so, he said, *"Real talk."* After kissing her forehead, he gently kissed her ear and worked his way down to her neck and chest, unbuttoning her Polo Rugby. He pulled her shirt over her head, unsnapped her bra and started playing with her nipples with his tongue. At the same time, his finger teased her clit. He worked at pulling off her sweat pants and thong and on his way up from doing so, he stopped at her middle and began licking her clit. Ezo ate the pussy for about a half an hour, then he turned her over in the doggy style position and continued to eat her pussy and asshole back and forth. After about ten more minutes of foreplay, he inserted his manhood into her, pumping slow and asking her, "Whose pussy is this, Niesha?"

She answered him by saying, "Yours, E, yours."

He told her that her pussy was good. While telling her, she responded and told him that she was about to come and that she wanted him to come with her. They did and afterward they both lay tired on the bed with Niesha resting on Ezo's chest.

"Damn, E, that was good. You ain't even put a condom on. I hope that I don't get pregnant," Niesha stated. Niesha loved E, but she wasn't ready to have children. She wanted to get her degree first, plus she wanted to see how long E would stick around.

"If you do, you'll just have to keep it," Ezo stated.

"You ain't have to tell me that. I was going to keep it anyway." Niesha rolled her eyes. She wanted to tell Ezo how she really felt in reference to the pregnancy thing, but she also knew that their relationship had only been made official a few hours prior. Saying the wrong thing could mess their whole relationship up, so for the moment, Niesha agreed along with whatever Ezo wanted.

"Do me a favor, Niesha," Ezo asked.

She looked at him seductively. She figured that round two

was on its way. "What?"

"Grab that half a blunt in the ashtray and my lighter. I need some smoke in me after that nut I just bust all up in you."

Niesha sucked her teeth and reached for the L *and* the light.

• • •

Knock, knock, knock. "What up?" Ezo yelled.

"Ayo, it's me, dogz, wake the fuck up, yo," Nitty bellowed.

"Aight son, breathe easy. I'm coming right now, just give me a minute." Ezo shook his head and bounced over to the edge of the bed.

While Ezo got up to put on his Nautica pajamas and his Nike slippers, he glanced at Niesha's beautiful body and gave her a kiss on the cheek. While doing so, she asked him where he was going.

"I'll be right back, I'ma go holla at Nitty real quick."

"Aight," Niesha said!

• • •

"Peep game, dogz, what we going to do? You know we have to go see your mans Ganga and Cano to get that work so we could go do our thing," Nitty reminded Ezo.

"Yeah, I know, dogz. Right now it's only like 10 o'clock in the damn morning, but I'ma get Niesha up so that she can bounce so we can do us."

"Aight. I'ma go and get a Dutch from the store."

"Take my keys, nigga, 'cause I might be busy."

"*Whatever*, you *sucker* for love."

"Fuck you, Nitty."

Ezo entered the room and found Niesha already dressed.

"Damn, baby-girl, you already dressed?" Ezo asked.

"Yeah, I'ma go home and get ready for tonight. Or did you forget?" She smiled at him.

"Nah, I ain't forget, ma." Ezo *did* forget. He actually had no idea what Niesha was talking about, *being ready for tonight?* He made another mental note to himself to lighten up on the trees.

"So what time are you going to pick me up?" she asked.

"I'ma pick you up around 7 o'clock, aight? So be ready when I call."

"Alright, E. I love you!" She kissed him on the lips.

"I love you too, Niesha!"

Ezo felt funny saying *I love you* because it was his first time really saying it to her. But that was something that he was going to have to get accustomed to sooner or later.

"Skee-yo, E," yelled Nitty from the living room.

"Yo, dogz, I'm in the shower," Ezo responded.

"Hurry up, nigga, before I light this smoke."

"Aight, I'm coming out right now. Ayo, do me a favor. Dial this beeper number, 917-753-8615. That's Cano's beeper number," Ezo shouted over the running water.

"Aight, I got you. Just hurry up, nigga."

• • •

By the time Ezo got out of the shower, Cano was already calling back. *Ring, ring, ring.*

"Hello, who is this?" Ezo asked after snatching the phone from Nitty.

"Yo, this is Cano. Who is this beeping me?" he questioned.

"Yo, this E. What up?"

"Ain't nothing, dogz. When are you trying to come through?" Cano asked. Cano had other customers to attend to as well. It was imperative to Cano and Ganga's operation to schedule every customer accordingly.

"Peep game, Cano, I have to take care of something tonight, so I'ma send Nitty to come get that, dogz. Aight, about what time though?" Ezo needed to be sure knowing that he had to prep Nitty a little bit earlier to insure an on-time arrival.

"Around 7 or 8 o'clock," Cano reasoned. Then he added, "Just tell him to beep me and put 112 on my beeper so that I know he's on his way."

"Aight, dogz. Oh, yeah, Cano, y'all still going to bless us, right?" Ezo was trying to come up in the streets and the only way to do it would be to get as much work as possible so that he could cover as much area as possible.

"Yeah, I got y'all. Just come through," Cano reassured him.

"Skee-yo, Nitty. Come to my room, dogz, I'm done getting dressed, plus I have to holla at you," Ezo shouted.

Nitty entered the room. "What up, dogz?" He gave Ezo a pound.

"Ain't nothing. It's just that I spoke to that nigga Cano and he said that everything is good for tonight. The only thing is that I ain't going to be able to come with you, dogz," Ezo informed his buddy.

Nitty immediately got upset. They were a team and teams don't move unless all are present. "Fuck you mean, *you ain't going to be able to come with me?*" Nitty's face had frowned up.

Ezo sighed. "Listen, dogz, I forgot that I told Niesha that I was going to take her out tonight, that's why."

Nitty walked away. "That's crazy, dogz. You knew we had some shit to take care of." Nitty re-entered Ezo's room and took a seat on his bed.

Ezo rubbed his face expressing his frustration and said, "Yeah, I know, that's my bad, dogz. As soon as I get back though, I'ma drop her off and come get you so that we can get this money right. *Real talk.*"

"I feel you, dogz. You go do you, dogz. Just make sure that you don't forget about the kid and our B.I."

"No doubt, dogz, but listen, all you have to do is beep Cano and put in the code 112. He's going to know you're on your way. Aight? Plus, they going to bless us on top of whatever we cop. I got a funny feeling this shit is going to work, dogz. We about to get this paper." Ezo smiled.

Nitty followed suit and showed off his pearly whites along with his homie. "That's what the fuck I'm talking about, dogz."

"Well stop talking and light up that smoke, nigga."

On the other side of town

Ring, ring, ring. "Hello," Cano answered his cell phone.

"Yo, Cano," someone spoke into his earpiece.

"Who's this?" Cano questioned.

"Ayo, it's me, Papito," his old comrade informed him.

Cano smiled. "Oh, what up?"

"Ayo, dogz, I got shot last night by some nigga from around your way named Ezo," Papito voiced.

"Word, that's my lil man," Cano made it known.

"You know that nigga, yo?" That bit of information caught Papito by surprise.

"Yeah, I know that nigga. We grew up together. Why, what up?"

"That's some crazy shit, yo, 'cause right before the nigga shot me and one of my peoples, the nigga Ezo was asking us, *where the work was at?* Talking about you and Ganga was pussy and that they going to rob you for everything. Then when I told him that I ain't know you, he started putting those hot rocks in me talking about he wanted everything."

Cano was short tempered and definitely hood smart meaning, *fuck everything and fuck everybody.* If it even seemed like a nigga was scheming, customer or not, homie or hated, friend or foe, it was better to be safe than sorry and in the projects, the rule was simple—*get a nigga before he gets you.* So after thinking about what Papito said, Cano's whole aura changed up. "I'm saying though, did y'all niggas give them my shit?"

"Damn, Cano, all you're worried about is your shit." Papito noticed that his lie was about to cover another angle, and he used it to his advantage.

"You motha fuckin' right, nigga. So did they get my shit or what?" Cano screamed through the phone.

"Yeah, they got everything except three packs that I had in my shorty's crib."

"Aight, hold on to that and I'ma get back at you when I'm done handling my B.I." Cano hung up the phone then turned to his man. "Ayo, Ganga, that nigga Papito and one of his mans got robbed and shot last night," Cano explained to his partner.

Ganga put down the controller to the Play Station 2 that Cano had set up in his living room and gave his right hand man his full attention. "Word, dogz? Stop playing."

"Nigga, I ain't playing. The shit that got me fucked up is that, the nigga said Ezo and Nitty did it with some funny looking nigga named Chuleta." Cano eyed Ganga.

Ganga shrugged his shoulders. "That's crazy, dogz, I've known that nigga Ezo all my life. We grew up in the same building. Yo, do you believe that nigga Papito?" Ganga asked.

"I'm saying, how the fuck that nigga know Ezo? Feel me?"

"Yeah, that's true, Cano. Why the fuck would Ezo want to stick him up for *our* paper when we were about to bless that nigga?" Ganga was a tad bit slower than Cano was which explained why Cano was the leader, but still, every once in a while, Ganga would try and make sense of whatever it was that would occasionally boggle Cano's mind.

"I don't know, but that's what we're about to find out, dogz. When that nigga Nitty come to see us tonight, we're going to have a surprise for his ass."

Ganga rubbed his hands together emphasizing the anticipation he had for what was about to pop off when Nitty showed up. "I feel you, dogz. Something gots to give."

• • •

Cano was very upset about what his man Papito had just told him, and he was about to do something to his other man for something *he* never even tried to look into.

• • •

Back on the other side of town
"Ayo, Nitty, it's about that time, dogz." Ezo glanced at his watch.

"Yeah, I know, dogz. I got that paper. I'm just waiting on the cab to come so I can bounce."

"Aight, dogz, be careful. Ayo, the address is 1581 West 156th Street. It's on Amsterdam Avenue, on the second floor, aight?"

"Aight. I got this, dogz, I already beeped that nigga Cano too. So everything is good so far. You just go and have a good time with Niesha, but remember, we got B.I. to handle."

"Ayo, just beep me as soon as you get back so that I know that you're safe." The two embraced one another then departed.

• • •

While Cano and Ganga waited for Nitty to come through, Ezo and Niesha were at the movies enjoying themselves.

Buzz, buzz, buzz. "Yo, who the fuck is that ringing my buzzer like that?" Cano yelled through the intercom.

"It's me, *Frank Nitty*," Nitty assured him.

"Aight, come up, son." *Buzz.*

Nitty approached the door and had no idea what was in store for him.

Cano whispered, "Ayo, Ganga, when I open the door, you grab that nigga Nitty and knock him in the head with the burner.

After I close the door, we're going to duct tape that nigga and torture his ass until he tells us where that nigga Ezo at."

Ganga seemed type hesitant at first. "Cano, you know that nigga Nitty ain't no sucker. He might even go hard and not tell us shit, feel me?"

"I guess we'll just have to see about that shit, dogz, when I put this hot coat hanger to his back," Cano said as he maneuvered the thin piece of metal around until it gave shape to his liking.

Knock, knock.

"Yo, hold on, I'm coming," Cano bellowed. He looked at Ganga. "You ready, son?"

"Yeah," Ganga nodded.

"Aight then."

Cano opened the door and everything went according to plan. Ganga hit Nitty in the head hard with his burner. Nitty fell to the ground, stunned because he wasn't expecting anything to happen, especially from Cano and Ganga.

Nitty curled up into the fetal position covering his head and hiding his face. "Ayo, what the fuck y'all doing? You bitch-ass niggas."

"You know what the fuck it is, yo," said Cano. "You and Ezo shot my man, Papito, in Douglas projects. And y'all stuck him for my shit, talking about *y'all want all my shit*," Cano explained to an injured Nitty.

Still covering and trying to make sense of the whole situation, Nitty said, "Ayo, you bugging the fuck out. We ain't rob your man for nothing. That nigga was talking greasy about some other shit, so my man Ezo told him to hold some hot lead. As a matter of fact, fuck you *and* your mans from Douglas," Nitty said frustratedly.

"Fuck *you*, you bitch ass nigga," said Cano.

"Ayo, Ganga, go get the duck tape so we can tie this nigga up and have some fun."

"Yeah, that's what the fuck *I'm* talking about," said Ganga running for the tape.

Cano was upset about what was going on, especially since he, Ezo and Ganga were associates since *mock necks* and *British walkers.*

After Nitty was secured, Cano started talking more shit. "Ayo, Nitty, dig this here, we're going to beat and burn shit down your ass until you tell us where Ezo at."

"Like I said, *Fuck y'all.* I ain't telling y'all shit. Do what the fuck y'all gotta do," Nitty mumbled over the loose duct tape that Ganga placed over his mouth.

Smack, smack was the sound of Cano's burner going across Nitty's head. "Ah, shit, damn, you hit like a bitch," Nitty laughed to keep from crying.

"Keep talking, nigga. Ayo, Ganga, pass me that hanger and that torch. I'm about to spell Cano on his nigga's back with that shit," Cano joked.

"Ayo, don't forget to write Ganga too." Ganga laughed.

• • •

Back at the movies, Ezo and Niesha were on their way out.

"Ezo, baby, what's wrong? You look like you have something on your mind." Niesha caressed his face.

Ezo turned away. "Ain't nothing, Niesha, it's just that I'm waiting for my man to beep me. That's my nigga and if something was to ever happen to him, I'll flip out, feel me?"

"Yeah, I know how you and Nitty are. Don't worry, he's aight," she comforted him.

"Ayo, stop a cab so we can go to the block. I really have to find out the deal with Nitty. After that, I'ma pick you back up so we can chill, aight?" Niesha agreed and responded with her tongue when Ezo planted a warm kiss on her lips.

A cab had pulled over. "Ezo, the cab, let's go," Niesha broke him from his trance.

"Aight, here I come." Ezo entered the taxi a moment after Niesha. Once he was comfortable, he tapped on the glass partition that separated the front and back seats and said, "Ayo, take us to 112th Street and First Avenue. Then to 112th Street and Lexington."

"Aight," said the cab driver. He pulled off.

Ezo was still zoned out. It took him a minute before he even realized that the cab he was in was the one he and Nitty always rented. He didn't realize it until he reached for the button to roll down the back window. That's when he noticed the rubber band he had placed around the door handle a day prior. He looked up at the driver and said, "Ayo, did my man Nitty call you, yo?"

"Yeah, I took him uptown to 156th Street and Amsterdam on the right hand side. He said he was going to beep me when he was ready, but he never beeped me and that was like three hours ago."

Ezo panicked. "Damn, son, check this out, take me up there after we drop my girl off. I have to find out what's good with my man."

"Aight!" said the cab driver.

Ezo was in another world. He also knew his man Nitty was always on point. All he kept saying was *I hope this nigga ain't get knocked*, but what he was about to witness was a lot more serious than that. Ezo was so far gone, and Niesha noticed it, that she didn't even bother to let him know that she was at their first destination, *her home*. She watched him for a moment and when his attention remained focused on whatever it was that was outside of the passenger side rear window, she simply blew him a kiss and mumbled to herself, "I hope he's okay."

"Yo, we here, Ezo," said the cab driver, waking Ezo out of his trance.

"Aight, dig this here, wait for me right here. I'll be back in about ten to fifteen minutes, aight?"

"Aight, Ezo," said the cab driver.

As Ezo was approaching the building, someone was exiting, so he didn't have to ring the intercom. When Ezo got close to the door, he could hear Nitty's voice. Nitty was cursing.

"Ahh shit, damn, stop yo, I don't know what the fuck y'all talking about. We ain't stick up y'all bitch ass man and his crew, yo."

By the time Ezo got to his man, Cano and Ganga had done Nitty dirty. They burned him with hangers, pistol whipped him and even threw rubbing alcohol on his wounds. They punished him. Nitty was hurt real bad, but he wouldn't give up his man.

On the other side of the door, Ezo was confused. He didn't know what was going on. All he knew what that his man was hurt and he felt that whatever was going on was *his* fault.

Ezo left the building and went around the corner to the fire escape so that he could see what was going on. When he reached the second floor and peeked in the window, he saw his man tied to a chair bleeding. He couldn't take what he was seeing, so without thinking, he fired two lucky shots into the window hitting Ganga in the head. When Ganga fell to the floor, Cano backed up against the wall, shocked at the sight of his man Ganga lying on the floor with his head missing. Nitty *came to* when he spotted his man Ezo climbing through the window with his 44 raised up, ready to pop off. When Ezo climbed all the way in the house, all he could think about was saving his man's life *and* his at the same time, with only four bullets left. He knew that Cano would kill him without even thinking twice. But it was a kill or be killed situation and he chose to get it cracking.

"Ayo, Ezo, shit ain't have to be like this, yo, but you stuck my peoples up and he said you was out to get me," Cano yelled from the rear of the apartment. Cano was sitting with his back against the wall and his knees pushed up to his chest. He fondled the grip and trigger of his weapon while he talked to Ezo. From the outside, it would've seemed like Cano was nervous. His hands were fidgety and his eyes were bloodshot red. But Cano wasn't scared. In fact, he couldn't wait to die. He always dreamed what it would be like at the pearly gates *or* at the door of the hell fire.

Ezo squenched up his face because what Cano had just said confused him. So he asked, "Who the fuck is your man?"

"My man Papito and his man that you shot from Douglas projects. You know who the fuck I'm talking about."

"Ayo, fuck your man Papito. Yo, I'ma pop that nigga's top if I ever see him again, but I ain't rob that bitch ass nigga, yo," Ezo bellowed back.

When Ezo looked at Nitty, Nitty gave him the look indicating that Cano was now standing behind the sheet rock wall in front of him. Ezo knew that if he shot through that wall that the bullets would go straight through, but he couldn't afford to miss. He let off two shots at the wall, one hitting Cano in the arm, the other striking his shoulder. Cano came out from behind the wall firing wild, missing Ezo, but at the same time, Ezo fired his last two shots hitting Cano in his chest. As Cano fell to the floor in front of Nitty, Ezo ran over and untied his friend. Ezo checked to see if Cano was dead while untying Nitty at the same time. Nitty was so hurt from being tortured that he could hardly walk.

Barely audible and in a shit load of pain, Nitty mumbled, "Ayo, Ezo, these bitch ass niggas was going to kill me, yo. That bitch ass nigga you shot from the west was these nigga's peoples. He told them that you shot and robbed them. I better not ever see that nigga, yo."

Nitty was on his feet now with one of his arms draped over Ezo's shoulder. "I feel you, son. I knew something was going on since you hadn't beep me. I got the cab outside, let's get ghost, yo."

Nitty stopped hopping along with his friend. He looked up at Ezo and said, "Ayo, Ezo, let's check this crib before we bounce. These niggas might have some money *and* work up in this piece."

"We have to hurry up though. You know the police are going to come up in this piece any minute now."

While the two searched the house, Nitty came across an open safe containing a brick and a half of coke *and* thirty-six thousand in cash.

Battered and bruised, Nitty held up the money in his hand and while trying to focus on the stack, by peering through two swollen eyes, Nitty stated, "Ayo, Ezo, we hit the jackpot, dogz, let's bounce, but let's exit the way that you came in."

"Aight, dogz." The duo hit the fire escape and made a successful getaway.

• • •

The next day at Ezo's house, Ezo was going through it because he had just killed two of his long-time friends that he had grown up with. After thinking about it for a second, he realized that at the same time, he had to save his man's life as well as his own.

Sitting next to Ezo on Ezo's bed, Nitty examined the drugs after counting the money over and over, several times. "Ayo,

Ezo, what are we going to do with this work, son?"

"I'ma call my man Tru from South Jamaica, Queens, I used to go to school with. That nigga is doing it big out there with his man Dawg. I know he'll let me rock until we get situated. How you feel though, Nitty?"

"I'm good, dogz. I knew you was going to handle them niggas whether I lived or died 'cause I would've done the same for you." Nitty smiled faintly at his brethren.

"Yeah, I know, dogz. Ayo, peep game, Nitty, this is going to be *our* lil secret. Nobody, I mean *nobody*, should know about last night 'cause that shit can come back on us." The look Ezo was giving Nitty told him that he was referring to being picked up by the cops and doing some serious prison time.

"Yeah, I know, dogz. Now it's time to get rich, dogz," Nitty replied.

"Let's go get some smoke and go see my man Tru and his man Dawg. It's time to get paid," Ezo concluded.

THE END

Look out for Eric Ferrer's 2nd short story in another publication. E-Boogie is a new comer in the literary field and is bound to be heard by any means necessary. For any questions, comments or concerns, kindly address your inquiries to tani-anunez79@hotmail.com or hit this author direct at eboogie1@hotmail.com..

THE BRONX
BADLANDS

by

Anthony "Big Ice Nitti" Bledsoe

Chapter 1

"A yo, shut that motha fucka up before the police or some-body hears that nigga kicking and screaming back there," I told D-Murder.

"Pull over, Ice, and I'll shut his bitch ass up for you," Beverly (A.K.A. Bev) said.

I pulled over to the curb as I was driving through Crotona Park, near the swimming pool and popped the trunk. Bev hopped out with an aluminum baseball bat that I had in the back seat of my black Seven Series B.M.W. and caught Paulie "The Psycho," trying to jump out of the trunk and make a run for it. Bev swung the bat one time and cracked Paulie's head wide open. He fell back into the trunk unconscious, bleeding heavily. She slammed the trunk lid, made her way back to the front seat of the Beemer and closed the door as I pulled off heading to University Avenue.

I parked the Beemer in the back of my man *Big Mike's* Auto Repair Shop on University Avenue. Drama, who was tall with a thick build and dreds, was my sister Becky's man. He pulled

Paulie from the trunk and dragged his kicking and screaming Italian ass into Mike's Auto Repair, where Mike himself was waiting for us with the door open.

Me, Bev, Rahiem and D-Murder entered the shop behind Drama and Paulie's begging and crying, scared ass.

"Yo, Drama, you and D-Murder tie that spaghetti, red sauce, sausage eatin' motha fucka to the bottom of the car lift. I got somethin' special in mind for this snake bitch," I said to them, seriously.

Before I ended Paulie's life, I thought back to what my father *Leon* had told me about the days he worked with Don Anthony, for over forty years, getting cocaine and heroin by the kilos. But I was also thinking about everything else that lead me to where I was now!!

My father and Don Anthony had seen and heard of each other around the Bronx neighborhoods ever since my father was a small time nickel and dime hustler back in the "70s," hustling on Tremont and Davidson avenues, also known as *The Bronx Badlands*. Don Anthony was just an *Associate* of the 187th Street Mozzo Crime Family on Crotona Avenue. The Mozzo family ran the entire Bronx area, but that soon changed.

They met each other while they both were doing a five-year bid in Elmira State Prison in Upstate New York. Don Anthony had already served two years in Elmira when he met my father. Their friendship started one day while playing chess in the outside *Rec Area* when an Aryan Nation member walked up on Anthony demanding cigarettes, basically trying to extort him, but Anthony wasn't having it. Anthony told the husky, baldheaded, tattooed extortionist to go fuck himself and my father got up and stepped between them. My father told the bald wanna-be extortionist that there would be no extorting anybody that was a friend of his. My father fought with two of the three Aryans stabbing one in the stomach and the other in the neck, while Anthony was stomping the other one in the head and face. A fourth Aryan came out of nowhere and stabbed my father in the back and upper arm. He also sliced Don Anthony in the face that started from his ear and went straight across to his nose.

My father and Don Anthony spent a month in the infirmary having their wounds attended to and spent the next six months in the hole. When they got out of the hole and were brought back to population, their bond was something like that of blood brothers, just from different mothers. They continued playing chess with each other and talking about the streets and what they had planned for when they hit the bricks.

Anthony went home first with a promise to my father that when he hit the streets he would be in a position to put my dad onto anything he wanted.

Two years later, Anthony had moved up in the Mozzo Crime Family and became a *soldier*. He was doing hits for the family like robbing truckloads full of fur coats, doing jewelry heists, extorting and protecting all of the after-hour spots that consisted of gambling, number running, bootleg liquor and prostitution. Anthony was feared by everyone in the neighborhood and he had set his sights on becoming the next Don of the Mozzo Crime Family.

My father came home three years after Anthony and Anthony kept his promise. Four years later, my father became the fifth biggest cocaine and heroin distributor in the Bronx, Harlem and Brooklyn, but it came with a price. Anthony expressed to my father the possible opportunities of becoming even bigger in the drug game if he, *Anthony*, became the *Don* of the family.

"You now that I'm down with you, Anthony, for anything

and I think I know what you're asking of me, but that could be an instant death sentence for me if someone ever finds out," he expressed his concerns to Anthony.

"No one will ever find out, Leon, trust me. I give you my word!"

"That's all I needed to hear you say," Leon told Anthony. "I'll do it!"

Chapter 2
THE DEATH OF DON MiKEY

The hit was to take place after the baptism of Anthony's son, Paulie. "Don Mikey will be going to his mistress' house on Central Park West in Manhattan after the baptism and he'll be with two of his bodyguards," Anthony told my father.

"What time is he supposed to arrive at his mistress' house?" Leon inquired.

"About eleven or eleven-thirty, but it's best that you get there early and wait on him, because I don't want you to miss this opportunity. There's no telling if we'll get another one like this," Anthony said flatly to him.

"I understand. Then he will die tonight, I promise you, my brother. I owe you big time for what you've done for me."

As Don Mikey's car pulled up to the curb of his mistress' building, the two bodyguards stepped out. One opened the Don's door, while the other bodyguard was holding open the front door to the building. Neither one of the bodyguards saw my father coming out of his hiding spot in the entrance of the alley on the side of the building. He was like a shadow of death, holding two twin four-five Browning pistols in both of his hands, moving rapidly toward the trio until it was too late. Leon was only five feet away from his target when he brought his arm straight up, shoulder level and shot the bodyguard that was holding the building's door, square in the forehead, blowing his brains out all over the front entrance door. He turned his attention back to Don Mikey and the other bodyguard who was now pushing the Don back into the car, trying to make a run for it. My father put six hot ones in the bodyguard's back and his body slumped onto the rain-soaked sidewalk face first. Don Mikey was in the back seat pleading for mercy with the assassin not to kill him, but his cries for mercy fell on deaf ears as my father shot Don Mikey five times in his face. All that was left of his grill was some facial bones and pieces of brain matter that were splattered all over the car's back seat and windows. My dad made sure that nobody saw his work. He slipped back into the shadows of the alley and disappeared.

My pops went into hiding for five months until he thought it was time to resurface, and he always kept his ears to the streets.

By then there was a power struggle within the Mozzo Crime Family and a lot of the older gangstas who were Don Mikey's friends and next in line to become the next Don all of a sudden were turning up dead or missing, never to be seen or heard of again.

It was a new era for the Mozzo Family and also for the New Don by the name of Anthony!

Anthony was now the *New* Don. He also kept his promise

to my father allowing my dad to become the biggest and largest distributor of cocaine and heroin in all the five boroughs. Don Anthony and my father promised each other that they'd take their private secret with them to their graves!

But eventually, the secret would be uncovered and it would cost one of them their life. The life to be lost was my father's, thirty years later!

Chapter 3
LOSING MY FATHER AND MOTHER

Before my father and mother were brutally murdered and tortured at the hands of a deranged killer *or* killers, my father showed me everything there was to know about his drug empire and introduced me to everyone that could be trusted within his cocaine and heroin organization. The last person I was to meet was Don Anthony himself.

My father informed the Don that he was retiring from the business and that *I* would be taking over all of the five boroughs' cocaine and heroin distribution and he asked him to give me his blessings. Don Anthony gave me his blessings and five strict orders/rules.

1. *You deal directly with me only.*
2. *Excuses are something that I never want to hear.*

3. Don't ever bring anybody to my house or speak my name to anyone.

4. If your ass gets knocked, do your time like a fuckin' man and keep your mouth shut.

5. And never turn against me, my son Paulie or the Mozzo Family.

"You have my word, Don Anthony, that my father's business and the way he has dealt with you over the years will continue the same way with me," I assured the Don.

Don Anthony said to my father, "I wish I had a son like you have here, who has a respect and appreciation of how the business is run."

The Don extended his hand and my father told me to go ahead. I bent down and kissed Don Anthony's ring and was officially in business. Don Anthony also extended his protection to me if needed.

Chapter 4
BLOOD IN MY EYES

Three months later...

I was at my loft in the *SOHO* District with my Puerto Rican and black girlfriend, Ursula, getting our smoke, drink and freak on.

"Ice, why you always have to do that shit?" Ursula asked.

"Do what?" I laughed questionably.

"Every time you want me to suck your dick, you always pull it out and hit me on my nose and forehead with it." Ursula frowned her face up as if she were mad, but the slight grin that crept on her grill told me otherwise.

I started laughing and said, "Okay, baby, I won't do it anymore, now, will you suck it?"

"You know I was in the first place," Ursula said smiling and getting down on her knees.

As she approached to suck my dick, I slapped my dick on

her forehead again and tried to stuff it in her nose hole. Ursula slapped the head of my dick like it was a bad baby and I stood there laughing my head off at the expression on her face.

I laughed so hard that tears were running down my face and I said, "Go ahead, baby, and suck it, I was just kidding around with you, that's all," I said, still laughing.

As Ursula was sucking my dick, I started eating her pussy out the way she liked it to be eaten in the sixty-nine position. She told me to do her favorite which was to throw her legs over my shoulders as I pounded her pussy out with my thick, long, nine-and-a-half inch dick. Ursula told me that every time I fucked her in that position, that she felt me in her stomach, so I stayed all up in her guts like that for about thirty minutes. I told Ursula to roll over on her stomach to do my two favorite things, one being, hitting Ursula's juicy Spanish pussy in the doggy style position. Then, sliding my dick in her tight little ass. I noticed that whenever I began to fuck Ursula in her ass, she really got into it and would start calling me the names I loved to hear from her like, *fuck that ass Papi*, or *tear that ass up Daddy* and that's when I'd go into overdrive and beat that ass and pussy up. But tonight, I'm going to tax that ass, because I took two Ecstasy pills and one Viagra.

I fucked Ursula's ass and pussy for four hours straight and she begged me to stop because I was hurting her. She said that I fucked her so long that she didn't have any more juices left in her body. Basically, I fucked her until her pussy went dry.

Ursula said, "Look at my pussy lips, Ice, they're swollen. I can't take anymore." She was laying on her back with her legs spread apart gently massaging her pussy lips.

It's true, her pussy lips *were* swollen and her pussy *was* dry, but my dick was still hard and I'd be damned if I didn't bust a nut up in that motha fucka. I opened the nightstand drawer, pulled out the K-Y Jelly, squirted some on Ursula's swollen pussy lips and asshole, put some on my rock hard dick, and commenced to tearing up her juicy tight ass and pussy until I busted my nut, *two hours later.*

I rolled off top of Ursula and onto my bed. I found myself sweating like a four-hundred pound fat bitch in labor and she asked me, "What the fuck was you on to fuck me for six hours straight?" She stared at me bewilderedly.

"It's you, babe," I said lighting up my *dro* blunt and looking down at my dick that was still a little hard and looking for some more action.

"Don't even think about touching my pussy," Ursula said jumping up out of the bed walking to the bathroom, kind of bowlegged, trying to get away from me.

I sat there on the bed watching her fat ass jiggle from side-to-side as she walked into the bathroom. My dick stood at attention immediately just by looking at her sexy ass, so I followed her to the bathroom and she screamed, "No more, Ice!"

I leaned her over the bathroom sink and with both of my hands, spread her ass cheeks apart and slid my dick into her swollen pussy until my balls touched her ass.

Later that night...

I was at my club on Fordham Road and Sedgwick Avenue near Jimmy's café called *Jazzy's* which was a restaurant and dance club, waiting for Don Anthony to show up.

As Don Anthony came through the door followed by six of his men, he greeted me by kissing me on both cheeks and calling me son, not son in a bad degrading way, but as a father would say to one of his children. I picked up on some sorrow in Don Anthony's eyes and asked him if everything was alright? He shook his head like he was ashamed to have to tell me what was wrong.

So Paulie came out of his mouth and said, "The police found your mother and father brutally murdered at their home this morning."

I went into shock, rage, then anger flared in my blood and I could almost swear I saw a slight smile on the face of Paulie and two of Don Anthony's bodyguards.

My father taught me to never let the next man see your hurt, because if he did, he'd use that against you in the long run. So I fought back my tears that were trying to surface in the corner of my eyes. I couldn't, however, help showing the blood and anger in my eyes.

He slid a folder over to me that he received from one of the homicide detectives that were on his payroll. Inside he said were the photos of the crime scene and for me not to look at them now, but to do so when I was in private. A tear ran down Don Anthony's face. I never thought that I would ever see a tear run down his face for a *black* man. I guess my father *was* truly his good friend.

"My detective friend said that the killer or killers didn't leave any evidence behind, but he believes that someone else did get killed in the house besides your mother and father because they found brain tissue on another part of the basement wall that didn't match your parents'. So your father probably took one of those bastards with him," Don Anthony said strongly slamming his fist down on the table hard.

"Son, please go home and sleep on this and don't try to do anything in the state of mind that you're in right now," Don Anthony advised me.

Paulie angrily excused himself and went outside with Joey *The Sleeper* to have a smoke and a talk with him.

"No disrespect is intended to you, Don Anthony, but

sleeping is the cousin of death and I don't plan on dying any time soon, so I'll stay up and handle this the best way I know how," I told him.

"You're just like your father," he told me. He then said, "If you need anything, just ask me and it'll be done. And if I hear anything, I'll get back to you ASAP."

Two hours later that same night...
It had been two hours since Don Anthony left my club and I hadn't moved since. After viewing the contents in the folder he left with me, I retraced everything of importance that my father told me about some of his enemies. There was short, fat, jheri curl, still having mutha fucka *Chulo*, the Dominican on 167th and Audubon. Big "T" Money, with his big fuckin' head, and mouth full of gold teeth who ran all of the Jefferson Housing Projects. "The hate those two felt for my father will come to an end, because I will kill both of those motha fuckas and anybody else that had something to do with my parents' death," I said silently crying by myself in my private booth in the corner of the club.

I made the necessary phone calls. I called my four child-hood friends, my cuzin Bev and my father's good friend from Harlem, and I asked all of them to meet me at my club ASAP.

Beverly...
Beverly, my cousin from Massachusetts, was the first one to show up.

Bev was a fine light-skinned black woman. She was five foot, eight, about a hundred and thirty-five pounds with a big ole fat ass and long black hair that reached the middle of her back. A couple of her men took her beauty for her weakness and they found out the hard way that Bev wasn't the bitch to fuck with! She laid down two of her ex-men and got away with it. But she got caught and arrested for the third one, who she threw hot grits mixed with lye on. As his punk ass was jumping around in pain from having the grits thrown in his face, Bev ran to the room and retrieved her Glock-40 pistol and shot him three times for giving her two black eyes and a broken jaw. All because she caught him fucking his baby-momma in *her* bed, in *her* house. They charged Bev with first degree manslaughter and sentenced her to nine years in Ludlow State Prison.

Bev did her time like a true gangsta and got out. Ever sine then she'd been working for me, doing special jobs.

At Club Jazzy's...

My soldiers and lifetime friends showed up one at a time. First D-Murder, my husky, crazy ass lieutenant, came through. Then Carlito, my slim, wavy hair lieutenant from Queens floated in. Then Rahiem, my tall, light-skinned Puerto Rican homeboy who had a mouth full of gold teeth arrived. Then Drama and my father's longtime friend Big Horse showed up thirty minutes after Bev. They all knew something was gravely wrong by the expression on my face and knew that the evening wasn't about fun and games. Bev was the first one to see the photos of her auntie and uncle's brutal murder and vowed revenge on everyone that was involved with their deaths. Then she threw up. I passed the folder around for everyone to see and it's safe to say that all of their faces were drained of blood after looking at the photos.

Horse, who was big as a house and about fifty-four years old, was my father's best friend. Horse had been hustling with my father from the beginning. So I asked him. "What's the deal, Horse, with that bitch ass nigga Big "T" Money? Is he still running his fucking mouth about my father?" I asked him like a snake shooting venom out of its mouth ready to attack.

"Yeah, he still talks a little bit of shit, but it all boils down to him still buying his heroin from off of one of our people. He thinks that he's not dealing with us, but he is. Do you think that he had something to do with your mother and father's deaths?" Horse asked me skeptically.

"It doesn't matter, Horse. Him and Chulo, that Dominican faggot from Washington Heights, are going to get their wigs pushed back, *just* because they hated my father and talked shit about him!"

"A yo, fuck *all* of them niggas!" D-Murder said. "Let's go kill every fuckin' body that you think killed your parents and let's go kill everybody that don't fuck with us. Yo, whatever you want to do, Ice, I'm down with you, playboy," D-Murder expressed seriously.

"Whoever did this violated our family in a major way, so let's go push some motha fuckin' wigs back right now," Bev said fuming.

"I'm with her," Drama said.

Rahiem agreed. "Let's go handle our business."

The only one that didn't say anything was Carlito, who ran the Queens operation. Maybe he was in shock from seeing the pictures, so I didn't think anything of his quietness.

"Put all of our soldiers on alert, because there will be a lot of blood spilled out there on the streets," I told them with a murderous look in my eyes!

Chapter 5
THE HIT ON DON ANTHONY

It had been two weeks and Don Anthony still couldn't come to grips with losing his very good friends, Leon and his wife Victoria. Don Anthony also found it very strange that his people hadn't gotten back to him with any kind of leads *or* information on the killings. There was rarely anything that he didn't know that went down on the streets, but this one situation puzzled him to the utmost.

While Don Anthony sat outside of his cappuccino shop, two Kawasaki-1100 motorcycles shot through his block doing wheelies. The passenger on the first motorcycle threw a bottle over to where Don Anthony was sitting and raced down Crotona Avenue's busy block popping a wheelie. His two bodyguards jumped up pulling their guns from their underarm holsters a minute too late. Don Anthony told his two enormous bodyguards to sit down saying, "They're just kids having a little fun."

Five minutes later, the two Kawasaki motorcycles with their passengers who were now strapped back-to-back with the driver and were holding *Baby-ohh-Wops* followed by twin black Cadillac Escalades with tinted windows, were creeping back through. Don Anthony's bodyguards saw the motorcycles coming down the block and stood up once again removing their weapons from their hoslters, fingering the safety switch *off* of their weapons and watched the two motorcycles approach. They didn't pay any attention to the two Escalades behind them. The two motorcycles picked up speed and as they got slightly past the bodyguards, the passengers cut loose their *OOH WOPS* on them. The bodyguards ducked for cover from the onslaught of bullets being fired at them, and as soon as they stood up to return fire, the twin black Escalades lowered their windows and caught the bodyguards off guard and riddled their bodies with automatic gunfire. The trailing Escalade came to a screeching halt and a young black male wearing gloves hopped out of the truck's rear door holding a 9mm pistol, ran over to Don Anthony who was cowering in the front entrance of his shop's door, and shot him three times.

The executioner hightailed it back to the truck and it sped off down the busy block, leaving confused and dazed neighborhood residents wondering, *Who would have the balls to do this to Don Anthony in his own neighborhood and in broad daylight?*

Later on that night...

I jumped out of my black-on-black 600, V-12 Mercedes Benz along with Bev on 110th Street between First and Second avenues in Manhattan. Nine trucks, ranging from Range Rovers, Yukon Denalis, Lincoln Navigators, Escalades and Suburbans along with seven soldiers to a truck inside, pulled up behind my Benz.

"It's plain and simple, niggas, we hit all seven buildings right now and kill each and every motha fucka that works for Big "T" Money. If you happen to run across "T" Money's ass, please bring him to me, but if he resists and acts up, then body his ass where he stands. Then its on to Chulo's Dominican ass, nah mean? This shit doesn't last another day *nor* night if we can help it. Do all of you follow me?" I barked at my solders.

Everybody responded with the sliding back and chambering a round in their weapons.

"I'll take that as a yes," I said.

"Horse, you take three trucks with you and hit the projects on 115th between First and Second. Flush them through the projects while me, Bev, Drama and D-Murder hit the 112th and First Street projects. The other four trucks will hit the backs and sides of the project buildings," I ordered.

Night of blood...

As me and Bev pulled up in front of the 112th Street projects, I hit Horse, Carlito and Rahiem on their Nextel two-way walkie talkie phones and told them to make it happen! I jumped out of the Benz holding two one-hundred shot 9mm Calicos, with my back-up gun, a Desert Eagle, in the waist of my Roca-Wear jeans. Bev had two fifteen-shot over and under clips for her Glock 40s. Drama and D-Murder's people carried AR-15s and A.K. 47s, and so did the rest of the crew.

Twenty minutes of gunfire resulted in forty-three of Big "T" Money's people being murdered, along with ten of my people being killed also and another fifteen being caught by police. But that still didn't stop us from going to 167th and Audubon in *Dominican Land* slaying more than half of Chulo's people either.

Chulo nor "T" Money were at their spots when we hit them, but the night was still young and this Bronx Badlands Nigga had nothing but pure revenge in my heart for those two pussy motha fuckas!

Chapter 6
THE SIT DOWN

"So, how are you feeling," I asked Don Anthony who was still hooked up to three machines, but in stable condition and doing well, the nurses told me.

"I've seen better days, Ice, much better days. If I were younger, I would have been out this damn hospital a week after I came in, but now I'm an old man, just barely hanging on." Don Anthony forced a smile.

"Don Anthony, you still have a good forty to fifty more years to live, who are you trying to kid?" I said smiling at him, trying to brighten up his day.

"You were always an honest young man, Ice, don't start lying to me now. You and I both know my days are numbered. I've been in this damn hospital for one month and my family has already been fighting to see who's going to be the next *Don*, like I'm already dead. If I had it my way, I would vote *you* as the new Don, Ice, but the rest of the crime families wouldn't hear of a Black Don running the Mozzo Italian Crime Family," Don Anthony said laughing, but I didn't find anything funny. "So who's running the family's business?" I asked him, because I needed to re-up.

"Paulie's in charge now," Don Anthony informed me, with some disgust in his tone. "I've arranged a *Sit Down* with you and him to discuss business. He knows the prices that I charge you, so there shouldn't be any problems there."

"Don't you think that Paulie's a little too hot headed to be running the family?" I questioned.

"That's my son, Ice, and even though he's not the brightest person on the planet, I do love him, plus he'll do what I tell him, until the day I'm laid to rest."

"Don Anthony, no disrespect, but I'd rather deal with you, because me and Paulie never see eye-to-eye on anything, why should he start now?"

"Ice, you're right, but Paulie's in charge now. He'll do what I tell him," Don Anthony assured me.

"If you say so." But I knew better.

Paulie...

"I asked you, Moo-Lees, to do one simple fuckin' thing and you fucked it up," Paulie said.

"I put three slugs into his old ass. How was I supposed to know he would survive the hit," the black hit man said to Paulie as he laid nailed down to the floor in an abandoned building in the South Bronx area, explaining and pleading for his life to Paulie.

"Because you were suppose to shoot him in the motha fuckin' head, you stupid black son of a bitch."

Frankie "The Switch Blade" leaned down, flicked open his

straight razor and sliced the black hit man's stomach open a little and dude let out a yell.

"Did that hurt, darkie? Well this is going to hurt you like hell even more," Paulie said to him evilly.

Joey "The Sleeper" poured sugar and rice into the slice that Frankie made on the black hit man's stomach. Frankie walked over to Joey with a box that held two large sewer rats that they caught earlier that day and pulled them out of the box by their tails. He placed them on the hit mans' stomach as Paulie quickly put a metal pail over the two large rats. The hit man was screaming and wiggling uncontrollably as the rat ate the sugar and rice, *through* his stomach because there was no other way out for them. Three minutes later, the screaming and wiggling stopped and the two large sewer rats emerged out of the black hit man's mouth with blood and guts all over them. The rodents then ran into a hole that was in the wall of the abandoned building.

ICE...

"Yo, cuz, that bitch T-Money just came back into town and he's in the projects as we speak."

"Who you with?"

"Me, D-Murder and Drama," Bev replied.

"Oh, yeah, Ice, Horse and Rahiem caught up with that rice and bean eaten motha fucka, Chulo too! They're holding his ass at the stash spot in the Dunbar Building on 148th between Seventh and Eighth avenues."

"Call Horse and tell him and Rahiem to bring Chulo's ass to the old "Loew's Paradise Theater" on the Grand Concourse. I'll be there waiting. And make sure y'all use the back door. And I want you three to snatch T-Money's ass up too, and bring him there also. And Bev, bring me four tubes of Super Glue, a bottle of one-fifty-one Bacardi, and a box of Philly blunts, so I can smoke my Dro and enjoy the show staring those two fagots."

At the old movie theater...
"Take the blindfolds off them," I said to Drama.

"What the fuck is going on here?" asked Big T-Money, looking around trying to figure out exactly where he was.

"Ice, so help me God, I'm going to kill your ass, Moreno," Chulo spit out harshly.

Big Horse punched him three times square in his mouth with one of his massive fists and Chulo spit out his two front teeth along with a glob of blood.

"Bev, roll this Dro up before the show begins," I told her and walked over to T-Money. I pistol whipped him upside his head until I saw blood leaking out of it from five different places.

"Now, which one of you pussy motha fuckas murdered my mother and father?" I asked the two of them angrily.

"What the fuck are you talking about?" T-Money shouted out to me, bleeding heavily from his head.

Bev walked over to T-Money who was being held up by D-Murder, and kicked him in the balls so hard that he doubled over onto the floor and threw up his lunch.

"I'll tell you two what. I don't give a fuck which one of you niggas did it, because in this theater you two motha fuckas will die."

Big-Bad-Ass T-Money started crying saying, "Ice, I didn't have anything to do with the deaths of your parents."

"Shut your lying ass, you bitch," Bev said as she smacked him across the mouth with her Glock-40. "Everybody knows that you were running your mouth about my uncle in a negative way," Bev told him, then smacked him again in the mouth with her gun.

"Yeah, but I didn't kill them," he was crying. "I was out of town taking care of some business," T-Money said with tears and blood running down his face.

"A yo, fuck that, nigga. Man-up," Chulo said to T-Money. "He's going to kill us even if we were lying *or* telling the truth."

"Oh, so your bitch ass been watching *Training Day* with Denzel in it. Okay, enough of the foreplay. Put those two bitches up on the stage and bring me the Super Glue and the One-Fifty-One Bacardi," I demanded Horse.

Everybody looked at me and I know they were saying to themselves, "*What the fuck is he going to do with that shit?*" T-Money started kicking and screaming at the top of his lungs for someone to help him as Drama, Horse, Rahiem and D-Murder dragged their two asses onto the stage.

Chulo said, "You need to check those fuckin' Italians, Ice, especially Paulie. He came to my spot last month talking about he's going to be the next Don and that he's taking over the distribution of the cocaine and heroin in the five boroughs real soon and he wanted me to be his right hand man in Washington Heights," Chulo relayed to me.

I started to think about what Chulo was saying and thought about the events that transpired over the months with my parents and Paulie's own father being shot up. Either way, Chulo and T-Money's asses were going to die, even if he was telling me the truth. I'll just put some people on it and see if what Chulo was saying is true, but for now, let the killing begin.

I felt like being creative just like the killer or killers did with my parents. So I started by Super Gluing Chulo's hands to the sides of T-Money's face and did the same with T-Money's hands to Chulo's face. I then proceeded to Super Glue Chulo-lips and eyes shut and duck taped the two of them together at the waist. Bev passed me the One-Fifty-One and I took a long swallow. I felt a tremendous burning sensation going down my throat and inside the pit of my stomach. I poured a quarter of the half gallon of Bacardi over Chulo's head and I know he wanted to scream out and swear that he had nothing to do with my parents' killings. So he tried desperately to removed his super glued hands from T-Money's face and T-Money was screaming in pain for him to stop. Bev passed me the blunt and I pulled out my solid gold lighter that I brought from the *Tiffany* store in the diamond district in Manhattan.

Rahiem said, "Oh, hell no, I know you're not going to do what I think you're going to do."

T-Money looked at me scared as a motha fucka as I lit the blunt that was in my mouth. I took a long, deep drag, then put my lighter to Chulo's hair and set it on fire. His whole head went up in flames and T-Money hollered and screamed at the top of his lungs. Horse, Bev, D-Murder, Drama and Rahiem all busted out laughing at the way Chulo was dragging T-Money all over the stage as his head was on fire. I stood back and said to myself, *"This is for you, Mom and Dad."* I walked up to T-Money as he laid on the floor with Chulo's head still on fire, pulled out the Desert Eagle I had in my shoulder holster, chambered a round, put it in T-Money's mouth just as he was about to holla again and put five slugs into his screaming bitch ass mouth. Then I put two in Chulo's burning head and left both of them dead on the stage. Afterward we walked out the same way we came in, through the back door.

Later on that evening at the sit down...

"Listen, this is the way it's going to be for now on," Paulie told me.

"Let me ask *you* something. Are you fuckin' telling me, or are you *asking* me?" I shot back.

"I'm telling you," Paulie said. "My father is no longer in charge of the family's business, *I* am," Paulie spit out.

"There's going to be some changes made as of today. The first order of business starts with you and those crazy ass prices my father was charging you for the heroin and cocaine."

I just sat back in the cut like peroxide and listened to this spaghetti and meatball, garlic bread eating bitch.

"My father is charging you thirteen grand on a kilo of cocaine and hundred-and-forty grand for a key of heroin. Those prices no longer exist for you."

"Yo, Ice, tell this linguini eating, fake fuckin' scarface, a hundred and fifty dollars worth of gel in his hair motha fucka to kiss your ass," Horse said angrily. "Your father would never settle for this bullshit he's trying to pull on you," Horse said fuming, leaning over me and whispering in my ear as I sat in a chair at the head of the table.

"I hear you, big fella, but I want to hear the rest of the bullshit he has to say," I replied to Horse.

"The prices as of now are seventeen-five for the coke and two hundred grand for the heroin," Paulie said.

"Are you finished?" I asked Paulie.

"Not quite. The family also wants to *TAX* every spot that you have in the five boroughs."

I clinched my fists tight under the table as this grease-ball bitch Paulie was talking out of his ass and I just wanted to Super Glue *his* punk ass like I did those two faggots a little while ago, but I kept my calm.

"We want sixty percent of every dollar that comes in to you," Paulie demanded, smiling and feeling himself like he just said something special.

"You know what? Who gives a fuck what the family wants and fuck what you want too, Paulie," I said exploding up out my chair making it crash to the floor.

Everybody in my crew *and* Paulie's crew drew their guns and it was a standoff for like three minutes.

Paulie said, "Have it your way, Ice, but we're no longer supplying you with the kilos you need until you come around to seeing things the family way."

"Now you listen to me and you listen good, you fake ass Don wanna-be. If you ever disrespect or dick tease my intelligence again, it'll be the last thing you'll ever try to do in your miserable life and please, don't take this as a threat, take it as a promise," I told Paulie staring at him with death in my eyes. Me and my crew backed out of Don Anthony's house holding our weapons in the ready position.

Chapter 7
THE MAKING OF A BLACK DON

I was at my club on Fordham Road having a power meeting with my new Columbian connect. It had been two-and-a half weeks since that fake bitch ass nigga Don Paulie tried to extort my business and I was without work. That was until I remembered the emergency number that my father left me of some Columbians he did time with. He said, "Only use this number if something happens to Don Anthony and you can't get any work." I used the number and the two Columbians were happy to hear from me until I explained to them what happened to their friend Leon and my mother.

For the next three hours we discussed business and everything was to my liking and we made a toast to a new-found relationship. Just as I was finishing up my business with my new connects, Salvatore walked into my club looking all nervous. I slipped my Desert Eagle out of my waistband, removed the safety switch, chambered a round and held it under the table as he approached, followed by D-Murder.

The Columbians asked, "Is everything alright?"

They proceeded to pull out their weapons from the brief-cases they were carrying which contained Mack-11s and said, "We're partners now so your beef is our beef." I liked what I heard form them because it was some true gangsta shit!

"Salvatore, what brings you to my neck of the woods?" I asked him.

Salvatore was Paulie's cousin, but Salvatore never liked Paulie and Paulie never liked him either. He said, "Salvatore's too soft to be in a crime family." But from the very first time I met Salvatore, we'd been cool with one another.

"Ice, can I talk to you in private? It's very important," Salvatore said, smoking his cigarette fast and looking around like he was waiting for someone to jump out of nowhere and bite his head off.

"Listen, Sal, anything you have to say to me you can say in front of them, alright?" I swung my arm, covering the area of my comrades.

"Okay, Ice, I know who killed your parents," Salvatore said to me nervously.

I jumped up from behind the table I was sitting at, holding my Desert Eagle in my hand and Salvatore jumped back looking like he wanted to run, but D-Murder grabbed him by the neck while the two Columbians pointed their Mack-11s at his face. Salvatore pleaded with me not to kill him. He said, "I had nothing to do with what happened. I overheard Paulie, Joe 'The Sleeper' and Frankie 'The Switch Blade' talking in detail about how they killed your father and mother and what they're going to do to you."

"Fuckin' Chulo was right. I should've checked those slicked

back, hair motha fuckas a long time ago," I yelled.

I snapped as anger came over me and I started walking around in circles waving my gun around. I calmed myself down for a moment and told Salvatore to tell me everything he overheard them say.

Salvatore started by saying, "Paulie had overheard a conversation your father and *his* father had one night in his cappuccino shop when he was just twenty years old. He said he heard his father thanking *your* father for doing the hit on *his* Uncle Mikey, Don Anthony's *own* brother. I guess that's why he always disliked you and your father so much," Salvatore assumed.

Salvatore continued and said, "Paulie also heard everything that was said in his father's den the night your father told Don Anthony that he was retiring from the game and turning over his drug operation to you, and that infuriated him. Only because he wasn't invited to the meeting and also because *his* father told you to deal with him directly like he wasn't capable of handling any of the family's business. But what I overheard Paulie, Joey 'The Sleeper' and Frankie 'The Switch Blade' talk about next was unbelievable and horrifying at the same time. They were talking about how they killed your father and mother. I assume that Joey 'The Sleeper' must have been the first one in the house because he talked about how he smashed your mother's teeth through her lips with his 'Street Sweeper' shotgun as she opened the front door. Joey said your mother must've thought that it was you because she called your name as she was unlocking the door, by then the door was halfway open and that's when Joey hit her in the mouth with his weapon and she fell to the floor. Then I heard all three of them laughing out loud talking about how your mother was on the floor bleeding heavily from the mouth and trying to pull her top lip that was imbedded into her teeth loose."

I grimaced as Salvatore was repeating the gruesome details of what he heard those three momma-mia, spicy meatball eating motha fuckas did to my mother.

"Then Frankie said he loved the way Jimmy 'The Gent' snatched your mother up off of the floor by her hair and hit her hard in the chin with the butt of his 20-gauge, sawed-off pistol grip Mossberg shotgun and she flew backwards like a rag doll. Then Jimmy's fat, sloppy, 300-pound ass asked Frankie why did he cut that black bitch from her forehead to her mouth like that, all the while laughing and patting Frankie on the back? 'Because the moo-lee bitch didn't answer your question quick enough when you asked her, *where's that piece of shit husband of hers,* that's why,' he said!

"After that, I guess everything went a little crazy," Salvatore told me. He said he heard Paulie's tall, skinny, beanie eyed ass say, *'That fuckin' moo-lee Leon must've been a real good shooter back in the days. Did you see the way he caught Jimmy straight through the mouth from twenty feet away? That's damn good shooting.'* Paulie said, when your father shot Jimmy, it caused Jimmy's trigger finger on his shotgun to move which blew the back of your mother's head off, because Jimmy had it pointed to her head as he walked her down the basement steps."

A tear started to form in the corner of my eyes as Salvatore relayed to me what he heard those three bitches talk about. But I held my tears back for the moment.

"I heard Joey say your father went rushing over to where your mother laid dead at the bottom of the stairs and with one blast from his 'Street-Sweeper' he dismembered your father's leg from his body. Joey started laughing and mimicking, I guess the way your father cried out in agonizing pain because Joey told Paulie, *'You should have been a punter for the New York*

Jets football team the way you kicked that black piece of shit moo-lee motha fucka in his mouth making blood and teeth fly out.' All three shared another laugh together.

"It was Joey and Frankie who duck taped your father to the basement's wooden support beam. Frankie then yelled out with laughter, 'X' marks the spot, then he sliced your father's face in the form of an 'X'. And it was Joey who put the razors in your father's mouth then duck taped it closed while all three of them repeatedly punched your father in the stomach and face so he could swallow the razors." Salvatore said, "But ultimately it was Paulie who killed your father by striking him repeatedly in his head with his own claw hammer until his brains were visible for all to see. Then I heard Paulie laugh and say to Joey and Frankie, *'I told you those black niggers don't have any brains in their head, because when I cracked that moo-lee's head open with the hammer, nothing fell out.'* Then all of them fell out laughing hysterically," Salvatore said.

"Enough," I yelled out to Salvatore who was visibly upset that he had to be the one to bring me that kind of news.

"How long did you know about this, Sal?" I asked him more upset than a motha fucka and pointed my gun in the direction of his face.

"I swear on everything I love, Ice, I just heard them talking about it today, about three hours ago," Salvatore replied shaking badly.

"Where the fuck are they now?" I asked Sal in a menacing tone.

"They're at the *Social Club* on Prospect Avenue and 163rd Street," Salvatore said, nervously.

"You better not be lying to me, Sal, *or* trying to set a nigga up, because I'll kill your ass even though I like you," I promised him.

"They're there," Salvatore assured me.

"As a token of good faith to our newfound business relationship," the two Columbians said, "we'll give those two, what's their names?"

"Joey the Sleeper and Frankie The Switch Blade," Salvatore told them.

"Yeah, those two, we'll give them a nice good ole fashion Columbian Neck-Tie and whatever else that comes to our minds," they offered me, meaning business!

One hour later...

We sat down the block from the Social Club on 163rd and Prospect for an hour and night time had finally arrived. The block was buzzing with people as usual for a summer night. I saw Paulie's tall, skinny ass, then Joey and Frankie Long Nose's funny shaped asses emerge from the club. As all three of them started to cross the street, I put my car in drive and gunned my black Seven Series BMW up the block. They stood in the middle of the street looking like three deer caught in headlights. I smashed the Beemer into all three of their asses and they went flying backwards in the air about twenty feet away, then they came crashing to the ground. The neighborhood parents saw what took place and snatched up their kids who were playing outside when I smashed my car into all three of the men. They ran to their buildings for safety.

The two Columbians jumped out of their truck, snatched Joey and Frankie out of the street, threw them into their Lexus LX-470 truck and drove off with them. I can only imagine what they were going to do with them.

Paulie started crawling back toward the Social Club screaming for help, as some of the neighborhood people watched in horror and disbelief to what was happening. Two soldiers from one of the five families heard Paulie's cries and emerged from the club only to be met by Bev's twin Glock 40s and Rahiem's A.K.-47. Their bodies were riddled with multiple gunshots. I jumped out the Beemer as Bev and Rahiem watched the front door of the Social Club and kicked Paulie in the face as hard as I could with my Timberland boots as he was crawling on the ground. While he laid there bleeding, I bent down over him and started pistol whipping him upside his head in the middle of the street in front of everybody until he was unconscious, then I threw his ass in the trunk of the Beemer and sped off down the block.

The end of Don Anthony's son, Paulie...

"A yo, shut that motha fucka up before the police or somebody hears that nigga kicking and screaming back there," I told D-Murder.

"Pull over, Ice, and I'll shut his bitch ass up for you," Beverly (A.K.A. Bev) said.

I pulled over as I was driving through Crotona Park near the swimming pool and popped the trunk. Bev hopped out with an aluminum baseball bat that I had in the back seat of my black Seven Series BMW and caught Paulie The Psycho trying to jump out of the trunk and make a run for it. Bev swung the bat one time and cracked Paulie's head wide open. He fell back into the trunk unconscious and bleeding heavily. She slammed the trunk lid, made her way back to the front seat of the Beemer and closed the car door as I pulled off heading to University Avenue.

I parked the Beemer in the back of my man *Big Mike's* Auto Repair Shop on University Avenue. Drama, who was tall with a thick build and dreds, was my sister Becky's man. He pulled Paulie from the trunk and dragged his kicking and screaming

Italian ass into Mike's Auto Repair, where Mike himself was waiting for us with the door open.

Me, Bev, Rahiem and D-Murder entered the shop behind Drama and Paulie's begging and crying, scared ass.

"Yo, Drama, you and D-Murder tie that spaghetti, red sauce, sausage eatin' motha fucka to the bottom of the car lift. I got somethin' special in mind for this snake bitch," I said to them, seriously.

"My father is going to kill your black, moo-lee ass, you son-of-a-bitch, fatherless and motherless punk, black motha fucka," Paulie said, hurting me to the core.

I picked up a tire iron and smacked Paulie across the mouth with it brutally hard, causing several of his front teeth to be knocked out and his lips to be split wide open.

"Fuck you and fuck your father. You motha fuckin' Italians don't run shit in the Bronx, *or* on these Bronx Streets. *I* do. Me and *my* crew run this shit out here, you pasta lovin' bitch."

I told Big Mike to hit the switch that lowered the lift. I saw the fright in Paulie's eyes as the car-lift started descending down towards him and he started crying and screaming that he was sorry. That he'd make it up to me.

I bent down and looked in his eyes and asked him, "How are you going to make it up to me when you killed my mother and father? Can you bring them back?"

Paulie had a look of surprise and disbelief on his face when I told him that. I backed away as the car-lift started crushing Paulie's body and I yelled for Big Mike to cut the switch.

"How does it feel to know that you're about to die?" I asked Paulie with tears of rage in my eyes.

Paulie's eyes were looking like they were about to burst out of his head and he was coughing up clots of blood from his mouth.

"Don't die yet, you selfish, backstabbing motha fucka. I want you to see this coming before you die."

Paulie's head was sticking out from the car-lift's blades and I asked Big Mike to pass me the fifty-pound sledgehammer. I raised it over my head and came down with it across Paulie's face with all the strength and power I could muster in my body. Paulie's whole face caved in with the one mighty blow from me.

Paulie's feet along with the rest of his body started trembling and twitching as blood squirted everywhere, even in my face. A minute later, that bitch's body stopped moving.

Chapter 8
THE END OF DON ANTHONY

"Ice, my son, how are you? How did the *Sit Down* go with Paulie," Don Anthony questioned me.

"Yo, Horse, bring Paulie in so he can see his father," I said and Horse dragged Paulie's dead corpse into Don Anthony's private hospital room and threw him on his bed.

Don Anthony was stunned then started crying, saying, "Why, Ice? Why did you have to kill my Paulie?"

"Because your precious little Paulie here killed my mother and father, *that's why!*"

"We could've straightened this out," Don Anthony said crying heavily. "But now that you've killed my Paulie, I'm going to have your black ass killed, you fuckin' moo-lee."

"That's what I came to talk to you about, Don Anthony.

There's no room for two Dons in the Bronx, so one of us *will* have to go."

Big Horse started laughing hysterically out loud. Me, Bev, Rahiem, Horse, D-Murder and Carlito pulled our guns out that had silencers on them and pointed them at the Don's body.

Don Anthony said, "I'll see you in hell, Ice."

"Well make sure that your old fuckin' ass ain't in the crime of the hustling game, because I'll have to kill your ass again," I promised and everybody fired on Don Anthony's helpless body as he laid in his hospital bed.

"Carlito, why don't you stay your snitching, cheese eatin' ass right here with the dead Don," I said and Bev snatched his gun out of his hand.

"Why?" he asked.

"Salvatore told me you gave Paulie and his two hit men my mother and father's address."

"That lying sack of..."

His sentence was ended right there, because I shot Carlito square in the forehead.

In the "Bronx Badlands," the weak get devoured and the strong become the "DON." I was now the Don of the Bronx Streets and the surrounding boroughs!!!

THE END

Stay tuned because Anthony Bledsoe is about to get it cracking with his debut novel, "The Problem" published by Amiaya Entertainment, LLC. He's a new writer but his pen game is vicious. For any further questions, comments or concerns, further your inquiries to tanianunez79@hotmail.com.

REVENGE, THE BITTER SWEETNESS

Urban Lit, handed to you on a chrome rim

by

Brandon McCalla

Chapter 1

His frantic escape had finally turned into a slow paced staggering. Two bullets had connected with his body. One entered the left side of his upper shoulder blade and nestled within him. The other slipped right into the back of his right thigh and went right out the front. He had run further than most men could have under the condition he was in with two bullet wounds. He was gasping for air and damn near on all of his limbs he was hunched down so low.

He turned a corner. Ran right into a garbage can, knocked it over, his body did a complete flip over it and he fell right onto his back. The pain was excruciating. He quickly rolled onto his stomach. He hadn't the use of his left arm and he was left handed, so he had to use the full strength of his right arm to lift himself up. "Arrrh," he screamed. Broken glass was in the garbage can and now *that* glass was stuck inside his right hand's palm.

His vision was blurry and it was dark, but he knew the area well and felt he could find someplace to hide. They were still after him, but they were almost a half block behind him. At least he thought they were. He wouldn't dare take the time to glance back to confirm shit. One of them had let off another series of shots.

BLAM!!! BLAM!!! BLAM!!!

Another bullet connected with his body as he began to move again. The bullet hit his face. The right side of it was burning like fire, but he was sure it didn't enter him. It only grazed him.

He moved the back of his right hand up to his face since his palm had broken glass embedded in it. He felt his warm blood leaking out of the side of his face as he teetered across the street. He was moving at a slow pace and he hardly had any equilibrium. He knew it was only a matter of time before the adrenalin left him, since blood was leaving him in abundance. He wouldn't be able to do anything but lie on the floor and await more bullets soon. Things seemed grim but he was a gully nigga. He wasn't gonna just lie down and die. He was gonna run till he dropped and crawl till he died. He wasn't gonna give them the satisfaction of his death, he wasn't.

He didn't even see the car; he hadn't much of his senses with him. He heard a horn honk, heard a car screech then he felt more pain. Ribs cracked, he heard them breaking inside him. Then his body was in the air.

His body impacted with the speeding vehicle. He flew right up onto the hood. He hit the windshield and the driver screamed as the glass shattered and splattered all over her.

"My God...!" she yelled in shock. She slammed on the brakes again; saw the man on the ground all broken up through her rear view mirror. She immediately unbuckled her seatbelt and jumped out the car. She was frightened. Didn't bother to even put her car in park and it began moving down the street just as soon as she hopped out it. She didn't realize her car was still moving. The night was grim, it had just begun to drizzle and it was like a haze was all around her, that or she was feeling faint and was slowly losing consciousness.

She felt her head and came to the realization that she was hurt. She had banged her head on the steering wheel and that had left her with a mean gash. She was bleeding. Before she could even wonder why her airbag didn't function, she heard her car crash. She turned and saw that it had hit a lamp pole. "No," she uttered in disbelief. What sort of night was she having? She had just gotten off from work and was gonna take a nice hot bath and enjoy her weekend.

• • •

The two men slowly walked up on the nigga they were about to execute. He had just been hit by a car and had already gotten shot a number of times. They were both breathing heavily. He had given them a good chase, but they were determined to do him in and had more than enough ammunition to do the job.

"Let's do this and go," one of the assailants worded to the other. "You hear those sirens. Don't think them ain't for us."

"I know," the other worded, cocking back a 9mm. He had an Uzi, but he had long since dropped it once the clip within it had run out of ammo. They were offered thirty thousand dollars to kill Darnell. Dude knew he could always get another Uzi. And besides, the serial numbers were scratched off the sub-machine gun *and* he was wearing surgical gloves. The authorities would be none the wiser.

Both men knew that whoever was driving the car was heavily injured or worse after that crash into the lamp pole. It was dark and they didn't see the woman till she screamed again. That was when they realized that she had gotten out of the car.

• • •

They were moving in, determined to kill the guy they'd been chasing for nearly twelve blocks. Both of the men turned in the direction of the woman first. Darnell had just gotten hit by a car and had a few bullets in him. They figured he wouldn't be getting up any time soon, if he'd get up at all.

The woman had screamed because she'd seen the guns. That wasn't the wisest thing for her to do because the guys with the guns didn't see her till she made noise.

The only light available was the lamp pole, but the lamp-light slowly winked out of existence. The car was damn near wrapped around the pole and smoking. It looked like it was about to explode.

"Get that bitch," one of the guys told the other. "We don't need any more witnesses. All the others were way too far away to see us. This one is looking dead at us."

"Right," the other one said. "Handle Darnell, I'll ice this bitch."

She couldn't move. She felt like she was paralyzed. *This isn't happening*, she kept saying to herself. *I'm a nurse, for Christ's sake. I don't deserve this. All I wanted to do was get home and take a bath*, she thought. She had a hard day at work. Now her day was worse, far worse.

She saw the guy clearly through the light rain and the lack of light within the darkness of the night. He was black, looked the spitting image of a thug. He was wearing a hooded sweat-shirt, his face was canopied but she saw his eyes clearly. They were narrowed and penetrating. His mouth was wrenched up in a snarl, she saw his yellow teeth. He was young, possibly not even twenty-one yet, but he was armed. Had some form of pistol and he was pointing it at her.

The other guy was going toward the man she'd hit with her car. She didn't know what to do. She had a can of pepper spray in her purse, but she was way too scared to reach for it. Her bladder got weak all of a sudden. She was about to piss on herself. But then she saw the guy she'd hit with her car, move, just a bit. He was struggling to rise. She could have sworn that she'd murdered him with her car. He ran right into it and slammed right into her windshield.

The guy saw her fumbling in her purse, but he thought nothing of it. He was a criminal but he hadn't ever killed a person before. His partner was a more seasoned gangsta and *he* was just a high school drop out and drug dealer, till recently. Now he was more than that.

Someone had given him a few guns and a whole lot of ammo and gave him a mission. Kill Darnell. And even though Darnell was their boss, they were hired by Darnell's drug supplier, a Colombian drug lord named Manuel. He had no last name, none anyone had ever mentioned.

Manuel was the leader of the Colombian Revolutionary Armed Forces, better known as the FARC. The FARC was a drug running crew of vicious killers. Darnell could attest to that. The two guys were friends of Darnell's once, his boys, his little drug dealing protégés who used to sell the product Manuel had fronted to Darnell in the mean streets of Brooklyn, New York.

It was betrayal but it was what it was. Manuel had offered the two guys far more money than Darnell could ever give them in one pop and had provided them with weapons. They made their choice and now Darnell was moments from death.

"Sorry, nigga," Darnell's former protégé said to him with his pistol pointed at Darnell's prone body, "but you were just holding us back and Manuel gave us an offer we just couldn't refuse."

The car exploded.

The guy turned around. He was shocked. "What the fuck!?" he blurted. The hood of the car had just erupted into flames. He quickly turned back to Darnell.

He saw the bullet as if in slow motion. It was spinning around as it traveled through the air cutting the space between the barrel it left and the middle of his forehead.

The slug went through the first few layers of his epidermis then it penetrated his skull. His whole body was thrown back from the impact. The projectile tore through gray matter then found a nice spot right in the middle of his brain.

His head exploded.

Darnell saw blood gushing out of the hole the bullet made. His former drug dealing protégé slowly fell lifelessly to the ground.

Darnell's whole upper left side was numb, so numb that when he initially got shot in his shoulder, his hand slowly began to swell. His swollen hand was still clutching the pistol he held, his Heckler and Koch .25 automatic. The car explosion had given him just enough time to turn his body around and let off one shot. One shot was all he needed. His left arm became lifeless once again falling feebly with the weight of the pistol.

Darnell was surrounded by a pool of his own blood. His body was broken up; he knew a few of his ribs were fractured, completely cracked in some places or worse.

• • •

The car exploded. Both she and the guy who had the gun pointed in her face turned to look. She wasted no time. She fumbled the pepper spray out of her purse and sprayed it right in the guy's eyes.

He screeched, but he didn't drop the gun. He used his empty hand, reaching for his burning eyes. The woman immediately kicked him in the groin area. The guy cried out in pain, but he reached and grabbed the woman's head. He wrung a good bit of her hair and pulled her head down. Then he swung his gun at the back of her head.

"No...!" she yelled. Then she cried out in pain. But she knew that he hadn't hit her like he wanted to. The pepper spray had weakened him. She had gotten him good. Directly in the eyes, and she knew his eyes were irritated and he had little to no vision. But he had a handful of her hair and she wasn't wearing a weave. He was trying to rip the hair right out of her scalp.

He felt her biting him on the arm. She was doing whatever she could to try to get away. He couldn't see shit, but he still had his gun and he had a handful of her hair. So he put the gun's tip right to the back of her head. "Bye, bitch!" he yelled.

She screamed again. Screamed for what she thought would be the last time.

BLAM!!!

A gun fired. But it wasn't her assailant's gun. It was somebody else's. The guy's fingers loosened from around her hair. He fell to one knee. He was clutching his other kneecap. Somebody had shot him right in the back of his right knee. His moaning was horrible. She backed away from him and cried more than she ever did.

The guy she had hit with her car was right above the guy who was just about to shoot her. He looked ghastly, almost dead. His eyes were hollow sockets and he was bleeding in a number of places. But he had a gun to the guy's temple.

"Just one question, Malik," she heard him tell the guy. "I just got one question. And you can answer or not, but regardless of the fact, you are as good as dead now. I never wronged you guys, ever!" The guy seemed to be gathering more strength, his voice was growing with volume. "All I did was made shit sweet for you niggas. And when any of y'all got locked up, I bailed you out the very next day, if not sooner."

Darnell grabbed Malik's head and yanked it back so that the nigga could look up at him, dead in the eyes. "One question. Who coaxed you niggas to get down with this. With the kidnapping. Who wants me killed? Who!? I could care less about why, I just wanna know who?"

The woman just watched. The light drizzle grew a bit more intense as the water beat down on her head. She was beyond words. Nothing like this had ever happened to her and she just wanted to run, but she couldn't. She heard sirens. They were getting close and she was glad because of it. Her car had exploded. And right in front of her face was a stand off between who knows whom. Drug dealers perhaps, killers, yes, they were definitely that. She knew these people weren't the scrupulous sort. She had the option to run, but she chose not to take it. She stood in the rain and watched and listened.

"If I tell you, you won't kill me, right?" Malik pleaded in question.

The man didn't reply.

All he said was, "Manuel..." Malik's eyes danced a bit and that was enough for the man. His eyes told Darnell all he needed to know. Malik's last thoughts were on Darnell being psychic because the last thing to be expected was Manuel and the FARC. Ironically, it was the first word that came from Darnell's lips. Darnell had never crossed Manuel before and vice versa. But the drug game was a dirty business. Who else had enough money to persuade betrayal but Manuel?

BLAM!!!

Chapter 2

She was so close to them that when the gun went off and the bullet went right between Malik's eyes, some of his crimson spit out of the hole in his head and splattered on her white nursing uniform. All she could do was gasp. Then she looked into the eyes of a man who should have been dead already, the man whom she hit with her car. Malik's body fell back and hit the asphalt ice cold with death.

The sirens were even louder now. The authorities were just a few blocks away, if that. The man fell to his knees. The drizzle had suddenly turned into a downright pour. The woman just stood paralyzed with fear and bewilderment, she was sure she'd need psychological treatment after what happened that evening. She heard the man say, "The authorities mustn't see me." He looked up with his sunken, defeated eyes. They locked with the woman's own which were wide from shock. "If they take me to the hospital, Manuel will finish the job my two former employees started. You gotta get me out of here."

"Huh?" She couldn't believe the words that came out of

the guy's mouth.

"You are a nurse. Help me..." The guy dropped face first to the wet pavement. The burgundy leaking from his shoulder and thigh wounds began intermingling with the rainwater and swirling, traveling toward some sewer drain the woman hadn't the care to look for.

She didn't know what she was supposed to do. Obviously this guy wasn't the sort of person she should know. And running away from the scene of a crime was a crime itself. How could she just leave her car right where it was? But then her car had exploded and the sirens were louder than she had heard them earlier. She saw the spinning red light atop the police vehicle. The rain was so intense. She was sure they couldn't see her.

She looked down at the man again and wondered how she was gonna take him anywhere and where would she take him. He looked like he was dead anyway and he looked like he weighed a thousand pounds at the moment. He was soaking wet, and so was she. This was the worst night of her life.

• • •

One of the detectives had just lit a cigarette. He barely got his Zippo lighter to function since it was pouring down raining. He looked at his partner and nudged his jaw toward the still smoking vehicle wrapped around the barely standing lamp pole.

"How fast do you think that sedan was traveling?" he worded with smoke seeping out of his mouth. His cigarette was already drenched. He flung it to the wet pavement.

"Kind of hard to say right now, Smithies, but this street has a narrow decline," Detective Barrows replied.

Detective Smithies nodded in agreement. "Yeah, we *are* on a damn hill. The forensics think the car hadn't a driver when it crashed. Ain't that some shit."

"This whole damn thing is some shit. You know, I've been doing this beat for damn near eight years, Smithies. I've arrested these two corpses a number of times. They ain't never been patted down without me finding at least a few bags of dope or some weed, if not for selling then their own personal use." Barrows saw Smithies nod in agreement.

"Yeah," Smithies added, "and that Uzi we found a few blocks down, the serial numbers were scratched off it. That was a professional job. Ain't no damn street hustler, no matter how successful, gonna know how to do it as clean as it was done. I used to work the beat up in Washington Heights before I got transferred. That Uzi smells like those damn spics. I'm talking Cubans or Colombian mafia stuff, Jeff."

Jeff Barrows puckered his lips and nodded in agreement. This sort of case was just the type of case he needed right now. He was going through a nasty divorce and two of his kids had a graduation coming up. Detective Barrows needed to get his mind off of his life. This case seemed like the sort of shit that could provide that. He wasn't gonna be half-ass on this one.

"First let's find out whose vehicle is kissing that lamp pole. Then let's see if we can find out who sliced off the numbers on the gun. You still got some connections in Washington Heights?"

"I think I can hunt down a few of the natives. I still know a couple of good scum in that district.

• • •

Sharon had dragged the guy by the arm in the rain and the dead of the night. He possibly would have left a trail of blood in his wake, but the rain washed away any bit of blood that leaked from his bullet wounds. Sharon wasn't certain a person could bleed as much as he was and she was a nurse and had seen all forms of injuries. The guy had been hit by a car also, her car. That might have been the only reason why she'd decided to do the craziness she was doing now.

She was huffing and puffing and as nervous as shit. Two police cars had just pulled up on the scene and she had just barely dragged the guy into a dark alley before the cops got out of their vehicles. The precipitation was heavy, but she saw the cops had flashlights and their guns were drawn.

After she'd dragged the guy into the alley, she dropped right next to him, balled up beside him and began to cry. What was she gonna do now? She wanted to just get up and run to the cops and tell them everything. She was just about to do just that. The guy then jumped up all of a sudden. Sharon was about to scream out, but he'd put a hand around her mouth. "Shhh," he said with a whisper.

The gun he held was right on the floor between the both of them. She looked at the weapon with huge eyes. She wanted to reach for it but hadn't the nerve. And besides that, the guy said, "Thanks," with a very weak whisper. "I need medical attention. How far do you live from here?"

"Not too far," Sharon uttered. Then she covered her mouth with a hand of her own. *I told him I lived not too far*, she thought. *I'm so fucking dumb.*

"Good," the guy worded. "I think I can walk, but I might drop dead at any minute. If I do I just wanna thank you."

"For what?" *For hitting you with my car?* Sharon cogitated.

"For dragging me into this alley," he worded as he staggered up. "If the cops got a hold of me, I'd be in worse condition than I am now. Manuel can have you killed in jail just as quick as out on the streets."

"Who's Manuel? Who are *you* for that matter?" she asked him.

"Get me someplace. Then patch me up. I'll talk when these ribs stop moving around in my stomach." *I'll talk, but talk about what?* Darnell thought. *I'm not quite sure what's going on.* He was in too much pain to situate all his thoughts, but he was thinking about his daughter. That alone gave him strength, the strength for revenge. He took another look at the woman. "You *are* a nurse, right?"

"I don't wear this uniform for nothing," she snapped at him. She thought he had grinned, but it was a grimace. Then he spit up some blood and clutched his midsection feebly. He was really in a bad situation.

They both saw the police flashlights buzzing around and a few more patrol cars had pulled up right around the murder scene. They both knew it was time to leave.

They moved as quickly as they could. She was scared shitless and he was damn near dead. But they were able to avoid any onlooker's eyes and the authorities, thanks to the heavy rain. Darnell was in so much pain that he hardly remembered how they got to the woman's house and once she opened the door, he dropped right within the threshold. It was all she could do to drag him inside her house. All of his blood was gonna ruin her fucking carpet.

• • •

The next couple of days were crazy for Sharon. She was a registered nurse who used to fantasize about being a doctor in her youth. She just wasn't rich or bright enough to situate herself in med school. But she was a beautiful woman who just turned thirty-one. She had no kids, lived alone and got her swerve on occasionally with some guy she found interesting at her job. But she'd never gotten deeply involved with anyone after her boyfriend who ended up being abusive.

She was in her living room about to perform an operation.

She used Vodka to rid the guy's wounds of any infections. It was the strongest thing she had. Stronger than any medication she'd smuggled out of her job. She did have some codeine and she gave him that to minimize the pain. But he was unconscious so she had to dissolve it in a spoon and force it into his mouth.

• • •

Sharon wasn't sure about his ribs but she did wrap them up. The guy told her his name but he didn't speak about much besides that. Though one time he had gained back his consciousness on that horrible night after they got to her house, he whispered, "Dial 911 and report your car stolen. Tell them that you couldn't find your keys since yesterday and you had worked a double shift within the last twenty-four hours." He said that for no apparent reason, but it was sound advice nonetheless. Sharon *had* worked a double shift ironically enough. When the detectives knocked on her door just ten hours later though, she was nervous, but she felt soundly about her alibi.

She didn't invite the two detectives within the house and they might have found that strange and were a bit suspicious, but they mentioned nothing about it. Sharon's story seemed legit. She had reported her car stolen once she got home from working a double shift at work. And her car keys were mysteriously missing, that was the only weird thing, but these things happened. The detectives knew about a series of odd burglaries in the area, window jobs, and all of the burglaries were for small items like jewelry and car keys, things that took people a day or two to notice missing at times. And Detective Barrows had already called her job and checked about her working schedule way before they'd even arrived at her home. They also got the 911 call verified.

Her car was stolen and used in a double homicide. That's what it seemed like. It seemed like drug-related criminology and violence, simple and plain. But the two detectives still speculated differently, and after they left Sharon's, they drove directly uptown, to Washington Heights. After they left, Sharon went right back to treating Darnell's wounds.

Darnell's face grazing was the least vicious of the three bullet wounds. That bullet barely nicked an ear and all she had to do after sanitizing it was dress it with some solution she had handy. The thigh wound was nasty, but she knew from her experience that it would heal up on its own in time. The bullet tore right through his flesh but at an angle that hadn't damaged any bone. The shoulder injury was the worse because the bullet was still lodged in one of the blades of his back. When the guy told Sharon to pull the bullet out, she nearly fainted.

"Hell, no," she yelled at him. "You need *real* medical attention...,"

Darnell cut her off. "Once I've healed up enough to walk without all this pain, I'm gonna go and kill Manuel and whomever else is involved in my daughter's death." Then she saw the moisture in his eyes, tears began to fall. "They murdered my daughter. Then they tried to murder me. I gotta stay alive till I get these mutha fuckas. I don't know why they did it but they are gonna die, all of them. And if I go to a hospital, I'll be dead before or after the operation. Manuel is the leader of a drug cartel. He probably has men at every hospital in the borough, the whole fucking city, just waiting for me to arrive, just waiting to murder me."

"My God," Sharon exasperated. "What did you do?"

"I don't know." Darnell held his head low. "My daughter's mother was Colombian. Her cousin got me the drug connects that made me what I am today some ten years ago, when we were both young and stupid. They tossed my daughter's mother right out a window, thirteen flights. It had something to do with her cousin because he died just two days later, with a slit throat. But that was two years ago and me and my daughter's mother, we were separated by then. I never got custody of my girl, but her Colombian grandmother was a nice lady. She died of natural causes and then I got my baby." Darnell took a deep breath. "Anna, my daughter, well, she spent most of her time at my sister's. I'm a drug dealer and well, you now. One day my sister called me screaming frantically saying that they kidnapped her. I asked who and she said Colombians. Shit, that could have been anybody. Manuel ain't the only Colombian. They were holding her for ransom. They called me. I asked them why. I told them I would give them anything. I had gathered my team up. All my thugs and drug dealers." His eyes narrowed Chinese thin. "Then I heard them slicing her throat over the phone..." Darnell was getting choked up. He rose up off the couch rather abruptly but moaned and laid himself right back down. "Then my own boys, my own men, they started blasting guns at me. They had betrayed me; sided with Manuel I guess; who else is behind this. All I could do was run. I don't know why. I never crossed Manuel before, never!"

Sharon's eyes were all full of tears. Darnell saw that she was shaking uncontrollably, but he hadn't the strength to do anything but cry himself. Then she said, "Turn around."

Darnell grinned. He knew it was gonna hurt. She hadn't any real surgical instrument and would probably use a kitchen knife and a fork to dig the bullet out of him. The bullet was right in his back on the left side and because of it, he barely had the use of his left arm, *and* he was left handed. But he knew once the bullet was out, he would be able to move a bit and then he would heal up enough to go to the Republic of Colombia and murder Manuel.

"Hand me that bottle of Vodka, and give me a few more of those codeines."

Chapter 3

The two detectives had found out a lot of shit. First off, once they got to Washington Heights, they found out that the Colombians were having an internal war. The heads of the FARC were in a bitter dispute. So many innocent people were getting killed in the crossfire. The FARC had many members in the U.S. and a lot of them were citizens. The FARC was considered a terrorist group, but they were more a drug cartel than anything. Nevertheless, with a bit of strong arming and whisperings from the ears of informants, the detectives got enough info to run with and situated their investigation.

"Let me get this straight," Detective Jeff Barrows spoke to his partner Smithies. They had just walked out of a bodega on 168th Street. The man who ran the store was a retired cocaine smuggler. He was still in the mix, however, and since he still sold a bit of coke here and there, Smithies would always shake him down for info. "The FARC is under new leadership and their new leader is murdering anyone who was loyal to the former leader, Manuel."

"Exactly," Smithies said while lighting a cigarette. "It's as simple as that," he coughed a bit. "I gotta give these muthas up." Then he laughed. Jeff Barrows just frowned at him.

"So they supplied those untraceable weapons to those street thugs and dealers to help them in their war, huh?" Jeff was trying to put all the 2's together.

"No," Smithies was still coughing. "It was more like an assassination. Look at all the homicides as of late in the city, all damn spics. And most of them Colombians, right? Put all that shit together and we can find out more. Those two kids were iced by bullets that weren't serial scratched. Those bullets came from an H&K .25 automatic that might have been used before."

"Let's get ballistics on it," Jeff told Smithies. "This whole FARC shit is more a job for the FBI. But we can see about the two murders. That nurse and that car are peanuts now when compared to all of this Colombian cartel bullshit. Those two kids were possibly pawns in this. They stole that car to help them in an assassination, maybe. Who were they after or was somebody after them?"

"Either way they both got iced by the same gun. I'd guess they were after the person and not the other way around. Those two punks weren't worth a professional assassin. But those two were worthless enough to murder someone for payment in this whole Colombian situation." After Smithies said that, they hopped in their car and drove off.

• • •

One week had slipped by. Sharon had taken a couple of sick days just so she could tend to Darnell, but then that turned into an indefinite leave of absence. She felt awfully sorry for him. His daughter murdered, his daughter's mother murdered and now they were after him. He had told her more about this Manuel person and some organization she'd read about in

Time magazine called the Colombian Revolutionary Armed Forces or the FARC. Sharon hadn't remembered much about the article she'd read but when Darnell was sleeping one day, she'd gathered information about them on the Internet.

The FARC were involved in bombings, murders, hijackings, kidnappings, extortion, and guerrilla and conventional military action against Colombian political, military, and economical targets. In other words, they were a group of terrorists. All she could do was sit staring at her computer screen in wonderment, "What the fuck!?" She went into her computer desk drawer and pulled out a box of Newport's. She found a lighter in the same drawer and put flame to a cigarette. She took one long pull for the sake of her nerves and began coughing violently.

Sharon felt somebody patting her on the back, turned and saw Darnell looking down at her, frowning. "I thought you quit smoking cigarettes over five years ago."

"I did," she said laughing a little, "but all of this FARC stuff has made me nervous as hell."

Darnell frowned at her again. "I told you to leave things be. Once I'm out of here I'm out of your life. Better for you." Darnell grabbed Sharon and forced her to stand. "This is not your situation..."

"This has been my situation since you jumped in front of my car," she yelled at him.

"Jumped in front," Darnell smirked. "You hit me." They both laughed. But then things got serious again. "Listen, I ain't really involved in the FARC. I'm just getting my product from someone affiliated with the organization. I have nothing to do with the movement. Shit, I'm a nigga. I just fuck Colombians, or did once."

"Your daughter is," she looked at him with sadness, genuine

sadness. "Your daughter was Colombian, or half anyway. Maybe her mother was involved in the movement? Do you have a picture of her, your daughter?"

"Where did you put my things?" Darnell asked her.

Sharon looked deeply into his eyes, smiling.

Darnell was very handsome and just a few years older than she was. He had a nice medium build and was six feet something or other. She liked average sized men with cute faces and he was that. He was also quite an intelligent man, possibly even attended a college or university. Who knew but him. He rarely spoke of himself. All he spoke about was killing Manuel and going to Colombia. Sharon felt it was an impossible mission. She figured Darnell was gonna go right to Colombia and get himself killed, possibly just as soon as he got off the plane.

She shook whatever thoughts she had off and went down to her basement where her washing machine and dryer were and got his clothes with the dried blood on them. She was gonna burn them, but she decided to wait till he was somewhat healed, and he was. He was able to walk around, though he did have a limp, and he grimaced and moaned a bit. But he was able to move his left arm now, with a wince or two, but he was able to do so.

When Sharon walked back upstairs with his things, which she had in a laundry basket, he reached within them and pulled out first his gun, and secondly his wallet. He showed a picture of his daughter to Sharon and she broke out in sobs and tears.

"She was so precious."

"I know," Darnell was wearing a pair of jeans and a shirt that Sharon had purchased for him since his clothes were beyond washing. "Here," he told her handing her a hell of a lot of money. "This should cover all the trouble I've caused you."

"You sound like you're leaving," she asked rubbing her eyes. She absentmindedly looked at the roll of bills he'd given her. They were all hundreds and she had about fifty or sixty of them.

"I am. I know a guy in Colombia, a guy that I can trust and I called him and made some arrangements. He'll have a car and a few weapons waiting for me when I arrive. I'm gonna leave tomorrow and do what I gotta do. I appreciate everything you've done for me."

"That's it?" Sharon said with wonder. "That's it? Just like that? You are gonna die. Getting yourself killed won't bring Anna or her mother back."

"I know," Darnell said, "but without my daughter, ain't nothing worth living for."

Sharon saw the tears forming again. Damn, she was really getting drawn in. It might have been his looks or the whole pity issue, but Sharon reached out to him caressing his face. Darnell pushed her back. He saw what she wanted in her eyes. Saw that glossy glare in her brown orbs.

She was a good looking woman, but she was way too honest for him. Too honest to stick his dick inside, *but then maybe she just wants to be held*, he thought. He allowed her to move in closer. He began moving his left hand's fingers within her hair. He heard her moan slightly. He lowered his face into her shoulder and smelled the fragrance of her flesh; he cast a long yearning breath upon her neck.

Sharon had been nursing Darnell back to health for a week. She had lied to the police for him, jeopardized her job and life for him. And she didn't even know him. He was a criminal. But he was human and very beautiful to her. He had compassion and he at least cared enough about her not to tell her enough to get her involved, though she knew she already was.

"I want you inside me," Sharon said softly in his ear. "I want you to have something to live for."

Darnell looked into her face, but he hadn't the chance to say what he was gonna say. Sharon had already moved in. Her thick lips merged with his and she penetrated his mouth with her tongue. It was such a sweet thing, her tongue. Darnell only needed that to enflame his desire for her.

Once he was healthy enough to walk around the house a bit, he sized her up; analyzed her nice plump rump and her well-situated perky size 34- or 36-C cups. She was only five feet, five inches and Darnell preferred his women taller, but her legs were toned and she had the nicest hips. Sharon was a dark brown delicacy. And she had invited Darnell to indulge in her delights.

The lust between the two was strong. Darnell knocked the computer monitor to the floor and placed Sharon right on the computer desk. She was breathing heavily and so was he. She knew that lifting her up quite possibly agitated his fractured ribs, but he didn't seem to care. Sharon cared little at the moment herself.

They were both looking into each other's eyes as they practically tore each other's clothes off. Sharon was the first person officially nude. Darnell spread her legs wide upon the desk, clutching her ankles like motorcycle handlebars. Then he slid his tongue from her nose, to her jaw, down her neck, slithered it through her rabbit trail and slipped it between the lips of her pussy...

...they had made love; Darnell was very tender with her. Maybe it was because he was still extremely injured and hadn't the strength to penetrate her as aggressively as she figured a man as rough as him would. But when he turned her around, with his mouth all a glisten with her secretions, he propped her ass up and entered her slow and methodically. She came instantly. It was the excitement of the moment and the time they shared, the whole life and death of their short experienced existence.

Eventually they found themselves on the floor. She had her legs wrapped up around his waist; he pumped within her with an easy vigor. Then he let out a loud moan of ecstasy and she did likewise. He didn't withdraw and she didn't give a fuck about it. Sharon swore afterwards that she felt every bit of his semen rocketing up into her. They both laughed at the comment. Both were drenched in each other's sweat and smelled like the other.

"I'm gonna leave in a couple of hours," he whispered softly in her ear. "I haven't any other words for you."

"I didn't expect any." Sharon just looked into his eyes as he lay atop her. "Come back. Don't die. You have something here."

Darnell said nothing else. Sharon had fallen asleep right on the floor next to the broken computer monitor. He looked at her as she was, naked on the floor, for a long moment before he walked out the room. He gathered his things. Darnell took in a good deal of air and breathed what remained of it out his lungs raggedly. "Now it's time to die," he uttered softly before he walked out the door.

Sharon would never see Darnell again.

• • •

Detectives Barrows and Smithies had gotten back the ballistics report and they weren't entirely surprised by what came up. The gun that murdered the two thugs was in a homicide investigation that had been going on for two years. It was just about to get swept under the judicial bureaucratic rug, but now Barrows was thinking. "This guy Darnell Abrams, he's associated with the two stiffs. They used to sell his drugs."

"Yeah," Smithies said with a cigarette dangling from the side of his mouth. "Darnell Abrams was taken in for questioning about a murder, but we ain't never found the gun. What sort of fool still keeps a gun involved in a murder around?"

"Maybe the gun had some sentimental significance, Smithies, I don't know. Maybe Darnell Abrams isn't as smart as we thought he was. Whatever the case, let's pay him a little visit." Barrows smiled. Things were working like greased wheels. Perhaps Darnell had murdered his two drug dealing companions, foul play or whatever, but then he thought about the FARC and Smithies added his two cents.

"I think the stiffs were gunning for Darnell and Darnell just got the best of them. I think they stole that woman's car just so he wouldn't see them coming." Smithies seemed very proud. He thought he had all the corners covered. He was about to speak more, but Barrows held him with a finger.

"Darnell was way out of his drug area. And the Uzi we found was almost five blocks away from the murder scene."

Smithies nodded his head. "Still, whatever it is, let's get this Darnell. Let's nail him for everything if we can, as many charges as we can think of."

Both detectives laughed. Little did they know their investigation stopped right then. Darnell was way too street smart to go back to his hood. Two of his most trusted dealers had tried to assassinate him and he had a Colombian drug cartel after him. He wasn't going anywhere near anyplace anyone would even think to find him.

Once he left Sharon's house with her smell still on his mouth and body, he tossed his pistol right down a sewer drain. Then he caught a cab and went directly to the airport. Darnell wasn't joking around. He was on his way to the Republic of

Colombia. He was still fucked up pretty badly, bandaged, bruised, punctured by bullets. But he was sorrow filled and angered, foamed up with hate, and revenge was the only thing that would sedate his disposition at the moment.

His death was imminent. He knew his demise was growing near. It was as close as his shadow, but his daughter would be avenged. He was gonna do away with Manuel, and he knew that was gonna be the last thing he'd ever do.

Chapter 4

Darnell's flight took him right to Colombia's capital city, Bogotá. He had already made arrangements with someone whom he thought he could trust. An Ecuadorian embezzler named Gatos Moraga. Gatos wasn't actually the trustworthy sort and Darnell was gambling with his trust because Gatos wasn't beyond selling his own mother if the price was right. But Gatos hadn't any love for the FARC since they were always muscling in on his business. That *and* it was whispered that the FARC had murdered his brother.

"Ahhh," Gatos said when Darnell completely walked out of the airport. "I told you to come by boat. The FARC have eyes and ears everywhere."

"How did you know I would arrive on this flight?" Darnell asked suspiciously.

"I have eyes and ears as well. But if you would have come by sea instead of by air...," Gatos let it linger. "I won't chastise you further, my friend. Come, my car is this way."

And so it was. Gatos hopped inside the most dingy

Mercedes Darnell had ever seen. It was at least thirty years old and looked nearly twice as old as that. But it drove well and they were soon riding down some dirt road in South America. "We must get out of Bogotá, my friend."

"Why?" Darnell asked.

"Because things are crazy here right now, friend. I'm talking revolution and terrorist bombings and all forms of military activity. You came here at the wrong time."

"There is no right or wrong time for death. Do you have that vehicle and the other things I asked of you?" Darnell wanted to get it over with.

"The guns are in the trunk, along with the infra red binoculars and the scuba equipment."

"Scuba equipment," Darnell blurted. "I didn't ask for..."

Gatos cut him short. "You didn't have to. I know what you are here for. Manuel isn't an easy man to walk up on and his mansion is a fortress. But I know of a way in. His property has a moat, but under the moat there is a hatch that leads right into the mansion."

Darnell knew that explained the scuba equipment, but it didn't explain why. So Darnell asked, "Why are you providing the extra help?" What he really wanted to say was *what makes you think I wanna get Manuel?* Darnell hadn't told Gatos the bitter details, hadn't told Gatos shit. Just that he needed a few things and a vehicle.

"Why?" Gatos looked at Darnell keenly. "Let's just say that any enemy of Manuel is a friend of mine. That and I see his death in your eyes and I heard Manuel's death on the phone in your voice. There is much you don't know, my friend. Perhaps you shouldn't know but know this, the FARC is responsible for your daughter's and wife's death and Manuel *is* the FARC."

"I wasn't married to her," Darnell muttered. "Who told

you about my daughter?"

"No questions," Gatos' eyes got very narrow, damn near Chinese. "Only revenge...!"

• • •

And thus they prepared for Darnell's revenge. Gatos drove them to a rundown shack somewhere in the bowels of Colombia. Three other South Americans were inside the place. They looked gully and hardboiled each having either an eye missing or an ear gone and numerous scars in many visible places upon their bodies.

"These three guys will help you. They are trusted comrades of mine and none of them are fond of Manuel." Gatos laughed. "Here is a map of Manuel's territory. He has heavily armed guards, but as you see on the map, we have all of their checkpoints and posts marked."

Indeed they did, Darnell saw. He wasn't proficient in map reading, hadn't ever been in the military and didn't know a damn thing about guerrilla tactics.

Darnell knew the mean streets of Brooklyn. He knew how to get down and dirty when he had to. He was ready to die for his daughter's sake and that alone gave him the strength to grin and bear the pain he was feeling. His ribs were killing him. The pain was almost unbearable. He still had some of the codeine Sharon had given him and gobbled up two of the pills while the five of them sat at a table and discussed Manuel's death.

Gatos had offered Darnell some coke. He refused at first, but Gatos insisted. "You look like you are half dead," he told him. "You are taking those pills for the pain, I'm thinking. Ain't nothing better than a line or two of the purest coke, this is Colombian nose candy. Snort as much as you like."

Darnell bent down over the table and took so much coke

up his nostrils that his brain literally froze. "Arrrrh," he yelled like an animal and shook his head till he felt dizzy. All the Colombians laughed at him. Then they all took a couple of lines and looked upon each other shaking their heads. They were about to do it. Staying alive hadn't much of a hold on them now.

"Let's do this and be done with it for the better or worse of things."

"Yes," Gatos said to Darnell. "This is what must be done and things should be done while they are ripe off the vine, yes?"

Darnell didn't give a fuck about anything Gatos said. "Let's do this."

Darnell left the shack with the three South Americans. One man drove the Mercedes, the other two were in the back seats with Darnell snapping clips within guns and placing on infra red goggles. Gatos stayed behind but he wished them luck, though they all knew that coming back alive was the slimmest thing. They had already put on the black scuba gear at the house. Gatos had briefed Darnell on how to use the small oxygen apparatus and the other things he provided that seemed quite useful in murdering a mutha fucka and espionage.

• • •

The four of them had to trek two miles in the deepest darkness Darnell had ever been in. Parts of Colombia were jungle terrain and all forms of nasty bugs were buzzing around them. He couldn't keep up with the men Gatos provided, but eventually they slowed their pace for him after a while. Darnell was breathing heavily; he was still very injured but he was determined and soon they were right upon the outskirts of the mansion.

The shit looked more like a castle to Darnell than anything.

It was a huge place and the gate they had to infiltrate was enormous, electrified and barb wired. But they were equipped for the challenge and they used grappling hooks and toe cables, shooting the hooks connected to the ropes up over the gate at a few sturdy tree branches upon the other side of the gate.

After the challenge of the gate, they had the moat. But that was where their scuba gear would come into play.

"Shit," one of Gatos' boys said in terrible English. "The guard has shifted up since we last snuck in here."

As soon as he said that, they saw two men approaching with flashlights and guard dogs. The dogs were already antsy and began growling and sniffing in the direction of Darnell and the men. They were crouching down in foliage but they were prepared. Two of Gatos' men had tranquilizer dart rifles and Darnell had a silencer on his 9mm pistol. He was also carrying an assault rifle, a 16 gauge shotgun and enough ammo for Scarface.

The tranquilizer rifles went off and both dogs went down with meek whelps. Darnell ran out of his hiding spot the moment the guards new what was dong on. "Die," he whispered.

TWOOP! TWOOP!

Two silent shots were fired from his pistol. Both bullets connected entering both heads. Both guards went down. Gatos' boys pounced on them just in case they were still alive. They slit their throats and dragged the bodies of both men and the dogs into the foliage. Things were going quite smoothly.

They all checked their scuba gear and dived into the moat. The moat was filled with piranha but they were prepared for everything. They tossed a few pounds of raw and bloody meat into one side of the moat and when the piranha rushed to devour, they jumped within the water on the other side.

Darnell wasn't the most astute swimmer, but he was incensed and his adrenalin was on overload. All four men quickly found the underwater hatch. They had to blow torch the thing open. Darnell was amazed that the fire from the welding equipment was intense enough to still ignite underwater. *You spics have state of the art shit,* he mused.

Once within the mansion, they took off their scuba gear. It was a bit bulky, the oxygen tanks, regardless of how small the tanks were. Then they were on the move, traveling through the lower levels. The plan was to split up, two men going east and up into the complex, two men going west, but staying within the bowels. The men going west were gonna plant plastic explosives throughout the mansion's lower levels. The detonation devices were timed and they figured that would surprise Manuel if anything wouldn't. And besides that, they were sure the explosion would knock out the power in the mansion, the reason why they all were equipped with infrared goggles.

Darnell didn't know any of the guy's names and they never bothered to ask him his. But he and the one he was with went up and east. They had the daunting task of murdering Manuel. *It seems oh so simple at this point,* Darnell thought. *You guys didn't need me to get this close to Manuel.* Darnell was getting a bit suspicious. But it was all about revenge to him and nothing else really mattered at that point.

The explosion came about five minutes after they'd entered the mansion, right on schedule. All the power blew with the explosives and Darnell turned on his infrared instrumentation. They were right by a door that would place them right within a main hallway. Darnell made sure his assault rifle was full of ammo and ready to fire.

"Are you ready?" the guy asked Darnell.

"Ready to die..." Darnell worded. "Let's do it."

Darnell kicked in the door. The hall was crowded with Manuel's men. They were all running with weapons, the explosion had definitely roused them up. It was dark within Manuel's home. Darnell and the guy chose their steps wisely using their night piercing equipment to move through the complex. They had plans on the interior and knew where Manuel's main chambers and his office were. Those were the two places to go searching for him. They had at least ten minutes of time before the reserve power kicked in, if that. Darnell figured that was all the time they needed.

"Who are you?" somebody asked in Spanish. Darnell knew little of the language, but he turned and ignited his rifle. More than a few bullets went through the guy putting him out of his misery.

"The shit's hitting the fan now," Gatos' man said to Darnell. Then it was just that, the shit hitting. Darnell had to actually reload his rifle, that was how much ammo he used and he had to at least kill a dozen or so men. Gatos' man got hit by a stray bullet. And Darnell took a slug in his right arm. It was only a flesh wound, nothing as serious as what he took in Brooklyn. But it was painful and he was still very weak from his previous injuries.

He found himself staggering alone, going up a long series of stairs, but he was cohesive enough to lead himself right to Manuel's bedroom, his main chambers. He tried the knob to the door. It was locked. Darnell splattered the door with a rain of bullets then kicked in the door's weakened structure.

He walked into the bedroom, found Manuel standing with a goddamn rocket launcher on his shoulders. He was a fat mutha and he was shivering because he was scared. A few hot looking Spanish bitches were running around the room screaming. They were half naked. Darnell ignored them. He didn't even see if they were armed or not. He figured all he needed to do was blast Manuel and be done with everything. After Manuel was dead, he could care less about what happened to him.

"Manuel," he yelled at the fat man.

"You," Manuel worded with a stutter. "I know you. You are the one who got my niece pregnant. The one who my nephew said it was okay to sell the cocaine to in America. What the fuck are you doing infiltrating my home?"

"Releasing a rocket from that launcher will kill us both," Darnell told him. "I could care less about my life. Do it. Let off a rocket." Darnell continued to move closer to the fat man.

"Why are you here causing all of this trouble?" Manuel yelled.

"You had your niece Mari killed. You had my daughter kidnapped and her throat slit and you paid my people to assassinate me. Why do you think I'm fucking here?" Darnell yelled. "You die right now mutha fucka!"

"What...!" Manuel blurted. It was something about the tone of his voice that made Darnell pause. "I never ordered any killing of my niece and I loved her and her daughter. You ass, you are a nigger. But you were a decent nigger. You never did my family harm and you always made money for me. Why would I kill my own blood for any hate for you?" Then Manuel's eyebrows arched. "You have been conned. It was Gatos. He has duped you. The FARC is at internal war for control of the movement. It's all political and he has done this. He has killed your family, your daughter, my family!" Manuel was screaming. "You are a fool. Drop your weapon. Let's figure this out."

"You are lying to me..." Darnell blurted. He was very confused. Some of the things Manuel was saying made perfect sense. But then he could be telling lies just to save his own skin. Darnell thought about things.

"Lying to you, huh? Listen, you are in Colombia. You traveled all the way from North America to kill me. Why didn't you contact me first? Do you know who I am? Yes, of course you do. I can see it in your eyes."

Manuel lowered the rocket launcher. Then he motioned to a chair that was right next to a desk in his chambers. "Sit, you asshole. If I wanted you dead, you would be dead. No attempted assassination, simply assassinated. And I would never harm family. That is more Gatos' way. Did he tell you about his brother? How he murdered his own brother, his own flesh and blood, did he?"

"I *am* confused," Darnell said honestly. All forms of thoughts were swarming around in his head. *Was this all a plot of Gatos'?* Darnell didn't know what was going on.

"The FARC is at war with itself and you are just a pawn within it. I will extract revenge for Mari's death and for her daughter Anna's. Yes, I know of my family. I know what Gatos had done."

"How do I know you are telling the truth?" Darnell asked. He was past anything feasible. His rifle fell clattering to the floor.

"You *don't* know, you damn fool. All you can do is trust that I won't kill you for being so damned stupid. That or you kill both me and Gatos," Manuel began laughing. He walked over to a bar in his chambers and poured a drink for himself. Then he poured one for Darnell. "Have this one last drink with me."

Darnell walked over to the fat man and took the glass he'd filled with liquor. He drained the glass with one gulp. Manuel just watched him warily. "Have another drink," Manuel said.

He was about to pour another drink, but Darnell stopped him with a raised hand. "You are right in one account, Manuel. I don't know if you are telling the truth or if Gatos has told the truth." Darnell quickly whipped out the 9mm he had nestled in his jeans. "I am confused, fat man." He laughed. "So confused and filled with the desire for revenge. So much so that I've decided to kill you both..."

Manuel dropped his glass in shock. It hit the floor, breaking into many pieces. He watched Darnell level the gun to his head. "I'm gonna make this painful just in case *you* are the liar."

Darnell shot Manuel in both kneecaps. The man fell screaming out in anguish. Darnell glanced to the left of him. One of the Spanish bitches were attempting to walk out the door. Darnell put a few bullets in her back. Manuel tried to lunge at him when he turned and did the woman in. Darnell was prepared. He smacked the fat man in the face with his gun. He then put another bullet in him, in his stomach. Manuel fell to the floor screaming agonizingly.

"You won't die from that gut shot. Not yet at least." Darnell laughed fiendishly. He walked over to the assault rifle he dropped, picked it up. Most of the women were all huddled in a corner of the room, petrified with fear. "No one is leaving this room alive!" he yelled. "No one..."

Darnell rained hell in the worst way, killing every woman his blood shot eyes could detect. He saved Manuel for last allowing the fat man to squirm on the floor. He was trying to crawl away, but Darnell had put a foot right on his head. "I'm gonna use every bullet I have on me. When they finally find you, you will be unrecognizable."

Darnell wasn't lying.

• • •

Gatos slowly raised a goblet filled with cognac up into the light of the clear blue sky. He was right outside the rundown shack. Not one mile away was a secret airfield where planes he owned would take off, bringing hundreds of thousands of dollars of illegal contraband to other places across the globe. Only one of his men made it back alive from Manuel's infamous mansion fortress. But the man told him that the fat man, Manuel was dead. Now Gatos was the leader of the FARC, the drug distribution portion of the terrorist group to be specific, but that was a very prestigious position to hold within the organization.

His brother was once the leader of the cartel till he had killed him, but then Manuel had taken over and Gatos was forced to play second fiddle. Now he was the leader. No one was around with enough experience to oppose him and none of Manuel's people were around to take the seat Manuel had left. Each and every member of Manuel's organization had been forced through Gatos' scheming to fight amongst themselves. Even the way Darnell and his men infiltrated the mansion was a testament to how many people he had within Manuel's regime.

"Now I am the boss," Gatos said laughing to himself. He drained the goblet empty. He heard something like a twig snapping. "Who is there?" Gatos said nervously. "Miguel...!" he then yelled.

Miguel came running with a shotgun in his arms. Miguel had suffered a bullet wound during the night Manuel got murdered. But he was well enough to blast off a shotgun if need be. "What is it boss?

"I heard something," Gatos worded with suspicion.

Before Miguel could respond, a silent bullet tore right through the back of his head. The hot piece of lead harpooned within him making a nice tunnel through his brain, leaving out of his cranium through the forehead.

Miguel's shotgun dropped then his lifeless body followed.

"Gatos," Darnell said with menace.

Gatos was about to say some plea, but Darnell shot him right in the hand that was holding the goblet. The glass exploded and if you looked closely, you could see the hole the bullet made in Gatos' palm.

"Gatos, don't speak. This isn't anything you can negotiate. I already killed Manuel and now you have to die. That way it doesn't matter who the liar is because the both of you will be dead."

BLAM! BLAM! BLAM!

Darnell thought about Sharon as Gatos' corpse hit dirt, cogitated that she was definitely something to live for, however, he was finished, mentally. Nothing anything the earth could offer could bring back his daughter.

His baby girl was all he had left, that and the streets, but he was only in the street for her. Not at first, because he was in the streets since dropped by the stork. The street was a means of making his baby happy. Nothing else mattered. He realized that now. Realized that the gun he'd just murdered Gatos with was at his temple for that very reason. "I know, Sharon," he said his last words. "You tried to give me something to come back to..."

Darnell would not be coming back.

BLAM!

THE BLOCK

by

Shareef

Prologue

"Gangster...I'ma gangsta, nigga! Ain't nobody gonna disrespect my gangsta and live to talk about it!" P-funk shouted down toward the man who was sprawled out on the concrete with blood oozing from the side of his head. The man was already dead, but P-funk's rage caused him to stand over the lifeless body and make his notorious statements. He also knew that there were other hustlers spread out in the street observing the violent transaction take place. He couldn't let a nigga front on him and get away with it. Especially not on *The Block*.

Standing six feet even, with a hard oak brown muscular body and a deep baritone voice, P-funk was a far cry from his old moniker of "Pee-wee"—and he was out to prove it. He knew that his reputation and his livelihood harbored not only on what he did, but what he said in the process of doing it.

"And make sure you relay that message to all them hustlers in hell...'cause when I get there I'ma still be gangsta!" P-funk yelled out before unloading six more shots into Slim's lifeless body. P-funk then spit on the cadaver and added, "Have your

275

fun down there now, 'cause the next time I see you, I'ma kill you again, nigga!"

After his brutally cold actions and statements, P-funk glanced around at the onlooking crowd and lifted his gun in the air. "I know ain't nobody seen shit, right!" He screamed out towards the crowd as they began to disburse looking in every direction but his. "That's what the fuck I thought!" Those were P-funk's final remarks before he calmly walked to the curb, hopped into his green 500 SL and sped off.

Chapter 1

It was a hot-hot summer. The hottest summer in over two decades. Everyone was out in the streets escaping the suffering heat of their apartments. Only a select few individuals in the 'hood were able to afford fans; they were a luxury that was treasured in the ghetto. On 102nd Street between First and Second avenues on the East Side of Manhattan's Spanish Harlem, times were surely rough in the heart of the ghetto—a place where fans were rare and air conditioners were unheard of.

The kids on the block didn't seem to mind the extreme heat because it was a time when none of the adults complained about all the water flowing from the constantly running fire hydrant—and those white men with big helmets and super-sized wrenches didn't come to turn them off either.

It was so much fun for the kids to sift through the trash bags by the curb and find an empty vegetable or other thick aluminum can. They would take the can and scrape it against the hot pavement until enough friction was produced to sever the remaining lid on the can. Once the lid was popped out, one would have a perfect cylinder that was open on both ends. No one ever needed or used a can opener. And no one could get a can opener from their apartments even if they wanted to anyway. Grandma didn't play that. "Boy, you bet'not take my good opener out in that street. You think money grow on trees...not here it don't." Grandma always watched over whatever valuables that were in the house. She couldn't afford to let anything happen to any of the things she needed on a daily basis. If something were to come up missing or broken, then we'd just have to do without it until some extra money passed through her hands.

Extra money in the 'hood was as rare as a goose laying a golden egg. It seemed only to be a fairy tale. But once in a blue moon, somebody's uncle would come through with a stash of cash that he would share with some kid's older sister or aunt, and a few nickels would always trickle down to the youngsters. Of course, the older sister or aunt would run off and disappear somewhere for a little while with the guy who had the money, but no one really cared about that. Everyone would be so busy trying to pick out the penny candy they wanted from *Mom & Pop's* corner store that their presence wouldn't be missed. It was on those occasions, on the block, that everyone would feel like one big family.

Sometimes, everybody didn't feel like family. Like when check day came and all of the loan sharks, boosters, hustlers and dope dealers came for their money. Every first of the month you would've sworn that someone was going to get killed.

"Bitch, you better give me my mutha fucking money for that shit I gave you."

"But Pudda, I...I gave you some pussy for that."

"Shiiiit, bitch. Ya pussy ain't no money. That was only an

278

advance for me to wait till today to collect what you owe me." Pudda scowled with his hand out, palm up expecting to get paid in full for the dope he provided.

There were situations like this that occurred every month right after welfare checks were cashed and the women would come sashaying up the block like they shit ain't stink 'cause they had more than a hundred dollars in their raggedy ass purse. But that money would be gone in less than a week. The only ones who had a few dollars left by the time the next check day came were the seasoned grandmothers. Grandma had been through it all before and she new exactly what she had to do to hold on to some pennies.

Those days in the 70s and early 80s were so routine and predictable that you didn't need a watch or a calendar to know what time or day it was. *The Block* was your timetable.

But in 1985 everything changed.

On one extremely hot summer day, everyone was out hanging in front of the tenement buildings on 102nd Street as usual. Some people roamed the block, walking up and down either side of the sidewalk gossiping, chatting or just plain ol' talking shit. Some schemed, some hustled, some walked into buildings, some peeked out of them—doing whatever it was that they were doing. And others, like Pee-wee, cooled off by playing in the fire hydrant.

Everyone was in their own ghetto mood. Sometimes people would get their entertainment by watching the passing cars slowly cruise through the block and pause by the hydrant to take advantage of a free car wash. This day was no different. Pee-wee was working the hydrant, using all of the muscles in his bony arms to steer the force of the water, when all of a sudden, out of the clear blue sky, a loud thud was heard and seen crashing down onto the roof of the car that he was spraying.

The car was sitting idle in the middle of the street enjoying the free wash given by the forceful thrust of water being shot out from the fire hydrant. Little Pee-wee was doing his thing.

When the body crashed onto the hood of the car that he was spraying, his arms jerked up in surprise and the can he used to tunnel the flow of water flew from his grip and into the street. Usually a can escaping someone's grip was a cue for one of the many surrounding youngsters to take their turn at the pump. Whoever was fastest to snatch up the can was next in turn. But this time, no one had rushed into the street to retrieve the can as it rolled with the force of the water.

Everyone on the block seemed to be frozen in motion as they looked toward the body laying limp on the roof of Pudda's brand new Cadillac. Pudda was even shocked as he hopped out of his vehicle, looked around at the staring faces, then looked up towards the roof of the six-story building where the body had to have fallen from—or be thrown from.

"What the fuck! Who the fuck!?" Pudda was more angry than anything. He looked at his dented in roof, scowled with a disgusted look on his face, and was in motion, pushing the twisted body off of his car.

Juanita, one of the females who was hanging out in front of the building where it all occurred, had screamed out to Pudda, "What the fuck are you doing man? Don't push her into the street like that. Look, that's Roxy," Juanita yelled with panic in her voice as she cut her eyes towards the boy at the hydrant.

When Pudda paused, he took a second look and realized that it *was* Roxy, his favorite customer, who was sprawled out on the roof of his car. He screeched in surprise, "Oh, shit, Roxy." He slowly blinked as he spoke with the realization of what had happened.

Although Pudda spoke while looking directly at the woman laid out on his car, he knew that she could not hear him. Her body lay twisted in an awkward position with her eyes stuck wide open in shock, staring up towards the way in which she had just come. She was dead for sure.

"Ma! Maaaaaa!" Pee-wee shouted out as he stood up from his stooped position behind the fire hydrant. He felt his feet rushing toward the body of his mother as she laid out on top of the luxury sedan, but his body wasn't getting any closer to her. He struggled and struggled, trying to free himself of all of the hands and arms that were preventing him from getting to his mother. All he could do was scream, kick and fight to get loose, but it was to no avail. The four sets of hands that held him were too strong to fight against. They had him in a solid grip. He screamed and struggled so much that he must have passed out because the next thing he remembered was waking up in his neighbor's bed soaking wet.

It took all four women from the building to hold little Pee-wee from rushing into the street and towards the dead body laying on top of Pudda's car. Once they saw that it was Roxy who had fallen to her death, Juanita, Romona, Tracy and Tha-Tha had all thought quickly and rushed over to the fallen woman's son, Pee-wee. They knew that it was not a good sight for a twelve-year-old boy to see. They grabbed him, covering his eyes and pulling him away from the horrific scene.

No one knew exactly what had happened, but everyone knew that trouble had come knocking, times were changing, and the block just wasn't going to be the same.

Chapter 2

By the time Pee-wee was eighteen years old, he had already murdered four men. He was never the same since his mother had jumped to her death. No one ever found out the complete details of what drove her to commit suicide like that that day, but rumors were abundant—*she owed the drug dealers more money than she could pay; she was so high that she thought she could fly; she had caught that new disease that makes you lose weight and die...* People were even saying that it was her little son, Pee-wee, who had driven her crazy and that she couldn't take it any longer and ended her life. The rumors were all speculative and gossip, but Pee-wee had heard all of them, and each one of them cut through him like a Samurai sword.

Whatever the reason was that his mother had decided to end her life, Pee-wee had acquired the attitude that he didn't care. He loved his mother and couldn't understand why she would do something like that, but as he had gotten older, he took to responding to her death by saying, "Man, fuck that bitch, she ain't do shit for me, but left me to fend for myself."

And that was how he dealt with any emotions that had crossed through his mind or heart ever since he was thirteen years old.

That first year after his mother had died, most of the folks on the block acted like they really cared. They would cook meals for him and invite him over to their house to eat. But the women who were his mother's best friends were only friendly until they realized that there was no big life insurance policy that Roxy left behind. And even that wasn't so much of the determining factor as was the fact that welfare stopped sending checks to the house as soon as the social worker, Ms. Fielberg, got wind of his mother's death. Even *she* didn't offer to take care of him. "You're thirteen years old now, boy, so you can take care of yourself. The best I can do for you is to have the agency continue paying the rent on this apartment you're staying in, but once you turn eighteen, you have to move out." That's what Ms. Fielberg said was the *agency's* policy. Even at such a young age, Pee-wee knew that she was a lying white bitch. She didn't even report the death of his mother to the agency. She kept it a secret so that she could pocket the monthly check and the food stamps they provided. It was the only reason Ms. Fielberg continued to let the rent get paid on time every month. But she knew that when Pee-wee turned eighteen, the agency would have required that is mother come into the main office to detach dependency, so Ms. Fielberg had to cease payment of the rent before then.

Everybody in the world thought that they were slicker than the next man. And all everyone cared about was getting over. Getting over and getting money...that was everyone's game. So little Pee-wee grew up to play the game, and he decided that he was going to play the game better than anyone else.

• • •

The first time Pee-wee killed a man, he was sixteen years

old. As a matter of fact, it was on his sixteenth birthday.

Pee-wee was standing on the corner of his block in front of Mom & Pop's grocery store when a car pulled up and parked right in front of him. The guy inside of the car looked like he was as mean as he was black. And he was as black as tar.

He parked his car, got out and headed toward the store's entrance. Before he entered, he turned to Pee-wee and said, "Come here, little nigga." He stood by the store's entrance and watched as Pee-wee took indecisive steps toward him. When Pee-wee was an arm's length away, the guy reached out and grabbed Pee-wee by the collar and threatened, "If there's so much as a scratch on my ride when I come out of this store, I'ma find your puny ass and chop you into little pieces, you hear me?" Pee-wee could only nod at the man as his feet dangled in the air.

As soon as the man let go of Pee-wee's collar, Pee-wee dropped to the ground, scrambled, got up and started running up his block. The man stood there enjoying a hearty laugh before he walked into the store to purchase a tall can of Colt 45 for himself.

Once the man returned to his car, he looked around, smiled, rubbed his elbow on the hood of his car and took a long gulp from the can of beer he held in his hand. He was proud of his white Caddy. Especially with the expensive wax job that he had gotten earlier that day. His Caddy sparkled in the sun and he knew that there wasn't going to be a drop of rain all week long. He knew that he could ride around profiling as clean as a whistle without worrying about his glossy shine on the outside, or the mink upholstery on the inside of his ride.

Black Mack hopped in his ride, started the engine and steered his pride and joy down 102nd Street, heading down toward First Avenue to pick up one of his ho's from the Metro

North projects.

As he rode down the block, he observed the many kids playing in the hydrant water. He knew that all he had to do was beep his horn at the streaming water and the kids would stop what they were doing. Everybody knew that when Black Mack rode by, all water games came to a cease. So he wasn't the least bit worried as he rode through the block with his convertible top down.

Mack was all smiles, showing off his diamond and gold teeth as he slowly rode down the street. There were quite a few fine sistas that he wanted to turn out that lived on that block, so he had to style and profile as he rode past.

He winked at this one fine sista that he knew was down on her luck and was just a step away from asking him if she could hop into his stable. She was a pretty, light-skinned Amazon and super thick in all the right places. Tracy was her name. Mack knew that he'd be the boss of all the Macks with her in his stable.

She waved his way and started to take a step in his direction. Then, just as Black Mack ran his thick pink tongue across his teeth, he felt a cloud of rain open up from the sky and drop down on him.

"What the fuck is...!" Mack couldn't even finish his statement because he was momentarily stunned into confusion, wondering if he had made a wrong turn into the Niagara Falls. He wanted to cus' out the world, but so much water had come rushing into his face that he could only spit out in gurgles.

He was so surprised at the event that instead of speeding up out of the rushing water, he had stepped on his brakes and put the car in park.

The only sounds in the surrounding area were of the many men and women who were previously standing around checking out his ride, shuffling back and forth ducking into buildings trying not to be seen.

Then there was the kid at the fire hydrant pump who was all smiles and laughter as he aimed the gutted out can in the direction of the man that had threatened him and lifted him into the air. He aimed such a powerful stream of heavy water that splashed all over Mack, that Black Mack felt like he was one of those Civil Rights activists back in the day.

Little Pee-wee was snatched up and thrown into the soaking wet seat in Black Mack's car so fast that he didn't even realize where he was at until he felt the cold wetness of the hydrant water soaking through his shorts, causing goose bumps to run down his spine and tingle his butt cheeks.

One minute he was hosing down the insides of the white Cadillac, and the next thing he knew, he was grabbed by the neck and thrown into its soggy front seat. The man who had gotten out of the car and grabbed him had done so with such violent speed that Pee-wee didn't compute the seriousness of the trouble he was in until he was pinned by the stranger's powerful arm as they sped down the block.

Everyone on the block who had witnessed what Pee-wee had done to Black Mack's ride, then Mack throwing Pee-wee into his car and speeding off down the block, felt relieved that Mack didn't pull out one of his guns and start shooting the block up like he was known to do. Everyone on the block knew that they would never see or hear from Pee-wee again.

But they were wrong....

Later that night, to everyone's surprise, Pee-wee came strolling up the block like he had been treated to a fried fish sandwich and fries. He even had a new swagger in his walk that wasn't there before. Some of the less seasoned men and women on the block looked at him as if he was a rabbit who had just escaped the fox's jaws. But the more experienced fellas on the block picked up on the new attitude right away. They looked at him as the rabbit who turned into a fox.

When Black Mack had grabbed Pee-wee up, he had full intentions of murdering the little mu-fucka who had nerve enough to funnel hydrant water in his direction—even *after* he had beeped his horn in warning that he was riding by. Black Mack had a rule not to harm kids, but he was so pissed that he was going to make an exception.

Mack drove down First Avenue with his arm tensed against little Pee-wee's chest, looking for a spot where he could drag the little bastard out of the car and leave him in an empty lot with a bullet in his skull. Pee-wee had put forth an effort to get loose from Mack's grip, even by biting him on his forearm, but the crushing backhand that Mack had smacked Pee-wee with had knocked him unconscious. When Pee-wee came to, he was laying in a pile of trash and dog doo-doo in a vacant lot. Pee-wee blinked and looked up to see Mack cursing and reloading the large gun he held in his hand, complaining, "Damn gun done misfired again, but I'ma put some brand new bullets in this mutha fucka."

Pee-wee didn't have anywhere to run, nothing to lose and nothing to live for, so he just stood up and decided to take his death like a man.

When Mack looked at the little mutha fucka standing there in front of him with his chest out, ready to take a bullet to his head without even flinching, he knew that he couldn't waste such a courageous little warrior. "Listen you little punk. I have every reason in the world to smoke your ass right here and no one would dare question me about it. But I'm going to give you a chance of a lifetime. I'm going to spare your worthless life for now, but you work for me from now on. One little slip up and you gonna wish I wudda blew your brains out right here. You hear me, lil nigga?" Mack scowled at Pee-wee while he held the 357 Magnum to the youngster's head.

As soon as Mack had gotten back into his ride with little Pee-wee, they drove straight to the Bendix Laundromat where Mack made Pee-wee take all of the mink car seats into the Laundromat to dry. He also made Pee-wee strip out of the smelly clothes he had on and wash the stench from them.

As Pee-wee did what he was told, Mack walked into a nearby grocery store and purchased another tall can of Colt 45. He then leaned on the hood of his car and watched as Pee-wee performed the tasks. After completing the duties at the Laundromat, they drove over to the Self-Serve carwash where Pee-wee was made to clean, re-wax, and vacuum the entire car dry.

Their next stop was one that they would both come to regret.

Mack had driven around Spanish Harlem looking for someone, *anyone*, who owed him money but tried to duck and dodge him. However, there weren't many people in the entire city of Manhattan who owed Black Mack money and didn't pay up. Shit, who would cross him after all of the examples he had made of the people who had tried his patience. The last bitch that owed him and wouldn't pay up, he had thrown off a roof. He didn't care that she begged for her life. And he surely didn't believe the nerve the bitch had when she tried to appeal to his tender side, saying that she had bore a son for him. Black Mack knew that he had laid his pipe in the bitch several times before, in order to squash some of her drug debt that she couldn't pay, but nobody was going to make him believe that he fathered any children— especially from a ho. Hustlers didn't get ho's pregnant. The bitch was just trying to get out of the shit she owed him. But she had better plead here case to the devil because as she fell from that roof, gravity surely wasn't pulling her ass up toward the heavens.

Not being able to come up with anyone who owed him money, Mack thought of a plan that would solve his dilemma of teaching the kid a lesson. At the same time, he figured that he could cut down some of his competition.

As he drove up First Avenue, he spotted one of his competitors, the infamous Pudda, hanging out in front of one of his dope spots. Mack parked his car on the corner of 116th Street, looked down at the attentive kid sitting next to him in the front seat and ordered, "You see that no-good pimp mutha fucka right there?" Mack pointed an accusing finger up the street and waited until Pee-wee nodded. "Here, take this small shooter I got and go blow that mutha fucka's brains out." He handed Pee-wee the .25 semi-automatic handgun that he kept in his ankle holster. He slid the chamber back so that all the little guy had to do was to pull the trigger.

After Pee-wee had gotten out of the car, Mack put the car in drive, ready to pull off in a heartbeat. He knew that if the little skinny kid wasn't fast enough, Pudda would gun him down in cold blood, kid or no kid.

But Mack was not disappointed. As a matter of fact, he was downright impressed as he watched little Pee-wee walk directly up to the man he had pointed out, aim the gun into Pudda's chest and unload shot after shot into the man's body. Pee-wee then lifted the gun to his own lips and blew on the muzzle— like they did in them western movies.

When Pee-wee returned to the car and got in as if he had just stepped out of the Boys' Club on the corner, Mack knew that he had a natural on his hands. The kid had gunned down Pudda in cold blood without so much as a flinch or a blink of an eye.

Mack felt a chill run down his spine when the kid got back in the car, but he attributed that feeling to the excitement that ran through his mind as he mentally counted up all of the money he would make from the spots he would take over once everyone got word of Pudda's assassination. And there was no doubt about Pudda's death, because by the time his corpse arrived at Metropolitan Hospital, his soul would already be dining with the devil.

As Mack steered his car across 117th Street, he reached over and snatched the gun from the kid's waist and sternly warned, "This here ain't no toy, and you ain't no cowboy. But I likes the way you handled that mutha fucka back there. What's your name lil man?" Mack requested.

"My name is little Pee-wee, that's what everybody call me." Pee-wee responded with the normal innocence of a kid, as if he hadn't just murdered a man in cold blood.

"Pee-what!?" Mack sneered. "I don't like that name, it ain't you. Don't let these pussies out here call you no damn Pee-wee. From now on your name is *P-funk* 'cause you the shit, lil nigga." Mack nodded toward the little guy as he drove. "If I hear anybody call you anything other than that, I'ma smack the living hell outta you. You hear me?" Mack commanded, then reached over and smacked P-funk in the back of his head to make his point.

"Okay, okay," P-funk flinched.

"Another thing...I want to know why you wasted all my damn bullets in that nigga back there like that? Shit seemed personal," Mack spoke to the sixteen-year-old's mind, feeling him out.

"Yeah, well, when I walked up on him, I caught a vision of my mother laying on the roof of his car all twisted up. I still remember seeing his face when my mom fell from a building on the block and onto the roof of his car. That punk had the nerve to try to push my mom's body off of his car like she was a piece of shit...I never forgot that," P-funk responded.

Mack almost lost control of his car when P-funk revealed the information to him. "What!" Mack swerved, then regained control of the steering wheel and looked over at P-funk. "You Roxy's little brat?" Mack asked surprised, but he didn't want an answer. He just drove on and reflected in his mind about some of the things that Roxy had said to him before she fell to her death.

Driving back down Second Avenue, Mack pulled over and kicked P-funk out of the car when they reached 105th Street. "I have to go see one of my ho's, so take your lil ass on outta here. But if I come to the block looking for you, your ass better be around, you hear me?" Mack commanded with a thick black finger pointed in P-funk's face. P-funk nodded before he hopped out of the car.

That was the end of little Pee-wee's innocence..., the beginning of P-funk's murderous rampage..., and the beginning of the end of Black Mack's life.

Chapter 3

P-funk had wiped out four old-time gangsters for Black Mack, and by the time Mack had ordered P-funk to hit his fifth victim, P-funk had become immune and addicted to killing.

So when he cornered Pretty Tony coming out of Ramona's building, it was nothing for P-funk to put two bullets in his head like Mack had told him to do.

Walking with the gait of a satisfied man who had just hopped out of some good pussy, Pretty Tony stepped out of the building directly into P-funk's path. He saw the look in P-funk's eyes and immediately turned back around to rush toward the back exit of the building. He knew that P-funk was carrying out hits for Black Mack, and that Black Mack was trying to get rid of all the old-time gangsters and hustlers so he could be the King of the 'hood.

But Pretty Tony's forty-two-year-old knees were no match for the youngster's speed. P-funk had him pinned against the back of the stairwell with a gun pressed against his head in an instant. Seeing the murderous look in P-funk's eyes, Pretty

Tony knew his demise was imminent so he desperately tried to bargain his way out of fate. He had some information that P-funk would surely be interested in, even though he knew that once he divulged the information he had to P-funk, Black Mack would hunt him down and kill him mercilessly. He'd rather take that chance with the odds and live to die another day.

He pleaded with P-funk. "Listen, man, I ain't do nothing to you. Why you gonna do me this way?" Pretty Tony said with a questioning frown on his face while on his knees looking up at the big gun pointed at him.

P-funk let the man babble because he wanted to let Pretty Tony make a fool of himself before he died. Secretly, P-funk didn't like Pretty Tony anyway. Pretty Tony was fucking one of the baddest bitches on the block, Ramona. And P-funk had a crush on Ramona ever since he was twelve years old. Ramona was fine, fine, fine—with her bowlegged self. She had a tight, petite, light bronze body with an ass that many a men would kill for. But she was stuck on Pretty Tony and his pussy eating lips. However, now that Pretty Tony was about to be a statistic, P-funk figured that he would have a shot with Ramona's fine ass.

"You done fucked over the wrong nigga, Pretty Boy," P-funk scowled at Tony.

"Wait. Listen. I didn't jerk nobody. I don't know what Black Mack told you, but it's a lie. I don't owe nobody. Here, look, I keeps me a stack of money." Pretty Tony reached into his front pocket and produced a wad of cash. P-funk immediately reached out and snatched the money from Tony's trembling hand. "Ill take that 'cause you won't need it where you're going," P-funk threatened.

"Wait, Pee-wee, wait," Tony desperately pleaded.

Upon hearing the name that people used to call him back

in the day when he was a lil nigga, P-funk felt infuriated and slapped Tony up side his head with the pistol that he held firmly in his hand.

"I'm sorry, man, I'm sorry, Pee-we...I mean P-funk. I slipped, man...I slipped because I wanna tell you about your mother. I knew Roxy, man. And I now what happened to her. I know who threw her off that roof...," Tony spoke quickly as thick globs of blood dripped from his mouth.

"What the fuck you talking about, you curly head nigga?" P-funk leaned in and whispered angrily. "That drug addict bitch jumped from the roof," P-funk said then spit in Tony's face.

"No. No. That's not what happened. It was Mack. Black Mack killed Roxy. He took her to that roof, gave her some dope, fucked her and then threw the bit...I mean your mother...he threw her off that roof because she didn't wanna give him her whole welfare check. Plus he was mad because she cussed his ass out in front of everybody, saying you was his son and he should be giving **her** money to take care of your bad ass. Black Mack is your dad, man. And he killed your moms because of it...tossed her right off this here roof," Pretty Tony revealed. He then looked up at P-funk and exhaled. He could tell by the look on P-funk's face that P-funk believed him, so he thought he could capitalize off of the revelation.

"So now that you know Black Mack is the enemy, you owe me one, nig..." Tony started to feel courageous and began to rise from the begging position he was in. But he wasn't even able to finish the statement he started, more or less rise to his feet. P-funk had quickly digested the information, shrugged it off, and pulled the trigger twice, splattering Pretty Tony's brain all over the back staircase.

Chapter 4

"I knew this time would come..., I didn't expect it to be so soon, but I knew it would come to this," Mack said as he sat in his white Caddy, too proud to beg for his life. P-funk was sitting next to him in the passenger's seat. It was three o'clock in the morning, heading toward a bright Monday. P-funk had flagged Mack down and told him to park up by the vacant lot so they could talk. When P-funk pulled out a snub nose .38 handgun and placed in to Black Mack's dome, Mack knew the time had come for him to pay the piper.

"Yeah, and it's way past due," P-funk scowled. "You should've *been* told me who you was. But instead, you used me to do your dirty work...now it's time to do my own dirty work," P-funk spoke to Mack without regard for the few people who straggled around on the block, stealing quick glances in their direction.

"Listen, lil nigga," Mack said, maintaining his gangsta status, "I'ma always be a gangsta. I've lived like one and I'ma die like one. So if you gots something to do —do it!" Mack spoke out of the side of his mouth while reaching into his shirt pocket to retrieve a Cuban cigar. He bit the end off of the large brown cigar and pushed in the lighter on his dashboard.

"Well at least you could tell me why. Why did you do my moms like that? She ain't deserve that—even if she was on dope." P-funk wanted to know what would cause a man to throw a helpless woman off a roof to her death.

"Listen, playa," Mack started to respond. Then he heard the click of the car lighter pop out so he reached over, grabbed it, lit his cigar and blew the heavy smoke into the air before continuing, "I'm about money and ho's. They don't mix and they don't match. Ho's make money and money doubles up. If a ho fucks wit' my money, then she doubles over." Mack felt proud to school the youngster even though he knew he was going to die.

"So why the fuck you ain't just put her ass to work instead of throwing her off that roof?" P-funk questioned.

"Man, listen. Your mother was a fine ho, but she wasn't no working ho...," Mack started to explain, but was cut off by a violent smack in the face. P-funk didn't appreciate hearing his mother being called a ho, so he wailed off and smacked Mack across the face with the gun. Mack's head tilted to the side with the force of the blow, but he was not fazed. He simply spit blood out from his mouth, along with five of his front teeth and continued. "Listen, nigga, if you didn't want to hear what I gots to say, then you shouldn't have asked. But I'ma finish anyway, then you can do what you gots to do."

Mack continued to school P-funk on how some women just weren't meant to be put on the ho stroll because women like his mother, Roxy, were too head-strong to lay on their back all day. They were the strong willed women who knew how to trap a nigga off. That's why Roxy gave up the pussy to Mack so often. She knew that she could support her drug habit and not worry about paying. And when she had gotten pregnant by the same fool that was supplying her, she just knew she had it made.

But Black Mack wasn't the average trick. He wasn't trying to hear shit about no damn kid. He just smacked the shit out of Roxy at the mention of a baby and kept it moving. But he had come back for more pussy from Roxy because she had it going on like that. However, enough was enough. And when niggas in the 'hood started talking about Black Mack getting soft and being pussy whipped, he knew that he had to send a loud and clear message. It just so happened that he chose Roxy to do it with. He figured that he could kill two birds with one stone. [Making an example of someone who didn't pay him his due, and getting rid of the one talking 'bout she had a baby for him.]

"There's one thing you need to remember, youngster," Mack relayed to P-funk as they sat in the smoke filled car. "The only thing that's gonna keep you alive in these mean streets is your reputation. You have to establish and keep you one mean fucking reputation to stay alive out here. So you gonna have to do some real hard shit to stay afloat. And it's not only what you do..., it's how you do it and what you say when you do it. That's what's gonna put fear in niggas' hearts. You gots to keep these niggas out here scared of you. Keep that in mind—Son."

Mack spoke those final words and spoke no more. He simply leaned back in his comfortable mink-covered seat and took one last long pull off of the cigar he held in his mouth. P-funk knew it was time to do what he had to do. He had no qualms about killing the man who had turned him out to the game. He had no qualms about murdering the one person whom he looked up to and respected. He fired six shots at point blank range right into his father's face.

Chapter 5

Years later...

P-Funk had acquired three apartments in three separate tenement buildings on the block. Money was coming in rapidly and he stayed on the rise, after taking over Black Mack's spots. There were six spots in all, and were all very profitable, every one of his spots in Spanish Harlem was bringing in five thousand dollars a day at a minimum. P-funk had it made. He had two brand new cars, a 2005 Mercedes Benz 500SL and a kitted out Lincoln Navigator sitting on 22's, and he had his pick of all the fine sistas in the 'hood. Ramona was his main girl and she was sitting on top of the world herself. She lived in building 311 on the fifth floor in a plush three-bedroom apartment with her daughter and her son. The son was courtesy of her relationship with P-funk. The apartment was furnished with every amenity that she could possibly want and need. P-funk came and went as he pleased and there were no arguments or complaints from Ramona, since she knew the type of relationship she was getting into when she allowed herself to become involved with P-funk.

• • •

When P-funk had first approached Ramona on some *I wanna get wit' you* shit, Ramona just knew that he was joking.

"Boy, I used to watch your mother change your diapers. You betta get outta my face wit' that." Ramona had shrugged off his initial advances.

"Shit, you only five years older than me so stop lying. Besides, I'm all grown now. I'm doing grown man things," P-funk persisted.

"Uhmmm, huunnn," Ramona responded with a sarcastic twist of her lips. "I hardly call what you out here doing *grown man things*," Ramona pointed out to him as they stood in the doorway of her building.

"Yeah, but what about this?" P-funk said as he reached inside both of his pockets at the same time and flashed a humogonously large wad of cash in each hand.

Ramona was caught by surprise because she had never seen that much money all rolled up in someone's hands. Even though the money was folded over in bundles, she could tell that it was all hundreds. Ramona looked at the money with raised eyebrows and thought about some of the things that she wanted to buy but couldn't afford. But since she wasn't a LBB (low budget bitch-who would've immediately hopped on their knees at the sight of a few dollars), she maintained her composure and spoke what was on her mind. "That don't make you no man," Ramona said after sucking her teeth and looking him up and down like she had an attitude.

But P-funk wasn't discouraged. He shoved the wads of money back into his pants pockets and shot back, "Oh, yeah, well what about this then," He said grabbing a handful of his crotch with his right hand.

"You see, that's why I wouldn't even fuck with you, Pee-wee," Ramona retorted with a frowned forehead and a flick of her wrist, as if she was swatting away a fly.

P-funk's smile immediately disintegrated from his face, and his hand instinctively moved from his crotch up to his waist, where he clutched the ivory handle of a .40 caliber semi-automatic handgun.

Upon seeing the switch up, Ramona looked at him with an air that said, *Boy, I wish you would*. She rolled her eyes and shifted her weight from one foot to the other in the process. When she saw that P-funk re-focused his senses by dropping his hand down to his side, then licking his lips and smiling at her, she squinted her eyes at him and said, "Oh, oh, that's what I thought. Nigga, you too crazy to get some of this pussy." Once she spoke, she turned around and walked toward the stairs in the building.

P-funk was stuck in place with his eyes plastered on Ramona's backside as she walked off. He noticed that she was taking her sweet ol' time sashaying down the hallway, and he soaked in every step she took. Ramona didn't have to put any extra sway I her walk or twist to her hips because she had a naturally sexy and seductive gait. And to top it off, her posterior was well rounded, firm and heart shaped. Walking up and down the three flights of stairs to her apartment all of her life had kept her in firm shape.

Staring behind her, P-funk's mouth snapped open and a drop of drool escaped his bottom lip, snapping him out of his trance. He wiped his mouth with the back of his hand. *I'ma get me some of that. Even if I have to kill the whole Spanish Harlem and be the last man standing...I'ma get me some of that,* he thought with confidence as Ramona disappeared up the steps.

But what P-Funk didn't see was the big smile plastered on

Ramona's pretty face as she walked away. She knew that he was watching her and she knew that she had it going on like that. She figured that if he wanted to flaunt his assets, then she could do just the same...and see who came out ahead.

It took a few weeks of P-funk's persistence to finally break down the barrier that Ramona had put around herself. He had finally gotten her to go out on a date with him...if you can call riding her around with him to pick up all of the money from his numerous dope spots a "date." But at least he wasn't stingy with his money. He proved that by driving down Fifth Avenue in Midtown and buying Ramona whatever she saw that she liked. P-funk must have spent over five thousand dollars in cash on her in less than an hour. That counted for something in Ramona's eyes, so even against her better judgment, she decided to take P-funk up on his offer of moving her and her young daughter, Charity, into his plush apartment on the fifth floor of the same building.

Ramona agreed not only because of how she felt, but her girlfriend, Tracy, had a lot to do with it also for Tracy had urged Ramona on.

"Girl, you better go 'head and get some of that money. These other niggas out here ain't giving you shit. Shit, if that nigga was feelin' me like that, I would've *been* rolling in one of them fly ass rides he got right now," Tracy suggested to Ramona.

"Yeah, but that nigga crazy Tracy. I don't want to be bothered with his shit," Ramona reasoned. "Plus he still a kid. You know we used to watch that boy running around on the block with a snotty nose before his momma got killed."

"Yeah, yeah, but fuck all that. He paid, ain't he? He rollin' in some fly shit, ain't he? He trickin' like a mutha fucka, ain't he? Plus he eat a good pussy," Tracy revealed, as she counted out all the benefits on her fingertips for Ramona to see.

"Wait, how you know all that?" Ramona questioned, knowing that if he had fucked with one of her girlfriends, then he was definitely out of the question.

"Girl, don't even start trippin'." Tracy knew exactly what her friend was thinking. "He used to fuck with apple-head Jackie from over in Old Metro North. She told me all about that nigga," Tracy explained.

Ramona listened to Tracy's explanation and smiled inside at the prospect of a good pussy eating nigga. Then she thought about her ex.

"Yeah, but like I said, that nigga is crazy as hell. You seen how he did Slim right in front of everybody. And word on the street is that he the one who killed Charity's father."

"Girl, you can't listen to every fuckin' thing you hear out here. Don't nobody know who killed Pretty Tony," Tracy responded.

"I don't know, I just heard..., but I do know what I saw with my own eyes, how he did Slim. And he ain't even have to do him that way. All Slim did was try to slide a counterfeit ten dollar bill at one of his spots to get a bag of dope. He ain't have to do Slim the way he did him for no damn ten dollars. I'm telling you, that nigga is crazy."

"Girl, you know that wasn't the only reason he did what he did. He was gonna let Slim get off easy by working in one of his spots for six months without getting paid. But when you came switching your ass up the block and Slim tried to holla at you, right there while P-funk was still scolding him, that's when P-funk snapped. Slim was dead with the first shot to the head, but P-funk was still talking shit and shot him again and again. Now that's That Gangsta Shit. I wish I had somebody that would kill over me." Tracy steered her friend in P-funk's direction.

That was how Ramona had made up her mind to start fucking with the crazy nigga P-funk.

That was seven years ago.

● ● ●

Now, in 2005, at the OG age of thirty-two, P-funk continued to rule his block and his dope spots with a brutal fist. No one dared cross him because the consequences were simply too high. He was able to last in the game so long because no one was stupid enough to try to snitch on him or even call the cops when he did something out in the open. Rumor had it that one of his uncles was a Captain in the 14th Precinct and kept him abreast of all the information coming out of his district. So no one dared turn states on P-funk. They feared for their life.

P-funk only had to kill two people within the last five years. One was a crackhead nigga named Slim who tried to get over on one of his spots with some fake *monopoly money* or some shit, and the other body he had to lay down was of some dope fiend bitch named Mo-Mo.

Mo-Mo worked in one of P-funk's spots. One day she was seen stepping out of a police cruiser down by P.S. 99 on 99th Street and First Avenue. The information was immediately relayed to P-funk, who in turn approached Mo-Mo inside one of his spots over in Wagner Projects. When P-funk walked into the spot, all of the workers knew something was up because P-funk never barged into any of the spots unless he was picking up some money, and the spot had just opened for the day so the money was just starting to come in. P-funk approached the manager in the spot and whispered something in his ear. Then he and the manager disappeared into one of the *restricted* bedrooms in the apartment. When P-funk walked out of the room with a machete in his hand, all of the workers stiffened, but they continued bagging up the work that they were

303

assigned. Every single one of the workers sat at a large round table completely naked—as was P-funk's policy for his workers inside all of his spots. No one dared to question P-funk's actions. P-funk walked right up to where Mo-Mo sat, and with both hands gripped around the heavy sword's golden handle, he swung the sharp blade with swift and deadly force. Mo-Mo's head severed from her body with the one precise blow. It happened so quickly that as her head tumbled and landed on the table in front of her, her hands still completed the task of sealing the bag of dope she had in front of her.

P-funk kicked her headless body out of the chair and said, "Get this snitching bitch out of here, and have me another worker in this chair in fifteen minutes." He then walked around the room, staring at the shocked faces of the four other women sitting at the large bag-up table and yelled out, "Anybody else got something to say to the police?" Of course there were no answers. The workers just sat there petrified, looking down into the glassy eyes of Mo-Mo's severed head on the table.

After his last example, P-funk knew that he wouldn't have to worry about anybody in any of his spots turning on him. He had made it known that he had eyes and ears everywhere, and he surely wasn't taking no shit. Anyone who violated would be the next example. P-funk's reign of terror was complete and there was no one who would dare stand up in opposition to him.

He was so confident in his status that he was caught off guard one day in front of the building when he slapped Juanita on her pretty ass cheek. Juanita, who had also lived on the fifth floor of the same building, was returning home from one of her weekly visits to Attica Correctional facility. She made the weekly trips upstate to visit her baby's father who was locked up for manslaughter.

Everyone on the block knew that Juanita didn't take no shit from anyone. She didn't fuck with any of the niggas on the block, even though her man had been locked up for the past ten years. Not only did she not want to violate her man's rep, but her focus was bigger than *the block*. She had plans and she wasn't going to get stuck in the cycle of being a hustler's wifey. The few people she did associate with, Tracy, Tha-Tha, and Ramona, were the only friends she had and she was happy to keep it that way. But even with them, she kept her distance because females always found a way of getting up under her skin. Plus, her friends seemed to be happy with their positions as a hustler's plaything. Ramona, who she was the closest with, had become distant because of the fool, P-funk, whom she was messing with. Juanita never did like the shiesty nigga P-funk and she made no secret of it either. So when P-funk played himself, one fateful night, by tapping her on her ass as she walked into her building, she had no hesitation in swinging her arm from down south and slapping him in the face with a loud *SMACK!*

P-funk was so shocked that all he could do was suck his teeth and spit on the ground in front of him. He then looked up at Juanita and threatened, "Bitch, I will fuck you up."

Juanita was never one to bow down, so she took a step back, planted her feet in place and threw up her hands in a defensive boxing stance. P-funk immediately reached for his heat, which for the first time wasn't where it should've been— in his waist. He took a step in Juanita's direction, but when he saw that she wasn't going to submit to him, he stopped in his tracks, looked around at the forming crowd, then back at Juanita. He pointed to her and said, "You won't be alive to see tomorrow, so show off all the fuck you want to now." P-funk really wanted to murder Juanita right then and there, but being that he had just come downstairs to get a little fresh air after a fabulous fucking session with Ramona, he neglected to pack his heat. He was reluctant to engage Juanita in a one-on-one fist-fight because even though he was a bonafide killer, he never really learned how to fight without a gun. And the way in which Juanita stood her ground, he wasn't sure if it would be a good idea to engage her in a fistfight.

The thought of Tom-Tom, Juanita's man who was upstate, had also crossed P-funk's mind. Tom-Tom had a notorious reputation throughout Spanish Harlem himself, but P-funk didn't care about that; he had to kill Juanita for what she did. His reputation depended on it.

Juanita was nowhere near a slouch. She had been born and raised in the same 'hood that produced many a gangsta. She was fighting guys since she was ten years old, so she knew how to hold her own. Ever since she was twelve she never lost a fight. Most of her opponents were thrown off guard due to her precious beauty. She looked like a young *Pam Grier*, with her sturdy legs and shapely body. But she could rumble with the hard rocks. P-funk looked at her and knew he had to put on a show in order to save face.

"Yeah, bitch, I'ma let you enjoy yourself tonight. On the strength of my girl Ramona, I'll let your ass live to see just one more sunrise."

However, Juanita wasn't one to let beef simmer. She wanted to finish things up right then and there. "What, you scared you punk ass mutha fucka? You had no business touching on me. And you better *never* put your filthy ass hands on me again."

"Fuck you, bitch! You's a dead bitch—and I don't give a fuck about that nigga you got up north, 'cause if he get out and talk shit over your dead ass, I'll kill his ass too," P-funk said right before he turned around and walked down the block, leaving the crowd wondering what his next move was going to be. P-funk simply wanted to retrieve one of his many weapons to redeem himself. Although the thought crossed his mind that Juanita's man Tom-Tom was going to declare war when he got home, P-funk didn't care about that at all. He knew that he had to murder Juanita that evening. And no one would do a damn thing about it. *Shit, Tom-Tom might never make it out of prison anyway—even if he did, he'd be a dead man before he even thought about steppin' to me.* P-Funk reflected as he walked down the block to one of his parked cars. He had everything all planned out. Or so he thought. The one thing that he didn't take into consideration was Juanita's nineteen-year-old son Tyrell, who was on the rise just a few blocks away.

• • •

One of the onlookers witnessing the altercation between P-funk and Juanita had stepped inside of an adjacent building and used his cell phone to dial up a number in the Carver Projects, which were located just a few blocks over between Park and Madison avenues. Nineteen-year-old Tyrell Crockett, a.k.a. Ty-rock, picked up his celly and moaned into the phone, "Speak."

"Yo, Rell, what's up? This is Ray-Ray. Check it, son, you gots to shoot over to the block A.S.A.P. That nigga P-funk is over here frontin' on your moms. He trying to violate her." Ray-Ray spoke quickly to his childhood friend, looking out for his behalf, but at the same time not wanting to be seen making the call for fear of P-funk's retaliation.

"Calm down, yo. What's up over there? I know ain't nobody fuckin' wit' mom dukes," Ty-rock exclaimed as he pushed the female, who was kneeling down between his legs, to the side and zipped up his zipper.

307

"On the real, son, that crazy nigga out here frontin' talking 'bout he don't give a fuck about your pops and shit. He even tapped your moms on her ass. That nigga straight up violated. But yo, your mom's a gangsta bitch for real, yo. She..." Ray-Ray babbled on in his excitement but was cut off in mid-sentence.

"Fuck wrong wit' you, nigga, calling my moms a bitch!" Tyrell interjected.

"Nah, man, my bad. You know what I'm saying, but Funk acting like he about to murk your moms or something, so you betta roll over here."

No more needed to be said. Tyrell was already out the door and on his way over to put an end to the stupid ass nigga P-funk once and for all.

Tyrell had heard a lot of shit about the nigga P-funk, but he didn't concern himself with the nigga's shit. Rell had his own shit going on. He was doing his thing on *his* side of town. Ty-rock, as he was known throughout Carver P.J.s, had Carver locked down on some *Nino Brown, New Jack City* type shit. And he wasn't no sleeper either. His reputation wasn't as far reaching as some of the other gangstas in the 'hood, but everyone throughout Carver knew and respected him. Even a crackhead knew better than to try to shortchange him a nickel.

Tyrell was satisfied doing his thing on his side of town without spilling out into another gangster's territory. He had heard of P-funk's success just a few blocks away, but Rell didn't step on anybody's toes because he wasn't going to let nobody step on his. But with P-funk disrespecting the game, Ty-rock thought that maybe it was time to change up. He grabbed two of his favorite toys and rushed out of the P.J.s.

As Tyrell approached the block where he grew up, he saw P-funk walking up towards his mother, who was standing in front of her building chatting with her girlfriend Tha-Tha.

P-funk had retrieved one of his handguns from out of his car that he kept parked up the block and headed toward Juanita as she stood in front of her building talking to one of her girlfriends. P-funk was glad that there were a lot of people in the area to witness what he was going to do to Juanita. That way, they would only talk about *his* treachery and not how Juanita chumped him.

As he approached her, he reached for his .40 caliber bulldog and clicked the safety off. He had full intentions of blowing her head off and unloading a full clip into her body.

Juanita looked up and saw P-funk at the last minute. As he approached with his gun drawn and pointed right at her, she could only stare at him and watch in slow motion as he opened his mouth to make one of his infamous statements before unloading his weapon. She knew she was a goner.

• • •

Tyrell walked stealthily, coming up behind P-funk. He saw P-funk heading toward his mother by the building and thought to himself, *Yeah, I'ma get him right in front of everybody so niggas know not to fuck wit' mines.... Plus, that fine redbone Tha-Tha is right there, and I want her to see that I'm gangsta...then maybe she'll know I'm doing grown things and fuck wit' a nigga.*

Through all the commotion, someone yelled out, "Watch out!" But neither one of the gangsters knew who had yelled out, or who they were warning. Both men maintained their focus. P-funk headed toward Juanita with a cold-blooded death stare while Tyrell headed toward P-funk with the stealth of an attacking cobra.

P-funk didn't know that there was a major threat lurking behind him, and Ty-rock couldn't see the heavy weapon in P-funk's hand, pointed at Juanita's dome.

As P-funk approached within five feet of the building, he started with one of his notorious statements, "It's past midnight, and the sun has risen..."

Ty-rock could hear P-funk saying something, but he couldn't make it out, so he continued his approach from behind as he cocked a slug into the chamber of the sawed off shotgun. He held the chrome pistol-grip Mosberg with both hands.

Bloom!

When the slug tore through P-funk's back, causing his stomach and intestines to spill out in front of him, he could only drop to his knees in disbelief as he saw a vision of the Grim Reaper appear and violently snatch his soul from out of his pained body.

One bullet had exited from P-funk's gun as the force of the shotgun penetrated his back, but the bullet went astray, hitting other than its intended target.

Everyone on the block looked on in awe as Ty-rock walked up to where P-funk knelt, frantically trying to shove his guts back into his stomach. Ty-rock stood over him, placed the shotgun on top of P-funk's head and pulled the trigger again. *Bloow!* P-funk's head split open down the middle into a pile of undistinguishable red globby matter.

Ty-rock glanced around at the onlooking crowd and yelled out as loud as he could,

"I'M THE NEXT BIG THING!"

Epilogue
[READY TO RE-LOAD]

Why Black Mack had to mess with that skinny kid minding his business in front of the store? Why Pee-wee had to flip and act like he had a chip on his shoulder? Why Roxy had to get pregnant, letting Mack go up in it raw? Why Pretty Tony had to be fucking Ramona? Why P-funk felt the urge to kill just to bone her? Why that one lady had to drop from the sky? Why young Tracy had to be so damn fly? Why that kid did a bid and wasn't there for his family? Why Tom-Tom had his baby's mom traveling up to Attica weekly? Why Tony's timing was wack when he came out the building? Why he got smacked by the stairs in the back right before P-funk went ahead and killed him? Why that black nigga had to violate? Why shit in the 'hood is at such a fast pace? Why my Caddy can't be so tight? Why I think every left turn I make is right? Why it took six shots to the face? Why some think he represent the black race? Why that bitch had to snitch? Why that shiesty nigga had to touch on Juanita's hips? Why them workers had to live like disciples? Why Ty-roc had to come and repeat the fucking cycle? Why Red Bone Tha-Tha had to be down for whatever? Why the wannabe Nino had to use a Mosberg to impress her? Why Ray-Ray had to call Rell while he was getting dome? Why a brotha gotta be Upstate going through hell when he should be representin' at home? Why The Block gotta be so hot with violence, drugs and cursing? Why we gotta call our sistas a "bitch" and each other a "nigga" and act like black life is so worthless?

Why I gotta holla in the 'hood while I swallow what's not good, sometimes I just wanna sing?

Why you can't respect my gangsta, when I rob and shank ya— and why can't I be "The Next Big Thing?"

• • •

Keep your ear to the street...'cause "That Gangsta Shit" ain't cease. Be on the lookout for:

"THE NEXT BIG THING" – [Part II of "The Block"] by Shareef.

Coming soon on Amiaya Entertainment LLC..."That Gangsta Shit Vol. III.

I thought he told you that we won't stop!

Author's end-note:

There's a "Pee-wee" in every one of us: Young innocence spurned and manipulated through environmental circumstance...

...and sitting beneath that thin layer of epidermis, that we call skin, lurks a "P-funk" awaiting metamorphosis— ready to explode into action: Given to brutal circumstances of "The Block"...

Then, there is that youngster "Ty-roc" who is right around the corner—ready, willing and in motion to take your place and become...

THE NEXT BIG THING.

Shareef

Be on the lookout for the upcoming debut novel by Shareef: *URBAN KARMA.*

If you think "The Block" was hot, "Urban Karma" will have you sunbathing on Mercury.

A hood tale of Love, Loss, Pain, Murder and Mayhem. It will make you laugh, it will make you cry—and it will make you reflect...

...because: What goes up—must come down. And what goes around comes back around...That is Urban Karma.

Shareef is an up and coming writer with great potential. He has the skills to pay the bills and is set to make his mark in this here writing game. Be on the lookout for his upcoming debut novel, "Urban Karma" to be released by Amiaya Entertainment LLC in the summer of 2006. Shareef is currently working on his website and e-mail address. In the meantime you can contact Shareef "Cinomill" Clark through Amiaya Entertainment—tanianunez79@hotmail.com.

IT WAS ALL GOOD
JUST A WEEK
AGO

by

A.K.A.   Big Rock

Chapter 1

Tuesday, 7:47

"Hurry up, mutha fucka!" Poncho whispered into the wind.

"Shhh! You want somebody to hear your stupid ass? I'm right here," Grim answered, rising out of the shadow.

"Alright, bro. Let's get this paper," Poncho said as he checked to see if his Glock was locked and loaded.

Grim didn't need to check; he always kept his shit cocked and ready to bust. The two seventeen-year-olds had plans of coming up that evening.

The winter months had the weather fucked up, but it was definitely jackin' season. Snow and the ice always made for good cover as lazy ass cops tended to stay inside rather than patrol the cold streets. The deadly duo had cased out the Jamaican weed spot for two weeks. On Tuesday evening at seven o'clock, a black Explorer pulled up out front with the same fat ass Rasta behind the wheel. He would blow the horn three times, then a dark-skinned, fake ass Bob Marley looking nigga would run out and grab two big bags off the back seat.

To the naked eye, it looked like two bags full of dirty laundry, but they were full of marijuana. Tonight though, instead of buying weed, the two friends planned to make a withdrawal.

With a solid kick from Grim's size twelve Timberlands, the door flew off its hinges. Running into the dual leveled half a double, Grim and Poncho stuck their guns into the faces of the only two people in the house. Sitting at the table weighing out the weed, neither one had a chance to react.

"Who da bumba-clod..." one started in a heavy Jamaican accent.

Before he could finish his sentence, Grim smacked the shit out of him with his Glock. "Shut your Rasta-farian ass up! Simon says to lay your bitch asses on the floor," Grim instructed as he waved his pistol.

Not wanting to be left out of the fun, Poncho started to beat the shit out of his prisoner.

"Quit fuckin' around, nigga, and tie them up," Grim said, as he tossed his partner a bundle of zip-ties. After wrapping up their wrists and ankles, the two tore through the weed spot.

They split up and searched the rooms until Poncho came across the stash. "Jackpot! I found it, Gee, let's roll out," he yelled upstairs.

Grim was upstairs going through the dressers of one of the scarcely furnished bedrooms until he ran across a thirty-two hundred dollar stash. Heading back down the steps, he snatched a bloody captive by his dreadlocks. "Where the fuck is the rest of the chips?" he demanded, stuffing the gun into his mouth.

"It ain't here!" the other Jamaican shouted. "Somebody comes to pick dat shit up...you just missed it."

Shit! They had missed the big payoff, so they settled for the money that they had in their pockets. Just then, a knock came from the back door. With Poncho covering him, Grim opened the door. "What up, fellas," the short dark-skinned man said as he stepped in, unaware of the robbery. Seeing the ski masked jacker behind the door probably made him piss on himself.

"Get the fuck on the floor!" Grim ordered as he shut the door and forced the man to the ground.

Taking the zip-ties, Grim bound his captive who was begging for his life. "Please, don't kill me...I just wanted to cop a pound of weed," He pleaded.

"Shut the fuck up," Poncho yelled as he shook his pockets down.

A thousand dollars later, they were running out of the spot and toward the dope fiend's Ford Escort that they parked one block over on Twenty-Fifth Avenue. Hopping in and pulling off, they both removed their ski masks. "Easy money, bro," Poncho said, thumbing through the money he had just taken from the pockets of their three victims.

"I told you, nigga, them dumb ass niggas be slippin', just waiting for a mu-fucka to come take that shit! It's some fire too!" Grim replied, referring to the pungent smell coming from the bags of weed in the back seat.

"Just don't get us pulled over, nigga," Poncho said, "and stop by the carry-out, I need some cigarettes."

•　•　•

Magic brought the ball slowly down the court, glancing at the clock and then at the man who was guarding him. The score was almost tied, with Beechcroft Cougar Squad down by three points late in the fourth quarter. Magic just gave his defender a smirk and with his lightning quick first step, he blew right past him. His move was so fast that by the time his defender even turned to guard him, magic had pulled up and let go of a fifteen footer....nothing but net. The large crowd went crazy, filling the gym with a thunderous roar. Being in foul trouble, the six foot, six inch point guard Deshawn "Magic" Phillips had to sit most of the game. That was most likely the reason they were down in the first place. But he didn't cry over spilled milk. He was in the game now and with forty seconds left, they were only down by one point. The Northland team tried to hold the ball and run out the clock by passing and dribbling. They ran off twenty seconds from the clock before Beechcroft's swingman poked the ball loose and got the ball back to Magic. Letting his teammates get down court, Magic dribbled the ball across half court. Scanning the floor, he called for a pick and roll. "You ain't ready for this shit, Casey," Magic whispered into his defender's ear. With seconds left, Magic put on his show. The high screen came from the blind side as he put his play into motion. Coming off the screen, Magic gave his defender a picture perfect Allen Iverson crossover that shook the shit out of him. As he came out of the move, he picked up steam as the defender converged on him. Instead of passing to the right or the left, Magic opted to use his God-given talent. Not missing a step, he leapt off of one foot and tomahawk dunked the ball, turning his defenders into instant highlight clips. The crowd lost their fuckin' minds! "This is my house, I own this place!" Magic yelled, holding his arms in the air to amp up the crowd.

The visiting Vikings had a chance at a last second shot, but missed the long range three pointer, protecting Beechcroft's unbeaten record. The police kept fans from rushing onto the court as the team rushed into the locker rooms.

The news crew surrounded the two-hundred twenty pound senior superstar for interviews before he could leave the court, forcing him to talk with the nosy reporters. "I see you guys are still undefeated. Any comments?" one reporter asked.

"Well, we just came out tonight and gave a hundred and ten percent, uhh, we played tight defense in the fourth quarter and made the big shots down the stretch," Magic said, trying to sound professional.

"Are you sure it's not because of the twenty-seven points that you scored?" another reporter questioned.

"Not at all. If I didn't have my team, we wouldn't have been able to pull this off," he answered back before he headed to the locker room.

But the truth was just that, Magic thought to himself as he stood in the shower. The crowds that filled the stands were coming to see him. The cameras that were there came to see what *he* would do next, all of them trying to get the inside scoop on what college he would go to. The bottom line, it was all about Magic, not about his teammates.

After his shower, Magic threw on his Sean John blue jean outfit and hit the door. The crowds had started to thin out a little, but there were still people lingering to get another look at the superstar.

"Good game, Magic," an older man said.

"I want to be like you when I get big," a little boy said, as he tried to dribble his miniature basketball.

"Just keep that up, little man, and you'll be better than me," Magic said as he gave the young fan some dap.

"Hey, Magic, what's goin' down? We are about to head over to Andrea's little party. You tryin' to roll?" Rick, his six foot, seven inch swingman, asked.

"Hell, yeah, we can do that," Magic answered as he headed over to Rick's Honda Accord. Magic didn't drive to games; he thought it was bad luck.

He decided to ride out with his nigga and party a little with his classmates. "Stop by the carryout so we can grab some beer, my nigga," Magic said, thumbing through his wallet.

Pulling up to Andrea's crib, Magic saw that the party was anything but little. Cars lined both sides of the street in the middle-class neighborhood of Summerset. Her parents were out of town, so people had free run of her crib.

"Hey, Magic, good game tonight," Andrea said as she answered her front door. "You too, Rick."

Andrea was one of Beechcroft's elite. She was a bad ass redbone with some big ass titties. Her parents had a little bit of money, so she stayed geared up and drove a little brand new Chevy Cavalier. That evening she had her hair in a ponytail making her resemble a light-skinned Aaliyah. Magic knew she fucked with the nigga Brad, but she did look on point that night.

She took the two cases of Bud Ice to put in the cooler, and they made their way to the festivities in the finished basement. Her party was stacked. There were people from all of the high schools on the north side of Columbus, Ohio. All of them were smoking weed and drinking beer. She had her cousin, Craig, behind the mini-bar trying to sell shots, but Magic didn't pay a dime for his liquor.... *"I don't know what you heard about me, but a bitch can't get a dollar out of me..."* Magic sang along with 50 Cent's, "P.I.M.P." They all got nice for about an hour and a half.

"A, what's up, Andrea?" Magic said, tapping her on her shoulder. "Somebody is in your bathroom down here. You think I can use the one upstairs?"

"I'm really not letting anybody up there," she said, biting her lip a little, "but I suppose you can use it." She walked Magic to the bottom of the steps leading upstairs, where she had people making sure no one went up. "He's cool; he's just got to use the bathroom," she said, turning to Magic. "Upstairs, all the way down the hall and to the right."

Magic had to piss like a race horse. "Ahh!" he let out as he drained his bladder. He exited out of the bathroom.

Andrea's shit was live as fuck. Forty-six inch flat screen and a mahogany wood bed and dressers furnished the room. Magic was scoping the shit out so tough that he didn't hear Andrea creep up from behind.

"You always were a nosy nigga," she said as she playfully pushed Magic onto her parents' king sized bed, "but tonight, I think it's safe to say it paid off." Pushing the door shut, she walked back over to him with her eyes full of lust.

"Damn, girl, what about...," Magic started.

"Shhh," she said, placing her finger onto his lips. "I've waited a long time to get you into the bed, and now that you're in it, we're going to fuck!"

Magic didn't protest. He was cool with her nigga Brad, but that nigga was going to have to share his bitch that night. She climbed onto the bed, taking her hand away from his face and putting it onto his hardening dick. Magic was peeling off his shirts while Andrea was undoing his belt and unzipping his pants. She looked up at him, flashing him a devilish grin before she put her hot mouth over his stiff dick. Stroking slowly as he smarted Magic up, Andrea worked with the skill of a professional. There was no way she was going to pull it off, but she tried her best to deep-throat his soldier.

"Oh, shit, man...that's the shit I'm talkin' about," Magic said as he laid back onto the bed. Magic let his hand wander down and started to rub on her titties. As he filled his big hands with her double D breasts, Andrea positioned herself so that Magic had total access to her goods.

Moving from her titties down to her belt buckle, he started

to undo her belt and pants. Sliding his finger down to her soaking wet pussy, Magic started to play with her clit. She started to squirm as he massaged her, but she never stopped doing her job. Magic used his long arms to slide her pants off of her hips, without disturbing her harmonious groove.

"You gotta stop before I nut in your mouth," Magic said, pulling her off. "Just let me hit it."

"That's what you want?" she whispered as she lay on her back and spread her legs. "Then come get this pussy, big daddy."

Magic stood up and dropped his pants, stepping out of them and crawling into the bed. He stared at her pretty pussy, before he rubbed his dick up and down her clit a few times and slid in.

"Ohhhh," Andrea moaned as she took the dick.

"Damn, girl, your shit is wet as fuck," Magic whispered into her ear, as he slid in and out of her. Feeling himself about to cum, he pulled out and started to lick and suck on her huge titties. Flipping her over from her back, Magic positioned her up on all fours so he could dig her out from behind. Andrea let out a shriek as Magic fell into the pussy. *This bitch can really take a dick*, Magic thought as he pounded her shit.

"Whose shit is this, huh?" Magic yelled as he pulled on her ponytail. "Whose pussy is this?"

"Yours, daddy...it's yours!" she yelled back in between her screams.

Had it not been for the loud music from downstairs, the whole house would have heard their fucking. Pumping as hard as he could for another five minutes, Magic pumped what seemed to be gobs of gooey juice all up in Andrea's pussy.

"Oh, shit," she said as she fell on the bed and stared at the ceiling, "what the fuck was I waiting for? Brad doesn't make me cum like that."

"That's because Brad isn't Magic, that's why. I got that Magic stick...you betta ask somebody," Magic arrogantly replied, wiping off his dick on her parents comforter.

"Well, after tonight, I don't have to ask anybody," she said, trying to fix her hair.

They both returned back to the party that was going on downstairs as if nothing had happened.

"What's wrong with you?" her girl asked, looking at Andrea's face.

"Oh, nothin', I just drank too much I think," she lied, acting like she didn't just get the shit fucked out of her.

Magic smiled inwardly as he called his niggas to come pick him up. It was almost one and Magic had enough of the scene. After almost twenty minutes, Magic got the call on his cell phone that his boys were out front. Magic dropped his cell phone number on Andrea's freaky ass before he headed out the door.

"What up, Magic, you tryin' to head over to the twins' crib with me?" Rick asked.

Before he could answer, Magic heard the *T.I.* anthem *"24's'...money, hoes, cars, and clothes, that's how all my niggas roll..."* blasting out of the speakers...*"Blowin' dro on 24's...,"* Magic sang along with the chorus as he headed to the source of the music. Walking over to the 1986 candy apple red Cutlass Supreme on chrome 24-inch Diablos, Magic balled his hand towel up and shot it into the hood like a basketball. This caused the occupants to rise out.

"Watch that shit, nigga! I don't need your sweaty ass towel fuckin' up my candy paint!" Grim yelled over the music.

"Shut up, bitch, I'll shit on that hood if I wanted to," Magic joked as he gave his nigga dap.

"I see y'all won tonight. What did you do?" Poncho asked

looking at Grim. "We could have come but we had that little business to take care of."

"Y'all know y'all wrong. Y'all should've waited for me. I can't stand them dred head mutha fuckas," Magic answered, "but a nigga dropped twenty-seven on those bums."

"What's up, Rick?" Poncho asked.

"Shit, just about to go to get some ass. Y'all niggas stay up. Good game, Magic, I'm out. I'll check you out tomorrow," Rick answered.

"Yeah, be careful and good game too. That late steal was on time," Magic replied, giving him the one armed hug.

With that, the trio pulled away from the crib. It was always cool to kick it with his classmates, but they were not the same as Magic. Besides fucking ho's and sipping beer, he had nothing in common with them.

"What did y'all niggas get?" Magic asked, as he turned down the music.

"We got like thirteen pounds and ten thousand dollars. We didn't get the big money, but fuck it, this shit will do," Grim answered as he passed a four-gram blunt to Magic. "This is that shit we got out of there. It's some mutha-fuckin' killa, too."

"Where are we headed tonight?" Poncho asked from the backseat.

"Let's hit the Seventh Heaven. That mutha fucka be jumpin' off every day of the week. We got a few dollars to blow, let's just go trick a little," Grim suggested.

"Then that's where we're headed," Magic said as he turned the music back up.

This was his real life...the streets. He loved to play basketball and dreamed of making the pros, but he loved money, guns, and fast women just as much. His road dawgs, Grim and

Poncho, were his crew. They had been running together since they met during the L.A. Gear League in the seventh grade.

Grim was gutter as fuck. At six foot, two inches, 195 pounds, he was far from small. He could have been big on the court, but he let the streets take him out of school as well as the basketball world. His dark skin and deep scar under his left eye gave him an intimidating look.

Poncho, on the other hand, was a pretty mutha fucka. He was gangsta, but all he worried about was his tight fade and gear. His high yellow skin gave him a look like he was mixed or something. But let him get his eyes on your money and he was coming to get it.

It didn't take long for them to get to the Seventh Heaven. They sat in the car finishing the giant blunt. The parking lot was full of cars and trucks, sitting on big shiny rims and coated with candy paint. It was also sprinkled with the luxurious rides that let the world know that Columbus had niggas who had big bread too.

"Damn, ain't it Tuesday?" Poncho asked as they all got out of the ride.

"Yeah, nigga, I told you this mutha fucka bang seven days a week. Pussy sells anyway you look at it. And these are some of the baddest bitches in the city working in there. Them niggas know how to pick the bitches, I'll tell you that much," Grim replied.

"As long as they ain't cardin' tonight. I don't have my fake I.D."

"Don't worry, my nigga be workin' the door," Magic said, "I got us covered."

Stepping into the plush strip club filled with gangstas waving dollars in the air, the three friends made their way to the bar. Grim and Poncho might have had trouble getting in without their fake I.D., but when they were with Magic, they were good.

Magic's face was like a ghetto coupon. He knew damn near everyone in there. They all ordered double Hennessey's with the two Bud Ice chaser, and Grim cashed in five hundred dollar bills for five hundred singles. They made their way to the large front stage where a chocolate beauty was making her money.

She was five feet, five inches, 140 pounds with a fat ass and no tits. She was on her back with her legs spread-eagled so that her toes were touching the ground by her head showing off the camel hoof that she called her pussy. All of the niggas flooded the stage with money. She finished off her routine on the golden pole, working it like a trainer fire chief, all to the sounds of Lucacris' *Pussy Poppin'*.

"Alright y'all, show your love for...Co-Co!" the M.C. said into the mic. The large crowd showed their love as the dancer raked in all of her dough.

As they sat at the table full of alcohol, the crew drank as they talked about the lick that went down earlier that evening. "Yeah, bro, I knew that shit would be easy, but damn, it was over before it started!" Poncho bragged.

"Peep this shit though, this mutha fucka knocks on the back door, but he don't know that we in there. So we let him in and laid his ass down too. The shit was too funny, Magic, I wish you were there," Grim added, pulling on a Newport.

"My nigga Marcus will probably snatch up at least five of them pounds from us tomorrow," Magic said as he turned back his shot.

Just then, a flawless dancer came up to their table. "Neeko told me to let you know that you were welcome to come back to the V.I.P. and drink with him," she informed Magic.

"What about my niggas?" he asked.

"Yeah, all of you can go back," she said before she walked away.

The fellas had never made it back behind the curtains. The front of the club was nice, but the V.I.P. behind the curtain was plush as fuck. The dimly lit room had only one stage, and it was in the center of the room. The stage was surrounded by glass tables with matching chairs adorned with soft maroon cushions that matched the carpet and drapes covering the walls. Two small groups sat close to the stage watching the yellow dime piece work the golden pole. Over at the table closest to the stage sat Neeko, the light-skinned drug lord who owned Columbus' north side. His crew, *The Fabulous Five*, sat at the table with him.

Future was the charismatic rapper, China was in control of the murder mami's, Menace was his gunrunner, and Shot Gun, the gold toothed assassin. All of them played vital roles in his organization, but tonight they were just relaxing.

"My man, young Magic," Neeko said, raising up to greet him, "what's going on?"

"I'm alright. I'm just out tryin' to relax a little bit after my game," Magic answered.

"I see you out there doing your thing," Neeko said as he festered for the waitress to bring more champagne. "What are you tryin' to do? Are you going to college or are you going to try to skip right to the pros?"

"I'm most likely going to college, but I'm not for sure exactly where though."

"I'm not sure any college will want you after my little nigga P.T. gets done with your ass on Friday," a voice said through laughter.

Standing up and walking closer to them, Magic saw that it was Lotto. He was a nigga that got it done on the city's east side. He was in attendance in the V.I.P. and was kicking it with his nigga P.T., who he referred to as Purtis Thompson, the six foot, five inch point guard from Brookhaven High School. They were undefeated as well and were playing Beechcroft on Friday night.

"Shit, that nigga can't hold my fuckin' jock strap. Them sorry mutha fuckas won't come close to winning," Magic said with confidence.

"Shit, my little nigga is this city's showpiece," Lotto woofed.

"That nigga ain't got it, cuz! I lead this city in scoring, assists and steals...not to mention turning mutha fuckas into instant posters," Magic said, slapping fives with Grim.

"That don't mean shit, youngsta! You ain't got no team; those suckas that you run up and down the court with can't fuck with them Bearcats. Those mutha fuckas is going to win the state," Lotto came back.

"Shit, how can they win the state if the title is coming home with me?" Magic asked.

"I see that you have confidence in your game, youngsta. Why don't you put your Velveeta where your mouth is?" Lotto asked.

"How much?" Magic asked.

"I got a hundred grand that y'all get y'all's shit beat in on Friday," Lotta challenged.

"Nigga, I ain't got that kind of money," Magic said.

"Aw, that's too bad, youngsta," Lotto teased.

"It still won't change the fact that I'm gonna personally destroy them Bearcats come Friday," Magic said.

"Fuck it. You say that you can guarantee a victory?" Neeko asked as he lit a blunt.

"Hell, yeah...I can't lose," Magic said.

"Then I'll put up your hundred grand," Neeko said, turning

to face Lotto. "I just love it when your ass is wrong."

"Whatever, Neeko," Lotto laughed as he headed for the door. "That's the fastest hundred grand that you ever lost. You might as well give me the money right now."

"Don't count that shit so fast, nigga," Neeko yelled, as he blew out a cloud of smoke. "I'll see you at the game Friday...and bring my money with you."

After Lotto left, Magic and his peoples sat at the table next to Neeko's. "Don't worry about that bet, Neeko, I got this shit in my back pocket. That nigga P.T. can't hold a match next to the torch that I carry," Magic answered him.

"I hope so, youngsta, I hate to lose at anything, but we won't talk about that shit anymore tonight. Just sit back and enjoy yourselves, your night is on me," Neeko said with a smile.

• • •

Chapter 2

Wednesday, 12:15 p.m.

"Why don't you sit down for one minute, Deshawn. I haven't seen you in almost two days. It seems like I only see you on TV," Mrs. Phillips said.

Magic was his mother's only son. They stayed together in a two-bedroom cape cod in Brittany Hills. Magic's father bounced out when he was three with a Mexican bitch and headed to California. He even had the nerve to show up at one of Magic's games last year. But Magic took that same hate and turned it into a deep love and respect that he had for his moms.

Mrs. Phillips worked the second shift at the hospital so she missed his games on Tuesdays, but never missed a Friday night. His schedule had him home at noon, so this was the only time that he got to see her through the week. She was fixing a sandwich for herself when Magic was on his way out the door, but at her request he stayed. He sat at the table and started to load bread with thin slices of turkey, ham and cheese.

"I saw your highlights last night on the news. Twenty-seven, huh?" Momma asked, starting a conversation.

"Yeah, I got into foul trouble in the second and third quarter. But I got my act together in the fourth. I think I hit for like fifteen straight down the stretch," Magic answered back, taking a huge bite of his sandwich.

"All that reaching that you do, it's a wonder you don't foul out every game," she looked. "You just need to relax a little and quit forcing the action. Anyways, that Coach K from Duke, Coach Huggins from Cincinnati and Coach Patino from Louisville sent you a bunch of mail yesterday. I put them all in the drawer."

"Well, I still don't know if I'm going to college or if I'm gonna try my hand with the draft. All across the country, they say that I'm the next Lebron James," Magic confided in his mother.

"Boy, you need to worry about life after the courts. You can't play ball forever," she said.

"You're right, I can't. But I can play long enough to take you out of the working class," Magic started, stuffing his mouth with more of his sandwich.

"If you say so...Mr. Man," she said as she sipped on her bottled water.

"Well, I do say so, and right now I say I'm about to be late for practice," Magic said. With that, Magic rose up, kissed him mom on the cheek and headed out the door.

• • •

After practice, the all-star guard showered and got into his 1999 gold Monte Carlo SS with the 20-inch chrome blades. Starting the engine, he started to bump his theme song, Jay-Z's _The Takeover_. "...*The takeover, the breaks over nigga...*," came the lyrics. He smoked a blunt and repeated the song all the way to their spot in the Kenmore Squares apartments. Pulling up to the friend's apartment in the rear of the complex, Magic hit his alarm and entered the spot. Walking into the kitchen, he saw the usual scene. Grim was at the stove cooking up dope with his Glock beside him on the counter. Poncho was sitting at the kitchen table sacking up the weed that they had jacked the day before.

"It's about fuckin' time you decided to show your face," Grim commented, not taking his eyes off of the oily cocaine.

"Yeah, nigga, this shit ain't as easy as I make it look. I'm so sick of baggin' this shit, it ain't funny," Poncho added.

"Fuck the both of you lazy mutha fuckas! I bet y'all don't get sick of countin' that money! Besides, I don't have the luxury of sittin' on my ass all day doing nothin'," Magic said, setting his Ruger on the table and reaching for the blunt. "Somebody has to make sure that the both of you niggas ain't stuck in this same spot in a few years."

"Fuck you, nigga! Not everybody grew up to be six feet, six inches, so we'll just leave that school shit to you," Grim said, leaving the coffee pot of dope to dry.

"But for real, my nigga, what the fuck were you thinking about lettin' that nigga Neeko put that bet on the game?" Poncho asked, as he bagged up another dub sack.

"Why not? That shit's a lock. Them niggas ain't got shit coming," Magic answered.

"I mean, do ya even understand who the fuck we were chillin' with last night? Them mutha fuckas are stone killers!" Poncho continued.

"Yeah, nigga, I knew who the fuck we were with. What do you think I'm doing out here? This is my city! That nigga is about to get paid fuckin' around with the kid," Magic answered back.

"Well, nigga," Grim said hitting the blunt," I hope for all of our sakes that you niggas bring y'all's A-game on Friday."

"You niggas really need to loosen the fuck up. That nigga Neeko is cool, and come Friday, that nigga is gonna be suckin' my dick for the hundred grand that I'm gonna win for his ass!" Magic stated.

"Like I said, my nigga, tell your teammates to bring their A-game," Grim reported. After Grim ended the conversation, the three of them held it down in the spot, selling green and dope to all that came through.

• • •

Chapter 3

Friday, 7:55 p.m.

The gym was jam packed with standing room only. The stands were filled with crazy fans screaming at the top of their lungs, rooting for their respective team. Every news camera from every station had their cameras rolling, not wanting to miss the next big play. Magic's mom was there faithfully in her *I'm Magic's Mom* sweater.

"Come on, baby, it's your time to shine!" she screamed as loud as she could.

It was just before halftime when The Fabulous Five rolled through with a team of fifteen niggas. Shotty motioned for the first two rows of the bench to clear out. Knowing who they were, the people wisely moved.

Almost ten minutes later, Lotto rolled up with his crew of ten and took rows on the other side of the court. They both gave each other the *What's up* head bob as the players took the court for the second half. Brookhaven was down by five points with four minutes left in the third quarter. Magic led all scores with twenty-six with P.T. close behind with twenty-two.

"You ain't got shit coming, P. You can't hold me," Magic whispered as he walked the ball up the court, talking shit the whole way. His move happened so fast that if you blinked, you missed it. Magic exploded to the hole and finished with a two-handed dunk.

"Ohhhhhh!" the crowd let out a sound of astonishment.

P.T. dribbled the ball up the court and ruled off a high screen and shot a three pointer...nothing but the net.

"L-E-T-S-G-O. That's the way we spell Let's Go..." the Brookhaven cheerleaders cheered, getting the crowd involved.

The game had so much electricity in the air, you could have plugged a TV into it. Brookhaven had the game tied with one minute left in the game with Magic bringing the ball up the court. "This is my game, nigga," Magic whispered to P.T. as he called for an isolation play.

Running the clock down, Magic put on his shiny suit. With a little bounce and a double crossover, Magic freed himself for a wide-open sixteen footer. The double team came, but it was for nothing as the shot dropped...nothing but the net. The crowd exploded into an uncontrolled roar!

"Time out!" Brookhaven's head coach yelled as he signaled for a T.O.

Taking the ball out, P.T. called for an isolation play of his own. "You ready for this shit, Magic?" P.T. whispered, talking his own brand of shit.

With ten seconds left, P.T. made an explosive move to the basket with the Cougar defense closing down on him. At the last second, P.T. kicked the ball out to a wide-open guard who took the three...nothing but the net! The horn signaling the end of the game was drowned out by the roar of the crowd. Even the police couldn't stop the stands from emptying out onto the court. Neeko and his crew didn't move. The look that came over his face couldn't be described. He took his gold Cartier frames off and ran his hands over his face. After China leaned in to whisper something into his ear, they all stood up and headed out of the gym.

Magic had his jersey pulled over his head as he sat on his ass under the basket, still filled with disbelief.

Although he was far from soft, he had to really fight the urge to cry. Even though he scored thirty-nine points, his cougars had lost by one fuckin' point! There went his undefeated season as well as his shine. The multitudes walked by patting him on the back, trying to lift his spirits.

"Good game, Magic."

"It's alright, you played your heart out, kid."

But their words did very little to ease his pain. None of the news cameras came over to interview him. No one wanted to talk to the losers. They all surrounded P.T., as he happily gave post-game remarks.

It wasn't until his mother's hand touched his shoulder that he broke out of his daze. "It's alright, baby. You did all that you could. You just fell a little short," she said as Magic stood to his feet.

"You're right, Mom, I'll be okay," Magic said as he placed his towel over his head and walked to the locker room.

The locker room was quiet as Magic walked in. The coach hadn't come in yet so it was just the players in a sulky mood.

Eventually, the coach came in and started to give his post-game talk. "Look, guys, you played your hearts out in what will most likely be the game of the year. You have nothing to be ashamed of; you did all you could to win. If only...," he started.

"If only *superstar* had remembered that he had other players on the court, we could have won!" Rick cut in.

"Fuck you, nigga! If your sorry ass would have closed out on that shot, we would have won and you would be kissin' my ass!" Magic yelled back.

"Alright you two, knock that shit off! We lost because we didn't play all the way through for four quarters. It had nothing to do with individuals! Now hit the fuckin showers so we can get the hell out of here!" coach shouted.

After he took his shower, Magic slowly left out of the building and got onto the bus. The ride back to Beechcroft was a quiet one, with no one saying a word. As he left the bus, he made his way over to Grim's candy painted Cutlass. Both he and Poncho were sitting on the trunk. Just as he approached the vehicle, a dark forest green 2005 Acura Legend with tinted windows pulled up on them. Although the car had stopped, the 20-inch chrome Zab Judah's kept on spinning. The green lights in its wheelbases flicked with each passing of the rotating blades. The sounds of Jay-Z's *Dope Man* poured out of the car as the driver and passenger doors opened.

"*They call me the dope man, dope man, I'm tryin' to tell 'em I'm what hopes floats man, ghetto spokes man...*" came Jigga's Man's voice.

Two men rose out smoking a blunt as they walked up to the trio at the Cutlass. "The mighty Magic, in the flesh," one started.

"Live and in mutha fuckin' color," the driver finished.

"Who the fuck are y'all...*itchy and scratchy*?" Grim asked, almost reaching for is heat.

"Ease down, cowboy," the driver with a deep scar on his cheek said. "We ain't come for all that."

"These niggas act like they don't know who you are, Ty-Ty," the blunt smoking passenger said with a chuckle.

"Shit, we don't know who the fuck *you* are either, *nigga*,"

Poncho said, hopping off the trunk.

But Magic knew who they were. The driver was Neeko's scar-faced protégé Ty-Ty and the long-faced passenger was his cousin Chin. Those niggas had a strange hold on the Short North's drug activity.

"What's up, fellas? I take it that Neeko sent you two to see me," Magic said, letting out a long sigh.

"The golden one speaks."

"Yeah, Neeko wants to see you...*immediately*," Ty-Ty informed him.

"If you haven't heard, I just lost a big game and I'm not in the mood for any more bullshit tonight," Magic replied.

Chin started to bust out laughing, causing him to cough up a lung from the weed smoke. Ty-Ty didn't smile one bit.

"I don't think you understand, Magic. Neeko wants to see you now," he started.

"Well, I don't know what to tell you. I'm not going anywhere tonight but home. Tell him I'll get at him tomorrow or something," Magic said.

Ty-Ty finally smiled, bending the long scar all over the side of his face. "Well if that's what you want me to tell him, I will. He didn't tell me to make you come, so with that said..., I'm out," Ty-Ty said as he climbed into his whip and pulled off.

"Bro, what are you doing? He already lost money fuckin' around with you. Are you really tryin' to piss him all the way off? You ain't supposed to be fuckin' around with a nigga like that," Poncho said, protesting Magic's decision.

"Fuck that nigga! I didn't tell him to bet on that shit! He did what he wanted to do with his money, so don't look at me like I'm supposed to kiss his ass because I lost a game! That nigga can suck my dick!" Magic fumed as he climbed into the Cutlass.

"I'm with Magic. Fuck that nigga. He bleeds just like us," Grim said as he gave Magic dap.

"Well, I'm with the fam too. I just don't like the way that shit went down, that's all," Poncho said as he sparked a blunt.

With that, the three friends pulled off into the night.

• • •

Chapter 4

Saturday, 1 p.m.

Magic woke up at noon the next day, tired and feeling like shit. He grabbed a couple of slices of cold pizza out of the fridge and hit the door. He was going to run to the carryout and grab some blunts and a six pack, that's the kind of mood he was in. As he walked into the street, a 2005 pearl white Mercedes CLS500 with tinted windows came to a stop right in front of him and rolled down the back window. China was sitting in the back seat.

"Get in the fuckin' car!" she said as she pointed the chrome Desert Eagle from her seat.

Menace, who was driving, hit the auto locks as Magic had no choice but to get into the back seat.

As much as he didn't want to, Magic still didn't want to be shot up in front of his mother's crib. "What's this about? Is it because I wouldn't come to the crib last night?" Magic questioned.

"Shut the fuck up, nigga!" China yelled, almost smacking

him with the Eagle. "Who the fuck do you think you are?"

"It's not even like..." Magic started.

"I said to shut the fuck up! If it were up to me, you would be coughin' up a lung by now, but Neeko has a soft spot for you," China yelled, putting the barrel to his temple. They pulled up at their Short North recording studio, instead of their strip club. "Just give me half of an excuse and I'll cook your brains! You got that, superstar?" China asked, warning Magic not to try anything funny.

Magic followed Menace up the main stairs with the deadly China bringing up the rear. Magic was led into a rear office that was filled with butter soft leather furniture, a bar and matching mahogany desk and meeting table. Neeko, who was staring out of the window, turned around, lit a blunt and let off his award winning smile. Even though he was a kingpin, he was still very young...maybe twenty-four or twenty-five years old. But he had the polish and savvy of an old school vet.

"Magic, my man, what happened last night?" he finally asked, pulling hard on his blunt. "I send my people to relay a message to you and you spit in Ty-Ty's face?"

"It ain't even like that, Neeko. My shit was really fucked up last night. We lost by one fuckin' point, the shit really got to me. Then Ty-Ty pulls up talkin' about come to the club...I just wasn't feelin' it. I lost you money and I knew that I would hear a bunch of shit about it, I..." Magic explained.

Neeko just held up his hand signaling Magic to stop talking. He got up, went to the bar to fix what looked like a triple Hennessey and came back to the giant desk. "First of all, I don't give a fuck what kind of mood your ass was in. When I call for you..., you come. Nicholas Banks shouldn't have to send his people to retrieve your sorry ass! My time is money, and you've wasted enough of my bread! Second, who the fuck are you,

Miss Cleo? How the fuck did you know what you would've had to hear when your ass got down to the club? Off the record, all I wanted to do is relax your uptight ass, and that's on my mama! I knew that your little loss would blow your mind, so maybe I had a couple of bitches to take some of that stress off your mind. You ever think about that? Shit, you scored thirty-nine fuckin' points. What could I have possibly been upset about? The money?" he asked, pausing to hit the blunt and sip his Hennessey. "I piss a hundred grand away every weekend, little nigga, I got cake! I wasn't even thinkin' about that shit!"

"Stupid mutha fucka," China said under her breath.

"You see, young Magic, all you did was find a way to piss me off. Now the streets are talkin', *How is Neeko just gonna let this little nigga treat him like shit? He just gonna let the little nigga cost him a hundred grand and call the shots too?* Those are just a couple of the questions that are on the top of the city's tongues right about now. What, you don't think that everyone knew about me and Lotto's bet? You don't think everyone knew about you turning your nose up at my request to see you last night? I can't afford to lose my grip on this city, Magic, not now...not ever. As soon as I let you get away with it, more niggas will try to get away with the shit. So it looks like I'm going to have to put my foot down, Mr. Phillips," Neeko continued explaining.

"So what does that mean?" Magic asked, looking at China and then at Menace, "y'all about to kill me?"

The three people in the room started to laugh, but Magic didn't find the shit funny.

"Nah, little nigga, I ain't about to kill you today. But how long you stay alive is completely up to you," Neeko said, with a devilish smile. "For your blatant disregard of the king of Columbus, that hundred grand that I lost last night just became the hundred grand *you* lost last night."

"You can't be serious. I don't have that kind of money," Magic protested, looking around the room.

Menace looked as if he could give a fuck, but China looked as if it made her pussy wet to hear her boss talk like that.

"That's not my problem, Magic," Neeko continued.

"You should've thought about that shit before you pulled that bullshit last night," China added to her bosses' words.

"What the fuck am I supposed to do," Magic asked, not having anything else on his mind.

"I think you need to be getting' up my scratch. The streets are watchin', and this will justify me lettin' your ass live," Neeko answered.

"It's going to take a while, Neeko," Magic started.

"I don't have a while, youngster," Neeko said, taking a heavy pull off of his fat blunt. "I'm going to give you seventy-two hours. Now that's the equivalent of three days. If I'm not paid by then, I'll be forced to send out for you like Chinese takeout, Magic. Now, I know that you think China is deadly, but when her and that Shotgun get together, it kind of scares the shit out of even me. I promise that you don't want to be at the other end of those two mutha fuckas."

"You better believe that shit, bitch!" China added, again acting like the situation would make her cum on herself.

"And you'll be watched closely, like all of my investments. If you or your mother try to leave city limits, you will be gunned down right on the highway. If you go to the police, trust and believe that nothing will stick to me, and I will invest every red cent I have to making you pay for it," Neeko continued. He walked back over to the bar and fixed another stiff drink for himself.

Menace was sitting on the couch rolling a blunt while

China stood by watching with murder in her eyes.

"You want a drink or something?" Neeko offered with sarcasm in his voice. "Maybe hit the blunt a few times?"

Magic's silence let Neeko know his answer.

"I didn't think so," Neeko continued with a smile. "Now if you don't have anything else to add, Mr. Phillips, I'll see you in three days!"

"Neeko, man, I'm...," Magic tried to talk.

"Get the fuck out!" Neeko ordered not even looking at Magic.

China took out her Eagle as Menace sparked the blunt. Magic had no other choice but to get up and roll out.

"Three days, bitch," China repeated as she walked Magic downstairs and out the door. "Now bounce your ho ass from around here!"

Magic just started to walk away. He was so dizzy that it felt like he was floating away. He got out his cell phone and called Grim...he was really in trouble and needed his crew. They were the only ones who could help him.

• • •

Sitting down at the table, Magic held his head in his hands. Grim was sitting next to him with his hand on his chin in deep thought while Poncho poured stiff shots of Remy Martin. Everyone sat in silence after Magic told them about the meeting that he just had with Neeko.

"Fuck that nigga!" Grim yelled as he threw back his shot. "I ain't got no problem with lettin' my gun bust at that bitch ass nigga!"

"It ain't that simple, Gee," Magic started. "If we miss him, that nigga will try some shit on my moms. Them niggas rolled up on me at the crib, so he probably already knows where she works. We gotta come up with something else."

"Let's just concentrate on getting' this nigga his paper," Poncho said as he uneasily sipped his drink.

"How much money do you have?" Magic asked.

"Hold up, Magic, fuck all those mutha fuckas. I say that we don't pay that nigga shit!" Grim interjected.

"That's stupid as fuck!" Poncho came back. "That kind of dumb ass logic is why Magic is in deep shit! It was never about the money, it was about respect, and more irrational decisions is gonna get somebody killed."

"Yeah..., that mutha fucka!" Grim said.

"Y'all niggas chill the fuck out! Really, y'all ain't got shit to do with this. I made this decision and I will deal with the consequences by myself," Magic said, trying to stop his friends from arguing.

"Nah, bro, we are all in this shit together...ride or die!" Grim said, hitting the blunt.

"Yeah, Magic, what kind of niggas do you think you run with? We all we got," Poncho added.

"We got about fifteen thousand left from that weed sting we hit. I've got, maybe another seven or eight grand," Grim answered.

"And I've got about fifty-five hundred at my crib," Poncho added.

"Alright, add my little three or four grand and we've got a little over thirty grand. That leaves us seventy stacks in the red. Any suggestions?" Magic asked. That put a silence on the trio as they all tried to come up with a solution to their problem.

"Alright, I got it," Grim announced after five minutes of silence. "Come one, let's take a ride."

The three of them piled into Poncho's Nissan Pathfinder and pulled away from the spot.

"*...You ain't no friend of mine, you ain't no kin of mine, what* *makes you think that I won't run up on you with the nine..."* 50 Cent's *Wanksta* blared out of his speakers as they rolled down Cleveland Avenue.

They rolled down the avenue smoking a fat blunt as Magic and Poncho tried to figure out what was going on in Grim's mind. Poncho was the pretty one, Magic was the arrogant one, but Grim was by far the live wire of the crew. Magic knew that whatever his partner had in mind was extreme, but this was an extreme situation. Grim made the signal for Poncho to turn down Sixteenth Avenue, and then pointed for him to park on the corner.

"There it is, fellas, given time. That nigga Neeko thinks he's Mr. Untouchable, so I know he got crazy shit in that mutha fucka."

"You're serious, aren't you?" Poncho asked.

"When do I joke about getting paper? Think about it, who the fuck would try to rob Neeko? Ain't nobody tryin' to fuck with that nigga so his guard will be all the way down. We can get in and out, wait a couple of days and then pay his bitch ass," Grim said with confidence.

"Fuck it, I'm down with it," Magic said as the Pathfinder crept away from the curb. "I don't see any other way to get this done."

"Hell, nah, there ain't no other way!" Grim said, "I damn sure don't plan on runnin' around robbing a hundred mutha fuckas trying to come up with seventy grand."

"Fuck it, that means that I'm in too," Poncho said, "but how the fuck are we gonna pull that shit off?"

"What the fuck is my name? Check this shit out. We gonna do this...," Grim started in on the plan.

• • •

Chapter 5

Sunday, 2:45 a.m.

It was almost three in the morning when the Ford Escort parked on Fifteenth Avenue. "Y'all ready to get this paper?" Grim asked as he tucked two Glock nines into his belt.

"You don't even have to ask me that shit, bro," Poncho answered as he tucked his twins into his waist.

"Well, let's get this shit done. Magic, stick to the script. That way no one can identify your tall ass," Grim said.

"I got you, Gee...bring up the rear. Don't forget who taught y'all niggas how to jack," Magic reminded is friend as he tucked twin forty-fives in his belt.

"Then show me what you're made of, gangsta," Grim said as he climbed out of the rental.

They were all dressed like bums, in head to toe rags from the thrift store. Poncho and Grim put phase one into motion. They left Magic near the car and walked into the alley, waiting for some traffic to walk by. After about ten minutes, a high ass dope fiend staggered by.

"What's up, man? I know that spot around the corner on Sixteenth got that A-1 critical work, but I don't know anybody on the inside. You think you can take me up to cop?" Grim asked in a disguised, raspy voice.

The dope fiend was so high that he could barely understand the question. "Huh? I don't know, man. They don't like me bringing new people to the spot," he protested.

"Look, man, I really need to get high. Come on and help a nigga out. I got almost three hundred dollars. I'm tryin' to spend at least two hundred on rocks. If you hook me up, you can keep the rest," Grim came back, flashing a roll of money. He banked on that one, knowing that most fiends wouldn't turn down free money.

Seeing the money, the fiend's eyes lit up like headlights. He reached out his hand, but Grim pulled it back. "Half now and the other half when we leave out...cool?" Grim asked.

"Yeah, but you're gonna have to give me the cop money right now. They're not going to sell you anything," he informed him.

Grim handed the smoker all but fifty dollars. The fiend counted out two hundred and put the remainder in his back pocket as they walked toward the house. They made their way to the side of the spot and gave a few taps on the door. Once inside the door, the plan went into effect.

The doorman recognized the old fiend and addressed him. "I thought I told you not to bring anybody new to the spot?" he asked as he turned his back upstairs in the kitchen.

"They're cool. They my peoples," the dope fiend vouched for them. That gave Poncho and Grim the opportunity to brandish their weapons.

"What the fuck are you tryin' to cop, old timer?" the doorman asked, not paying attention to the trio on the landing.

Grim took the six steps with one leap and stuck the gun to the doorman's head.

Leaving the side door unlocked, Poncho ran up the steps and started on the crowd control. "Lay on the fuckin' floor," he yelled as he waved his two Glocks. "Y'all know what this is."

Grim roughly threw his captive on the floor and held his pistols on the four men that occupied the kitchen and living room.

"Y'all gotta be the dumbest mutha fuckas in the city! Do y'all know who the fuck y'all are tryin' to rob?" the short, husky nigga asked.

"Tryin? Y'all niggas are shut the fuck down!" Grim stated. "I don't give a fuck who y'all think y'all are, fuck around and be leakin' up in this bitch!" Almost on cue, Magic came through the side door. "Took you long enough, nigga," Grim shouted. "Take those zip-ties out of my back pocket and tie these niggas up." Taking to it like a fish takes to water, Magic bound up all five of the men on the floor. Grim knelt down next to the dope fiend and removed the money that he gave him from his pockets. "Thanks for holding onto that for me, Pops," he said with a smile. "P, strip all these bitch ass nigga's pockets!" Poncho started to shake down their pockets as Magic tore into the kitchen cabinets and drawers.

"You gotta be fuckin' kiddin' me!" the light-skinned nigga said as Poncho pulled his necklace off. "Y'all niggas is gonna have to kill my ass!"

This comment pissed Grim all the way off. He took one of his Glocks and started to beat the shit out of him. The blood started to pour out of gashes that were opened in his face. "You punk bitch!" he shouted as he pounded his face. "Now, which one of you mutha fucka's is gon' tell me where the dough is?" Not getting a response, Grim walked over to the closest prisoner on the floor. "We are going to be here all fuckin' night if that's what it takes," he yelled as he began to pistol whip his next victim until blood ran out of his grill.

Poncho and Magic completely destroyed the kitchen and living room, leaving nothing unturned. But all they found was dope and a few thousand dollars that was in their victims' pockets.

Grim turned to give the next nigga his ass beating. "It's upstairs...it's upstairs! Don't fuck me up, man, please!" he pleaded before Grim even touched him.

Smack! Grim hit his previous victim one last time. "Where the fuck is the dough, nigga?" Grim asked, holding the gun to the crying man's temple.

"It's upstairs in the last bedroom, in the closet," he cried.

"Shut your bitch ass up!" Poncho yelled as he kicked him in the mouth, drawing instant blood. "Your boss wouldn't like all that whining...now would he?"

"Stop fuckin' around, P," Grim said as he turned to run up the steps. "We're almost home free."

Pop, Pop, Pop! Pop, Pop! When Grim reached the stairs, he came under heavy fire! *Pop, Pop, Pop!* The bullets continued to rain down from the top of the steps. Grim pulled back just as the bullets turned the wall into Swiss cheese.

Magic upped his twins and let off round after round and then took cover as the AK-47 started to rip holes into the bottom of the steps.

Poncho heard the shooting stop and emptied both clips toward the top of the steps. The loud shots echoed off the walls of the large living room.

Magic had dropped both clips and popped two fresh ones in. The gunman let loose from the AK-47, giving away his position. Magic took aim and let loose bullets from both guns right through the floor until he heard a loud cry.

"Ahhgg," the voice yelled as the loud klump signified a body hitting the floor.

"I got that mutha fucka!" Magic yelled.

"Come on, bro, let's go," Grim yelled as he cautiously scaled the stairs.

Upon reaching the top, Grim turned the corner to see a nigga badly wounded by the gunshots. The blood was gushing out of the three holes in his chest and the one in his leg, He tried to talk, but the only thing that came out was a bloody bubble. He struggled to reach for his weapon, but Grim stepped on it, stopping his effort. "That's your ass, Mr. Postman," he sang as he pumped half a clip into his head, neck and chest. The blank look on his face let all of them know that he was dead.

Magic hadn't seen a bloody corpse in years, but it was something he could never get used to. The blood poured professionally from his open wounds, saturating the thick tan carpet in the hallway.

"Snap out of it!" Grim yelled, seeing his partner's shock from looking at the lifeless mess. "Check that room right there."

They all split up and searched the three rooms. Magic tore into the small bedroom, starting with the closet. He searched the room for almost five minutes when he heard Grim's voice.

"I hit the dirt!" he yelled.

Running into the back room, Magic saw Grim in the closet. His feet were spread against the walls, holding him up in mid-air. As Magic got closer, he saw that Grim was getting money out of the attic.

"Here, take this shit, bro," he said, handing down six plastic Kroger bags full of money rolls. Dropping down, Grim started his dash out of the room, with Magic and Poncho close behind him. After hopping over the dead body, they ran down the stairs and headed for the door. "Pull the car around to the end of the alley, Poncho," Grim said as he tossed the keys.

"Man, what the fuck did you say my name for?" Poncho asked.

"Don't sweat that shit, bro," Grim said as he turned to his captives. "Ain't nobody going to be around to tell about it."

Magic and Poncho looked at each other for a second before running out the door and disappearing into the night. Grim walked back over to the men that were tied up on the floor. He stood in the middle of them as he gave every one of them two slugs to the back of their heads. Blood splattered all over the white walls. Grim turned and left out of the house. Running down the alley, he jumped into the back of the waiting Escort. "I'm in...roll out!" he yelled, as Poncho hit the gas. The trio sped off as the sounds of police sirens could be heard in the distance.

● ● ●

Magic was awakened the next morning by Poncho tapping his legs. They had switched the cars and went back to Magic's crib. Since it was so early in the morning, the three friends stayed the night in Magic's fully finished basement. When he woke up, his partners were counting stacks of money and weighing up the dope. "Wake your punk ass up and help us count this money," Poncho said, pulling on the blunt.

"Nigga, put that shit out before my moms comes down here and flips the fuck out!" Magic said, as he wiped the cold out of his eyes.

"Man, chill out with that shit," Grim said. "Moms left about an hour ago...she went to church. Just get your ass over here and help us count this money."

"How long y'all niggas been up?" Magic asked.

"Not long. Your mom yelled down to tell us she was

leaving," Poncho answered.

Magic started flipping through the channels when he came to channel 10 news. *"...And the police are still trying to figure out what actually happened early this morning at this Sixteenth Avenue house. Now what is clear is that there are six dead bodies that were found bound at the feet and wrists,"* the reporter said.

"I was asleep when I heard a bunch of shots coming from across the street. That place has been nothing but trouble since those drug dealers moved in. I just hope that the police shut that place down," the neighbor across the street said. *"Now police have no suspects, but they do say that this is a known crack house and that there have been numerous complaints from neighbors about the traffic,"* the reporter chimed back in.

"This is an ongoing problem in the neighborhood, we just don't have enough officers to patrol all of the streets. We just ask if anyone has information or tips about this, call our tip line." The homicide detective said.

"Once again, six people are dead, killed execution style in the house behind me. Once I have more, you'll be the first to know. Reporting live, this is Shelley Crenshaw, 10 TV. Eyewitness News," she reported.

The shit was all over the news. The trio had taken a regular lick and turned it into a gruesome murder scene. Magic hadn't felt any type of way when it all happened, but after seeing it on the news, he felt his stomach tighten. *How the fuck did he let this happen?* This whole situation was because of Magic's bad decision and now he was responsible for six dead people. He took the blunt and pulled on it hard, trying to ease his mind.

"Snap out of it, nigga," Grim said, "that shit had to happen like that. All one of those nigga's had to say was that it was three young niggas and one of them was six feet, six inches. How much thinking do you think it would take to put that shit together once you drop a hundred grand on Neeko's desk? At least now, it's still a mystery. He will think that one of his rivals took a shot at his title, not us. Just relax, we're almost out of this hot water."

He was right...as usual. Magic couldn't take a chance of there being any way that Neeko could find out that they were behind that shit. If taking money wasn't bad enough, leaving five of his workers split open was enough to get all of their heads busted for sure. The poor dope fiend was just in the wrong place at the wrong time.

After smoking two more blunts and an hour later, they had finished their count. "Damn, bro, that mutha fucka was loaded," Grim said, hitting a Newport.

"That stack brings the total to fifty-seven grand. Them mutha fuckas had fifty stacks stashed up in the attic and almost seven in their pockets."

"Plus, they had damn near a brick in the kitchen," Poncho added.

"So with the thirty we already have, that's like eight-seven thousand. We can bump off some of the work to make that hundred and still have some recovery money left over for us," Magic said with a tone of relief.

"I told y'all niggas that spot was puttin' up silly numbers," Grim said. "By Monday, Magic, you can pay Neeko's dumb ass with his own fuckin' money! Is that gangsta or what?"

"Yeah, bro, that's all the way hood!" Poncho shouted, giving Grim hard five after hard five.

Magic just sat staring at the pile of money...blood money. Paid for with the lives of six people. Were they innocent? No. But Magic didn't feel that they deserved to die by *their* hands. But fuck it, that money just saved Magic's life. *Fuck Neeko and his bitch ass squad! That nigga will get his fuckin' money and that would be that.*

The trio headed to their Kenmore Square dope spot to push the dope. They still had two days to get up the thirteen thousand that they were short. But with a few calls, they could easily push the A-I dope that they had jacked. It was almost ten o'clock that night when Magic got a call from Andrea.

"What's up, Magic? What are ya doing?" she asked.

"Shit, just runnin' around making a few moves. What's the business?" Magic said as he reached for the blunt.

"I'm not doing anything. I'm just sitting here in my bathrobe. My parents won't be home until tomorrow night. Why don't you come by so you can blow my back out?" she said.

"Damn, girl, you don't hold back your words, huh?" Magic asked.

"Shit, when you get fucked the way that I did last week, you just gotta come out and say what you want," she answered.

Magic felt his dick start to get hard. "That's cool, Drea. I could be there in an hour," Magic said.

After another half an hour, Magic gave his partners dap and headed out of the door. "I'll get up with y'all tomorrow," Magic said. He stopped by the store to get some blunts and beer on his way to his appointment with the lovely Ms. Andrea.

• • •

Chapter 6

Monday, 7:30 p.m.

The trio pulled up to the studio at almost eight o'clock in Magic's Monte Carlo. He had called Neeko at six, but was instructed to come by at eight. They all tucked their guns and proceeded into the building. Seeing them pull up on the monitor that was hooked to cameras positioned all over the outside of the studio, Neeko sent down the goon squad to greet them. They were all searched thoroughly before they were allowed to advance past the lobby. They also searched the suitcase that Magic had filled with money. "They had these on them, Shotty," one of the goons reported.

Shotty took a silver tray that sat on the table and gestured for the goon to drop them in it. "Alright, y'all follow me," Shotty said as he led the way upstairs.

The room was filled with about twelve of Neeko's lieutenants and captains, all of them smoking weed and drinking. As the trio walked into the room, a silence fell over everyone. All eyes were on Magic and his niggas as Shotty walked the tray with the guns on it over to the table behind Neeko's desk. With a slight raise of his hand, the room emptied all except for the fabulous five.

"Please, fellas," Neeko started, "why don't y'all have a seat." The trio had a seat in the chairs that sat in front of Neeko's desk. Magic sat in the middle chair with the case full of money on the floor in front of him. Future, Shotty, Menace and China sat at the meeting table behind them. "Fellas, you want a drink or something? Shotgun, why don't you hook my guests up with double shots of some of that Louis XIII?" Neeko said, smiling.

Shotty fixed them all healthy shots of the top shelf liquors and brought them over to the three friends. Taking a seat on the couch behind them, Shotty started to break down some weed.

"Neeko, here is the money that I owe," Magic said, setting the case on the desk. "I really apologize for any inconveniences that it may have caused. I didn't mean any disrespect by my actions over the weekend."

"Magic, we got off on a good foot on Tuesday. We kicked it real tough. I allowed myself to make a wager on your basketball game and lost," Neeko began. "Like I told you, it had nothing to do with money. Your direct actions are what got me upset...are what got my family upset. They wanted to do some really foul shit to y'all, but I knew there were other ways to handle things."

This part of his speech made Grim's face tighten up. Magic saw his nostrils flare and his jaws clench at having to sit and listen to Neeko's arrogance. Magic knew that if Grim had his gun, he would've pulled it out by now. *If only his bitch ass knew that he was being paid with his own fuckin' money.*

"I really didn't think that you would come up with it all," Neeko said as he opened the case and lit a blunt, "but here you are, three days later with a hundred grand. If I knew you got it done like this, I would've put you on a long time ago. How did you get it?"

"You know, I'm not the smallest nigga out here. Me and my crew eat good too. This shit put a cramp on us, but we got it together," Magic said quickly off the top of his head as he tossed back his shot. This caused Neeko and his crew to laugh, like something was really funny.

"This guy...," Neeko said as he passed the blunt to Magic, "he comes in here and drops a hundred on my desk like it's nothing...I should have asked for more. But sadly, I can't accept this money, Magic, my man. It would be against my principles."

Magic was shook, and so was his crew. *What the fuck did he mean, he didn't want the money? Did they just kill six people for nothing?* He was sure he had heard wrong.

"What are you talking about?" Magic asked, "I got your money together, just like you requested. I lost a lot of sleep this weekend trying to get you this bread. And now you say you don't want it? What's this shit about, Neek?"

Neeko made another hand gesture to Shotty, and his assassins brought him the whole bottle of Louis. After pouring another shot for himself, he lit the Newport. "I didn't want it, plain and simple. It's like I said, *I* made the bet...not you. You proved your point. You can stomp with the big dogs and pay your own way. I respect that. So go ahead and keep your money...you've earned it," Neeko explained. The three just continued sitting, stuck in a confused state. All Magic could do was toss back his drink. "Now, if you gentlemen will excuse me," Neeko continued, shutting the case, "I have an important meeting to attend to."

"Now why don't y'all argue with that," Magic said as he

gave Neeko dap, "but I really need you to take this money, Neeko. I'm a stand up nigga and I wouldn't feel right leaving with this money."

"I wouldn't hear of it. It's yours...take this and have a good time," Neeko said as he handed Magic the case. "Shotty, please show my guests to the door and fellas, feel free to stop by the club tonight. We gonnna have a party for one of my niggas."

"Yeah, that'll work," Magic said. "We can be through there a little later."

Shotty and two others walked the trio downstairs and gave their guns back to them. As he showed them to the back door, Shotty flashed them a gold toothed smile. "We'll see y'all at the club a little later, fellas," he said and pulled off.

They all rode in complete silence not wanting to talk. Magic stopped at the red light at Hudson and Fourth. He looked around the car as he lit a Newport. "Y'all think that nigga knew something?" Magic asked to no one in particular.

Before either one of his passengers could answer, a dark blue Suburban pulled to a screeching stop preventing Magic from pulling off. China's smile and Shotgun's gold teeth were the last thing that Magic saw. They both hung out of the window and started to let off bullets from extended clips loaded into their AK-47s. The trio tried to duck, but the SS was ripped apart by a barrage of gunshots.

"...*On any raw night, I perform like Mike, anyone, Tyson, Jordan, Jackson...,*" The lyrics of *Biggie Smalls* pumped out of the Suburban speakers. After emptying their clips into the Monte, China hopped out armed with her Desert Eagle. She ran up on the passenger side and stuck the Eagle into the car. All three men were alive, but badly bleeding. "You dumb mutha fuckas really thought Neeko wouldn't know that y'all robbed him?" she asked before she let shots into the car. *Pop, Pop, Pop, Pop,*

Pop, Pop, Pop, Pop, Pop, click! She reached into the back seat and grabbed the case full of money. "We will be keeping our money after all, fellas," she joked as she hopped into the truck and pulled off bumping Puff Daddy's *Victory*. *"...Where my niggas is at, where my niggas is at, where the fuck my bitches at, where my bitches is at...we got the real live shit..."*

• • •

Big Rock is an ill writer from Columbus, Ohio. Keep an eye out for the material he's preparing to drop on the literary world. For further qustions, comments or concerns, e-mail Big Rock up at tanianunez79@hotmail.com.

Attention

Aspiring Authors

Amiaya Entertainment, LLC is looking for participants who are willing to contribute a short story to our "Gangsta Sh!t" series. "That Gangsta Sh!t Vol. III" will be our last installment of this trilogy. Volume one was crazy. Volume two was bananas. We're trying to shut sh!t down with volume three. *If* you're gangsta enough.

Do you have what it takes to write something that'll make the readers wince? Can you lace a joint that'll cause your reader to cringe? Can you bring the streets to your fans in the form of a short story? Check it, everybody already knows what happened in volume's one and two; we need '5' more people to help us end this thing with a 'bang!'

If you think you have what it takes to impress our bosses, holla at us over here at www.amiayaentertainment.com or give us a call at 212.946.6565.

To see if you qualify, send us the first two chapters or sections of your story. Your story must be about 10,000 words, no more than 13,000 and no less than 9,000.

The stories that are accepted will be owned and published

by Amiaya Entertainment, LLC exclusively. All authors will be credited for their work and given a fee. The first portion of the fee will be provided to you once your story is submitted, accepted and edited. The remaining portion will be sent to you with a copy of the book once it's complete.

Your stories must be typed, double space. The deadline is August 1, 2006 and the book will drop shortly afterward.

Authors, writers, essayists, journalists and wordsmiths, look at it for what it is. It's a promotional tool for some and for others, it's a dream come true. We're the 'Interscope' of this book thing; all y'all have to do is bring the pain. Holla at us if you think you can handle it. Oh yeah, that sh!t better be gangsta. Don't miss out on your opportunity to become a part of one of the fastest growing independent publishing companies around.

Can't stop, won't stop!

One!
Amiaya Entertainment, LLC....

Fan Mail Page

If you have any further questions, comments or concerns,
kindly address your inquires in care of:

AMIAYA ENTERTAINMENT
P.O.BOX 1275
NEW YORK, NY 10159

tanianunez79@hotmail.com

Coming Soon

From
Amiaya Entertainment LLC

"SISTER"
by
Thomas Glover

and

"SOCIAL SECURITY"
by
Shalya Crape, Gene Johnson, Brenda Christian,
T. Benson Glover, Mary Woodward- Austin.

www.amiayaentertainment.com

Flower's Bed

The Most Controversial Book Of This Era

Written By

Antoine "Inch" Thomas

Suspenseful...Fastpaced...Richly Textured

PUBLISHED BY AMIAYA ENTERTAINMENT

From the Underground Bestseller "Flower's Bed"
Author Antoine "Inch" Thomas delivers you

NO REGRETS

It's Time To Get It Popping

AVAILABLE NOW FROM
AMIAYA ENTERTAINMENT
ISBN# 0-9745075-1-2

"Gritty....Realistic Conflicts....Intensely Eerie"
Published by Amiaya Entertainment

A Diamond IN THE ROUGH

JAMES "I-GOD" MORRIS

PUBLISHED BY AMIAYA ENTERTAINMENT, LLC.

TRAVIS "UNIQUE" STEVENS

NY

I AIN'T MAD AT ya

PUBLISHED BY AMIAYA ENTERTAINMENT, LLC.

ALL OR NOTHING

MICHAEL WHITBY

PUBLISHED BY AMIAYA ENTERTAINMENT, LLC.

A STORY THAT WILL HAVE YOU ON YOUR TOES FROM BEGINING TO END...

AGAINST THE GRAIN

G.B. JOHNSON

PUBLISHED BY AMIAYA ENTERTAINMENT, LLC.

HOE-ZETTA
VINCENT WARREN BRINGS YOU ANOTHER "HOT" NOVEL FROM AMIAYA ENTERTAINMENT
AVAILABLE NOW FROM
AMIAYA ENTERTAINMENT
ISBN# 0-9745075-8-X
VINCENT "V.I." WARREN
PUBLISHED BY AMIAYA ENTERTAINMENT, LLC.

So Many Tears

AVAILABLE NOW FROM
AMIAYA ENTERTAINMENT
ISBN# 0-9745075-9-8

Teresa Aviles

PUBLISHED BY AMIAYA ENTERTAINMENT, LLC.

A WOMAN'S WILL TO SUCCEED FROM THE LOW'S OF THE GHETTO TO THE TOP OF THE GAME

A ROSE *Among* THORNS

JIMMY DA SAINT
PUBLISHED BY AMIAYA ENTERTAINMENT, LLC.

The Gangsta Sh!t Vol.II

ORDER FORM

Number of Copies

A Rose Among Thorns	ISBN# 0-9777544-0-5	$15.00/Copy	_____
That Gangsta Sh!t Vol. II	ISBN# 0-9777544-1-3	$15.00/Copy	_____
So Many Tears	ISBN# 0-9745075-9-8	$15.00/Copy	_____
Hoe-Zetta	ISBN# 0-9745075-8-X	$15.00/Copy	_____
All Or Nothing	ISBN# 0-9745075-7-1	$15.00/Copy	_____
Against The Grain	ISBN# 0-9745075-6-3	$15.00/Copy	_____
I Ain't Mad At Ya	ISBN# 0-9745075-5-5	$15.00/Copy	_____
Diamonds In The Rough	ISBN# 0-9745075-4-7	$15.00/Copy	_____
Flower's Bed	ISBN# 0-9745075-0-4	$14.95/Copy	_____
That Gangsta Sh!t	ISBN# 0-9745075-3-9	$15.00/Copy	_____
No Regrets	ISBN# 0-9745075-1-2	$15.00/Copy	_____
Unwilling To Suffer	ISBN# 0-9745075-2-0	$15.00/Copy	_____

PRIORITY POSTAGE (4-6 DAYS US MAIL): Add $4.95

Accepted form of Payments: Institutional Checks or Money Orders
(All Postal rates are subject to change.)
Please check with your local Post Office for change of rate and schedules.
Please Provide Us With Your Mailing Information:

Billing Address_____

Name: _____

Address:_____

Suite/Apartment#: _____

City:_____

Zip Code:_____

Shipping Address

Name:_____

Address:_____

Suite/Apartment#:_____

City:_____

Zip Code:_____

(Federal & State Prisoners, Please include your Inmate Registration Number)

Send Checks or Money Orders to:
AMIAYA ENTERTAINMENT
P.O.BOX 1275
NEW YORK, NY 10159
212-946-6565

www.amiayaentertainment.com

Soul Quest Records
presents
International Vocalist
MelSoulTree

FEATURING

MelSoulTree

 IN STORES NOW!!!
www.MelSoulTree.com

Melissa Thomas, born and raised in the New York City Borough of the Bronx is both beautiful and talented! **MEL-SOUL-TREE** (Melissa Rooted In Soul), a sensational R&B soul singer (with a strong background in Gospel music) is signed to the international **Soul Quest Record Label**. This vocalist has been described as having "an **AMAZING** voice that is **EMOTIONALLY CHARGED** to deliver the goods through her **INCREDIBLE** vocal range."

MelSoulTree can sing!! (Log on to www.Soundclick.com/MelSoulTree to hear music excerpts and view her video "Rain" from her self-titled debut **CD**). **MelSoulTree** has performed worldwide. She has established musical ties in France, Germany, Switzerland, Argentina, Uruguay, Chile, Canada and throughout the U.S.

LIVE PERFORMANCES?
MelSoulTree's love for performing in front of live audiences has earned her a loyal fan base. This extraordinary artist is blessed, not only as a soloist, but has proven that she can sing with the best of them. **MelSoulTree's** rich vocals are a mixture of **R&B, Hip Hop, Gospel and Jazz** styles. This songbird has been blessed with the gift of song. "Everyone speaks the same language when it comes to music, and every time I perform on stage, I realize how blessed I am."

PERFORMANCE HISTORY
MelSoulTree has worked with music legends such as: **Sheila Jordan, Ron Carter, The Duke Ellington Orchestra, The Princeton Jazz Orchestra & Ensemble, Smokey Robinson, Mickey Stevenson, Grand Master Flash** and the **Glory Gospel Singers** to name a few. This sensational vocalist has also recorded for the **Select, Wild Pitch, Audio Quest, Giant/Warner, Lo Key** and **2 Positive** record labels. She tours internationally both as a soloist and as a member of the legendary **Crystals (a group made popular in the 1960's by Phil Spector's "Wall of Sound")**. **MelSoulTree** is known affectionately as the "Kid" or "Baby" by music legends on the veteran circuit. "Working with the **Crystals** has afforded me priceless experience, both on stage and in the wings being 'schooled' by other legendary acts while on these tours." According to **MelSoulTree**, "performing and studying the live shows of veteran acts is the most effective way to learn to engage an audience and keep my performance chops on point at the same time."

MUSICAL INFLUENCES
Minnie Riperton, Phyllis Hyman, Stevie Wonder, Marvin Gaye, Chaka Khan, Natalie Cole, Rachelle Farrell, CeeCee Winans, Ella Fitzgerald, Whitney Houston, Alicia Keys, Mariah Carey, Yolanda Adams and many others… "A lot can be learned from new school and old school artists…good music is good music! I want to be remembered for bringing people **GREAT** music and entertainment!!

FOR MelSoulTree INFO, CD's & MP3 DOWNLOADS VISIT:
www.MelSoulTree.com , www.Itunes.com & www.TowerRecords.com
For booking information please contact **Granted Entertainment at: (212) 560-7117.**

Support the Soul Quest Records **MelSoulTree Project** by ordering your CD TODAY!

MelSoulTree's "Mel-Soul-Tree" <u>**CD ALBUM**</u>/ISBN# 8-3710109095-7 *$16.98*/Per CD_____
10 Songs + 2 Remixes
*** *SPECIAL "MAIL ORDER" PROMOTION* ***
FREE "FIRST CLASS" SHIPPING <u>**ANYWHERE**</u> IN THE UNITED STATES.
FREE Autographed POSTER when you buy **2 or MORE** MelSoulTree CD Albums.

Hurry! This FREE Poster Promotion is available while supplies last!!!
Please allow 7 Days for delivery. Accepted forms of payment: Checks or Money Orders.

CREDIT CARD ORDERS can be placed via www.CDBaby.com/MelSoulTree2
OR
Call CD Baby at: **1 (800) Buy-My-CD**
NOTE: Credit Card Orders <u>will be</u> charged $16.98 + S&H. Credit Card orders are NOT eligible
for the FREE poster offer.

Please provide us with your BILLING & SHIPPING information:

| BILLING ADDRESS |

Name:_____
Address:_____
Suite/Apt.:_____
City: _____ State: _____ Zip Code: _____

| SHIPPING ADDRESS |

Name:_____
Address:_____
Suite/Apt.:_____
City: _____ State: _____ Zip Code: _____

If you are ordering 2 or MORE CD's... Please list the name(s) that should be signed on the FREE
autographed poster. _____
Send Checks or Money Orders <u>along with this form</u> to:

Soul Quest Records
244 Fifth Avenue, Suite K210
New York, NY 10001-7604
www.MelSoulTree.com

We thank you in advance for your support of the Soul Quest Records MelSoulTree Project. www.MelSoulTree.com